T0171651

BEYOND BETRAYAL
BEYOND HUMANITY

BEYOND BETRAYAL
BEYOND HUMANITY

A Fictionalized Biography

HELGA SCHWEININGER

Order this book online at www.trafford.com
or email orders@trafford.com

Most Trafford titles are also available at major online book retailers.

© Copyright 2012 Helga Schweininger.
All rights reserved. No part of this publication may be reproduced, stored in a retrieval
system, or transmitted, in any form or by any means, electronic, mechanical, photocopying,
recording, or otherwise, without the written prior permission of the author.

Jones Harvest Publishing
5400 East State Road 45
Bloomington, Indiana 47408

First Printing

Printed in the United States of America.

ISBN: 978-1-4269-6364-3 (sc)
ISBN: 978-1-4269-6365-0 (e)

Trafford rev. 03/12/2012

 www.trafford.com

North America & International
toll-free: 1 888 232 4444 (USA & Canada)
phone: 250 383 6864 ♦ fax: 812 355 4082

ACKNOWLEDGEMENTS

I am very grateful to my husband, Ferdinand, without whom Lieschen's story would not exist. I would also like to thank my daughter Irene, my parents who shaped and guided my childhood and paved the foundation for my artistic endeavor, and my generous parents-in-law.

Further I would like to express my special gratitude to Dr. Pat Kubis who taught me basic rules and who gave me the initial encouragement, and to Dr. Louise Vernon who taught me perspective and discipline and who believed in me to be a good writer.

I would also like to extend my appreciation to my writing colleague and good friend Nima Isner, and to instructors Joan Talmage Weiss and Shirl Thomas for their support. Further I would like to thank all my family members and writing colleagues and personal friends. Sincere thanks to everyone.

CHAPTER 1

Fear gripped Lieschen when gunshots jolted her from her sleep. She would never forget that evening thirteen years ago, which had turned her life topsy-turvy and would remain upside down for a long time. Lieschen was only five years old when that evil monster had paved the way for a relentless path.

The evening had started out as many evenings before. Lieschen had gathered for dinner with her loving parents, her petite grandmother, and her mother's sister, Aunt Klara. They had taken their seats around the oblong dining table in the luxuriant formal dining room at the Reinking Villa in Mariatrost, a suburb east of Graz in Austria. The pleasant spring air drifted in through the open window while dusk settled outside. Lieschen could hear crickets chirping in the hilly countryside.

While Frau Emma, their long-time cook, served Veal Braten with rhubarb sauce, spiced tomatoes and cucumber and dill salads, Lieschen noticed a huge black spider with a red cross crawling up the kaleidoscopic coral-beige wallpaper behind her mother. "Look!" she called, pointing her index at the spider.

"Don't look!" Elisabeth Reinking, Lieschen's mother, cautioned the moment she turned and saw the spider.

"Why not?" Lieschen thought the spider had a beautiful red cross on its back. The classic crystal chandelier above the dining table enhanced the spider's features.

"Because a black spider with a red cross is a bad omen," her mother said and touched Lieschen's hand lovingly. "My darling, it means bad luck."

"We'll put it out. Don't worry, my Princess," Walter Reinking, Lieschen's aristocratic father, assured with his strong authoritative voice.

"We will," her mother echoed and pulled back her hand.

Reinhard, a tall, middle-aged butler, came to serve wine.

"Reinhard, will you put out the spider on the wall over there." With his right hand, Lieschen's father indicated the spider.

"Jawohl, Herr Reinking." Reinhard promptly took out the spider. Then the family enjoyed the main course of their meal, followed by baked cinnamon apples for dessert. All the while they chatted about the day's events. Lieschen recounted her exciting day in kindergarten. Rope-jumping with her friend Ingrid Leitner had been the main event. "I jumped higher than Ingrid. It was the first time I jumped higher!" Lieschen lifted her silver fork with a spiced tomato up high to indicate height, but the tomato dropped on the white damask table cloth. "I'm sorry!" She looked at her parents, then picked up the slice of tomato with her fork, and put it into her mouth.

Her mother smiled without reproaching Lieschen for the red stain the tomato had caused on the table cloth. Her father did not reproach her either.

At bedtime, her mother read *Little Red Riding Hood* at Lieschen's bedside.

"Mommy, will you sing for me?" Lieschen asked when her mother closed the story book.

"Sure, my darling." Her mother put the story book back on the white, Danish bookshelf. Then she sang the lullaby *Schlaf Kindlein Schlaf,* and together they said the Lord's Prayer.

After this regular bedtime ritual, her mother bent over the silky, pink down comforter and gave Lieschen a tender kiss on her cheek. "Sweet dreams, my darling," she said tenderly, turned off the light of the mushroom-shaped lamp on the white Danish nightstand beside Lieschen's bed and walked out.

Lieschen looked after her mother until the door closed. Then she rolled over toward Nipo, her big furry brown teddy bear, tucked him in, and drifted off to sleep.

When shots jolted her, her head jerked on the pillow. In the darkness she called, "Mommy! Mommy!" Her mother did not respond, but a short while later Lieschen heard a loud bang, followed by a louder bang and a clattering zz-um zz-um of a motor. She had never heard such a strange noise during the night. She crawled deep under her down comforter, pulled up her knees to her stomach, clutched Nipo, and listened.

Finally she heard footsteps. "Now Mommy is coming," she told Nipo. She straightened her knees, pushed back the down comforter, and lifted her head from the pillow.

The bedroom door opened, and pale shafts of light streamed in from the hallway. "Mommy, why didn't you come when I called you? I was scared, really scared because. . ." Lieschen stopped talking because Aunt Klara stood in the doorway.

Lieschen let go of Nipo and sat up in her bed. "Where is Mommy?" she asked.

Aunt Klara's head bobbed as if standing in a rain-shower, shaking off raindrops. She switched on the ceiling light in Lieschen's bedroom and stepped over to her bed. Looking at Lieschen, her aunt's lean face stretched. She seemed to be listening for something.

It occurred to Lieschen that her aunt had changed her dress since dinner. Why? She wondered and asked again, "Where is Mommy?"

Aunt Klara put her slender, knotted hand on Lieschen's Danish headboard. "My Dear, your mother has fallen ill. Your father had to take her to the hospital." Her aunt's soft-spoken voice quaked.

"I heard shots!" Lieschen said.

Aunt Klara's bluish-green eyes narrowed.

"And where is Grandma?"

"Grandma went home."

Lieschen dropped her legs over the edge of her bed.

"No, my child, you have to sleep now." Aunt Klara put her hand on Lieschen's shoulder to make her lie down.

Lieschen would do no such thing. She bounced out of bed and ran across the soft carpeting into the spacious, elegant hallway, where night lights jutted out between Baroque paintings on the walls. Aunt Klara scurried after her.

A little ways down, Lieschen pushed open the door to her parents' bedroom and clicked on the light switch. "Mommy! Mommy!" she screamed. She could not see her mother, but she saw blood on her parents' crumpled white pillows and bedsheets, and on the plush, emerald carpeting. She had never seen so much blood, except one time when her father had shot a deer which was bleeding profusely.

Aunt Klara grabbed her. Lieschen kicked and pushed with her hands and feet. Her aunt's grip tightened as she lifted her into her arms and carried her back to bed. "You have to sleep now." Aunt Klara put her down abruptly and pulled up the down comforter. She turned away from Lieschen's bed, pommeled to the door, switched off the light, and closed the door from the outside.

Lieschen heard a click and a scraping sound. She hopped back out of bed and, in the darkness, stumbled over to the door and tugged at the bronze handle. It would not open. Her aunt had locked her in. Nobody had ever locked her in. Lieschen's heart pounded like a fire engine in her chest.

After an agonizing while, she crawled back to bed and clutched Nipo with her shivering hands. Her ears strained for some noise, any noise, but there was only silence. Ominous darkness and silence. Lieschen thought of the black spider with the Red Cross, and strange thoughts crept into her little head: was Mommy bleeding like the dead deer?

A week earlier, on April 11, 1955, on Lieschen's fifth birthday (thirteen years ago), her father had taken her on a hunting trip to his estate in Stainz, located forty kilometers west of Graz. It was Lieschen's first hunting trip where she had witnessed her father shooting a deer, and where she had seen the deer bleeding profusely. She felt sorry for the dead deer, lying motionless between tree trunks, shrubs, colorful wildflowers, and scattered leaves. She loved animals, but she loved them alive, not dead.

Mommy could've been bleeding like the dead deer.

This thought circled in her head until she was too exhausted to think and fell asleep.

In the morning, rays of light filtered through the eggshell-colored drapes. Lieschen hopped out of bed and tiptoed across the playful shadows on the soft carpeting. She turned the bronze handle. The door opened. Somebody must've unlocked it while I was sleeping, she thought.

Barefoot, in her pink nightgown, she headed for the breakfast nook, a large pastel-pink alcove with an arched entrance. At the rectangular teakwood table, her father sat alone hunched over a morning paper and a cup of steaming coffee. He had not noticed her. To Lieschen, he appeared downtrodden. She had never seen him sitting like that.

Her father was not only tall with a regal stature, he was also known as a powerhouse in his pharmaceutical field; and coupled with the aristocratic crown of his ancestry, it made him a giant. That's how people talked about him, but to Lieschen he was her loving father, and she had been very fond of him, just as she had been very fond of her mother. She kept staring at him for a little while, then asked, "Where's Mommy?"

Her father looked up. "You startled me, Princess. I didn't hear you come in." His eyes shifted toward Lieschen's feet. "Ah, you aren't wearing your slippers; that's why I didn't hear you." He reached out with his strong hands. "Come to me, my Princess!"

Her father's voice sounded as though coming from a remote cellar. His short, clipped mustache twitched on his stern, oval face. "Your mother had a heart attack during the night and died," he said.

Ice water ran instantly inside Lieschen. Her father pulled her close and held her. "Did Mommy bleed like the dead deer?" she asked.

Her father released her. His expression stiffened, but his shrewd, dark-gray eyes remained steady. "What makes you think that your mother was bleeding?"

"Because I heard shots, like when you shot the deer. And I saw so much blood in your bedroom, but Mommy wasn't there."

"I didn't see blood or hear a shot. Why don't we go and see." Her father took her shivering hand and led her toward the bedroom.

Lieschen pulled ahead. The moment she opened the door, she gaped because her parents' bed was nicely made up, and she could not see blood anywhere. Bewildered she asked, "But Pap, I saw so much blood!"

Her father put his right hand on her shoulder. "You had a bad dream. That's what it was. It wasn't real."

"It was all real, I saw it!" Lieschen's eyes blurred while she stared again at the beautiful silk bedspread with its circular mauve pattern, and no blood anywhere.

"Bad dreams can seem real, but in reality they're not. Let's get out of here. Come on, my Princess." Her father led her out.

In the wide hallway, they sat down on two of the twelve Baroque chairs, lined up like soldiers under the paintings along the high walls. The Baroque depictions on the ceiling did not match the paintings on the walls.

Her father moved his chair close to Lieschen's and said, "You have to be brave now and forget this bad dream. And you must never talk to anybody about it."

Why not?"

"Because a bad dream is a bad omen."

"Like the black spider with the red cross?"

"Yes. Something very bad could happen to you and to me if you talk to anyone about your bad dream. You must promise me that you will never talk to anybody. You will understand this better when you grow up."

Lieschen wanted to understand now, not when she grew up.

"Aunt Klara promised to be a good mother to you." Her father smiled a little now.

"I don't want Aunt Klara. I hate Aunt Klara!" Nobody could take the place of her loving mother; especially not Aunt Klara who, like a cruel witch, had pushed her into her bed, then locked her bedroom door.

"What did you say?" Her father looked shocked.

"I don't want Aunt Klara as my Mommy." Lieschen's feelings against her aunt had grown razor sharp during that horrifying night.

"You will learn to like her. I promise. Give it a little time. And I will always love you very much. Very, very much!"

They went back to the breakfast nook. Lieschen's place had always been between her parents. Now, her mother's chair was empty.

Frau Emma came in. Looking with sad eyes at Lieschen's father, she asked, "Herr Reinking, what do you wish for breakfast?"

"A small serving of bacon and eggs with fresh plums. And a glass of orange juice. And for my Princess . . ." he motioned toward Lieschen.

Frau Emma offered her fresh fruit, compote, eggs, croissant with butter and marmalade or honey, and hot chocolate, the things Lieschen usually liked for breakfast, but she would not eat or drink anything. She sat at the table, all forlorn. Nobody else joined them.

Lieschen thought of *Little Red Riding Hood,* the story her mother had read to her the previous evening; and she thought of the lullaby her mother had sung; and the prayer they had prayed together.

She folded her hands *Albrecht Duerer-fashion.* She was hardly two years old when her mother had taught her how to pray. As teaching example her mother had used a replica of *Albrecht Duerer's Praying Hands* on the wall next to the piano in their music room.

Lieschen prayed silently, "Dear God, please bring Mommy back to me." Her mother had told her that God loved her and would always speak to her heart when she prayed. She listened for God to speak to her, but couldn't hear anything.

Her father watched her while he ate part of his serving of bacon and eggs with fresh plums. Then he explained he had to take care of business and left Lieschen in Frau Emma's care.

Lieschen wandered out into the fruit orchard, adjacent to the vegetable and flower garden behind their luxurious villa. She sat down in the swing, under the old cherry tree, where her parents used to rock her. During those happy days, Lieschen would dangle her feet high in the air, and sing and laugh. Now her feet would not move. She sat motionless, waiting for God to speak to her and bring her mother back.

She could not hear God, and her mother did not come back, but Aunt Klara came to talk to her. Lieschen did not respond to anything her aunt said.

In the evening, instead of listening to her mother's bedtime story, singing a lullaby, and saying the Lord's Prayer, she folded Nipo's hands the way her mother had taught her. She prayed with Nipo and sang to him the lullaby *Schlaf Kindlein Schlaf.*

The following morning, during breakfast, Lieschen asked her father what would happen to her mother.

"Your mother will be buried." Her father explained the burial procedure. Aunt Klara did not make any comments, nor did Uncle Gustav and Aunt Sylvia, who had flown in from Lucerne, Switzerland, for the funeral; and they had joined them for breakfast.

Lieschen wondered why she couldn't be dead with her mother and devised her own plan.

Two days hence, hundreds of people huddled around her mother's gravesite, a newly opened rectangular hole in the ground, with a large heap of brown earth on one side. Some people carried cameras, some held flowers-roses, carnations, daffodils, irises, daisies, lilies-and a few held open umbrellas to catch the drizzle. Lieschen, her relatives, and Father Cassedi carried no umbrellas.

Standing between her father and Aunt Klara, Lieschen looked over at her grandmother's lean, ashen face, which was partly hidden behind Aunt Klara and Uncle Gustav. Her petite grandmother seemed downtrodden when she leaned forward and said to Lieschen, "My precious darling, you have to be brave now and . . ." she squeezed her swollen eyes shut and stopped talking. Lieschen wondered why.

Drizzle came down in silvery droplets while the pallbearers lowered her mother's casket into the grave.

Father Cassedi, dressed in his usual dark suit and white Roman collar of a priest, stood poised while the pallbearers placed the casket at the bottom of the earthly hole. Then he made the sign of the cross. "The earth is the Lord's and the fullness thereof."

That moment, Lieschen tore away from her father and Aunt Klara, and leaped into the grave, on top of her mother's casket. "Mommy, can you hear me?" she whispered. "I want to be with you!"

In a scurry, her father, her relatives, and Father Cassedi stooped down and reached for her.

"Child, what are you doing?" Aunt Sylvia choked.

"I want to be with Mommy," Lieschen replied, clasping her mother's casket.

Her grandmother stretched out her fine, wrinkled hands as far as she could. "My precious darling, come to me!"

"Jump in Granny!" Lieschen looked up at her.

"My sweet child, you must come toooo meeee ..." Grandma lost her voice.

"Only if you jump in." The next moment Lieschen saw her grandmother tumbling to the side. Her fmgers that sparkled with diamond rings dangled over clumps of dirt. People carried her grandmother away. Lieschen wondered why.

"Get that poor child off the coffin!" came a distraught voice from the crowd.

Her father kept reaching for her. "My Princess, you must give me your hands!"

Lieschen would not.

Father Cassedi said with a pacifying tone, "My child, in the name of Jesus Christ, let me lift you out of this grave. It's not your time to be buried."

Lying flat on her tummy, Lieschen clung to her mother's casket. She had no intention of letting go.

Father Cassedi talked to the pallbearers, and they lifted the casket back out of the grave.

"Mommy, Mommy, I want to be with you!" Lieschen clutched her mother's casket as hard as she could, but her father and Aunt Klara removed her and, together with Uncle Gustav and Aunt Sylvia, led her away.

That was the end of her mother's burial as far as Lieschen could remember, but it was also the beginning of her relentless path and search for the truth.

CHAPTER 2

Warm droplets sprayed over Lieschen's shoulders. Her hands still trembled from the nightmare that had revived the scorching memories of the fatal night thirteen years ago. Lieschen wished her nightmares would go away and stop reminding her of that excruciating time. During her growing years she had tried to uncover the truth concerning her mother's suspicious death and the disappearance of her grandmother. To this day she had not succeeded. Soon she would graduate from St. Germain, the gymnasium she attended, and then she would intensify her investigation. She could never find peace without knowing the truth.

She turned off the shower and tried to think of happy memories with her mother and her grandmother to block out her acute pain which her nightmare had revived. There were many happy memories-when her mother had taught Lieschen the piano scales, or when she had taught her to paint and make depictions come alive; and Lieschen loved when both of her parents had taken her horseback-riding, or skiing, or on other trips; or when they had rocked her in the swing under the old cherry tree in the fruit orchard next to their vegetable and flower garden behind their villa.

Occasionally her grandmother had joined them; or Grandma had taken her on train rides to castles or to see Lipizzaner horses. Lieschen would never forget one fiaker ride, a horse-drawn cabby, to the Eggenberg Palace on the western outskirts of Graz, where they attended a ballet performance in honor of the aristocratic society. "Aristocracy is our ancestry," Grandma had proudly explained.

Lieschen could not understand the meaning of aristocracy, but she had enjoyed the ballet performance together with her grandmother.

Then the awful night had cut off everything. Now Lieschen reached a point where she could no longer keep the heartwrenching secret of that treacherous night bottled up. Her nightmares kept getting worse, always intensifying her pain. She could no longer keep the promise to her father. She would talk to her best friend, Ingrid Leitner.

She finished drying herself with a soft, pale-pink towel, slipped on coral silk underwear, stepped into her study and dialed Ingrid's number on her desk phone. The telephone rang seven times before Ingrid answered.

"You need to talk to me half past midnight?" Ingrid sounded sleepy and surprised. "You seem out of breath. Did you dance on your rooftop?" she asked with a drowsy tone.

"No joking, please." Over the years, Lieschen had grown accustomed to Ingrid's goofy and sometimes sarcastic sense of humor, which was part of her fun-loving, self-confident spirit; but now was not the time for fun or humor. "I need to talk to you about a serious matter," she said.

"A serious matter half past midnight?" Ingrid's sleepy voice sounded a little irritated now.

"Can we talk in school, during break? I'll explain everything," Lieschen said. "It's about a tragic secret."

"See you in class." The phone clicked.

Lieschen went back to her bedroom and slipped on her new dress which her father had bought for her the previous day. He had told her that he had bought this special dress at the French couturier *L.a Grande Boutique.* Her father would sometimes surprise her with such unexpected tokens of love, but this time the beautiful new dress had caused an argument between her father and Aunt Klara. Lieschen had overheard the argument the previous evening when she was about to enter the living room. She stopped abruptly behind the half-closed door when she heard Aunt Klara chide, "Such expensive dresses will only make Lieschen vain."

"Leave this up to me!" her father had retorted.

"Conniving aunt!" Lieschen had seethed behind the door. She would have liked to face Aunt Klara and tell her that she was a cruel witch, but she knew her father would censor her; therefore, she refrained.

She decided to wear her beautiful new dress out of spite for her aunt, and she also thought it might help her lift her spirits. During the last year of study at St. Germain, students had a choice to wear class uniforms or personal attire. Lieschen alternated between class uniforms and her own dresses and skirts and blouses.

In front of the three-winged dresser mirror in her bedroom, she examined herself in her new dress. The tulip-pattern on the coral chiffon fabric complimented her slender figure, her long chestnut curls, and her big hazel eyes. She was aware that this beautiful dress highlighted her good looks. "Pap has such good taste," she murmured looking at Nipo, her furry brown teddy bear, who was sitting at the right side of the mahogany dresser in front of the dresser-mirror.

Ever since Nipo had experienced the dreadful night with Lieschen, he remained close to her, almost like a personal confidant. Lieschen would talk to him about many things, especially about her feelings for her father, which vacillated between love and doubt, and sometimes even hate when her suspicion escalated. She felt her father truly loved her, and she loved him. She only wished from the bottom of her heart that he had not harmed her mother and her grandmother. She kept telling herself she would soon find out. Her main goal after graduation was to find the truth.

She stepped out of her upstairs apartment in her father's villa and descended the wide, ruby-red carpeted steps. At the bottom of the stairway she hopped on the marbled floor tiles in the hallway. The ruby-red and white diamond-shaped tiles gave off a speckled sheen; but everything was quiet. Mouse-still. Why? Lieschen wondered. The mornings usually stirred with activities.

She walked toward the breakfast nook and looked in. The dainty fingers on the Mattriesen clock on the wall next to the window showed twenty-seven minutes past five. "I didn't realize," she mumbled to herself. Her nightmare had thrown off her timing. She regretted that she had called Ingrid that early. "I should've checked the time before calling Ingrid!" she reproached herself, but it had already been dawning outside, that's why she did not think that it was that early.

She entered the breakfast nook and sat down on the carved teakwood chair. Leaning against the tall honey-colored back cushion, she reminisced. While her mother had been alive, parties with high-society guests had been the norm. Her mother had often played the piano in the music room for the guests. Lieschen had resented these parties because guests had claimed her mother's attention, and she had to go to bed without a bedtime story, or a lullaby, or the Lord's Prayer together with her mother. And on such mornings the hallway and the breakfast nook usually had buzzed with guests. After her mother's death the parties had stopped; and there were no more butlers, only a few servants. Frau Emma, their long-time cook, had also assumed the function of Nanny for Lieschen. And there was a housekeeper, Reserl; and a few gardeners; and occasional extra help.

Looking through the window, Lieschen saw Joseph, their regular gardener, and two helpers, Christopher and Leo, working in the fruit orchard behind their vegetable and flower garden. She was aware that the gardeners often started work early, just like her father and Aunt Klara.

Morning light splashed across the silverware and Auergarten china on the embroidered linen table cloth, reflecting the rays of the rising sun. Frau Emma and Reserl routinely set the breakfast table in the evenings. They used specific Auergarten china for breakfast, while they alternated various Auergarten sets for dinner.

"You're up early," Frau Emma's voice came through the arched doorway.

"I woke up early because of a nightmare," Lieschen said.

"Another ugly nightmare. Umm . . ." Frau Emma wiped her hands with a fresh, green kitchen towel, draped over her short, rounded arm. The color of the towel reflected the shade of her veridian linen dress which she wore with a starched, lace-fringed, white apron.

"Very ugly." Lieschen let out a woeful sigh.

"Forget your nightmare and look at your lovely new dress." Frau Emma's smile formed a few wrinkles around the small, amber eyes on her full round face. To Lieschen, Frau Emma's chubby appearance manifested her good-natured personality.

"Good morning." Aunt Klara joined Frau Emma in the doorway.

Aunt Klara's slender appearance and her lean, pointed face contrasted Frau Emma's full figure. While her aunt's soft-spoken voice and her looks always reminded Lieschen of her grandmother, she could not understand why, in reality, her aunt had turned into a witch during the fatal night when her mother had died. Frau Emma and Aunt Klara discussed dinner; and they talked about the preservation of the early harvest of cucumbers in their vegetable garden. When Frau Emma returned to the kitchen, Aunt Klara sat down opposite Lieschen. With her knotted hands, glinting with diamond rings, she motioned toward the window. "Did you notice the beautiful sunrise?"

"I noticed." Lieschen had noticed the golden sun climbing like a huge ball defying gravity.

Frau Emma served coffee with Schlag for Aunt Klara and hot chocolate for Lieschen, their habitual drinks for breakfast.

"Where is my father?" Lieschen asked since he did not join them.

"He went to the Plant early." Aunt Klara reached for her large, brown-rimmed glasses, which she had put on the table earlier. As usual, her aunt had her graying hair piled in a bun in the back of her thin face; and she wore subdued make-up.

"I got up early, but I didn't see Pap."

"He left before five." Aunt Klara reached for her cup of coffee with Schlag. The whipped cream looked fluffy like fresh snow.

Pap must've left while I took a shower, thought Lieschen because she had not heard him drive out of the garage. She knew, however, that he sometimes inspected his entire Pharmaceutical Plant before employees arrived for work. The Plant was located at the flanks of the River Mur in the center of Graz, a twenty-minute drive from their villa in Mariatrost.

Aunt Klara set down her cup, unfolded the *Grazer Zeitung,* and put on her glasses. Before she started reading, she glanced at Lieschen without saying a word about her new dress. Her aunt's bluish-green eyes appeared blurred through the thick glasses. Lieschen thought she might as well look into an impenetrable ocean. That's how she perceived her aunt's eyes.

Aunt Klara lowered her head and began reading the front page of the *Grazer Zeitung.* A special calmness and quality of assured self-confidence surrounded her aunt's demeanor. She was known as a dignified person, but to Lieschen she was not dignified because of the way she had treated her during the treacherous night when her mother had died.

Frau Emma peeked in. "Would *it* be okay to serve breakfast?"

Aunt Klara turned to Lieschen, "My Dear, what would you like?"

Lieschen turned to Frau Emma and said, "Butter croissant with strawberry marmalade, but no eggs. And no sausage or bacon."

"Orange juice?"

"Yes, please."

"Okay. Honey is already on the table, if you like some." Frau Emma indicated the jar of honey.

Lieschen nodded.

"For me the usual," Aunt Klara said.

"Bitte." Frau Emma went back to the kitchen.

Peering over the top of her spectacles, Aunt Klara remarked, "You look so happy today. I'd like to share your happiness."

"Sure, you would." Lieschen shot a distrustful glance at her aunt. She wished so badly to be happy, but pain and sadness often eclipsed her happiness.

"Is it because you've found your own apartment?" Aunt Klara asked.

Lieschen took a deep breath and said, "I don't see why I should've to look for another apartment. We have this huge villa, and I know my father likes having me at home."

"The situation is different now. You're grown up and ..." Aunt Klara hesitated.

"Different, and what?" Lieschen dug her fingernails into her palms, a nervous habit she had acquired after her mother's death.

Aunt Klara took off her glasses and dropped them on the table. "My Dear, your father and I want you to be a grown-up, independent young lady. Toward that end, it would be best for you to move out. And there're other reasons why it would be best for you to move away from home."

"What other reasons? I don't believe that my father feels as you do. If he did, why wouldn't he tell me himself?"

Aunt Klara touched her glasses with both hands. "Do you realize that you wouldn't be with your father now if your mother were alive?"

Lieschen felt her cheeks blazing up. She believed her conniving aunt had just told her the biggest lie. 'Why wouldn't I be with both of my parents?"

"Because of circumstances."

"What circumstances?"

"The point is moot . . ." Aunt Klara's voice tapered, as if she wanted to retract what she had just said. Nonetheless, she continued at a low voice, ". . . because your mother is no longer alive. So we will not discuss this subject further."

"I don't believe you. You just want to have my father and the entire villa for yourself," . . . like a self-centered witch! Lieschen did not have the nerve to say out loud the last part of her thought. At St. Germain she had been taught to honor parents, grandparents, and elders, but sometimes she could not reconcile her upbringing with the anguish over the events in her life.

"I've told you the truth. And it would be best for you to move out," Aunt Klara repeated with calm emphasis.

Frau Emma served breakfast and poured more coffee for Aunt Klara and hot chocolate for Lieschen. She also brought a glass of orange juice for Lieschen.

As soon as Frau Emma left, Lieschen drank the entire glassful of orange juice. Then she challenged Aunt Klara, "I want to know why I wouldn't be with my parents if my mother were alive!"

Aunt Klara looked up from the soft-boiled eggs she had begun eating. "Destiny has reversed the course. One day you will learn that you cannot swim against destiny. Destiny is something we cannot control. Nor can we change it."

"I understand the meaning of destiny. Why won't you explain what you really mean?" Lieschen's stomach cramped.

"One day I may tell you more, but for now my main concern is your welfare." From a small pitcher, Aunt Klara spooned more Schlag into her coffee.

"I don't believe you." Lieschen sipped hot chocolate, but choked. She dropped her cup and grabbed the white linen napkin on her lap to cover her mouth. When she stopped choking, she placed the crumpled napkin back on her lap and exclaimed, "You're making up these stories for your own benefit, otherwise you would explain. Just as you've never explained what happened to the bloodstains in my parents' bedroom the night you locked me in and Mommy died."

Aunt Klara cast an uneasy glance at her, as though she were looking at a warped plate. "Your father has shown you that there were no bloodstains. And our discussion is closed for now. You have to go to school, and I've to go to work."

"You are so heartless!" Lieschen exclaimed through quivering lips. Then she blurted out, "I know you had something to do with my mother's death." She wanted to say murder, but the word got stuck in her throat.

"Stop making false accusations or something severe will happen." Aunt Klara grabbed her glasses.

Lieschen could see that her aunt understood very well what she meant. She was amazed that she had rattled her aunt's usual calm. "I'll find out, I guarantee. And this is my father's house, not yours. You cannot tell me to move out."

"It's only a suggestion."

"I love my apartment and my painting studio, and you want to take it all away from me. Why should I give it all up for your sake?"

"Not for my sake, for your own. An overdose of luxury and comfort can be harmful. One should never crave luxury and comfort to the sacrifice of one's personal welfare and moral values."

"What do you mean? I have moral values!"

Aunt Klara dabbed her mouth with her napkin. "One day you'll see for yourself what I mean. Life holds many secrets. And people carry a myriad of misconceptions. You can be sure, by and by you'll find out."

"You're so deceptive, I can't take it." Bouncing from her seat, Lieschen scraped her knee on the carved leg of the teakwood table. She grabbed her cup and splashed the remaining hot chocolate into her aunt's face.

Aunt Klara covered her face with both hands.

Lieschen glared at the streaks of brown chocolate seeping through her aunt's fingers, onto the sleeves of her light-gray Styrian costume. "I'm not going to do a thing without talking to my father," she exclaimed and headed upstairs to her apartment.

In her study, she looked through the picture window beyond the blossoming old cherry tree. She regretted what she had done to her aunt but sometimes her temper, coupled with her desolate emotions, got the better of her."But dear God, Aunt Klara is such a witch!" she uttered a moment later. For an agonizing while, she kept gazing at the invisible God. Then she turned away from the window and got ready for school.

CHAPTER 3

Walking on cobbled stones along the arched walkway in the St. Germain courtyard, Lieschen glimpsed instructors and students through the vaulted windows of the old cloister. The spirit of learning emanated through these windows and thick walls.

In addition to the obligatory curriculum, students could enroll in music, the arts, science, and foreign languages. The English language counted as obligatory. Lieschen had chosen French as her second foreign language. She had also enrolled in her favorite subjects of art and music. And Mother Marisa, Mother Superior of St. Germain, and all sisters and instructors, incorporated the study of the Christian faith and the wisdom of the testaments in the curriculum.

Walking by Sister Gertrude's class, Lieschen looked in through the open door and saw a student standing beside the emblem on the wall behind the catheter. She remembered the wording of the emblem: *Life on earth is not the end of this world. God's universe is unlimited and eternal.*

One time Sister Gertrude had talked about this emblem during class instruction, and Marianne Bosch, a fellow student, had asked, "Does this mean for all of us?"

"Unless you commit a deadly sin," Sister Gertrude had replied. That warning stuck in Lieschen's head.

At the end of the walkway, she entered her classroom. Professor Brand, their history instructor, was arranging class material behind the lectern. He paid no attention to her, but a few students gazed at her.

It's my new dress, thought Lieschen. She would have liked to tell her classmates that she was wearing this dress mainly in defiance of Aunt Klara. However, in previous years, even when she was wearing a uniform, some classmates had treated her as if she were not one of them, as welcome as a skunk in a dining room. Ingrid had told her that some students could not relate to her because of her father's fame and riches and because of his aristocratic lineage. "Be patient, it'll change," Ingrid consoled her. "You're kind and caring. Our classmates will eventually respond to your true nature."

With Lieschen's philanthropic ways, and with Ingrid's help, her relationship with most classmates had improved over the years. Lieschen was glad. She ended up having good relations with most students, although her father expected that she mainly associated with aristocratic children. On the other hand, her mother had encouraged her to mingle with all children and with all people to experience God's richness of life on earth. "God created a variety of people for His purpose. We're all God's children, and we have to appreciate one another," her mother used to say. Two of her mother's best friends, Ingrid Leitner's mother, and Werner Kurzweiler's mother were not from the aristocracy either.

Holding a stack of sheets in his hands, Professor Brand faced the students. His short, slim stature, dark flat hair, and big glasses above his slightly crooked nose made him look like a sentry without a hat. "This quiz concerns the reign of the Hapsburg Dynasty, which will be part of your final exam," he announced and instructed two students to distribute the quizzes.

Lieschen tried to decipher the jumble of letters that appeared as clear as mud in her head, like a rain puddle during a storm. The argument with Aunt Klara and her nightmare preoccupied her troubled heart and mind.

After a short while, Professor Brand alerted the students, "You have five more minutes."

Lieschen answered as many questions as she could, guessing most of them because she could not concentrate, and she had run out of time.

"Don't forget to put your name in the upper right-hand corner," Professor Brand reminded the students when it was time to turn in the quizzes.

Lieschen jotted down her name and handed in the quiz. Professor Brand redistributed the sheets to different students for correction. Lieschen received the quiz of Heidi Strauss. Heidi had clone well, but

Lieschen worried that she might have flunked the quiz. She had been a good student, especially in her favorite subjects of languages, music, art, sociology, history, geography, and literature, but today she could not do well in any quiz. The moment she heard Werner Kurzweiler report the best grade for her, she knew that Werner had received her quiz and had corrected her answers.

Normally flunking such a quiz had no serious consequence; and normally Lieschen did not believe in cheating; however, this quiz comprised part of the final exam before graduation, and her father would be furious if he found out that she had flunked an exam concerning the Hapsburg nobility, their ancestry. With a thankful smile she glanced over at Werner.

Much time had passed since Lieschen had enjoyed riding her gold bicycle with Werner, or playing with him in his tree house when they were little. For Werner, this friendship had developed into much more. "You're the only girl I'd ever want to marry," he had told Lieschen. "I love you more than I could ever tell you with words. I would die for you."

This concerned Lieschen because her feelings for Werner were not like that. Playing with him as a child had been like playing with a brother, and it had never changed. Now, Lieschen saw in Werner a big brother, and she adored him. She always wanted to have a big brother and missed not having any siblings.

When the recess bell rang, Lieschen and Ingrid left the classroom together. Strolling along the cemented path on the St. Germain school grounds, between chestnut trees and flowers, Lieschen apologized to Ingrid for having called her so early.

"Don't do it again!" Ingrid smiled. "By the way, your dress looks chic."

"Danke." Lieschen was glad that Ingrid did not hold the early telephone call against her.

"Now tell me about your problem."

Lieschen stumbled over a twig on the path. Her knees buckled. To break the promise to her father never to talk to anybody about the fatal night made her feel guilty.

"No need to fall down." Ingrid cackled.

When Lieschen regained her balance, Ingrid said with a mischievous smirk, "Did you climb on your rooftop last night trying to measure the universe with your yardstick? And you didn't succeed? Is that your problem?"

"I'm not talking about something crazy like that. I'm talking about a tragic secret."

"I believe the universe is tragic. And it's secretive, and beautiful, and mysterious." Ingrid stopped cackling when she looked at Lieschen's tearful eyes. "Now, now, I'm listening," she said.

Lieschen felt as if steel jaws clammed her throat. "I wanted to tell you a long time ago," she managed to utter.

"Tell me what?"

"I couldn't. I just couldn't."

"I thought you wanted to tell me now." Ingrid squinted her eyes. "If you prefer telling me later, that's okay . . . the day after tomorrow, or the day after the day after tomorrow ..."

Ingrid had never let Lieschen down when she needed her but, in her present condition, Ingrid's goofy sense of humor irked her.

"Serious, tell me. I really mean serious. Never mind my teasing. You know me."

Lieschen hesitated for another moment, and then her words began spilling through her tense lips as if a waterfall had broken loose inside her mouth. She told Ingrid the whole tragedy of the fatal night.

The mischievous residue on Ingrid's face vanished like darkness during lightning. "I can't believe it." She grabbed her thick brown braids and tossed them over her broad shoulders.

"I've never told anybody." Lieschen's tongue felt sticky because she had broken the promise to her father.

"Here I thought you were on top of the world, having inherited your mother's beauty and talent, and your father's riches. That's what my Mom used to say about you."

"In the first place, the money and riches belong to my father. In the second place ..."

"But you're his only daughter, his only heiress, heiress to a ton of riches," Ingrid interrupted.

"Whatever that means. Sometimes I feel like crawling into a sinkhole."

"Why a stinkhole?"

"I said sinkhole."

"Small difference."

Lieschen looked at a cluster of daisies, interspersed with an array of rhododendrons and begonias that formed a symmetrical pattern and filled the space between trunks of the chestnut trees on both sides of the pathway. When she felt a bee humming into her left ear, she flicked her hand until the bee flew away. Then she said, "None of my father's riches could ever replace my mother."

"1 wouldn't doubt that." Ingrid looked deadly serious now.

"And the way I've lost my mother, and also my Grandma, I feel I've lost part of my roots under treacherous circumstances." A woeful sigh escaped Lieschen. "I mean my father has been good to me, but he wouldn't allow me to talk to anybody about that fatal night, which made me more and more suspicious as I grew older."

"I can hardly imagine what you must've gone through. I mean, what you're still going through ..."

"And to this day I don't know what really happened. On that awful night when Mommy died, Aunt Klara locked me in my room, as I told you. Since then, I couldn't stand her, but my father made me accept her as my surrogate mother."

"Your aunt is known to be a good, respectable person. Just as your father is known to be honorable?"

"That's the irony." With her fingers Lieschen wiped the tears on her cheeks and turned to look across the meadow, where she saw handicapped children playing near a statue of Friedrich Schiller. A few of the children held out their hands and played with the rivulets of water squirting from the Schiller fountain.

"Did you ask your father about the shots you heard, and the bloodstains you saw?" Ingrid asked.

Lieschen turned back. "My father insists there were no shots and no bloodstains. He said I had a bad dream, as I told you."

"Quite a bad dream. Somebody probably cleaned away the bloodstains during the night after your aunt had locked you in your bedroom. That's how it appears."

Lieschen felt dizzy.

"What was wrong between your parents?"

"I don't know. That's what I'm trying to find out."

"I'll help you."

"Danke."

Ingrid tried to tuck her white blouse into her veridian linen skirt. "Look at me; I've got to lose weight." She struggled to close her skirt's zipper.

Lieschen did not mind the distraction from their painful conversation. "Hans likes you a little chubby," she said.

"I can never be sure. Anyway, you mean if my fiancé likes me the way I am, I shouldn't worry about losing weight?"

"I think you look fine."

"I'd like to lose at least five kilo." Ingrid pointed at a bench under a nearby lime tree along a gravel path, about twenty meters off the main path. "We got sidetracked," she said. "Why don't we sit down over there so we can talk better?"

They walked over and sat down on the wooden bench under the lime tree. Robins and finches chirped in the luscious spring branches above.

"I want to have courage, but look at me!" Lieschen held out her quivering hands.

"Jesus!" Ingrid touched Lieschen's hands with hers. "You must ground that sucker."

"I wish I could."

"You have to. You can't fall apart." Ingrid pulled back her hands and Lieschen dropped hers on her lap. Then Ingrid asked, "Why did you wait so long to tell me?"

"Because I wanted to keep the promise to my father. He must never find out that I talked to you. All hell would break loose."

"If he's guilty of murder, hell should break loose."

Lieschen's hands fluttered on her lap like a mouse in an owl's jaw.

"Couldn't your mother have committed suicide?"

"She could've, but I don't think Mommy would've abandoned me." Lieschen could not stop the tears flowing from her eyes.

"Big puzzle. Are you sure you didn't dream about the shots and the bloodstains, as your father said?"

"During that awful night, everything was real. I'm sure it was all real."

"So you think your father invented the bad dream as a cover-up?"

"I'm afraid so. Otherwise, why would Aunt Klara have locked me in my bedroom? And why did she change her dress? At dinner, she wore a blue dress. Then, when she came to my bedroom, she wore a black dress."

"You mean her blue dress might've been splattered with blood?"

"It might've been. When I question my aunt, she always gives me evasive answers. And she tries to brush me off. Always."

"I understand that you're determined to find the truth."

"1 cannot find peace unless I know the truth, and I believe I have a right to know."

"Of course, you do."

"I don't think my nightmares will stop either unless I know the truth."

"You think your nightmares will stop if you find out what happened? What if your father or your aunt had murdered your mother?"

"Despite everything, I cannot picture my father, nor Aunt Klara, as murderers . . ." Lieschen's quivering hands felt very cold.

"I don't know if we can picture murderers. My cousin Erik says that most murderers appear like normal people." Ingrid paused, and then asked, "Have you seen your Mom's death certificate?"

"My father has shown it to me. Cardiac arrest is listed as the cause of Mommy's death."

Ingrid's eyes narrowed. "With your father's money, couldn't he have bought any death certificate?"

"*My* father always emphasizes aristocratic dignity." Lieschen felt a strange urge to defend her father. She did not know why, but these mixed emotions added to her torment.

"You suppose your father had committed a noble murder? A dignified crime?"

"Ingrid, please, don't be sarcastic."

"I mean, you don't know what went on. Your father and your aunt might've wanted to get rid of your mother because they were in love. Triangle love isn't for everyone, you must know." Ingrid snickered a bit.

"That occurred to me," Lieschen sighed.

"I don't think your father could've divorced your mother."

"I don't know if he could or couldn't have."

"Such a scandal could've ruined his reputation and social standing. His dignity and nobility. We've just talked about it." Ingrid took a lime leaf that had fallen on her lap, and dropped it on the green grass. Then she asked, "How is your father's relationship with your aunt now? Are they in love?"

"My aunt is very important in my father's personal life and in his Pharmaceutical Company, but I don't know if they're in love. I've never caught them making love, if that's what you mean."

"I don't mean making love. Being in love doesn't just mean making love. Not in my book."

"I don't know if they're in love."

"Your aunt was never married, was she?"

"No, she wasn't."

"And she's now fifty-something?"

"Fifty-four."

"Still young. And she has her own bedroom, you told me."

"Two rooms down from my father's bedroom. I mean from my parents' bedroom. My father is still sleeping in the same bed, in the same bedroom where he used to sleep with my mother. He just took out all of Mommy's clothes from the closet, except her beautiful wedding gown." Lieschen paused, then said, "And most of the other things in our villa are the way they used to be during Mommy's lifetime, like the paintings in the hallway, the Baroque ceiling, the library, the music room, the game room, and all the other rooms. Everything's the same. My father hasn't changed anything."

"It seems your father loved your mother."

"I thought so too."

"And where is your Grandma?"

"I've searched in our clinic in Mariatrost, and everywhere I could think of. I've talked to Frau Ritt and Frau Orlando, Grandma's neighbors, and I've talked to some of Mommy's friends. Nobody seems to know."

"Or no one might tell because they're afraid of your father. Could that be? Everybody knows your father is very powerful."

"1 don't know," Lieschen inhaled deeply.

"Perhaps your grandmother knew what happened to your mother and also died mysteriously?"

"By God, I hope that didn't happen."

Five male students, including Werner Kurzweiler and Ingrid's cousin Fritz Probst, walked up to them and exchanged a congenial Servus.

"How did you score on your Hapsburg quiz-a-ra?" With a screwed up face, Fritz winked at Ingrid as if that quiz had been for the birds.

Lieschen noticed acne on both sides of Fritz's rounded nose, on his protruding cheeks, and on his low forehead. She had not noticed the acne before.

Ingrid gave a thumbs up sign.

"Good for you. But who's counting." Fritz swooshed his right foot forward, as though pushing away some pebbles, or something. Then he said, "After graduation, I won't set my precious feet into another classroom. Not in my lifetime." He screwed up his face some more. "Studying is for the birds."

"Perhaps birds are smarter than we are and don't need to study," said Wolfgang, another student.

"So we should learn from birds," Ingrid giggled.

"We just need to grow wings." Fritz pulled up the left sleeve of his Prussian-blue shirt and displayed a fashionable, new Swiss watch on his hair-covered wrist. Ingrid looked closely at the watch. "Nice," she said.

"Birthday present from my folks."

"Now you won't be late anymore." Ingrid winked at Fritz with her left eye.

Fritz patted his brownish, wavy hair. "I'd also have to reprogram my internal watch."

"I thought it's your prerogative to be late," Wolfgang said.

"That's it. I have a right to choose my prerogatives."

To Lieschen, it sounded as though Fritz held a license for being late all the time.

"Of course, you have to guard your reputation," Werner said.

"You bet." Fritz gave an exaggerated nod.

"Never mind who you keep waiting," Ingrid snickered.

"Never mind," Fritz nodded.

While Fritz continued talking and joking with Ingrid and the other students, Lieschen whispered into Werner's ear, "Danke for correcting my quiz."

"Bitte." Werner smiled his contagious smile, while his clear blue, expressive eyes accented his sympathetic oval face and thick auburn hair; but his quizzical expression told Lieschen that he had recognized something was bothering her.

"Must be nice to be in love," Fritz chuckled.

"Will you hush!" Werner cast an angry glance at Fritz.

"Don't you agree?" Fritz looked at Lieschen with a twisted grin. The other students also chuckled.

Lieschen felt embarrassed and annoyed and did not reply.

Slipping his hands into his sand-colored trousers, Werner said to Fritz, "Let's go on, you insensitive hobo."

Fritz laughed out loud. "Hey, I'm glad you're a sensitive hobo." Lieschen was familiar with the expression *hobo,* a regional idiom for fellow.

"You'll excuse me," Werner said to Lieschen, and he and the other young men strolled on.

Lieschen knew that Werner was patient and kind, and his tall, straight walk reflected his upright character. Only when someone angered him did he become a bit condescending, as just now with Fritz.

"I've such a funny cousin. When Fritz comes over to our house, we often roll with laughter," Ingrid said.

"Good for you." Lieschen had calmed down. Her hands were no longer shaking.

"Listen, I can ask my cousin Erik to investigate for you," Ingrid suggested then.

Lieschen had never met Erik. She only knew Ingrid's cousins Jakob and Fritz. Jakob worked in her father's pharmaceutical lab.

"Erik is now a detective with the Criminal Investigative Division at the Grazer Police Department," Ingrid disclosed.

"Don't ask him. He might leak information."

"I wouldn't worry about that. If your father is guilty, he should reap the just rewards." Ingrid paused. "Nonetheless, I'm sure Erik would keep things hushed," she added.

"It's too risky. Don't talk to him. Don't talk to anybody."

"How can I help you if I cannot talk to the people who could help you with the investigation?"

"You helped me by listening and talking to me." Lieschen felt better since she could talk to Ingrid about her bottled-up pain. "I have to investigate my own way," she said then. "In private."

"Do you intend to become an amateur private eye with professional status?"

"I don't need a title. I'll start by asking my uncle in Lucerne. Uncle Gustav is my mother's brother."

"I didn't know you had relatives in Switzerland."

"I haven't seen Uncle Gustav and his wife, Aunt Sylvia, since my mother's funeral. But, from time to time, we talk by phone. Uncle Gustav works in his own architecture firm in Lucerne."

"You never told me."

"I don't know why I never told you. Now you know."

"So your mother has one brother, your Uncle Gustav, and one sister, your Aunt Klara."

Lieschen nodded, "Yes."

"Now I've a clearer picture." Ingrid checked her wrist watch. "We better head back."

Werner was talking with a few students at the entrance to their classroom. He held a glass of water in his right hand and offered it to Lieschen. "Hope this will help you feel better."

Lieschen drank the whole glassful. "Danke," she said and handed the empty glass back to Werner.

At home, she called Uncle Gustav from her study. Since her father and Aunt Klara had gone to a business meeting in Stainz, they could not eavesdrop, and Lieschen could talk without inhibition.

Uncle Gustav answered on the third ring. "How nice to hear from you, Lieschen." He sounded surprised.

"How *are you*, Uncle Gustav?"

"I just came home from work. We're busy, and we're healthy. So we're fine." Uncle Gustav's warm baritone voice had not changed over the years. "How is school?" he asked.

"I'll graduate next month."

"I know. You've undoubtedly become a mature young lady."

Lieschen was not sure. "Uncle Gustav, may I ask you a question?"

"You may."

A knot formed in Lieschen's throat.

"Go ahead," Uncle Gustav urged.

"It concerns my mother and my grandmother," Lieschen finally said. "I'd like to ask you in person."

"Why, of course. When will you come to see us?"

"I'd like to come after I graduate from St. Germain, if that would be all right?" Lieschen was surprised over this spontaneous exchange. It just happened. She had not planned it that way.

"We'd be delighted to have you come. Your graduation date is when?"

"June 12."

"Would you like to catch a flight right after your graduation, or the next day, the thirteenth?"

"The thirteenth." The moment Lieschen said the thirteenth, a red light flashed up in her head because the number thirteen might mean bad luck. But I can't be superstitious, she warned herself the next moment.

"I'll send you the flight ticket as part of your graduation gift. We'll also have a surprise waiting for you."

"That's very kind of you, Uncle Gustav." Lieschen's spirits rose.

"Do you still paint?"

"Yes, I love to paint. I'd like to be an artist." Ever since her mother had taught her how to paint, art had been Lieschen's passion. And after her father had given her the upstairs apartment with the large painting studio for her twelfth birthday, Lieschen often spend hours on end sketching and painting, while she occasionally neglected her studies.

"I'm sure you have inherited your mother's artistic talent," Uncle Gustav said.

"I don't know." Although Lieschen would happily follow in her mother's artistic footsteps, she felt uncertain whether one could inherit artistic talent. "How is Aunt Sylvia?" she asked.

"She is fine. She went to the hairdresser this afternoon. Things girls like to do, right?"

"Right." Lieschen smiled a little into the receiver. "Would you say hello to Aunt Sylvia."

"Of course. She'll be delighted that you called. We often talk about you. Since we have no children, we like to think of you as our child too. After all, your mother and I have always been close."

Lieschen knew.

"We'll send you the flight ticket, and we'll look forward to seeing you on the thirteenth, next month. Good luck on your final exams."

"Danke. Good-bye Uncle Gustav." Lieschen replaced the receiver and stepped out of her apartment. Half-way down the stairway, she began singing a song she had learned at St. Germain: *Life's a carousel, like ocean waves, storming, ebbing, rising, falling . . .* With her hands in the air, she felt like conducting an orchestra.

Frau Emma came out of the kitchen, holding a potato in one hand and a knife in the other. Her smile turned into a wide grin.

At the bottom of the stairway, Lieschen hopped onto the marble tiles and tap-danced. She had taken lessons in tap-dancing at St. Germain, and right now she wanted to hold on to her happy sentiments and shut out the sad events of her life. The conversation with Uncle Gustav, and his cordial invitation, had uplifted her spirits.

When she stopped dancing, Frau Emma said, "I haven't seen you so joyful in a long time. And you sang like a nightingale."

"I just wanted to capture this happy moment." Lieschen breathed fast from tap-dancing.

"Whichever happy sentiments you captured, make sure you hold on," Frau Emma said.

"I would like to." Lieschen longed to be happy. "What are you cooking?" she asked. "It smells good."

"I'm baking Apfelstrudel, and for the main dish we'll have Wienerschnitzel with potato pancakes and mixed salads."

"I mean what is the sweet, spicy smell?"

"Cinnamon and cloves in the Apfelstrudel."

"Can I have a slice right out of the oven?"

"Sure. It should be ready in about fifteen minutes." Frau Emma returned to the kitchen.

Lieschen loved Frau Emma's Apfelstrudel, especially hot out of the oven; and she felt hungry. One time, she had watched Frau Emma measure together the ingredients, and she had helped kneading the dough. She intended to make her own Apfelstrudel one day.

She went out into the orchard and meandered over to the old cherry tree. The wooden seat of the swing under the cherry tree was chipped, as though mice had gnawed off small pieces; but Lieschen would not want it changed for a new seat because the original swing reminded her of the happy days when her parents used to rock her in this swing. She dropped into the seat and began moving her feet when Frau Emma called her from the portico. She held a bouquet of red roses in her hands. "These roses have just arrived for you."

Lieschen wondered who might have sent her roses. She hopped off the swing and hurried over to Frau Emma. "Fraulein Roswitta from the Mariatrost Florist brought them."

Lieschen knew Fraulein Roswitta because she used to buy flowers at the Mariatrost Florist for different occasions. Especially in winter when they did not have flowers in their own garden, Lieschen would buy yellow daffodils for her mother's grave. She reached for the small envelope between the roses and pulled out the note. The cursive looked familiar. She began reading.

Dear Lieschen!

Whatever has caused you discomfort and pain, I feel with you, and I hope these roses will cheer you up. They come from my heart, which is always with you.

Always!
Fondest love,
Werner

Lieschen looked at the red heart which Werner had drawn around her name. She appreciated his caring ways, but she wished he would love her like a brother, the way she loved him. She took the roses from Frau Emma and inhaled the delectable fragrance.

"Love roses?" Frau Emma inquired.

"Kind of-" Lieschen carried the bouquet to her apartment, prepared a crystal vase with fresh water, and carefully arranged the roses. She set the bouquet on the elongated Danish coffee table in her study. The fresh color brightened the entire study, while the delectable fragrance laced the air.

I better do my homework, she reminded herself again and pulled the chemistry book from the Danish bookshelf. She also picked up a notepad and a pen from the adjacent desk, carried everything out to the balcony and dropped it on the oak table. Then she leaned her elbows on the oak railing and looked at the majestic alpine mountains, bathed in the afternoon sunshine. She also saw a few riders exercising horses in the rink at her father's nearby horse stables.

Study! Study! She reminded herself and dropped into one of the four oak chairs around the table. She opened her chemistry book and began to study in earnest.

A short while later, Frau Emma brought her two slices of Apfelstrudel. "Mmm, tastes good." Lieschen swallowed the first bite.

"If you want more, let me know. I'll finish preparing dinner." Frau Emma left again.

Lieschen continued studying and making notes, while munching the delicious Apfelstrudel. She had almost finished the second slice when her father called her from the study.

The business meeting must've been short, thought Lieschen. She put her pen next to the notepad and stepped inside, where she found her father standing near the bouquet of red roses by the Danish coffee table. "Who sent you these roses?" he queried.

Lieschen told him.

"Young lady, we have to have a talk. Let's sit down." Her father settled on the mustard-colored couch behind the coffee table. Lieschen joined on one of the two matching chairs.

They looked at each other for an intense moment. Then her father spoke with an emphatic tone, "As the son of an insignificant textile merchant, Werner is not fitting for you. No commoner's blood will soil our heritage. We've talked about this before."

Lieschen's breathing came in sudden spurts. "Pap, I've also told you that I don't see any difference between commoners' and aristocratic blood. God doesn't define blood types as common or aristocratic. Neither does medical science."

"My dear Lieschen, you're almost nineteen years old. By now you must understand that you cannot spoil the aristocratic blood in our veins. It's our pride. Our ancestry. Our heritage and great joy!" Her father's shrewd eyes lit up while he made these statements.

"The Hapsburg aristocracy ceased to govern in 1918. It's now 1968, and Austria is a democratic Republic." Lieschen could not understand why her father clung to a concept which had been outdated.

"Aristocracy doesn't cease over night. Since it is our family heritage, it will remain in our blood and continue to exist. *And* you have to respect and appreciate our heritage."

"I do respect and appreciate our heritage, and I know many good people from the aristocracy. By the same token, I know many good people who aren't from the aristocracy, as for instance Family Reichert. Their children intermarried with aristocratic children. They have children and grandchildren. For them, it hasn't been an issue."

"What other people do is their business. Just don't forget ..." Her father took a deep breath, and then said with a sharp tone, "Don't ever mock the sanctity of our blood!"

"What matters to me is the heart and soul of a person. The character and personality, not the bloodline." Lieschen was amazed how firmly she defended her opinion against her authoritative father.

"My dear Lieschen, you have *a* lot to learn." Deep lines etched on her father's high forehead.

"We just have a difference of opinion." Lieschen felt she did not have to learn anything to have her own opinion and her own feelings. "And Werner's Mom and Ingrid's Mom, were Mommy's best friends," she said.

"That was a long time ago." Her father waved his hands away from his chest, as if he did not want to be reminded of that reality.

"Werner is my dear friend." Lieschen found her father's point of view quite disturbing.

"I do not wish for you to be *seen* with Werner. People could get the wrong impression."

"What impression is that?"

"That you might be engaged to him. People do get such impressions, you must know."

"If they do, I don't care. I know Werner is a good person, and I'm not doing anything wrong." Lieschen's agitated breathing accelerated.

"In our social position, you *have* to care. Our heritage and our business are of uppermost importance, and you have to be very selective in choosing the right friends and the right husband. They have to be from our nobility."

"What do business and nobility have to do with love?" Lieschen gnawed on her lower lip.

"Everything. For you, business, nobility and love have to merge, and your husband has to be well qualified to carry on our business."

"Pap, did you feel that way when you married Mommy? She was an opera singer, a pianist, and a painter. As far as I know she had no interest in business."

Visibly taken aback, her father replied, "My marriage to your mother was different."

"How was it different?" Lieschen saw another opportunity to question her father.

"It was not like most marriages."

"I'd like to know how your relationship with Mommy was different. Why won't you tell me?"

"Because there is nothing to tell."

"Pap, that's not a satisfactory answer."

"You might say we had genetic differences."

"What genetic differences? And did you discover them before or after you got married?"

Her father's troubled eyes turned away. When he shifted back, he said with an edge in his voice, "Do not pry!"

"I have to know what was wrong between you and Mommy." Lieschen squeezed her fingernails into her palms. "I have to know!"

Her father leaned forward on the couch and clasped his knees with his hands. "Let me give you one word of advice, as your loving father ..."

"I don't want advice. I want the truth. Our truth. Please Pap!"

"In certain circumstances you have to accept what happened and live with it." Her father's eyes became laced with a dark, mysterious veil.

Lieschen put her hand on her heart. "Pap, I know you're hiding something in there. Why won't you tell me what it is?" She inhaled deeply and asked, "How did Mommy die?"

"You know how your mother died." Her father made an abrupt motion with both hands to curtail the conversation. In a moment, he carried on, though. "Rehashing painful events won't change them. The past is gone. Let's talk about the future. Your future. Our future. That's what matters now. We're alive, and your mother is not." Her father put his hand on Lieschen's. "I will help you select a husband with the right qualifications, so that your future will shine."

Lieschen pulled away her hand. "I will choose my own husband," she insisted.

"If you're thinking of Werner, the answer is no!" Her father projected a forceful **no.**

"I'm thinking of love." Lieschen crossed her legs. "Only I know who I can love."

"You can always learn to love a husband who has the right qualifications." Her father's tone became somewhat tempered.

"I don't believe love for a husband can he learned, or negotiated, or arranged like a business deal."

"You're very naive. We'll talk more about this when the time is ripe. Just don't forget . . ." Her father ran his left hand over his forehead, then continued, ". . . since you're my only child and heiress, people will keep an eye on you. That's the nature of the beast. And you have to carry on our noble principles."

Lieschen sighed. "Pap, you know I'd like to pursue an art career." She reasoned she could follow her passion with an art career and, at the same time, sidesteps her father's expectations.

His thin lips under his shortly clipped mustache twitched. "That is out of the question." He rose. "I have to go now." He bent over and patted Lieschen's shoulder. "All you need to do is follow my advice and guidance, and you won't go wrong." He smiled his authoritative smile and exited.

Lieschen thought her father had very unreasonable expectations. His attitude greatly disturbed her. After all, she was grown up, and her father had to relinquish his control over her. She cast another glance at the beautiful roses from Werner. She would never let her father disrupt their friendship.

CHAPTER 4

Lieschen entered the formal dining room at their villa. "Good evening," she said, looking at her father and Aunt Klara seated at the dining table.

They returned her greeting, and Lieschen sat down on her chair. She reached for the white linen napkin next to her Auergarten plate and put it on her lap. Two days had passed since she had the disagreement with her father over the roses from Werner. The previous evening, they did not have dinner together because her father and her aunt had been out. Lieschen now hoped for a conciliatory reunion.

Frau Emma served roasted veal with almond rice, red cabbage, dill sauce, and spinach salad.

As soon as Frau Emma left, her father picked up a forkful of roasted veal from his plate and said, "I believe our Xiron formula will soon reach a major breakthrough in the treatment of cancer." His enthusiastic tone told Lieschen that he did not hold a grudge against her, and she was glad.

"We had an exciting day," Aunt Klara said.

"You're approaching phase III, aren't you?" Lieschen had only limited knowledge of this revolutionary formula.

"Yes, our most critical phase." Her father swallowed the roasted veal he had been chewing.

"Why is this critical?" Lieschen thought all development phases should be equally critical.

"In this final stage we have to be careful that no information leak to a competitor." With his silver fork, her father picked up a bunch of red cabbage from his plate.

"Ah! I thought something might explode." Lieschen laughed at her own clumsy thought.

Aunt Klara laughed too and said, "Something might explode if information leaks out." She ground a little pepper over her dill sauce, and then offered the peppermill to Lieschen's father. Since he did not want pepper, she held the peppermill toward Lieschen. She did not want pepper either. Sometimes she liked pepper, at other times she did not. Aunt Klara put down the peppermill and resumed eating.

"When will you depart for Venice?" Lieschen asked her father.

"I had to coordinate the timing with Dr. Prinz Senior, Professor Mondschein from the Intrapolar Institute, and Dr. Schwarz from Kripschach. We're leaving in the morning."

"Tomorrow morning?"

"Yes, earlier than scheduled." Her father dabbed his lips with his linen napkin.

Lieschen scooped up a forkful of spinach. She enjoyed spinach now. As a little girl she had neither liked salads nor cooked vegetables, but she had acquired a taste for it; and she had learned that salads, vegetables, and fresh fruit are important for a healthy diet.

After she swallowed the spinach, she asked her father, "Why don't you fly? You used to fly to such meetings."

"We have to stop at the Angus Ranch to select cats, dogs, and mice for research. And perhaps one small ape. Dr. Prinz will make the selection."

With a sinking feeling in her stomach, Lieschen said, "Couldn't there be other methods used in research? Isn't testing animals inhumane?" Living in harmony with nature and animals and plants and everything alive was very important to her. At St. Germain she had learned reverence for all living things.

"Would you rather have people tested?" Her father observed her closely.

That sounded awful. "There must be a method other than testing people or animals," she said.

"At present, we don't have other methods." Her father's shrewd gaze reflected his decisive character. At age fifty-eight, he was the powerful chairman and widely respected chief executive officer of his own pharmaceutical enterprise, *Reinking & Co.,* one of the largest in Austria.

They had almost finished their meal when her father glanced at her with a challenging expression.

What does this mean? Lieschen wondered, glancing back.

A frown formed on her father's high forehead above his thick eyebrows. "I've been waiting for you to tell me!"

"Tell you what?" Lieschen could not remember that she was supposed to tell her father anything in particular.

"There's nothing you have to tell me?"

Did Pap find out about my conversation with Uncle Gustav, or with Ingrid? But why wouldn't he have said something sooner? Since Lieschen did not know what to tell her father, she said nothing. She just kept glancing at him.

"Why haven't you told me that you wanted to move out? Why did Aunt Klara have to break such news?"

"Pap, I don't want to move out."

"I considered it proper to tell you," Aunt Klara budged in.

Lieschen wanted to say something awful to her aunt, like you're such a conniving witch! But she knew better and refrained.

Frau Emma collected the plates and served dessert of chocolate souffle with raspberry compote. The dessert looked appetizing, but Lieschen's stomach felt cramped, and she could not *eat* anymore. *She* despised Aunt Klara for wanting to drive a wedge between her and her father, and for luring her away from home.

With a sharp tone, her father said, "I don't consider your actions proper. If you have such plans, you talk to me!"

"Pap, I'd like to talk to you alone." Lieschen felt her cheeks burning.

"We can go horseback riding after dinner. Then we can talk."

"But Walter, the Kramers are coming over. I thought you wanted to play chess with Albert. And Gwendolyn and I were going to play cards," Aunt Klara said with a dismayed expression.

"Call and ask Albert and Gwendolyn to come later." Lieschen knew Herr and Frau Kramer well. They had been friends with her father and Aunt Klara for as long as she could remember. They were also descendants of the Hapsburg nobility and lived on a nearby ridge where the road curved at a sharp angle. Herr Kramer owned and operated a brick factory in Weiz, a suburb east of Graz. Lieschen knew that her father sometimes had political meetings with Herrn Kramer at his factory.

She headed upstairs and slipped on coal-colored jodhpurs, a pullover of the same color, black boots, and a crimson English riding jacket. She was anxious to tell her father that Aunt Klara had been trying to undermine their relationship.

While they sauntered along the sloping path toward the stables, Lieschen's eyes wandered over shades of pink, blue, yellow, white, orange, and purple wildflowers, scattered across the rolling countryside like splashes of color on a huge green pallet. Her soul identified in a tender way with the harmony and beauty of nature, but her nerves did not. When she could not stand waiting any longer for her father to resume their conversation, she turned toward him and said, "Pap, I thought your home is also my home. That's what you told me. Why do you want me to move out?"

"Aunt Klara told me that you wanted to move out to be independent."

"Aunt Klara always tries to come between you and me. Since I'm grown up and will graduate soon, it's getting worse. And I think I know wy.

"Why?" Her father raised his eyebrows.

"I believe Aunt Klara is self-centered and jealous. She wants you and the whole villa to herself, and I should disappear as if I had never existed." A knot formed in Lieschen's throat.

"I think you misunderstand. I know Aunt Klara has tried to be a good mother to you."

Lieschen choked. "She pretends. She's been hurting my feelings ever since Mommy died."

"You know that's not true. Have you ever thought that you might not understand Aunt Klara?"

"I understand very well what she's trying to do. I don't know why you always support her. Do you love her more than me?" The knot in Lieschen's throat intensified, and tears began rolling down her cheeks.

"Aunt Klara is very important for you, for me, and for my Company, and I'm fond of Aunt Klara. But you, my dear Lieschen, you're very special to me!" Her father put his powerful arm around Lieschen's shoulder and pulled her close.

His arm comforted her, but she deeply resented his fondness of Aunt Klara. A vision of her mother appeared in her mind. "Pap, please tell me how Mommy died," she asked quickly as though this moment could slip away. She had asked her father many times, she had lost count; but she would never give up until he would tell her the truth, or she would find out one way or another. She had to know the truth.

Her father withdrew his arm. "I've explained as much as I can explain. And I've shown you the death certificate."

"A death certificate can be forged." Lieschen hoped her father would not jump on her for this comment.

He stopped walking. "How then do you believe your mother died?"

"How should I know?"

Her father resumed walking and turned to look over his right shoulder. Lieschen kept his pace and looked to the other side, across the sloping meadow, where her mother's body lay decaying in the Mariatrost Cemetery, at the bottom of the hill.

After sauntering and reflecting for a little while, she turned to her father and said, "I only know that the bloodstains which I saw during that gruesome night had disappeared by next morning, and you said I had a bad dream when I heard shots and saw bloodstains."

Her father's head shot back. His mustache twitched. 'What the devil are you implying?" His jarred voice bounced like a cougar bouncing after a prey.

Lieschen had never seen her father like that. "Pap, please tell me if Mommy was murdered, or if she committed suicide, or what happened." She felt her own agonizing sigh deep inside her.

Large crevices formed on her father's face as if it was plowed over, and his pupils took on an obscure glow.

They walked on in silence until her father resumed talking with a controlled tone. "You know your mother died of cardiac arrest."

Since Lieschen was getting nowhere with her interrogation, she disclosed, "Aunt Klara told me that I wouldn't be living with you if Mommy were alive."

"When did Aunt Klara tell you that?"

"At the same time when she told me that you wanted me to move out.

"I'll have to have a talk with Aunt Klara." Her father accelerated his pace.

Lieschen kept up and requested, "Pap, please tell me the truth how Mommy died."

"I've told you everything I can tell you, and I want to consider the matter closed. For once and for all!"

It sounded as though her father's heart had frozen over when it concerned her mother. Lieschen would certainly not consider the matter closed. "And I cannot understand why I've never been allowed to see Grandma since Mommy's funeral?"

"You know your grandmother has been too ill to see visitors."

"I'm not any visitor. I'm Grandma's grandchild. Or do you say this to keep me at arm's length while, in reality, Grandma is not alive?" Lieschen was amazed at her courage, to talk in such a straight-forward manner with her authoritative father.

"Your grandmother is alive and very ill," her father replied.

"Does she have a contagious disease?"

"You have to talk to Aunt Klara about your grandmother. She's your aunt's and your mother's mother."

"Aunt Klara always brushes me off." Lieschen's sad voice resonated across the colorful countryside.

"Then I cannot help you in this matter."

More than ever, Lieschen realized that she had no choice but to investigate her own way.

As they neared the stables, her father said, "I want you to know that I love you very much. I always have, and I always will. You're my flesh and my blood. My only child." Her father's voice sounded soft and warm now.

It surprised Lieschen that he was no longer angry over her interrogation. "I love you too, Pap." She felt it deep in her heart, but the uncertainties concerning her mother and her grandmother fractured her love for her father.

At the stables, Lieschen breathed the warm, racy scent of manure that mingled with the sweet smell of hay. She was fond of horses, especially of her white Lipizzaner, Grande, whom her father had given her while her mother had been alive.

Currently, her father had thirteen horses-three Lipizzaner, two white Hanovarians, two English Hackneys, two Swedish Halfbreds, two Arabian stallions and one Spanish foal.

Lieschen was deeply fond of Grande. She would keep him alive for a hundred years if she could, because through Grande, she was able to relive the happy rides she had experienced with both of her parents. Grande and the old cherry tree in their garden, where her parents used to rock her in the swing, held some of her fondest memories and remained anchored in her heart.

Ralph Gruber came out of one of the stables, holding a pitch fork in his hands. Ralph was a short, lean, young fellow with a sallow complexion, shining dark eyes, and dark, curly hair. Along with one helper, he was in charge of the Reinking stables. Sometimes the gardener's helpers, Christopher and Leo, also assisted Ralph.

Her father instructed Ralph to bring out Grande for Lieschen, and Spike, a deep brown English Hackney, for himself. Her father usually alternated among different horses, while Lieschen routinely rode Grande.

"I'll be right back." Her father walked toward the brick arena with its red tile roof. The arena was located on the west side of the stables.

In a short while, Ralph led Grande toward Lieschen and inspected the horse's hooves for mud and rocks. Lieschen stroked Grande's bridge, but he nipped her hand. "Don't be grumpy." She pulled back.

Ralph looked up from his crouched position. "You know he's sometimes cranky." It sounded as though Ralph wanted to defend Grande.

"Is it because he's getting old?"

"Irregardless, horses are like people. Young or old, sometimes they're cranky." With a questioning expression, Ralph looked at Lieschen as though she should know that animals have emotions like people.

Lieschen thought that Grande's mood might improve if she left him alone for a little while. "I'll go see Figaro."

With excitement shining in liis eyes, Ralph said, "Herr Reinking promised that Figaro will be me racing horse." He tossed aside a small rock which he had picked off Grande's hoof.

Lieschen knew. Her father bad told her. He had promised to reward Ralph's good work and sponsor his fondest ambition of racing horses. "I wish you good luck." She smiled and walked off toward Figaro's stall. Figaro lifted his proud head above his shiny bay body and bushy mane. He examined Lieschen with his curious, somewhat fearful eyes. She gently talked to him and stretched her hand over the railing, coaxing him with a few sugar cubes which she had pulled from her pants' pockets; but he would not come to her.

Lieschen went back to Ralph and Grande. Her father had already mounted Spike. She patted Grande's neck before Ralph helped her into the saddle. Grande's mood seemed to have improved. Lieschen did not want him to throw her off, as he had done once before.

Grande trotted next to Spike on the rugged trail, alongside the gingerly prattling Rinden Creek that seemed to split the Mariatroster Woods in two. A slight wind rustled the leaves of trees - oak, beech, linden, birch, ash, elm, poplar, and others. Some of the luscious branches intertwined above the trail along the Rinden Creek and formed a junglelike canopy. A few pine trees peeked through the deciduous trees; and purple, blue, red, orange and yellow wild flowers splashed the rich undergrowth and filled the air with a delicious scent.

Suddenly Lieschen heard cupping sounds, as if mysterious invaders were approaching from some underground cave. A short while later, she glimpsed riders galloping toward them. Among the riders she recognized Sigi Prinz, who was general manager at her father's pharmaceutical plant. She had occasionally seen Sigi at the Plant when she had stopped by and, from time to time, he had been invited for dinner at their villa, sometimes with his parents, sometimes alone.

Sigi was tall, slender, and handsome, except his crooked nose protruded a litde on his elongated face. As the son of Dr. Eugene Prinz, one of her father's closest friends and business associates from the aristocracy, Sigi enjoyed a special status. Next to Aunt Klara, he was the most important person in her father's company. Her father had trained Sigi to be general manager.

The riders broke their gallop and exchanged greetings with Lieschen and her father. Sigi's Prussian-blue riding suit and patented, shiny black boots stood out from the other riders, who wore casual clothing. Lieschen had seldom seen Sigi wear casual clothing. He talked with his boss, Lieschen's father, about the business trip to Venice. While they talked, Lieschen noticed that Sigi's dark-brown hair was plastered down with gel or something. It had a jet-black sheen. During the conversation, the other riders listened in. Lieschen had not met any of them before. When one of the riders coughed, Sigi said with an annoyed gesture, "Feel free to ride on. I'11 catch up with you later."

The riders seemed to be taken aback. "Enjoy your company," sneered one blond rider. He cast a long glance at Lieschen, and then spurred his stallion, so did the other riders.

Walter and Sigi continued their business talk about the scheduled meetings with Tortellini Enterprises and Granero Corporation in Venice. Then Walter suggested, "Why don't you join us on our ride."

"Be delighted." Sigi's grin showed his even white teeth that contrasted with his dark eyes and dark-brown hair. He kicked the flanks of his brown stallion to align him with Spike. Lieschen trotted with Grande on the other side of her father. At this stretch, the trail provided enough space for three riders next to each other.

"I thought you were going to see Swan Lake at the Opera Haus this evening?" Walter asked Sigi.

"1 have two tickets for the eight-o'clock performance. My cousin Angelika wanted to see Swan Lake, but she contracted the flu." Sigi looked over at Lieschen. "Would you care to join me, Fraulein Lieschen?"

"Tonight?"

"Yes, tonight. The performance starts at eight."

Lieschen wanted to see Swan Lake, and she was caught up with her studies, but she was not sure if she should accept Sigi's invitation. She turned to her father for his reaction.

"If you like to see Swan Lake, go ahead. It should be a good performance." Her father gave an approving nod. He had been very selective about the men with whom she could associate. Sigi seemed to be an exception, and Lieschen accepted his invitation.

CHAPTER 5

Lieschen regarded her reflection in the dresser mirror in her bedroom. The emerald satin gown, which she had selected for this special evening, accented her slender figure while it covered up her shapely, long legs. She turned to Nipo on the right side of the dresser mirror and asked with an excited tone, "What do you think? Looks chic, doesn't it?"

Nipo seemed to echo Lieschen's thoughts.

From the quaint jewelry box on the dresser, she selected a set of a gold necklace with a pyramid-shaped emerald pendant and a matching gold bracelet which her father had given her for her eighteenth birthday. She closed the necklace behind her neck and put the bracelet on her left wrist, below the tiny frills of the three-quarter-long sleeves of her emerald satin gown. Then she touched up her eyebrows and eyelashes with a little mascara. She never wore any other makeup, although she liked a tasteful application of lipstick and makeup on other ladies.

When she heard a car pull into the circular driveway in front of their villa, she peeked through the west-window in her study and saw Sigi parking his midnight-blue Porsche at the curbline next to the rose-bed, which resembled an elongated, colorful knoll, sprouting with beautiful pink, white, yellow, and red roses. A grassy border inside the raised curb framed the rose-bed.

Lieschen watched as Sigi climbed out of his Porsche. Dressed in a tailor-made black tuxedo, white shirt, and Prussian-blue bow-tie, he looked suave, like a dark prince. His hair was no longer slicked back, but his dark features reminded Lieschen of a boy who had sliced open the belly of a frog years ago. She did not know why Sigi reminded her of that boy who had caught a green frog at the edge of the Hilmteich, a community pond in Mariatrost. Lieschen and Ingrid had been playing hide and seek between trees in the adjacent park. That boy had also been dressed in a black tuxedo. Crouching down, he had slapped the frog, belly up, on the wet ground at the edge of the pond. The little frog had desperately tried to escape, but the boy would not let him. Lieschen had waved for Ingrid to join her. They hid behind the trunk of a large oak tree and watched as that boy ferociously tore at the frog's legs. Lieschen wanted to scream because she felt sorry for the helpless little creature, but Ingrid motioned for her to keep quiet. When that boy failed to rip the frog's legs apart, he held it down with his knees and, from his pants' pocket, pulled out a pocket knife. He opened the blade, spread the frog's legs far apart and sliced open its belly.

"Murderer!" Lieschen had screamed, and she and Ingrid had run away.

Looking now at Sigi, and thinking of that ugly boy, struck Lieschen with an eerie feeling. She was aware that Sigi and that boy could not be one and the same because Sigi was now twenty-nine years old, about ten years older than Lieschen, and that ugly boy was about Lieschen's age. She did not know why the comparison entered her mind.

She turned away from the window, slipped on her emerald shoes, grabbed the matching purse, and headed for the stairway. Halfway down, she swung around because she had forgotten to apply perfume. She did not feel complete without a moderate application of perfume and always wore the same fragrance, Egus de France. Suddenly she tripped. The seams of her beautiful gown ripped. "Oh, no!" she exclaimed, gripped the carved wooden banister and hastened back upstairs.

In her bedroom, she slipped off the torn emerald satin gown and gazed at the ripped seams. She was sure neither she nor Frau Emma could mend the badly torn seams in a hurry. She glanced over at Nipo on the dresser mirror. "Look!" she uttered. Her excitement had dampened. She took a deep breath and tossed the gown on her bed, on top of her embroidered bedspread. She turned and stepped over to her mahogany closet. From a number of gowns neatly hanging inside, she selected a black velvet gown with small pleats from the knees to the ankles. She slipped it on and glanced over at Nipo again. "The evening doesn't start out right," she uttered.

Nipo seemed to agree. Nipo always seemed to agree.

Lieschen remembered that one heel of her matching black velvet shoes had come loose, and she had forgotten to have it repaired. She decided to wear her emerald shoes and purse, which gave a brisk accent; and Lieschen thought that her gold necklace with the pyramid-shaped emerald pendant and the matching gold bracelet looked exquisite with the black gown.

She responded to a knock at the door. Frau Emma peeked in. "You look gorgeous," she said.

"I don't feel gorgeous."

"Why not?"

"Come, see." Lieschen showed Frau Emma the ripped seams of her emerald gown on the bedspread. "That's why." She explained how it happened.

Frau Emma touched the torn seams. "Perhaps you shouldn't wear your lovely Princess gown tonight," she said and made an insightful gesture with a wrinkled facial expression.

"Why not? I'm wearing my emerald purse and shoes. Look!" Lieschen pulled up the pleats of her black gown and lifted her right leg to show Frau Emma.

"Looks fine."

Lieschen could not follow Frau Emma's train of thought, but she did not have time to ask more questions because Frau Emma pointed at her wrist watch. "Your escort is waiting."

Downstairs, Lieschen found her father and Sigi seated behind the coffee table in the living room, talking and sipping aperitifs. Sigi's shiny dark eyes rolled over her. "How enchanting you look, Fraulein Lieschen!" he complimented her. His smile showed his splendid white teeth.

"You should be on your way," her father said. He and Sigi rose, and all three proceeded toward the exit.

In the hallway, under the painting of the Hapsburg Dynasty, Sigi stopped to look at Lieschen's gold bicycle in the ornate glass cage. "How fortunate you are, Fraulein Lieschen, to have such a noble father who buys you such extraordinary gifts," he commented.

Lieschen smiled at her father and, together with Sigi, stepped outside into the falling dusk.

On the way to the Opera Haus, at the intersection of Mariatroster Kay and Karl Rainer Strasse, Lieschen's hands landed on the dashboard because Sigi had slammed his foot on the brakes to avoid hitting a jaywalker. An elderly man in haggard clothing had stumbled into the hood of Sigi's Porsche.

"He must be colorblind." Sigi cast an irritated glance through the front windshield.

Lieschen opened the door on her side and hopped out. "Can 1 help you?" she asked the elderly man as he held on to the hood. Lieschen could not see his eyes behind his dark glasses, but she could see his scarred cheeks.

"Just don't see so well. My eyes, my eyes ..." He removed his hands from the hood and tried to straighten up on the worn asphalt. He appeared unsteady.

"Would you like that we call an ambulance?" Lieschen worried he might be hurt.

"No." The elderly man compressed his lips; and after a moment he said, "God bless you," and walked on.

"God bless you too." Lieschen thought this gentleman badly needed God's blessing. She watched till he had crossed Karl Rainer Strasse, and then climbed back into Sigi's Porsche.

A cynical twist showed on Sigi's lips. He shifted the clutch and pushed down on the accelerator. Lieschen thought he would get a ticket if the police saw him driving so fast.

Inside the Opera Haus, red-cushioned chairs and gilded decorations in the spacious auditorium sparked with reflections from the brilliant chandeliers above. And Lieschen noticed men in elegant suits and tuxedos with bow-ties, and women's brocade, velvet, and silk attire adorned with sparkling jewelry. She thought her evening gown and accessories and *exquisite* jewelry was appropriate for the air d'elegance.

A young man, presumably a student, ushered them upstairs to a balcony for which Sigi had tickets. Inside the balcony, the fragrance of jasmine bouquets pricked Lieschen's nose. The perfume seemed to be coming from the two women seated in the front of the two rows of red-cushioned chairs.

Sigi inspected his tickets, then looked at the two women and said with an edge in his voice, "I regret to inform you that you're occupying the wrong seats."

The middle-aged of the two ladies snatched open her black evening purse, extracted two stubs and compared the numbers with those of their seats. "Smart guess!" she snapped with a boisterous tone. "Why don't you put on glasses and double-check the numbers on your tickets."

Again Sigi compared the numbers without glasses. Lieschen had never seen him wear glasses. "I had requested two adjoining seats!" He shook the tickets with his right hand, as though the mix-up was the tickets' fault.

"The seats are joining behind each other," the middle-aged woman snickered. She adjusted the collar of her wine-red brocade gown, then turned to the young companion next to her and said, "Can't always have what you want. Hmm!"

Hmm! echoed in Lieschen's ears, like a drumming reflex.

Sigi offered her the chair in front, and she sat down. "I'm sorry for this incongruity," he said and settled behind Lieschen.

The two women put their heads together. Lieschen heard them whisper something about her gold bicycle and right away she knew they had recognized her.

The photo and the write-up in the *Grazer Zeitung* had illustrated Lieschen as *Princess with a Golden Bike*. She assumed people still recognized her because of that article, although it had appeared in the newspaper when Lieschen was little. She remembered when her father had read the article to her. It began: *Lieschen Reinking, aristocratic daughter of industrialist Walter Reinking, emerges in full golden splendor.*

After her father had read the entire article, Lieschen had asked him, "Pap, am I rich now like you're? Mommy always said you're very rich and important."

"Of course. As my only child, you carry my blood. You will follow in my footsteps, and I will direct your life. Only you, my dear Lieschen, can carry forward our bloodline and our pharmaceutical industry."

"1 will carry forward," Lieschen had replied although she did not know what she would carry forward. She could not understand everything her father had said, but carrying things forward sounded good to her.

The middle-aged woman tapped Lieschen's hand. "You're Fraulein Reinking, aren't you?"

"Yes."

"I had the privilege of doing your mother's hair. I'm Frau Lenz from the Lenz Hair Salon."

Lieschen immediately extended her right hand to greet Frau Lenz in their traditional manner.

"What a coincidence!" Frau Lenz said. Lieschen thought so too. Frau Lenz shook Lieschen's hand vigorously and said, "You resemble your mother as if cut from one cloth."

Ah, that's why Frau Lenz recognized me, thought Lieschen.

"I knew your mother since the days when she began her career right here at the Opera Haus. Let's see-that was in 1948, in the fall season."

"Did you always do my mother's hair?" Lieschen's curiosity rose.

"She wouldn't have anybody else do it."

"Where is your salon located?" Lieschen intended to visit Frau Lenz at her salon. She hoped to get information concerning her mother's death. What an unexpected channel!

"Near the Health Department," Frau Lenz replied. "When you go up Sporgasse, it's the second shop next to the Weidinger Butcher Shop."

"I believe I know the location." Lieschen remembered the butcher shop from strolling by. She had never shopped there, though. She and her family usually shopped at the Krenn Butcher Shop in Mariatrost. In any case, she resolved to visit Frau Lenz as soon as possible during business hours. Now was not the time to ask intricate questions.

The lights faded. Graceful dancers in pastel-blue and caramel satin appeared like nymphs on a celestial sphere while Tchaikovsky's music charged the air. Fraulein Katharina Gringos, the prima ballerina in white, made her debut.

During intermission, Sigi invited Lieschen for a drink. "We have to celebrate our first evening out," he emphasized.

Lieschen wanted to talk to Frau Lenz and get to know her better; therefore, she declined Sigi's invitation. His disappointed expression showed that he was not accustomed to taking No for an answer. "In this case, you will excuse me." He rose and stepped out.

Frau Lenz introduced her daughter Mariella.

"What an interesting place to meet." Mariella leaned over to shake hands with Lieschen.

"I should say," Frau Lenz nodded, then said, "Your mother was such a great Opera singer and pianist. What a misfortune that she had to die so young. And the wicked rumor that's floating around. Oh, how wicked! What a shame! All that suspicion!"

Blood surged into Lieschen's head.

"Mamma, these are rumors." Mariella nervously played with her large golden bracelet, which matched her golden necklace and looped earrings. The custom jewelry accented Mariella's battleship-gray velvet gown.

"All right. We'll leave it at that." Frau Lenz looked uneasy.

When Sigi returned, he handed Lieschen a shiny fan. "A souvenir expressly designed for you."

"Danke." Lieschen opened the folds with a pattern of pink cherry blossoms and began fanning her burning cheeks.

Just as Sigi settled on his seat behind Lieschen, two strangers entered and greeted Frau Lenz and Mariella with a colloquial *Servus*.

"My husband and my son-in-law," Frau Lenz introduced the two gentlemen.

Lieschen gave a courteous nod and continued fanning her hot cheeks.

Herr Lenz and his son-in-law settled next to Sigi in the second row. They explained that their appointments had delayed them.

When the lights dimmed, majestic dancers returned, and Tchaikovsky's vibrant music recharged the air.

Lieschen folded the fan on her lap and watched while Frau Lenz's statements buzzed in her head.

In the middle of the performance, Sigi slipped his hands and arms around Lieschen's shoulders. She felt uncomfortable and moved forward. His hands followed. A whiff of alcohol crept into her nose. The next moment, Sigi's hands clasped her breasts. "How rapturous!" he chanted into her left ear.

Lieschen gasped. She clutched her purse and fan and walked out. Sigi followed and, with a reproachful tone, challenged her, "Where're you going?" Without replying, Lieschen proceeded along the courtly hall and down the stairs. Sigi kept pace. "Where're you going?" he raised his voice.

"Home," Lieschen snapped.

"Don't you like the performance?" Sigi looked as though she was out of line.

"Not any more." Lieschen could not believe that he thought he had done nothing wrong.

"Can I invite you for a glass of wine or a Cappuccino? Or for cinnamon ice-cream with fruit topping at the Gaier Cafe? Then we could return to this eloquent performance."

Lieschen gazed at him. His dark pupils glowed. "I wish to go home!" she repeated, resolute to take a taxi.

"What a pity!" Sigi mumbled. "Notwithstanding your wish is my command."

They proceeded toward the exit.

"What do you wish to do now?" Sigi asked outside the Opera Haus. He sounded as if nothing had happened.

Does he think I'm stupid? Or is he drunk, or half-drunk, or what? Lieschen did not know, except she felt offended and very uncomfortable. "I want to go home," she repeated once more.

"If that's what you really wish, I shall take you home." Sigi's head shifted to the side, and he mumbled under his breath, "Stupid game of pursuit and retreat."

Lieschen heard it. His attitude incensed her. That was not the Sigi she knew. Or does he have two personalities? Sister Gertrude had told students in class that there are people with two or more personalities. If Sigi was such a person, that scared Lieschen.

Approaching his Porsche, she saw a young woman in a tight-fitting crimson dress, bracing her hands against the hood. Her shapely figure and her straight red tresses cast a conspicuous shadow under the tall parking lantern. "I thought you had a business meeting!" she huffed, her sharp gaze fixed on Sigi. Her painted eyelashes fluttered like butterflies' wings.

It took Sigi a moment to catch his breath and speak. "Of course I had a meeting, and we'll talk later," he declared firmly.

The young woman attached herself to the hood of Sigi's Porsche like a lioness.

"I wish for you to leave right now!" Sigi's harsh tone echoed through the star-sprinkled night.

The young woman glared at him. "You'll pay for this!" She turned and stalked away in her high heels.

It was obvious that Sigi knew her. Perplexed Lieschen wondered, is she a girlfriend? Or could she be a prostitute? The provocative clothing might be an indication that she wanted to advertise her beautiful features. Lieschen remembered when Sister Gertrude had told them in class about ignorant women in provocative clothing. "They're selling their bodies for money," Sister Gertrude had explained. "They're called prostitutes, or whores, or tramps. They're misusing their gift from God, their precious lives. Only Jesus Christ can help them find their way back to our Heavenly Father and to eternal life."

"She's the niece of my friend," Sigi explained inside his Porsche. "Sometimes she exerts too many rights, and I have to put her in her place."

Lieschen doubted that. No matter what, she wanted to go home and be away from Sigi.

His engine soared. The tires squeaked. Along Mariatroster Kay, where the Mariatroster Hill started to climb, Sigi veered into a dark shadow under a large oak tree and turned off the engine. "Here we're!" he ejaculated as though they had reached a summit.

"What's wrong?"

"I have to tell you something very important." He wrapped his right arm around Lieschen's shoulders.

A creepy feeling came over her. "Why do you have to tell me here? And now?"

"Because my passion for you is killing me." He pulled her into his arms and kissed her.

His kiss felt like the touch of a creepy spider, unlike anything Lieschen had imagined for her first kiss. And he smelled of alcohol. "Please drive me home!" she requested with a pleading tone because she felt trapped. Her agitated breathing came in gasps.

Sigi ignored her. He took her hand and put it on his heart. "You must feel my passion for you!" Lieschen pulled back her hand.

"I had to wait too long to hold you in my arms." He stroked her hair gently. Then he pulled her head into his armpit and kissed her again. She tried to push him away, but he would not let go. With the heels of her shoes, Lieschen dug into his legs. His left hand swished down and removed her heels from his legs, pulled up the pleats of her gown, and pressed his hands between her legs. She trampled and kicked and screamed, "Let me go!" Sigi's chest pounded. He began caressing her thighs and knees. They wrestled.

Lieschen strained for the door handle, but could not grasp it. Sigi's fingers probed on up between her knees. When Lieschen finally seized the door handle, she thrust open the door, hurled herself out, and staggered away. The engine of Sigi's Porsche howled after her as she fled along the ascending road. When she looked back, streams of headlights flashed over her. She took an abrupt turn into an adjacent clover field where her high heels got stuck in the soil. She could no longer move her feet. She pulled and pulled but could not remove the high heels from the soil. Afraid that Sigi might catch up, she slid her feet out of the shoes and, with her hands, pulled the shoes out of the soil.

Carrying the shoes in her hands, she bolted on through dark clover-, wheat-, barley-, and potato fields. Sticks and stones pierced her silk stockings. When she stumbled over a mole hump, she halted. She could no longer hear or see Sigi's Porsche and tried to catch her breath. Stars glittered like dazzling jewels on the wondrous sky. The sickle of the moon hung between the stars, beautiful and bright.

"God, why is Sigi such an awful man?" she asked the moon and the stars. Was this really his other personality, or was it alcohol that made him act so badly? She staggered on up the hillside. Fields turned into rolling meadows. When she glimpsed lights at her father's horse stables, she knew she would soon be home; but as she approached their villa, she suddenly felt like vomiting because Sigi's Porsche was parked in their driveway.

Sigi might tell Pap and Aunt Klara a false story, and they night believe him and end up blaming me. Lieschen's stomach turned over.

When she managed to collect herself after having stopped vomiting, she tottered to a fence post at the corner of their fruit orchard, adjacent to their flower and vegetable garden. From there she could clearly see Sigi's silhouette in his Porsche. What now? She sighed. Her feet felt cold, and they hurt. She tossed her shoes over the fence, pulled up her gown, slipped her toes into the mesh of the chained links of the fence, climbed up, and dropped down on the inside. She picked up her shoes and, in her silk stockings, scrambled to the back entrance of their villa. There she wondered how she could get inside. During the struggle, she had left her purse in Sigi's car, with the keys in her purse.

She stepped under her balcony and contemplated climbing up. Somehow she should be able to get into her apartment through a window, she thought, but she had not left any of her windows open. She would have to break a glass pane, and that would wake up her father and Aunt Klara. I cannot do that, she concluded. That was not a good idea.

Suddenly she heard the engine of Sigi's Porsche and hobbled back to a fence post at the corner of their fruit orchard where she could see Sigi drive off. She felt an odd sense of relief and swayed over to Frau Emma's window. The inside shutters were half-closed, and the room was dark. Lieschen wanted to ask Frau Emma to let her in and scratched the glass pane with her fingernails. Frau Emma did not respond. Lieschen scratched harder. Then she knocked and finally lights flashed on and the inside shutters lifted.

"Who is it?" Lieschen heard Aunt Klara's voice as she opened the window.

Lieschen did not say anything.

"Who is it?" Aunt Klara called in a louder tone.

"It's me." Lieschen dreaded to talk to her aunt, who stretched her head through the shaft of light.

"What in the world are you doing at Frau Emma's window?"

"Would you let me in? I forgot my purse in Sigi's car. And my keys are in my purse."

"Why didn't you ring the doorbell?"

"I didn't want to wake you up. Or Pap." Lieschen tottered over to the main door, wondering why it had to be a night when Frau Emma had gone home to her grown-up children. She used to go home only once or twice a month.

The moment Aunt Klara opened the door, her eyes shifted from Lieschen's disheveled hair to her muddy, torn silk stockings, and to the dirty emerald shoes she held in her hands. "What on earth have you been doing? Look at your beautiful shoes, all covered with mud!"

Lieschen was so tired, cold, and emotionally drained, she could hardly think of anything to say. And she could not tell her aunt what happened. "The heel came loose," she mumbled; but her aunt's expression told her that she did not believe her. Then Aunt Kiara stared at her muddy feet.

All her life, Lieschen had been taught to be clean. Although she felt exhausted, she stepped across the driveway to the grassy border at the foot of the rose-bed and wiped her muddy shoes and feet on the green grass. Then she pulled out her white lace handkerchief from the pocket of her gown and cleaned her feet some more to avoid tracking dirt inside. Holding the soiled lace handkerchief in her right fist and her muddy shoes in her left hand, she hobbled back to the door.

Aunt Klara only said, "Go to sleep right away. You have to get up early in the morning."

Lieschen was glad that her aunt did not have a fit and call her father. She mumbled "Gute Nacht" and tiptoed along the marble tiles to the stairway, and up to her apartment.

In her bedroom, she dropped the muddy shoes and the dirty lace handkerchief on the carpet and collapsed on top of her torn emerald gown on her bed. Her tongue felt swollen. Sigi must've bitten my tongue, she assumed. She felt hurt, humiliated, cold, and resentful, but she did not feel like crying. This event had been unlike anything she had ever experienced.

After a while, she dragged herself up, undressed, and tossed her muddy, torn stockings into the wastepaper basket. She also picked up her soiled lace handkerchief and dropped it into the wastepaper basket. When she wanted to take off her jewelry in front of the mahogany dresser, she realized that she had lost her gold necklace with the pyramid-shaped emerald pendant. Looking at Nipo, she uttered sadly, "I don't know where I lost my necklace. Perhaps in Sigi's car or perhaps in the countryside." Carefully she put the bracelet into the ornate jewelry box and lugged herself into the bathroom. She filled the tub with warm water, added lavender bubble cubes, and cuddled under the fragrant foam. She thought of the beautiful performance and the exciting encounter with Frau Lenz; but then, oh then! What an awful evening it had turned out to be. Sigi had turned into a despicable person. She did not ever want to see him again. But how would that be possible?

Lieschen also thought of Werner, who had wanted to kiss her many times. Since she did not want Werner to kiss her, he respected her wishes and remained her dear friend, always caring for her and loving her; but Sigi did not care how she felt. He would have taken everything he wanted, including her virginity.

CHAPTER 6

In the morning, Lieschen found her purse on the kitchen counter and asked Frau Emma who had put it there.

"Aunt Klara had put it there before she left with your father," Frau Emma told her.

Lieschen wondered whether Sigi might have dropped it off. "I thought my father had left for Venice?" she asked then.

"He had to go to the Plant before going on his trip," Frau Emma explained.

"I see."

After breakfast, Lieschen took the Strassenbahn to St. Germain and arrived five minutes late. Professor Kinki, her math instructor, was talking to a student and did not notice her late arrival. Other students did not pay attention to her either. She wore her class uniform and quietly took her seat. They did not have a quiz, only preparation work for the final math exam. Lieschen could hardly wait for the recess to tell Ingrid about her experience with Sigi.

As soon as they exited the classroom during the first intermission, Lieschen told Ingrid, "You won't believe what happened last night."

"Did you dance on your roof again?"

"No quirks, please!"

"Okay, I'm all ears."

Lieschen took a deep breath and said, "Sigi tried to rape me last night."

"You must've really danced on your roof," Ingrid cackled.

"Why can't you be serious when I'm telling you something serious? I'm not telling you a kukameni story!" Lieschen gulped.

Ingrid stopped cackling. "Because I thought you couldn't be serious! Did you go out with him or what?"

"We went to see Swan Lake at the Opera Haus."

"And Sigi tried to rape you at the Opera Haus?" Ingrid squinted her eyes.

"No, on the way home." Lieschen explained why she went out with him and how it happened.

"Was he intoxicated?"

"I'm not sure. He left during intermission. When he came back, he smelled of alcohol, but I don't know if he was intoxicated or semi-intoxicated or what."

"Now I'm beginning to understand. You must know that he's a pro when he's intoxicated. He becomes a different person when he drinks too much alcohol."

"How do you know?"

"He raped Petruschka when he was intoxicated. Alcohol changes him. Not that he's a virgin otherwise."

"How do you know all this?"

"Petruschka told me. You know I'm good friends with Petruschka."

"I know."

"She told me that it happened when he came back from flying his twin-engine Cessna plane. He drank beer and Schnapps. When he mixes the two, his brain gets haywired. Then, while Petruschka practiced her guitar, Sigi ripped the guitar from her hands, pushed her on the Persian rug, tore off her dress and underwear, and raped her."

Lieschen clasped her cheeks with both fists. She also knew Petruschka, but they were not friends.

A group of students jogged behind them. "Excuse us," said Marianne Bosch, a fellow student from their class.

"Running match?" Ingrid smiled at Marianne. She and Lieschen stepped out of the way on the cemented path.

"Daily dose of exercise." Marianne smiled back and, together with the other students, jogged on.

"Sigi has his good sides too, Petruschka told me, and she loves him dearly; but you can imagine she never wanted him to rape her."

Lieschen shook her head and said, "You know my father says he's the best manager."

"He must be smart to be general manager in your father's company."

"I think he's smart, but he's also bad-bad, bad, bad ..."

"At least he didn't succeed in raping you."

"I thank God for that."

"You should." Ingrid paused, then continued, "You know people have different impressions of Sigi. Some say he's a gigolo or a Casanova, some say he's a good person because he feeds squirrels and birds, others say his heart is made of steel, and others say he's very intelligent and smart, but reckless and cunning . You take your pick."

"I had my pick. I'm just so sorry I went out with him. But as I told you my father had encouraged me, and I wanted to see Swan Lake. And since I was caught up with studying, I accepted his invitation." Lieschen could think of only one positive outcome: meeting Frau Lenz. As soon as possible, she would go and see Frau Lenz at her hair salon.

"You can't change anything. In the future you'll know better," Ingrid said.

They exchanged greetings with a few more students corning from the opposite direction.

"Does your father know that Sigi attempted to rape you?" Ingrid asked after the classmates had passed.

"He'd never believe it. He's so biased in favor of Sigi and his family. I know he wouldn't believe it. That's why I don't even tell him. And I wouldn't know how to tell him."

"Tell him you can prove it with fingerprints on your knees."

"Be serious!"

"Talk about being serious, how's your investigation concerning your Mom and your Grandma coming along?"

"I called my uncle in Lucerne, but I want to talk to him in person."

"Is he coming for a visit?"

"No, I'll fly there after graduation. My uncle will send me a flight ticket as graduation gift."

"Swell."

"I felt so happy after talking to my uncle because he said I'm always welcome in their home. I'm like their own child."

"Good for you."

Lieschen knew that Ingrid meant in earnest now what she said. She usually could discern whether Ingrid was serious or goofy. They headed back to class.

When Lieschen came home from school that afternoon, Frau Emma and Reserl worked in the garden, tying tomato vines to wooden sticks. No one else was around. And since her father was out of town, Lieschen headed for his office and looked for the vault key behind a large box of staples in the middle desk drawer, where she had previously found the key. She could not find it. Did Pap take it along to Venice? Could he suspect that I'm encroaching? she wondered when the door suddenly opened and Aunt Klara came in.

Lieschen felt her face flushing.

"Did you find your purse?" Aunt Klara asked.

"Yes, danke. How did you get *it?*"

"Sigi dropped it off." Without saying anything else, her aunt left again and closed the door. Lieschen had neither expected Aunt Klara to come home so early in the afternoon, nor had she heard her arrive. That was why she had not expected that her aunt would butt in like that. I better watch out! she warned herself and walked out of her father's office. She was determined to inspect all documents in her father's vault to unearth clues concerning her mother's death and her grandmother's disappearance. She had previously searched and inspected some documents without finding any evidence. She wanted to search more and look specifically for new documents.

When Lieschen found Aunt Klara in the kitchen, she told her that she would take the Strassenbahn back to town to pick up her black velvet shoes at the Frederick Shoe Repair Shop. She also had in mind to see Frau Lenz. She was anxious to talk to Frau Lenz and, time permitting, go to the Health Department to investigate further.

While waiting for the Strassenbahn, Lieschen crossed the street to the Witt Bakery to buy Vanillekipferl, her favorite kind of cookies. Frau Witt, the baker's brunette, middle-aged wife, offered Lieschen an extra chocolate cookie which she started munching while Frau Witt packed her order.

On the wall shelf behind the counter, Lieschen also noticed fresh Pumpernickel bread and Farmers bread, the two kinds of bread Aunt

Klara and Frau Emma used to buy there, along with croissants, French rolls, and biscuits.

Just as she exited, the green street car screeched to a halt. Lieschen crossed the street, climbed the metal steps, and slipped into an empty window seat in the second row. Two boys occupied the front row behind the glass enclosure of the conductor.

At the Sporgasse stop, Lieschen got off and ascended the narrow business street, lined with shops on both sides. When she reached the Frederick Shoe Repair Shop, she entered through a small doorway.

"Turned out fine as new," Herr Frederick said with his coarse voice while he showed Lieschen the shoes.

She inspected the heels. "Looks good," she nodded and paid for the repair. Herr Frederick packed the shoes into a brown bag.

From there, she headed toward Frau Lenz's Hairsalon and had no problem funding it. Through shining glass doors, she could see Frau Lenz and other hairdressers and patrons. In her mind, Lieschen rehearsed questions which she intended to ask Frau Lenz. The moment she stepped inside, Frau Lenz and two other hairdressers looked up. Their gazes multiplied in the wide mirrors.

"Will you have a seat," Frau Lenz offered, indicating the bright yellow chairs around a small glass table in the front corner, to the right of the entrance. "I'll be with you shortly."

Lieschen sat down and put the brown bag with her shoes on the floor. While she watched the hairdressers fashioning their patrons' hair, she continued formulating questions. She was anxious to talk to Frau Lenz.

"How nice of you to come!" Frau Lenz said as she joined Lieschen. She continued talking while she sat down. "It's probably going to rain tonight. Do you like rain?"

I didn't come to talk about rain, thought Lieschen. "Sometimes," she replied. Then, right away, she switched to her main objective. "Frau Lenz, I came to ask you about the conversation we had at the Opera Haus concerning my mother's death."

"Ah!" Frau Lenz curled her bright red lips. "People blabber. You mustn't believe rumors."

What a slap in my face! Lieschen assumed that Mariella had probably advised her mother not to talk about the rumor because they might get in trouble.

"Why did you leave Swan Lake in the middle of the performance?" Frau Lenz turned the questioning around.

"I didn't feel well." Lieschen was not about to tell Frau Lenz the real reason.

"When will you and Herr Prinz get married?" Frau Lenz's mouth remained open, as though she could not wait to hear the news.

Lieschen did not know how Frau Lenz found out Sigi's identity. "Herr Prinz is general manager at my father's Company, but we don't have a personal relationship," she contested while trying to control her irritation. Ingrid had warned her that Frau Lenz and some of the hairdressers in that salon spread gossip.

"You went to the Opera Haus together, and Herr Prinz cuddled you out of no personal relationship? Hmm!" Frau Lenz's lips curled in amusement.

Now Lieschen knew that Frau Lenz had noticed Sigi's transgression. "It was an engagement through my father," she said quickly. The next moment, she wished she had not said that either, but she could not take it back.

"Did your father engage you to Herrn Prinz?"

"It was an engagement for that evening."

"I didn't know that you could be engaged for one evening?" Frau Lenz's amusement coupled with a facetious twist on her short nose.

Lieschen broke up the meeting and left. "What a disaster!" she mumbled as she walked out.

She proceeded up Sporgasse to the Health Department, which was located a short distance from the Lenz Hair Salon. At the information booth of the Health Department, she asked a white-haired male clerk, "Could I talk to the person who issues death certificates?"

"Try Room 103, down the hall. If you can't get the information there, you have to go to the Coroner's office." The clerk's lips hardly moved while he talked.

Lieschen thanked the clerk and went down the hall to Room 103, a stuffy room that smelled as if the files of deceased people carried an imprint of their passing. A tall chipped ladder on wheels reached up to the ceiling, where it ran along a railing for access to the top files of the old steel cabinets. A thin blond woman with a lean face offered her services. "How can I help you?"

"I need a copy of my mother's death certificate, please. And I'd like to talk to the clerk who issued the death certificate."

"You have to fill out a formal request." The clerk handed Lieschen a preprinted form and a pen.

"Why do I have to fill out this form?" Lieschen worried her father might get wind of what she was doing. While he was in Venice, he could not; but upon his return, he might find out and hell would break loose.

"Legal requirement," the clerk explained.

"Red tape," Lieschen mumbled and filled out the questionnaire without recording her address or telephone number. One of the questions seemed odd: when did you last talk to the deceased? I wish I could've talked to my deceased mother, thought Lieschen. She waded through the questions, and then handed the form and pen back to the clerk, who made notations on a sheet of paper. With that sheet in hand, the clerk spun the ladder to a shelf marked R-1955 and climbed up the chipped steps.

Lieschen figured out that R stood for names beginning with R, and 1955 was the year when her mother had died.

While the clerk pulled out one of the top drawers and checked the files, Lieschen heard a raspy voice, "I'm a Minister, who're you?" She turned, but could not see anybody.

The voice repeated, "I'm a Minister, who're you?" Now Lieschen spotted a green parakeet on the ledge of a cabinet, way in the corner. The parakeet repeated the same question.

Lieschen replied, "1'm a parakeet."

The parakeet dipped his head and looked at her as if to contest what she said.

The clerk climbed down the ladder and informed Lieschen, "We have no record of your mother's death. I recommend that you go to the Coroner's office."

Lieschen picked up the brown bag with her shoes from the Frederick Shoe Repair Shop. Before leaving, she turned to the parakeet and said, "Bye-bye Minister."

"Bye-bye parakeet," replied the green parakeet.

"He learns fast," the clerk said with a smile.

It amazed Lieschen that a parakeet could be so smart.

At the nearby Coroner's office she had to fill out another questionnaire. Again, she left the spaces for her address and telephone number blank.

The clerk, a young tall man with glassy blue eyes, accepted the form and promptly found her mother's record. He showed Lieschen that cardiac arrest was listed as the cause of death.

"Can I talk to the doctor who issued the death certificate?" Lieschen requested. She was so glad that she had tapped into concrete information.

The clerk pulled out another file and informed her, "The medical examiner, who had issued your mother's death certificate, retired seven years ago."

"Where does the medical examiner live?"

"We're not allowed to give out addresses of employees, active or retired."

"Could you make an exception?"

The clerk rolled his glassy blue eyes. "Lady, you must know there are **no** exceptions when you're dealing with *our office.*"

How cold and ungiving! Almost as death itself, thought Lieschen and asked, 'What is the examiner's name?"

"You can see it right here on the record." The clerk pointed his long finger at the signature and the print underneath. "Dr. Paul Tschingelbaum."

Dr. Stanislaus Weitzinger was her father's physician. Lieschen could not see any connection and thanked the unfriendly clerk for his help.

On the way out of the Coroner's office, she remembered that somewhere she had seen or heard Dr. Tschingelbaum's name. She had to find him.

CHAPTER 7

During the night, Wednesday to Thursday, Lieschen's father returned from Venice, together with two guests who joined them for breakfast. Her father introduced the trvo gentlemen, Herr Brentano and Herr Reiterhorn from the Granero Corporation in Venice.

Lieschen appraised their age between forty and forty-five. Herr Reiterhorn was sedately dressed in brown. He had short, dark hair and aqua eyes. Herr Brentano had umber hair and deep olive eyes above a fleshy nose. He wore a beige gabardine suit. His chubby appearance contrasted with Herr Reiterhorn's tall and lean stature.

Lieschen's father and the two gentlemen discussed the convention they had attended in Venice concerning the Xiron formula. They talked while eating sausages, and bacon and eggs with warm butter rolls; and they drank coffee and prune juice. Aunt Klara ate hot oatmeal, sprinkled with cinnamon sugar, and coffee with Schlag. Lieschen had opted for an omelette with raspberry marmalade, and her usual hot chocolate and orange juice.

"We'll have a tour at our plant today," her father told Lieschen. "Herr Prinz will be the tour guide."

"I see." Lieschen's food got stuck in her throat. She felt nauseated just hearing Sigi's name.

"And how did you enjoy the performance of Swan Lake? Sigi told me it was a most enchanting evening." A rich smile covered her father's lips.

Lieschen wondered when her father had talked to Sigi. Probably by phone from Venice, she assumed. Because of her nausea, she put her hand over her mouth. She had no desire to vomit in front of everybody. She did not answer her father's question.

Walter turned to his guests and said," As you know, Herr Prinz Junior is general manager at our Plant."

"We're looking forward to meet Herrn Prinz Junior," Herr Brentano acknowledged this preliminary introduction.

"He is a fine gentleman, just like his father whom you met," Walter pointed out.

Herr Reiterhorn and Herr Brentano gave another nod of acknowledgement.

"We can proudly say, like father like son."

Lieschen felt more nausea; and she felt like screaming, Pap, stop that! I can't take it! Yet she knew when her father had a deeply rooted opinion about someone or about something, nobody could change his mind. Sigi and his family had a preferred status in her father's heart, and she did not know how to change that.

"In the evening, we have a dinner engagement," Walter looked at Lieschen. "Both, Herr Prinz Junior and Senior, and Frau Prinz, will join us. And after dinner you can see the new performance of the Eggnest. Sigi has tickets."

Lieschen stuffed a forkful of omelette into her mouth. Then, with a full mouth, she said, "I have an art meeting this evening."

"Are you an artist?" Herr Reiterhorn asked.

"Yes." Lieschen shook her head up and down while chewing the mouthful of omelette.

"In that case, art meetings are very important." Herr Reiterhorn seemed to have picked up on her consternation. He turned to Lieschen's father and emphasized, "Herr Reinking you must be very proud of you daughter? Art is very special!"

"As a hobby, it is okay; but not as Lieschen's main profession."

"I see," Herr Reiterhorn retracted.

Lieschen's father turned back to her and said with a firm tone, "You can attend the art meeting another time."

"I can't. Not this art meeting." Lieschen gazed at Aunt Klara who did not say a word. Most of the time her aunt made no comments during such dissents. Lieschen turned back to her father and said, "The speaker is a renowned artist; I couldn't miss this meeting."

"Who is the speaker?" Her father picked up the last sliver of bacon on his plate.

Lieschen had to invent a name. Quick! She came up with "Frau Liliana Kressig."

Her father frowned. "I haven't heard of her works."

Since her father was only interested in classical music and classical art, he would not recognize contemporary artists, Lieschen speculated. "Oh yes, she's well known in the art field." She swallowed her white lie along with the omelette she had been chewing. Although she hated lies, she would do whatever it took to avoid going out with Sigi ever again.

Her father observed her, but said nothing else. After breakfast, while he and Aunt Klara, together with Herrn Reiterhorn and Herrn Brentano, drove her to school-on route to the Pharmaceutical Plant-they talked about her graduation.

"A big turning point in Lieschen's life," Aunt Klara said.

Lieschen looked forward to this milestone in her life's journey. Before getting out of her father's Mercedes in front of St. Germain, she wished everybody a nice day.

During recess, Lieschen wanted to talk to Ingrid about her predicament for the evening but could not because Ingrid met with her fiance' Hans. She decided to call Ingrid later at home.

In the afternoon when she came home, Frau Emma showed her a huge bouquet of yellow roses, with one red rose sticking out in the middle of the bouquet. A fine-grain, butter-colored linen envelope addressed to her propped against the crystal vase on the mahogany coffee table in the living room. Has Werner sent me roses again? Lieschen wondered and reached for the envelope. Quickly she opened it and exclaimed, "Not from him!"

She began reading: Dear Fxaulein Lieschen!

I feel compelled to communicate in writing since my heavy work schedule prevented me from seeing you in person. In your wildest dreams you cannot imagine how much anguish I suffered since our enchanting evening at the Opera Haus.

Enchanting! In disgust Lieschen read on.

Because I love you from the deepest well of my longing heart, I know you will understand my passion for you.

Ants began crawling under Lieschen's skin. Sigi was the only person who had caused such an eerie itching sensation under her skin, especially under the skin of her arms.

Sigi closed his note with underlined statements:

You are the star of my life! My only star! My golden jewel! I desire to carry you in my arms for the rest of my life and remain forever dedicated to you with bottomless love and affection, Sigi.

Lieschen tore the note and the envelope into celian pieces and tossed everything into the wastepaper basket. "You can have the roses, if you'd like," she told Frau Emma, who was dusting off the window sill.

"You don't like yellow roses?" Frau Emma crumpled the dust cloth in her hands.

"I don't like the roses because Sigi Prinz sent them." Lieschen thought of all the pain and shame he had inflicted upon her. She detested Sigi beyond description.

"Would it be okay to leave the roses here on the table?" Frau Emma asked Lieschen.

"The waste basket is fine too."

Frau Emma wrinkled her nose.

Lieschen went upstairs to her apartment and, from her study, she called Ingrid and told her of her predicament for that evening. "I've to get out of this dilemma. Are you busy this evening?" She did not wait for Ingrid's answer before she continued. "What I'm trying to say is can we go to a movie?"

"Yes, we can. I'd like to see *Hortner's Rock,* the new American release."

"Okay, I'd like to see that movie too. But most of all I need to get away from home. I'll be at your house at seven."

"Okay. Ciao."

While driving to the Annenstein Theater with Ingrid, Lieschen said, "I don't know why Sigi can't understand that I don't want to go out with him ever again. He's like a sticky pest. Like a leech. I don't know how else to describe him."

"That's close enough," Ingrid cackled. "He probably thinks you're his chance to your father's fame and riches."

"It's pitiful. You should've seen the note he sent me today, together with a bunch of roses. He writes like blown-up silken dough. I can't show you the note because I tore it up."

"He probably wants to play games with you, as he does with some other girls." Ingrid slowed her blue Volkswagen behind a maroon Citroen.

"Whatever games he's playing, he won't play them with me."

"Good for you." Ingrid shifted gears. "Hans can't understand why your father lets him masquerade as general manager in his reputable company."

"I can't understand it either." Lieschen took a deep breath. "As I've told you, my father thinks Sigi is one of the most honorable gentleman, and the best manager. Accomplished, distinguished ..."

"As we've talked before, people have different opinions about Sigi. Hans' brother Martin knows Sigi well. He says that Sigi is arrogant, cunning, disdainful, power-hungry, reckless, and so on. And he toys with women.

"Wow!" Lieschen inhaled deeply, then said, "Whatever people think or say, I don't want to have anything to do with Sigi anymore. From my experience, he's turned into a poisonous glue. Sticky! Horrific!" Lieschen scratched her forehead and said, "I just don't know how to change my father's perception of him."

"Keep trying."

"Yeah, good luck for me!"

They arrived on time at the Annenstein Theater and waited for their turn behind other people at the ticket counter.

Lieschen enjoyed *Hortner's Rock,* together with Ingrid. When she returned home, everything was quiet in their villa, except night lights flickered on the walls between the paintings in the hallway. She tiptoed up to her apartment.

"Now I won't have to see Sigi before I graduate. Then I'll visit my relatives in Switzerland, and Sigi can fly a kite," she said to Nipo while she undressed.

Chapter 8

"Would you like to go horseback riding before dinner?" Lieschen's father proposed when she returned home from St. Germain the day after she had gone to see the movie *Hortner's* Rock with Ingrid. Usually she came home before her father and Aunt Klara came home, but today she had studied with Ingrid on a math assignment and came home late.

"Yes, I would," she replied. Horseback riding seemed a welcome relief from the steaming numbers in her head.

While they trotted along the rugged trail in the Mariatroster Woods, next to the gurgling Rinden Creek, Lieschen told her father that she had done well on her final English and Science exams.

"Good." A complacent smile showed on her father's lips. "Do you have a graduation present in mind?" he asked.

"May I wish for anything?"

"Within reason."

"By whose definition?" Because Grande started nibbling at a bush, Lieschen pulled at his reins. She tried to break Grande's habit because her father had told her that nibbling at bushes was not good for horses.

Her father turned back his head and asked, 'What did you say? I couldn't hear."

By the time Lieschen and Grande caught up with her father and Spike, she decided not to repeat what she had said to avoid precipitating an argument. She would have liked to ask her father again about the true cause of her mother's death and the whereabouts of her grandmother. These painful revelations, and the removal of Sigi from her life, would be her greatest graduation present, but she knew she had to solve these excruciating enigmas her own way.

"You can tell me what's on your mind. I'm your father!"

Don't I wish! Lieschen sighed.

Spike broke into a canter and Grande followed. Needles of a fir tree swished against Lieschen's gaited blue riding pants and jacket. Abruptly, Grande stopped and raised his forehead. He reared, neighed, snorted and let out a shrill whistle.

"Don't throw me off." Lieschen clasped Grande's mane and clutched his flanks with her knees. "Prr . . . Prr . . ." she hummed into his ears.

Her father turned his stallion around and yelled, "Grande, stop it!"

Grande lowered his forelegs, but continued snorting and pawing the dirt with his hooves. Lieschen stroked his neck and continued purring into his ears. Though Grande was sometimes moody, Lieschen could not understand why he had burst out just now, almost as if he had followed her train of thought and was sad and upset too.

"Let's ride back since Grande seems to be having a difficult time," her father said.

"Okay." It took Lieschen a while to get Grande to cooperate.

At the stables they left Grande and Spike in Ralph's care and sauntered along the hilly path toward their villa. Suddenly Lieschen halted as if facing a red traffic light.

"What is it?" Her father almost bumped into her because he was a step behind her. They gaped at each other, and Lieschen questioned, "Sigi?"

Her father's exulted smile stretched wide. "We postponed our dinner engagement, so that you could be with us," he said.

"How kiiiind oof yoouuu . . ." Lieschen's tongue got stuck on her palate.

Sigi hopped out of his midnight-blue Porsche and strolled toward them.

Lieschen felt as if pulled into the spin of a cyclone.

"Did you have a nice ride?" Sigi extended his hand to greet her while displaying his dazzling white teeth in an enticing smile.

Lieschen did not say anything; and she did not shake hands with Sigi either.

"You have to excuse me for a quick trip to the bathroom. Her father walked on. Lieschen followed. Sigi seized her hand. "Can l have a word with you, Fraulein Lieschen?"

She yanked away her hand. "If you think your smile can wipe away your evil deeds, you're grossly mistaken."

Her father had disappeared through the oak doors.

"You misunderstood." Sigi shook his head indignantly.

Misunderstood rape or attempted rape? Lieschen's disdain for Sigi cramped her throat, her stomach, her bones, her whole being; and ants began crawling under her skin.

"If you believe I wronged you, you have to forgive me. I would never hurt you. Never ever would I hurt you! How could I possibly hurt you? I only feel the purest motives for you: to protect and love you from the deepest well of my burning heart."

He must be sick if he thinks rape is normal and part of love. Or was he really that intoxicated that he didn't know what he was doing? Whatever, intoxicated or not, the deed was awful. Lieschen swallowed hard.

"You're the most precious jewel of my life." Sigi put his hand on his heart. "Did you read the note I sent you?" he asked.

Lieschen did not reply. Ants crawled wildly under her skin now, like a thousand hornets stinging her all at once.

Frau Emma called, "Dinner is ready."

"Let's have a pleasant meal." Her father's voice came through the oak doors.

"I'm not hungry." Anger and resentment added to Lieschen's frustration, which echoed in her voice.

"Why aren't you hungry? You haven't eaten." Her father examined her.

"I don't feel well." Why can't Pap see how unhappy I am in Sigi's presence? Lieschen let out a woeful sigh.

"If you don't feel like eating, at Ieast sit down with us. Herr Brentano and Herr Reiterhorn will also join us. Herr Dr. Prinz Senior has an unexpected speaking engagement, therefore he and Frau Prinz won't be here this evening."

"Aren't we supposed to change out of our riding clothes before dinner?" Lieschen liked the equestrian look, but for Sigi she would change into old, tattered clothes and smear soot on her face, so he would leave her alone.

"Today is an exception," her father smiled.

"You look charming in your riding suit." Sigi's dark eyes rolled over her.

If I just could hide in a cuckoo's nest and spit down at Sigi, Lieschen wished. Against her gut feeling, she joined her father, Aunt Klara, and Sigi at the dinner table in the formal dining room. Some unspoken words seemed to flow between Lieschen and Aunt Klara, almost as though her aunt were sympathetic to her dilemma, as unbelievable as that sounded.

Herr Brentano and Herr Reiterhorn, respectively dressed in navy-blue and light-gray business suits, arrived and joined them.

Frau Emma served Pollo a la Cacciatore-Italian-style chicken with browned rice, wine sauce with slivered hazelnuts, red beets, tender endive salad, deep-red tomatoes, and juicy cucumbers. To drink, they had light and dark beer. No wine. Lieschen did not care to drink beer or wine, or other alcoholic beverages, except to clink glasses and have tiny sips on social occasions. But right now she lifted her glass of dark beer. "Prost!" she said and drank half the glassful at once before anybody else cheered.

Her father scrutinized her.

"Cheers!" Sigi lifted his glass, looking surprised. Herr Brentano and Herr Reiterhorn also lifted their glasses and cheered.

Lieschen noticed that her aunt was observing her with an astonished expression. Probably because I've never done anything like that, she thought. She had been trained to be a proper young lady, and a proper young lady did not drink alcohol in large quantities, regardless of type. Lieschen also ate wine sauce with hazelnuts, hoping the wine sauce would further help to calm her anxiety. She had heard that alcohol calmed people's nerves. She was afraid she might otherwise smash a plate on Sigi's head, and her father might smash one on hers in response.

The gentlemen talked about the revolutionary cancer formula Xiron, and about politics, one of her father's passions. Lieschen had not much interest in politics. To this day, she had not attended any of her father's political functions. He had not encouraged her either. He had expressed that politics should be in the domain of men, considering only a few exceptions.

Lieschen drank more beer and yawned frequently. Her father drew her into the conversation by switching the topic to customer relations. "We have to increase our customer base in Vienna and other parts of Europe," he said. "Our current undertaking in Venice is a fruitful step." With his hands, he motioned toward Herrn Brentano and Herrn Reiterhorn. Then he pointed out, "And, of course, we have to expand our base overseas and prepare for the distribution of Xiron."

"Most important," Sigi agreed.

"Growth and expansion are necessary for a successful pharmaceutical enterprise like yours," concurred Herr Brentano.

Herr Reiterhorn gave a nod.

"Can you see the importance of this endeavor?" her father asked her. She replied with a slow nod and said with a hiccup, "I'm very tired. I'd like to be excused."

"You can give us the courtesy to stay until we've finished eating." Her father's eyebrows furrowed. "You have been drinking too much beer, and you're not used to it."

"I'll get used to it." Lieschen held her right hand against her stomach because she continued to hiccup.

"Lieschen has homework to do for tomorrow," Aunt Klara said. "We have to realize that she has her finals before graduation."

Lieschen stopped hiccupping. My aunt is defending me? She could hardly believe it. "I have a lot of studying to do," she said. She would have used any excuse to get away from Sigi.

"When will you graduate?" Herr Reiterhorn asked.

"In two weeks."

"In this case, last-minute studies are very important," Herr Reiterhorn accentuated.

"Yes." Lieschen cast a grateful glance at Aunt Klara and Herr Reiterhorn. She rose and left with a fleeting "Gute Nacht."

Did my aunt have a change of heart? She wondered as she headed upstairs to her apartment. In her study she stepped over to the picture window and looked beyond the old cherry tree at the darkening sky. She folded her hands and prayed, "Dear God, please take Sigi to Jupiter or to Pluto and never let him come back. Dear God, you know Sigi has tried to rape me."

CHAPTER 9

A large, cheerful group assembled in the carefully tended, flower-lined courtyard at St. Germain. Lieschen stood poised next to Ingrid, among graduates, relatives, friends, and the faculty of St. Germain. Since Lieschen's black cuff around her white silk blouse felt tight, she loosened it. All female candidates wore the same formal attire—white silk blouses with black cuffs, and cobalt blue, pleated linen skirts. Male students wore tuxedos.

Mother Marisa, dressed in a dark-blue habit with a white bib, stepped behind the lectern and greeted all in attendance. In her commencement speech, Mother Marisa underscored the students' accomplishments and the importance of their individual contribution to the future of Austria and the world. Other sisters and instructors followed with different allocutions and, at the grand finale, Mother Marisa congratulated each student with a handshake. Sister Gertrude and Sister Margarita awarded the diplomas.

Upon Lieschen's turn, Mother Marisa shook her hand and said, "Well done. God be with you."

"Thank you, Mother Marisa." Lieschen bowed her head, then marched over to Sister Gertrude, who handed her the diploma. Stepping off the podium, she spotted Werner lifting his right hand with a thumbs-up sign. He smiled his contagious smile to which Lieschen had grown accustomed. With the diploma in hand, she waved to him. Then she took her place next to Ingrid.

After the ceremony, on the way to the parking lot, her father reached into the jacket of his charcoal, double-breasted linen suit, pulled out a gold ring with two keys, and dangled them in front of Lieschen's nose.

"What does this mean?" she asked, although she had an inkling.

"You'll see in a minute." Her father withdrew the key and urged, "Come, come!" He led the way to a new silver-gray Porsche, parked among an array of cars behind the cloister. Standing next to the Porsche, adjacent to her father's Mercedes, her father handed her the gold ring with the two keys. "Enjoy!" he smiled.

Lieschen felt her eyes blazing at the sight of this magnificent new Porsche. "Oh Pap, danke!" She embraced her father and recalled when he had told her that she would not get her own car until she graduated from St. Germain. "My car. It's mine!" she whispered under her breath with a sense of exhilaration that resonated in her veins.

Aunt Klara handed her a St. Christopher safety charm. "Far safe driving," she said.

For the first time since her mother had died, Lieschen gave Aunt Klara a hug. The recent incident with Sigi during dinner, in which het aunt had helped her get out of that sticky dilemma, had helped to improve their relationship. Lieschen turned toward her new Porsche. With her fingers she touched the metallic surface of the silver-gray hood and glanced through the front window at the chocolate-gray leather upholstery.

"Why don't you open the door and have a seat." Her father became a little impatient.

Lieschen unlocked the door and scooted into the driver's seat. The leather upholstery felt firm, but comfortable. She put the St. Christopher safety charm into the glove compartment and stuck the key into the ignition. Her father stepped close and explained the different features, gadgets, and gear shift. In fascination, Lieschen paid close attention. The Porsche appeared different from her father's Mercedes and his Jeep, the two cars she had occasionally been allowed to drive under her father's supervision. He had been very particular with his cars and usually hesitated to let Lieschen or Aunt Klara or anybody else drive them. He did not want a chauffeur either and routinely drove his own cars.

Leaving St. Germain under a cloudless sky, Lieschen looked through the rear-view mirror and saw her father following in his Mercedes, with Aunt Klara on the passenger seat beside him. Lieschen also cast a glance back at the rusty pink facade of the cloister. She would never again sit in any of the classrooms, but she would go back to visit Mother Marisa, Sister Gertrude, Sister Margarita, and other sisters and instructors.

Firmly holding the steering wheel of her new Porsche, she enjoyed the feeling of having possession and control. She fumbled only a little with the gear shift. A short distance down the road she already drove like a pro, twisting, turning, breaking. The chemistry with her new Porsche felt great.

At home, during their special graduation dinner, her father said, "Sigi would like to test-drive your Porsche."

No! Lieschen's heart screamed. Her happiness cracked into a thousand splinters. Instantaneously. She had just swallowed a bite of Wienerschnitzel, which seemed to come back up from her stomach.

"Since Sigi has owned a Porsche for many years, you can count on his expertise. And should you need help, he will always be at your side."

Over my dead body will Sigi be at my side! Lieschen wailed, her stomach churned, and ants crawled under her skin.

When her father mentioned another dinner engagement with Sigi, Lieschen's cup ran over. She took a deep breath and announced her visit to Uncle Gustav and Aunt Sylvia.

Her father's expression darkened. "I will not allow you to go on such a trip."

"Uncle Gustav has sent me a flight ticket, as part of my graduation present."

Her father rose from his chair and proceeded toward the door. He did not leave, however. He turned back, anger shining in his agitated eyes. "Why didn't you tell me earlier?"

"I never found the proper occasion." Sometimes Lieschen patterned her speech and her behavior after her father's vernacular, which included diplomacy.

"You may not go on this trip," her father repeated with a stern expression. He turned to Aunt Klara. "Did you know about this?"

Aunt Klara shrugged.

Lieschen looked at the appetizing Wienerschnitzel with potato dumplings, delectable salads, and rhubarb sauce on her plate, but she could not eat another bite. She was still holding her fork, however. She asked her father, "Why shouldn't I visit with my relatives?"

"Because I have other plans for you." He moved back toward the table and sat down.

"Which plans?"

"I want you to work at our Plant and attend the AKA Business College in fall. I've researched colleges and universities. I consider the program at the AKA Institute compatible with our enterprise. You'll be well equipped with this type of study."

"Pap, you know I'd like to follow an art career." Lieschen could never work at her father's Plant with Sigi presiding as general manager. She could not possibly work with and respect a man who had evoked so much pain and shame in her.

"My dear Lieschen, I've made it clear that your first obligation has to be to me and to our pharmaceutical enterprise. You're allowed to develop art as a hobby, but that's the extent. An art career is out of the question."

"I'm grown up, and I've graduated. Now I should be free to make my own decisions. And I should ..."

"I've enrolled you at the AKA Business College for fall," her father interrupted.

All without my knowledge and consent! Lieschen was more resolved than ever to visit Uncle Gustav and Aunt Sylvia. She realized that she could be as strong-minded and determined as her authoritative father. She would even return her beautiful Porsche, if that were a condition.

"Contrary to what you might believe, my health is deteriorating." A gray veil clouded her father's eyes. "I have to be able to look with confidence into the future. I want you to be happy. And you and your husband will have to carry on our business and meet all the challenges in conformity with the integrity and highest reputation for which we stand."

That's a mouthful to swallow, thought Lieschen and asked, "And who is that husband supposed to be?" She already had a nauseating hunch.

"A respectable businessman from our aristocracy." A proud gleam overshadowed the gray veil in her father's eyes.

Aunt Klara reached for her white linen napkin on her lap. Her diamond rings twinkled with brilliance against her knotted hands while she dabbed her mouth.

"Are you referring to Sigi?" Lieschen squirmed on her chair.

"You have a keen sense of intuition." A joyful expression lit up her father's face.

Lieschen spiked the fork she was holding into the Wienerschnitzel on her exquisite Auergarten plate. "How unfair!" she exclaimed and thought of Sigi's ugly fingers creeping up between her legs.

Suddenly she burst out, "Sigi is loathsome. He contaminates our relationship. He is phony. His heart, his tongue, his hair, his nose, his fingers, everything's phony. He flatters and deceives ..." She could not find words bad enough to describe Sigi's detestable character, and she could not hold her emotions in check.

Her father's lips twitched. "You have a strange sense of humor."

"Humor? I am dead serious."

"I cannot believe hearing you talk in such a derogatory manner about a respectable gentleman?"

Aunt Klara coughed and crumpled the napkin in front of her mouth, as if curbing the words she intended to say.

"Respectable? That's what you think." Lieschen wanted to tell her father about Sigi's attempted rape, but she felt so ashamed, and she knew her father would never believe that Sigi was capable of such a horrible deed. Her father could only see Sigi's positive sides. He might even say I made up a story. "It's all an illusion," she sighed. "I'm so sad that you cannot recognize Sigi's fake character."

"What in the world are you talking about? I have known Sigi and his family for a lifetime. The impeccability of the entire family speaks for itself. And I have personally trained Sigi for our business. He is highly qualified." Her father's pride over his so-called achievement resonated in his voice.

Lieschen's cheeks burned. Her stomach shriveled. Ants kept crawling and stinging her under her skin.

"I can forgive your attitude because you're young and naive, but you have to trust in my judgement." Her father checked his wrist watch. "And now I've to be off to attend a conference, and we'll talk more later." He rose and stepped to the door.

At the threshold, he turned back. "Let me make it clear: you will not go on that trip!"

Her father's strong, authoritative voice resounded in Lieschen's ears. She did not say another word; she had already made up her mind.

CHAPTER 10

At seven-thirty the following morning, Lieschen boarded a DC6, a plane of Austrian Airlines, at Thalerhof, the airport of Graz. She had written a note for her father and had left it next to his breakfast plate, asking him again to let her be independent and make her own decisions.

In Vienna, she transferred to Swiss Air and experienced a delightful sense of freedom. This exhilaration, however, seemed short-lived. The moment she boarded Swiss Air, worries crept up. What will Pap do now?

One and a half hours later, the plane touched down at the airport in Zurich, Switzerland, and taxied to gate twelve. Queued among passengers in the aisle of the airplane, Lieschen tripped on a metal strip, but managed to regain her balance in the high heels of her rusty beige leather shoes, which she wore with an ivory linen suit, a crepe blouse, and a rusty beige leather purse.

Shortly after passing through Customs, she spotted her relatives in the waiting area. Aunt Sylvia held a large bouquet of vibrant red roses. Lieschen had no problem recognizing her relatives and was happy to see them. Both Uncle Gustav and Aunt Sylvia gave her a warm hug, and Aunt Sylvia handed her the bouquet of roses. "Danke." Lieschen inhaled the delicious fragrance.

"Let me look at you." Uncle Gustav stepped back. "What a stunning resemblance to your mother."

"Amazing," Aunt Sylvia agreed. "The same big hazel eyes and beautiful long chestnut curls. And so grown up!" Her aunt's small, green eyes dampened.

"Do you have luggage?" Uncle Gustav asked then.

"One suitcase."

"We better get in line over there." Uncle Gustav indicated the luggage area.

While strolling over, he inquired, "How was your trip?"

Lieschen recounted a few pumps over the Alps. While they talked, she noticed a few lines on her uncle's high forehead and white sprinkles in his copper-brown hair. Other than that her uncle's serene face and medium-heavy, tall stature had not changed since she had last seen him during her mother's funeral. And Aunt Sylvia's rosy cheeks and short, wheat-colored hair still crowned her short build. In her high heels, her aunt barely reached up to her uncle's shoulders.

"We've had sunshine for three long days, after a whole week of rain," Aunt Sylvia said. "And today, the sun has been waiting for you."

"I need sunshine," Lieschen smiled. In more than one way, she thought. When her suitcase came trundling along, she picked it off the rolling belt. Uncle Gustav helped her.

On the curving two-way asphalt road between Zurich and Lucerne, Lieschen gashed into Aunt Sylvia's backrest because Uncle Gustav hit the brakes. His Mercedes swerved. Lieschen squashed the beautiful roses she was holding on her lap, and thorns penetrated through her clothes and stung her abdomen. She rearranged the roses, wrapped two buds that had fallen off in tissue paper, and put the buds into her purse. She intended to dry them and keep them as souvenir. The rest of the roses seemed okay.

"These little creatures don't know that it's dangerous on the road," Uncle Gustav said after he realigned the steering wheel.

"When they sense danger, they curl up and think their long spikes can protect them. Of course, if they get under the wheels, they're lost." Aunt Sylvia looked at Lieschen over the beige backrest.

'What is it?' Lieschen had no idea what her relatives were talking about.

"A little porcupine." Aunt Sylvia motioned toward the rear window.

Lieschen turned and looked out. "I hope it's not hurt," she said when she saw the porcupine crawling over the embankment.

"Thank Heaven we aren't hurt either," Aunt Sylvia said with a rather unnerving tone.

At the shoreline of the Vierwaldstaetter Lake, Lieschen saw colorful paddle boats and big steamers.

With his left hand, Uncle Gustav indicated the direction of the Matterhorn and asked, "Do you remember our snow fights?"

Lieschen recalled the big snowballs her mother had made to throw at her father. She nodded.

"Wasn't it fun?"

"It was," Lieschen said while bittersweet memories pricked her heart.

Uncle Gustav glanced at her through the rear-view mirror. "And how was your graduation?" he asked.

Lieschen related the exciting events; but she did not mention her new Porsche. She might have to give it back because of the conflict with her father over Sigi; therefore, she thought it was better not to mention it.

"Are you interested in carrying on your father's pharmaceutical business?" Aunt Sylvia asked.

"I'd prefer an art career."

Uncle Gustav gave an approving nod. "Just like your mother. When she played the piano, the notes rolled like the flowing waters of a mountain stream. She always combined harmony and emotion in engaging performances."

"And she had a magnificent voice," Aunt Sylvia added. "Remember when she sang with the Salzburg Symphony Orchestra?"

"It was special. And, of course, she liked to paint," Uncle Gustav said. Then, looking at Lieschen again in the rear-view mirror, he asked, "Or perhaps you might want to study architecture in my Company?"

She wondered why her uncle came up with such an idea. "Thank you, Uncle Gustav, but I just would like to be an artist," she said.

"Do you still play the piano?" Aunt Sylvia asked.

"I haven't played for quite a while. I quit taking lessons two years ago. But sometimes I regret that I quit."

"You have a good foundation, you can always build on your foundation," Aunt Sylvia said. "And if you'd like to be an artist, why don't you enroll in an art school?"

"I'd have to convince my father or do it against his will. He wants me to carry on his pharmaceutical business. He says it's my primary obligation."

"It's understandable from your father's point of view since the business has been in your family for several generations, and you're his only child. Nonetheless, it's your life," Aunt Sylvia said.

"That's how I feel." Lieschen turned to look at the residential area on the green hillside. A short while later, her uncle slowed and veered into a long driveway in front of their one-story, bungalow-style, brick home with its raised foundation. Under the foundation were garages, a room for mechanical handicrafts, and a big storage room. Lieschen remembered the layout from her last visit with her parents when she was four years old. During that visit, she had picked out a huge red apple from a bin in the storage room.

She looked at the big elm trees and pockets of white and pink hydrangeas, bushy lavenders, and violet sage that skirted both sides of the driveway. The color of the rusty stucco walls seemed different, though. They had changed into a fashionable coral-beige. They used to be a soft spring green.

In front of the garage, Uncle Gustav tooted his horn. "Our maid Isolde will be right out to help with your luggage," he said to Lieschen and scooted out of his seat. Aunt Sylvia eased out on her side. Lieschen was careful with the roses while she climbed out of the back seat. Her abdomen still hurt a little where the thorns had stung her.

"Make yourself feel at home." Uncle Gustav stepped back to the trunk and opened it. Lieschen offered to help with her luggage, but her uncle waved her off. "We'll take care of it." In a short while, he returned to the driver's seat and tooted the horn louder than before.

Moments later, Lieschen saw a young maid in a mint dress and white apron coming through the shining oak doors of the upper landing. She hopped down the steps like a pony on a joy ride between bright red and pink rhododendrons in large flower pots. The beautiful flowers skirted the steps inside the white iron railings along the serpentine-shaped stairway.

"Didn't you hear when I honked the horn the first time?" Uncle Gustav cast a reproachful glance at the maid.

"I'm sorry, Herr Chef, I was talking on the telefon. Herr Meindl wants me to ride down a massage for you, Herr Chef," the maid explained apologetically.

"What message?"

"I rode it down, Herr Chef. Very careful."

"Can't you remember?"

"It's about an architectural plant. I rode it down with black ink."

Uncle Gustav tilted his head. "This is our maid, Isolde, and this is Fraulein Lieschen, our niece. We've been telling you about Lieschen's visit," he said to Isolde.

"I'm very happy pleased to meeten and welcomen you, Fraulein Liesichen." Isolde's squeaky voice carried a high pitch.

"I'm pleased to meet you too." While shaking hands, Lieschen noticed pronounced freckles on the nose and cheeks of Isolde's cheerful, young face. Her brown eyes were a shade lighter than her thick, brown braids.

Uncle Gustav took Lieschen's suitcase out of the trunk and handed it to Isolde. "Take it to Lieschen's room. And the roses too, will you."

"I will, Herr Chef." Isolde took the suitcase in one hand, and Lieschen handed her the bouquet of roses to carry in the other hand.

"Put the roses into the large antique vase on the dresser," instructed Aunt Sylvia.

"Jawohl, Frau Chefin. Me makin a nice bouquelet," Isolde promised and headed up the stairs.

"Isolde wants to be a great cook," Aunt Sylvia said. "The other day she made strawberry cake with fresh gooseberries and lemon juice. She had followed a special recipe, she told us."

"Uughh . . ." Lieschen imagined the taste of fresh gooseberries with lemon juice.

"She substituted gooseberries because she had eaten the strawberries," Uncle Gustav said.

"The cake was edible after we added a kilo of powdered sugar," Aunt Sylvia smiled.

"She has a heart of gold, but the battery to her brain somehow got disconnected." Uncle Gustav wrinkled his high forehead.

"She lost her parents when she was two. And people mistreated her as a child. Poor soul," Aunt Sylvia said.

"How sad!" Lieschen thought Isolde's strange behavior probably resulted from having been mistreated.

They climbed the stairs and entered through the varnished oak doors into a hallway with animated wallpaper of soap bubbles in small clusters. They walked along a tan-colored runner with a sprightly leaf pattern and entered the spacious living room. Lieschen felt the plush, caramel colored carpeting under her feet while she crossed over to the picture window to look out.

"Does this look familiar?" Aunt Sylvia motioned toward the shimmering surface of the Vierwaldstaetter Lake.

Lieschen nodded. Although fourteen years had passed since she had been standing in that same spot with her parents, *it* did not seem so long ago.

"The lake sometimes shines like a thousand dewdrops on golden satin, especially in the moonlight, or during a sunset," Aunt Sylvia smiled.

"Moonlight, sunset, and dewdrops. Why don't we sit down?" With his hands, Uncle Gustav indicated the bluish-gray cushions of the couch and matching chairs.

While Lieschen settled into the velvety softness of a chair, she noticed an interesting oil painting above the brick fireplace. "Is this Lucerne?" she asked.

"It's a depiction of our capital, Bern. Our nephew Robert painted it," Aunt Sylvia explained.

"We have a nice art community here in Lucerne. Robert is a member." Uncle Gustav edged back on the couch.

"Robert is an architect. He works for your uncle's firm," Aunt Sylvia said. "And he paints city scapes in his spare time. He has painted many versions of Vienna, Salzburg, Munich, Heidelberg, Paris, Stockholm, Rome, Madrid, and other cities. And, of course, Bern, Lucerne, and Zurich. He even painted the American Statue of Liberty."

"In New York Harbor?"

"Yes. It's one of Robert's favorite paintings. One day, Robert wants to visit New York Harbor, and he wants to travel throughout the United States. He says it's the country of liberty, dreams, and visions."

"I would also like to travel to the United States, and to Canada, South America, Africa, Japan, Russia, China, India, all parts of Asia and the Middle East and other parts of the world. And, of course, I'd like to get to know Europe really well," Lieschen said. At St. Germain, she had studied the history of many countries, and she had heard inspiring particulars about different cultures which she found fascinating. She wanted to explore them.

"I'm sure you'll have a chance to travel." Uncle Gustav ran his hand over his high forehead. "Which painters do you like?" he asked then.

"My idols are Vincent Van Gogh, Claude Monet, Albrecht Duerer, Paul Klee . . ." Lieschen could not think of all the painters whose artwork she admired.

"At the Mongrit, they currently have originals by Claude Monet on loan from the Louvre or from some other museum in Paris," Uncle Gustav said, kindling Lieschen's curiosity.

"Here in Lucerne?" she asked.

"Yes, the Mongrit is the largest art gallery in our community," Aunt Sylvia pointed out. "It used to be called Montreal while it belonged to another gallery or a chain of galleries. Now, the official name is Mongrit."

"I'd love to see the original Monet paintings." Lieschen inhaled deeply.

"Why don't we call Robert and find out more," Uncle Gustav suggested.

"Good idea," Aunt Sylvia nodded.

"I'll go to my office and call Robert." Uncle Gustav stepped out.

"The paintings from Paris are on loan for a limited time only," Aunt Sylvia explained.

"I wouldn't want to miss this opportunity to see them."

"Robert, our nephew, is familiar with all exhibitions. He knows many of the local artists too."

"I'm looking forward to meet Robert."

"He is a noble, talented young man. He is the right hand man to your uncle in his architecture firm. He started to work part time during school breaks while he attended the Technische Hochschule in Salzburg."

"I see."

After he graduated, he began working full time for your uncle." Aunt Sylvia paused. "Have your father and Aunt Klara never mentioned Robert?"

Lieschen reflected. "No, they haven't," she said and wondered about her father's reaction to her note and to her trip. What will Pap end up doing?

Uncle Gustav came back. He sat down and said, "Robert will be here shortly." They continued talking about the Monet exhibit. When the door bell chimed, Uncle Gustav went to open the door.

"Hi, Robert. Come in," Lieschen heard her uncle say. "We need your help."

"Happy to help."

Then Lieschen heard some mumbling, but she could not make out what they were saying.

The moment Robert entered the living room, sparks ignited Lieschen's heart. Robert resembled Michelangelo's David with his tall, muscular build, curly dark blonde hair, and refined facial expression; and his tan trousers and adobe-colored sport shirt enhanced his muscular build. However, it was not only his good looks and his rich, pleasant voice which ignited Lieschen's senses. She did not know what was happening.

Uncle Gustav introduced them. "This is my nephew Robert Schweitzer, and this is my niece Lieschen Reinking."

"I'm very happy to meet you," Robert said as they shook hands.

"Nice to meet you too." Lieschen made a courteous nod while trying to conceal her strong emotions.

"Have a seat." Uncle Gustav motioned for Robert to sit down.

He slipped his car keys into his trouser pocket and settled next to Uncle Gustav on the couch. Looking at Lieschen with a peculiar tenderness, he asked, "How can I help?"

"Uncle Gustav and Aunt Sylvia told me about the Monet exhibition. I'd like very much to see it." While talking to Robert, Lieschen felt herself blushing. She had never experienced such an embarrassing emotion.

"I'd be happy to take you there."

"Danke."

"Would you care for a drink?" Aunt Sylvia offered Robert Himbeersaft. "That's what you see in our glasses."

"Himbeersaft would be grand." Robert crossed his legs and wrapped his hands around his knees.

Aunt Sylvia called Isolde and instructed her to bring raspberry juice for Robert.

"When do you think you could take Lieschen to the Mongrit?" Uncle Gustav asked Robert.

"When would be a good time?"

"How about tomorrow? For a refreshing start." Uncle Gustav turned to Lieschen with an inquiring glance.

"If it isn't inconvenient?" She shrugged.

"Tomorrow should be fine." Robert smiled.

Lieschen noticed a tinge of blue and hazel in Robert's mysterious, gray eyes; and she sensed an invisible magnetic pull which she could not understand.

Isolde came in, holding a glass of lemonade.

"Did you drink the Himbeersaft?" Aunt Sylvia questioned.

"The bottle broken. I'm so so sorry! I swear I'm so so sorry." Isolde cramped the glass of lemonade in her right hand.

"Lemonade is fine too." Robert reached for the glass.

Isolde released her cramped fingers and handed Robert the glass of lemonade.

"Danke." He drank a little.

They chatted a bit longer about the exhibition, then arranged for Robert to come for breakfast the following morning and take Lieschen to the Mongrit.

After Uncle Gustav escorted Robert to the exit, he came back, but he did not sit down. He looked at Aunt Sylvia and suggested, "Why don't we show Lieschen her room so that she can get settled in."

Entering her assigned bedroom, Lieschen could hardly believe her eyes when she saw a large, framed color photograph of herself with her parents on the mahogany dresser, next to an antique vase with the bouquet of vibrant red roses which Aunt Sylvia had given her at the airport.

"How precious!" She stepped close and touched the bronze frame of the photo.

"We took this picture at the Vierwaldstatter Lake during your last visit with your parents."

"I remember." Lieschen had not wanted for her uncle to take pictures because she had not been allowed to take swans into a paddle boat. She loved the swans and wanted to take them for a boat ride. Now she was deeply grateful for this photo.

Isolde looked in. "Frau Chefin, you're wishin on the telephon."

"You'll both excuse me." Aunt Sylvia hurried out.

"We hoped the photo would be a nice surprise for you." Uncle Gustav's eyes brimmed.

"It's priceless. Especially since my mother is no longer alive." After a moment of silence, Lieschen mustered the courage to ask, "Uncle Gustav, do you know how Mommy died?"

"It seems you haven't been satisfied with the answers you've been given."

"No, I haven't." The bitter memory singed Lieschen's heart as if needles had reopened the wound. "Was Mommy murdered, or did she commit suicide?" She stared at her uncle.

"Your assumption of foul play has some merit." Uncle Gustav ran his hand across his forehead.

"I knew it. I knew it."

"I said some merit. The situation isn't that simple. And I'm not sure you really want to know."

"I do. I want to know so badly." Lieschen squeezed her fingernails into her palms.

Uncle Gustav tilted his head. "And I'm not sure you should know."

"Oh yes, I should. Please, Uncle Gustav! I've been burning to find out what happened to Mommy, and how she died."

"Okay, at your own risk."

Lieschen nodded anxiously.

Uncle Gustav hesitated for another moment, swallowed hard, then said, "Your mother loved another man before she married your father. The marriage to your father had consequently turned into failure."

Lieschen clutched her cheeks with clenched fists. This revelation hit her like a sword slashing her soul. Never had she expected anything like that.

"I believe we shouldn't go on. You get the picture."

"I want to know everything. Please, Uncle Gustav."

"All right." Her uncle took a deep breath. "When your mother wanted to divorce your father, she insisted that you live with her. Your father insisted that you live with him. The custody battle between your parents escalated ..."

Aunt Klara told me the truth. Lieschen choked as another awful idea crossed her mind. She looked at her uncle and uttered, "Am I the cause of Mommy's death? Am I to be blamed?"

Uncle Gustav made a vigorous gesture with his hands. "Don't ever think that!"

"If I caused Mommy's death, I have no right to live." Dizziness blinded Lieschen's eyes. She dropped into the chair by the mahogany table. Her head slumped forward on the embroidered tablecloth. Her chest filled with burning sawdust. That's how her chest felt.

"You're drawing the wrong conclusion. In the first place you hadn't been born when your mother had the relationship with the man she loved. Even after you were born, you couldn't have prevented or changed anything."

Lieschen buried her head in her arms, on the table, and sobbed bitterly. Her heart wrenched.

Uncle Gustav waited.

When Lieschen raised her head and wiped the tangled strands of hair out of her face, her uncle resumed in a low voice, "You see, I shouldn't have told you."

Lieschen tried to collect herself with all the willpower she could muster. "I had to know."

"Listen to me! You must never blame yourself. It wasn't your fault that your mother loved another man," Uncle Gustav repeated with strong emphasis. "Your maternal parents wouldn't allow your mother to marry the man she loved because he was not an aristocrat. That caused all the pain and suffering."

"God, no!" Lieschen wiped her eyes and cheeks with her fingers. Uncle Gustav retrieved a beige linen handkerchief from his pants' pocket and handed it to her.

"Danke." She dabbed her face with the handkerchief. Uncle Gustav's revelation seemed to mark an end. The happy relationship with her parents seemed to be a dream of long ago, almost too beautiful to have been true. And Lieschen was no longer certain to what extent she could blame her father or Aunt Klara. But she felt certain that her father did not want her to visit her relatives because he did not want her to find out about his tragic relationship with her mother. She even felt sorry for her father now.

"It was a big mistake for your mother to marry your father, but it's much too late for such a remedy. Much too late . . ." Uncle Gustav took another deep breath. "Of course, your father's insensitivity to your mother's feelings also contributed to the dissent. Before your mother died, she complained that your father ignored her feelings."

Ignoring feelings seemed to be a flaw which her father would not or could not recognize and rectify. Lieschen knew first hand from her own experience.

Uncle Gustav tilted his head and said, "Your parents' marriage lacked God's blessing."

"Why?"

"God's blessing follows a sincere heart, not a pretentious relationship."

Lieschen dug her fingernails deep into her palms. "But I believe both of my parents loved me?"

"That's why neither your mother nor your father would've given you up.

After a brief silence, Lieschen asked, "Uncle Gustav, how did Mommy die?"

"When I last talked to her the day before she died, she told me that she could no longer live with your father. Then I heard from Aunt Klara that your mother had died of cardiac arrest."

"Do you believe that Mommy died of cardiac arrest?"

"I don't know . . ." Uncle Gustav's voice trailed, and Lieschen sensed that her uncle would not tell her all he knew. The fatal events of that treacherous night flashed before her eyes and she felt faint. *I can't falter now after urging my uncle to tell me everything!* she reminded herself and tried to hold up.

"No matter what we do, we cannot bring your mother back."

Lieschen nodded sadly. "And I could never see my Grandma since Mommy's funeral. Uncle Gustav, where is my Grandma?"

"I don't know."

Just then, Aunt Sylvia came into the room and said, "It was Robert's stepmother, Karmen, calling about the Ball this coming Saturday. She wanted to know whether they should cook the venison in wine or with bilberries."

"What did you tell her?"

"I suggested cooking it in wine and serving bilberry sauce as a side dish."

"Sounds good."

"Lieschen will come to the Ball with us, won't you?" Aunt Sylvia turned toward her. "What in the world happened?" Her eyes opened wide as she gazed at Lieschen.

Uncle Gustav explained.

Aunt Sylvia's expression became compassionate, and her eyes returned to normal. "People's lives are sometimes tangled in a way which is difficult to understand. And difficult to solve." She paused, then said, "I suggest that you come to the Ball with us next Saturday. It'll take your mind off these sad events."

"Which Ball?" Robert's image appeared in Lieschen's mind, and her sadness became somewhat muted. Aunt Sylvia explained, "Every year, local business people arrange a Geschaeftsball at the Prinz Wilhelm Hotel here in Lucerne. The next Ball of this sort happens to be this coming Saturday."

"It's a large business banquet with a ballroom dance," Uncle Gustav clarified. "You have them in Austria as well."

Lieschen knew. "I'd like to come along." She felt a hint of a smile as Robert's image lingered in her mind and in her heart.

"Good. But now we better leave you alone, so you can unpack and get settled in. Whenever you're ready, come out and we'll have dinner," Aunt Sylvia said.

Although Lieschen felt drained, she unpacked, and then joined her relatives and Isolde in the large dining room, around the oval birch dining table. A white linen table cloth with elaborate white stitching covered the top. Lieschen had never eaten a combination of Paprika-chicken with spiced sour cream, stuffed cabbage, and roasted chestnuts, but she liked it. Despite her heavy heart, she ate a bit of everything, including dessert of a fluffy Sachertorte with Schlag and strawberries.

"You must be tired. We understand if you'd like to go to bed," Aunt Sylvia said when everybody had finished eating and nobody was talking.

"Tomorrow you'll feel better," Uncle Gustav assured.

"You will, because Herr Chef sayin." Isolde pointed her index into the air. "Herr Chef always right."

Lieschen thought Isolde was cute in her own way. She thanked her aunt and uncle for the fine meal and for everything and went to the bedroom.

Standing in front of the beautiful photo of herself with her parents, she reminisced about the events of the day - the excitement of seeing her relatives and meeting Robert; the dreadful discovery of her parents' futile relationship, and still not knowing how her mother had died; and not knowing the whereabouts of her grandmother; the uncertainty over her father's reaction to her trip; and she thought of her dear friend Werner, who wanted to know when she'd come back. She could not tell him because she did not know.

In bed, she could not fall asleep for a long time while all these thoughts and worries kept circling in her head. Yet, to a degree, they became eclipsed by spirited sentiments for Robert. She wanted to understand these curious new feelings and wondered if she was falling in love.

CHAPTER 11

Seated next to Robert in his classic, Geranium-bronze sports car, on the way to the Mongrit Gallery, Lieschen sensed the same magnetic pull which she had experienced the previous day, as if all of her senses had been lit by a magic beacon. In a peculiar way, Robert helped ease Lieschen's afflicted heart.

"Look at this bustle." Robert indicated the sidewalk along Mering Strasse, a narrow business alley, where children hopped about among parents and friends. Life seemed a merry coaster in front of cafes, delicatessen shops, boutiques, and souvenir-, jewelry-, and other specialty shops. Cars drove at a slow speed.

"Not all shops are open," Lieschen remarked when she noticed that some of them were closed.

"Not all of our shops open on Sundays," Robert said.

"In Graz, none of our shops open on Sundays. They close Saturday afternoon, usually at two, and reopen Monday morning at eight."

"I believe tourism makes a difference."

"We have tourism in Graz, but not as much as you have here," Lieschen said. Then, touching the wine-red dashboard, she asked, 'What make is your car? It's so different."

"It's a Talbot, an old British sports car with a BMW V8 engine. I purchased it from a British businessman through Uncle Gustav's business connections."

"It's very attractive."

"Danke-schoen. As far as I know, it's a rare model," Robert acknowledged and accelerated behind a police car. "As you can see, some of our streets are congested and narrow," he said then.

"We have the same problem in Graz. That's why some of our old streets are no longer open to car traffic."

"It would solve the problem here too. In any case, I'm very happy that you came to Lucerne." Robert cast a tender glance at her.

Again Lieschen felt this magnetic pull. If this means falling in love, it's beautiful, she thought.

A short while later, Robert maneuvered his Talbot into a parking lot in the back of the mint-colored Mongrit Gallery and parked between a white Audi and a barn-red Peugeot.

"I appreciate that you drove me here." Lieschen turned to climb out of her seat.

"My pleasure."

Outside, Robert locked the car-door, slipped the car keys into his charcoal trouser pocket, and led the way inside to a deep-blue grotto. "Here're Monet's masterpieces." He indicated the paintings hanging on three walls inside the grotto.

Lieschen stepped up close and, mesmerized, viewed *Monet's Waterlilies.* Robert stayed with her.

"Guten Morgen, Herr Schweitzer," came the voice of a middle-aged man of medium height, wearing a formal beige suit.

"Guten Morgen, Herr Oberbauer." They shook hands, and Robert introduced Lieschen. "Herr Oberbauer is the administrator of this Gallery," he said.

"I'm pleased to meet you." Lieschen also shook hands with Herr Oberbauer.

"Fraulein Reinking? Did I understand your name correctly?"

"Can I assume that you are an artist?" Herr Oberbauer examined Lieschen with his inky gray eyes.

"I'd like to be an artist," she replied, a little embarrassed. She did not know *why* she felt embarrassed. Sometimes shyness interfered with her manners.

"Are you here in Lucerne for a visit?"

"I'm visiting with my relatives."

"Familie Schmidt," Robert clarified.

"Your boss?"

"Yes."

"Enjoy your visit." Herr Oberbauer said to Lieschen.

"Danke."

Turning to Robert, Herr Oberbauer said, "Listen my friend, we've just sold your painting of the Schwarzenbergplatz in Vienna. You can pick up your check anytime. The customer paid cash."

"Cash always comes in handy. I'll be in tomorrow, if that's all right?"

"Quite all right. I'll be expecting you." Herr Oberbauer's heels clicked away on the hardwood floor; and Lieschen congratulated Robert on the sale of his painting.

"In today's art world one never knows when a painting will sell. I'm sure you know that art isn't only in the eye of the beholder. People must have the means to pay for a work of art. Nowadays, things are expensive."

Money, money, money! The whole world seemed to revolve around money. Lieschen wished it were not so.

At closing time, when Robert took Lieschen home, he did not stay. He was in a hurry to leave.

Chapter 12

With a sketch-book and a pencil, Lieschen set out to stroll on foot to the Mongrit Gallery. Uncle Gustav and Robert had started work early and could not give her a ride.

Fleecy clouds traversed on the morning sky while the sun struggled to break through. Lieschen felt comfortable in her cobalt-blue linen skirt, white linen blouse, and flat cobalt-blue leather shoes. She enjoyed getting to know Lucerne on foot. Aunt Sylvia had pointed out some sites to watch for, especially a little church called La Chiesa Santa Maria degli Angioli, patterned after a church in Italy.

Beautiful frescos of the Virgin Mary with the Baby Jesus and many angels decorated the walls and the ceiling of this quaint church. Well preserved after hundreds of years, the artist had long since died, but his artwork transcended time. Lieschen would have loved to watch the artist work on these magnificent frescos. Since it had happened hundreds of years ago, she could not watch because she could not transcend time.

At the Mongrit, she made study sketches of Monet's *Waterlilies* and of his painting of a *Sunset*. She became so involved that she did not feel hungry and skipped lunch. Early in the afternoon, she ventured to other sections of the Gallery, where several paintings of local artists caught her attention. One of the paintings was an old steam engine puffing through green meadows, titled Steam *Engine* by Karl Volper. Others included: *Farmer Plowing a Field* by Ilse Tropf; and *Green Night* by Bernhard Arndt, who had carried his night premise to metaphysical interpretations, with varied green and dark-blue nocturnal colors. Lieschen enjoyed in particular *Green Night*.

Back in the Monet Grotto, she turned abruptly when she felt somebody standing beside her.

"I didn't mean to scare you," Robert smiled.

"You didn't scare me." Lieschen was very happy to see Robert. "How was your day?"

"I visited La Chiesa Santa Maria degli Angioli on my way to the Mongrit." Lieschen told Robert about the beautiful frescoes.

"I believe the church is modeled after St.Francis' Church of Assisi."

"I didn't know," Lieschen replied, then showed Robert her favorite paintings of the local artists before they left the Mongrit.

"It's very kind of you to take me home," she said as soon as they had settled inside Robert's Talbot. "You must be tired since you started work early."

"Challenging work usually keeps me going. And I just picked up the check for my painting of the Schwarzenbergplatz in Vienna." From the inside pocket of his brown tweed jacket, Robert pulled out an envelope with the check and showed it to Lieschen.

"Congratulations," she said with a smile.

"Danke schoen." Robert slipped the check back into the envelope, and tucked it away in the inside pocket of his tweed jacket. Then he started the engine and veered into traffic. Before heading home, he suggested a side trip to the ancient Chapel Bridge. "It was built in 1333. An example of Switzerland's architectural candor," Robert pointed out.

Lieschen liked the idea of a side trip.

As they approached the bridge, she read a sign on a tall iron post: *River Reuss* and she saw people wandering in both directions on the wide, long bridge. Robert parked nearby, and they strolled over to the bridge. About midway, they leaned their elbows on the railing, bent over and looked down at the grayish-green swiftly flowing stream. "The waters still flow as they did in the Middle Ages," Robert remarked.

"Nature and art live on," Lieschen agreed. Her tone of voice was laced with a melancholic touch.

"While we have to die. Difficult to understand, isn't it?" Robert glanced at Lieschen.

She nodded. Her mother's picture appeared in her mind, and she wished there were no final partings on earth.

On the way home, Robert inquired, "You will come to the Geschaeftsball on Saturday, won't you?"

"My aunt and uncle have invited me."

"You couldn't disappoint them. And I look forward to dance with you." Robert smiled tenderly at her, slowing at an intersection.

She smiled back, feeling wonderfully alive. She longed to dance with Robert. During this short time since they met, her spirits renewed. Every morning she looked forward to see Robert, like tulips longing for the sunrise.

The following day, after work, Robert picked up Lieschen again at the Mongrit and showed her the countryside.

While strolling along a grassy path in a fruit orchard on the outskirts of Lucerne, Lieschen noticed the golden glow of the setting sun reflecting on green apples and pears. Some fruit had begun ripening. A ladder against a crooked trunk of a pear tree blocked part of their path. Walking around the ladder, Robert said, "The times together with you are the most precious of my life."

"I like being with you too," Lieschen whispered, feeling the same magnetic pull she had felt from the moment she had met Robert.

"Do you like our countryside?" Robert asked as they sauntered on.

"It's similar to Mariatrost, where I live."

"I've never been to Mariatrost. As a matter of fact, I've never been to Graz. But I would like to visit you in the future."

"I hope you will." Lieschen thought she would show Robert all the interesting sites she could think of - the Stadtpark with its magnificent statues and lakes; the Schlossberg; the Eggenberg Castle where her grandmother used to take her for concerts and ballet performances; Maria Strassengel, the historic Church where Ralph's father served as assistant deacon; the old University; the stud-farm Piber, where Grande, her Lipizzaner had been bred; and museums, and other interesting sites inside and outside the parameters of Graz. Suddenly she thought of her father and wondered how he would react to Robert. She still had not heard from him since she had left on this trip.

"The only part of Austria I know is Salzburg. I lived there during Hochschule," Robert said.

"Did you like Salzburg?"

"Who wouldn't?"

"While my mother was alive, we used to go to Salzburg often. After my mother died, my father never took me there anymore." Lieschen wondered whether the man her mother loved had lived in Salzburg.

"Can you remember your mother well?" Robert observed her closely. Lieschen nodded with a sad touch.

"I'm sorry; I didn't mean to make you sad." Robert switched the topic and asked, "Do you sometimes go for walks where you live in Mariatrost?"

"Sometimes, but more often I go horseback riding. We have nice riding trails in our Mariatroster Woods." Lieschen tripped over a string of roots across the grassy path. Robert caught her elbow. She stumbled into his arms. The magic flame intensified, and Lieschen shivered with delight.

Robert let go of her and asked, "Are you okay?"

"Yes." Lieschen felt embarrassed.

They strolled on.

"When you go riding, do you go by yourself?" Robert asked.

"Sometimes, but usually with my father or with my friend Ingrid." Lieschen did not mention Werner. She would explain their special relationship later.

"Since you enjoy horseback riding, we could go riding here. If you'd like?"

"We could?"

"Yes. I usually go to the Kipplinger Stables. They rent horses by the hour, or by the day."

"Do you often go horseback-riding?"

"I can't always find the time, nor the money. But for you I'd find both."

"Danke." Lieschen felt jubilant.

"You're so sweet." Robert's intimate tone made her heart glow.

A furry white rabbit lunged out from the fruit trees and crossed in front of them. Lieschen stopped abruptly. "He scared me." She glanced at Robert.

"We should head back. You're probably hungry, and Uncle Gustav and Aunt Sylvia are waiting."

Lieschen wanted to stay with Robert in this idyllic fruit orchard. As much as she loved animals, she was angry at the white rabbit for having disrupted their intimate moments.

Robert took Lieschen home and stayed for dinner. After an enjoyable meal of Naturschnitzel with <u>dill</u> sauce, red beets, and Hauptelsalad, and dessert of raspberry tarts, they drove to the Kursaal to attend a chamber concert with music by Johann Sebastian Bach. The musicians' instruments included string, flute, and oboe; and a young female harpist in a classic Viennese costume played a harp solo. Lieschen savored the concert together with Robert and her relatives.

This delightful evening resonated in her slumber during the night.

CHAPTER 13

Aunt Sylvia took Lieschen shopping. On the way to the boutiques, they dropped by Uncle Gustav's Architecture Firm.

"How unique!" Lieschen remarked as they climbed the wide, short flight of stairs flanked with iron florals and fish statues on both sides of the stairway.

"You must tell your uncle. Robert designed the building, and your uncle built it." Aunt Sylvia's tone revealed her pride.

On the upper landing, Aunt Sylvia led the way inside to the architectural hall and offices. The light coming from the walled windows gave the work space a buoyant look. Lieschen counted seven individual drawing tables with designs of small and large model homes and other building projects. One of the architects looked up, but Lieschen could not see Robert.

Uncle Gustav's office was closed. Aunt Sylvia knocked lightly at the door, then carefully opened it. Lieschen could now see her uncle and hear him talking on the telephone. He motioned for them to come in and sit down.

They crossed the shortly clipped, moss-green carpet and sat down on the two oak chairs opposite her uncle at his wide oak desk. As soon as Uncle Gustav finished his telephone conversation, he replaced the receiver and pointed his right hand at the wall behind his desk. "Recognize this photo?" he asked Lieschen.

"It's an areal depiction of your home."

"You've just passed your test. Wouldn't you like to work here and become an architect? You must know that art and architecture are related," Uncle Gustav pointed out.

"Your building and your offices are truly special and unique, and I know I could learn a lot from you, but I really would like to pursue an art career."

"You've made up your mind?"

While Lieschen nodded, the phone rang again. "You'll excuse me." Uncle Gustav answered the call and right away asked the person on the line, "Can I call you back?"

Just then another light started blinking on the telephone, indicating more phone calls.

Aunt Sylvia whispered, "1 know you're very busy. We only came to say hi and show Lieschen your Company, but we don't want to keep you from your work. We'll be on our way to do some shopping for Lieschen."

Uncle Gustav covered the speaking part of the receiver and said at a low voice, "Enjoy. I'll see you later."

On their way out, Lieschen saw Robert coming up the stairs. He carried a large attache case. "I have to pick up two drawings for my next appointment," he explained.

"You're all so busy. We won't interrupt your schedule," Aunt Sylvia promised. Lieschen was delighted to see Robert, if only for a moment.

From there, Aunt Sylvia drove Lieschen to the Lucerne Modehaus, a boutique on Mering Strasse, where she tried on sapphire-, pastel pink-, and various shades of blue and green gowns, all the while wondering which gown Robert might prefer. Lastly, she slipped on an emerald satin gown, which she had put aside on a separate chair. She hesitated to try on this gown because the style and the color resembled the emerald gown she had ripped on the evening when she had gone to see Swan Lake with Sigi. Could it mean bad luck if I select this gown? She hesitated a moment longer, then tried it on and moved back and forth in front of the tall mirror.

"It's gorgeous on you. Just gorgeous. And the color seems tailor-made for you." Aunt Sylvia sounded enthusiastic.

"I like it too." Lieschen did not mention the reason for her hesitation. Aunt Sylvia paid for the gown, and Lieschen thanked her aunt.

They sauntered farther down Mering Strasse, looking into windows that displayed clothing, jewehy, souvenirs, postcards, shoes, purses, and other fashion and utility items. At a small restaurant called *Die Zeitschnuppe,* they entered to have lunch.

Aunt Sylvia suggested Veal Cotelettes with dumplings, dillsauce, and mixed salads; and Lackerli, a spiced honey cake with lemon icing, for dessert. "When your uncle and I come here from time to time, that's our usual choice," Aunt Sylvia disclosed.

Lieschen was hungry and relished the meal. The atmosphere was semi-formal.

Back home, she compared the emerald color of her new gown with her own emerald purse and shoes, which she had brought along on this trip. The hue of the gown was a trifle less intense than that of her purse and shoes, but they fit fine together. She had all she needed for the Ball and looked forward to dancing with Robert.

Saturday finally came, and Lieschen dressed for the Ball. She touched up her eyebrows, and curled her eyelashes with a little mascara. She wondered whether Robert might like lipstick or other makeup. If he did, she would begin wearing it. She wanted very much to please him, and she was grateful that he had come into her life at such a critical time when she tried to overcome the agonizing revelation concerning her parents' futile relationship. In a way, Robert helped her work through that pain. Could God have a special reason for bringing Robert into my life? She wondered. When she heard a knock at the door, she responded. Aunt Sylvia peeked in and said through the half-open door, "Uncle Gustav is waiting."

"I'm ready." Quickly Lieschen applied a little Egus de France perfume behind her ears and on her wrists, and followed her aunt.

At the Prinz Wilhelm Hotel, a tall waiter escorted them into the grand ballroom. What a silly face! thought Lieschen because the waiter's maladroit expression resembled a toad's with owlish eyes. His dress code was classy, though - black pants, a crimson double-breasted jacket, and a white shirt with a black necktie.

People in elegant attire drifted about. Lieschen thought her new emerald gown, as well as her aunt's metallic bronze satin gown and her uncle's Prussian-blue, double-breasted linen suit fit well for this festive Ball.

People chatted while smoking, eating, and drinking. The aroma of cigarettes, cocktails, and coffee fused. Flickering candles and small bouquets of flowers in tall crystal vases on damask table cloths embellished the tables. Diffused lighting in the color of blue Enzian ejected from the walls. Lieschen also noticed musicians in white shirts with cobalt-blue bow ties and silver jackets fine-tuning their instruments on the elevated rostrum behind the round parquet dance floor.

The tall waiter with his silly expression assisted Lieschen and her relatives in taking their seats. Most of the tables were already occupied. For starters, Uncle Gustav ordered hors-d'oeuvre and a bottle of Chardonais Champagne. Lieschen concluded that the waiter's professional attitude obliterated his weird expression. She did not mean to be unkind. She never wanted to be unkind - and was glad that she had not made any derogatory remarks to her relatives about the waiter's bizarre expression.

When the waiter returned with a tray of hors d'oeuvre, Lieschen and her relatives picked Russian eggs with caviar, tiny herrings, anchovies, slices of red and green tomatoes sprinkled with herbs, smoked sirloin, garnished cheeses, small round butter balls, and a few other delectables. Lieschen's English China plate looked like a colorful disk after she had filled it with hors d'oeuvres and, to her, they tasted delicious.

The waiter poured Champagne for Uncle Gustav just as Robert arrived. Lieschen pictured Michelangelo's David dressed like Robert in his double-breasted, charcoal linen suit, white shirt and black bow tie. She was sure Robert and Michelangelo's David would look like brothers alongside each other. Robert handed her a small bouquet of three fresh Edelweiss, held together with a pink bow.

"Danke." Lieschen adored the dainty flowers that looked like off-white velvet stars.

While the waiter pulled out the empty chair for Robert to sit down next to Lieschen, she carefully put the bouquet of Edelweiss on the damask tablecloth, near the burning candle and the small vase with white and pink carnations.

"How is Monika?" Aunt Sylvia asked Robert.

"Not well. Doctor Ambrosius told her she had to stay home."

"That's too bad." Uncle Gustav took an unusually deep breath.

"Doctor Ambrosius instructed her to take a different medication for a few days and come back to see him on Wednesday."

"Hope that she feels better soon." Aunt Sylvia looked worried.

"I hope so too," Robert said with a serious expression.

Uncle Gustav proposed a toast. "To Monika's health."

Everybody joined, so did Lieschen, although she had never met Monika. She assumed Monika was Robert's sister.

Whisps of smoke in hues of yellow, orange, and purple vaporized like a colorful fog at the sides of the rostrum as the musicians began playing the Danube Waltz.

"Would you care to dance?" Robert invited Lieschen.

She nodded gracefully and rose. Finally the time had come when she could dance with Robert.

"Emerald is very becoming on you," he complimented her while they turned round and round among other dance couples on the shining parquet floor.

"Danke." The emerald color of the gown no longer reminded Lieschen of the horrifying evening with Sigi. During these happy moments, Sigi did not even exist.

"Do you dance a lot?" Robert asked.

"Not a lot." Lieschen paused, then explained, "About four months ago was my last dance outing with my father and Aunt Klara when they had taken me along to the Jaegerball in Graz."

"Did you enjoy the Jaegerball?"

"There were many fun activities, like blindfolding dancers, who had to recognize their partners. The mood was folkloric."

"Do you prefer a casual or a formal dance?"

"1 think each has its own charm. I like in particular tap-dancing and Viennese dances."

"I like your charm too." Robert pressed Lieschen slightly toward him. His closeness blazed inside her.

After the Danube Waltz, the musicians played a Rheinland Tango, then a variety potpourri. Robert and Lieschen continued dancing until the musicians announced a short break.

On the way to their table, a stranger of medium height approached. Robert exchanged greetings with the young man, whose shortly clipped golden hair crowned his round face. "This is my artist friend Karl Volpert," Robert introduced him to Lieschen.

She recalled having seen Karl's painting at the Mongrit and asked, "Did you paint the Steam Engine, which is on display at the Mongrit?"

"Many people take notice of my paintings. I currently have seven on display at the Mongrit," Karl said.

"I see." Lieschen had not noticed Karl's other paintings.

The orchestra resumed playing the Rapsurka Loreal, and Karl requested formally of Robert, "You will permit me to steal Fraulein Reinking for this dance?"

Robert looked at Lieschen with an expression that seemed to say, "If you like to dance with Karl, go ahead."

She went dancing with Karl while Robert remained standing along the wall where the blue Enzian lights jotted out. His arms folded across his chest, he observed them. Lieschen could see him from the dance floor. When the orchestra stopped for another break, Robert strolled toward them. "I'll escort Fraulein Lieschen back to the table," he said.

Karl raised his golden eyebrows. "New flame?"

Robert did not reply. Lieschen could see that he felt uncomfortable. She continued dancing with Robert, and occasionally with Uncle Gustav and with one other friend of Robert named Rudi Maxim, but she did not dance with Karl anymore. At eight-thirty, when the musicians announced a half-hour break, Robert and Lieschen returned to Uncle Gustav and Aunt Sylvia.

"Good timing. I don't know about you, but my stomach is telling me something." Uncle Gustav put his hand on his growling stomach. "I feel hungry too," echoed Aunt Sylvia.

Robert and Lieschen joined in the selection of venison with bilberry sauce, rice a la ragu, and variety vegetables - steamed carrots, tender green beans, and fresh mustard-horseradish. Lieschen also ate a good portion of the dessert of Salzburger Nockerln with Maraschino cherries from a large serving, which they shared. During dinner, a few of Uncle Gustav's business associates and friends dropped by to say hello and chat a little.

After this stimulating meal, Robert suggested a walk in the fresh air. Lieschen liked the idea. Her relatives did not come along.

At the exit, Karl Volpert and a robust, tall man with thick brown locks stepped in front of them. They made it appear accidental, but Lieschen heard Karl whisper to Robert, "Forbidden territory!"

The robust man slurred, "Where y-y-ou gooing?"

To Lieschen, he appeared drunk, although she could not be sure. His drawling speech made her assume that he was drunk.

"Just for a little walk." Robert made an abrupt gesture with his hands, indicating that the two men had no right to block them. They did not step out of the way. With his right hand, Robert made another firm motion and guided Lieschen around the men through the exit.

"D'y-y-ou h-have my p-p-ermission?" the drunken man stammered as soon as Robert and Lieschen were outside. Robert ignored him.

A short distance from the exit, Lieschen heard the drunken man garble something in a loud voice, but she could not make out what he was saying. She only understood Karl when he said, "Robert is a careful planner."

"Robert did y-you hear m-my qu-question?" the drunken man challenged Robert once more in an even louder voice.

"Excuse me," Robert said to Lieschen and hastened back.

"Heinz, will you shut your drunken mouth and back off? You can't even see straight."

Lieschen realized that Robert and Heinz had been acquainted, and that Heinz was really drunk.

"I c-c-can see what you-u-u're do-ing," muttered Heinz accusingly.

"It's none of your business what I'm doing."

"How c-cute y-you-u are w-when y-you-u are angry . . ." Heinz mellowed his accusation.

Karl did not make any more comments.

When Robert rejoined Lieschen, he apologized for the incident, and they strolled on. Lieschen had a difficult time with her high-heeled emerald shoes to keep her balance along the gravel path under the gas lanterns.

"Would you care to sit down for a little while?" Robert indicated a wooden bench under one of the blooming acacia trees.

"Okay," Lieschen nodded, and they sat down. Just then a spooky noise crept up. Both turned to look, but could not see anybody or anything. Shortly thereafter the noise stopped.

"Perhaps a mouse," Robert smiled.

"Perhaps," Lieschen echoed, but she did not think that it was a mouse.

"Look at this beautiful sky." With his right hand, Robert indicated the profusion of stars. "Can you see the sickle of the moon near the Great Bear? It seems the moon is guarding the Great Bear, doesn't it?"

Lieschen had never thought of the moon guarding stars.

"And over there ..." Robert motioned toward the east, ". . . the brilliance of Venus. Can you see?"

Lieschen's eyes followed the direction of Robert's hand.

"And the Big Dipper. And a little over to the right, the Little Dipper."

Lieschen looked from one cluster of stars to another. "I don't know much about stars," she admitted.

"At one time I wanted to be an astronomer, but my uncle convinced me to be an architect."

Now Lieschen understood Robert's fascination with stars. "Do you like being an architect?" she asked.

"I enjoy it. And I also enjoy you in a special way." Robert nudged his right hand behind her on the wooden backrest. Although he barely touched her shoulders, her pulse accelerated. His closeness illuminated her whole being, as if his heart were beating inside her.

Now Robert will kiss me! Lieschen thought. She had been yearning for this moment. Although she would have liked to initiate a kiss to show Robert how much she had grown to love hisn, she could not do that because her code of ethics would not allow it.

"To be near you is like a wonderful dream come true," Robert whispered.

Lieschen wanted it to be real, not a dream. Dreams reminded her of too many bad things.

"I hope I'm not boring you."

"No!" God how can Robert think that? She breathed deeply.

"I'm glad." He pressed her shoulder a little closer. She wished time would stand still, but she could not understand why Robert would not kiss her. It seemed a perfect moment. Could he consider it immoral to kiss a girl before the wedding? This must be it, she soothed her longing heart.

The spooky noise could be heard again, stronger than before, as if footsteps were sneaking up.

"Ghosts in disguise," Robert joked.

Perhaps Robert doesn't kiss me because he worries that Karl and Heinz followed, Lieschen thought then.

"Should we go back?" Robert lifted his arm from her shoulders and moved forward on the bench.

"Okay," Lieschen replied regretfully.

Their delightful evening came to a close when the Ball broke up at midnight. It had been such a fleeting evening. Lieschen wanted to hold on. When she looked for the Edelweiss which Robert had given her, she could not find them. Robert and her relatives helped look for the Edelweiss, but they had disappeared.

Could Karl and Heinz have taken them? After the incident by the exit, Lieschen had not seen them anymore.

Back home, she was still sad about the loss of the Edelweiss. She wanted to press and keep them, as her mother had done with many flowers. Her mother's book of flowers included Enzian, Edelweiss, Almenrausch, orchids, roses, carnations, lilies, forget-me-nots, irises, daffodils (her mother's favorite flower), poppies, cornflowers and many others. Her mother had written personal notes or brief poems beside or below each flower. Her mother had frequently leafed through this book. Many times Lieschen had watched her mother. And since she found out about her parents' tragic relationship, she wondered whether the man her mother loved had given her all of these flowers, which she had so carefully pressed and preserved. After her mother's death, the book had disappeared from the book-shelf in the family library. Lieschen had searched everywhere, but could not find it. When she questioned her father and Aunt Klara, they told her they did not know what happened to the book.

Lying under the warm down comforter, with the bedside lamp burning on the nightstand, Lieschen longed to be near Robert. Her curiosity for intimate love had been powerfully aroused. She visualized the night of their honeymoon when Robert would finally kiss her and make love to her, and she would be able to caress him and wake up in the morning beside him - always beside him. She could not help her yearning and hoped to God that it was not another bad dream.

CHAPTER 14

Seated at the breakfast table with Aunt Sylvia and Isolde, Lieschen jumped to her feet when Uncle Gustav came in and told her that her father was on the telephone waiting for her. She rushed over to her uncle's private office and grabbed the receiver. "Hi, Pap!" she said loudly and pressed the receiver close to her ear while she sat down on her uncle's leather chair behind his large oak desk.

"Are you enjoying yourself?" Her father did not sound angry. His attitude surprised Lieschen, especially since she had made this trip despite his objection.

"Pap, I'm very happy here. I'd like to stay for a year and attend the RAIK Art Institute. It's a famous art school, with an excellent reputation according to your standards." Lieschen craved for her father to agree. She could not leave Lucerne and be away from Robert.

"I will not permit you to stay." Her father's voice changed.

"I cannot leave," Lieschen said.

Silence followed.

When her father resumed, his tone of voice sounded deep. "I thought I'd made it clear that you're enrolled at AKA."

"We can postpone AKA."

"We cannot."

"Why not?"

"Because I will not permit it."

Lieschen was determined to stand her ground. "Pap, I'm grown up. It's my life. I believe ..."

The phone clicked.

Slowly Lieschen replaced the receiver, propped her elbows on the desk, and held her head with both hands. What is Pap going to do now?

A few minutes later, Aunt Sylvia looked in and said, "Won't you come back to finish breakfast?" Lieschen followed her aunt.

"No meal is no good if it's gettin cold." Isolde shook her head as though Lieschen should know better.

"I'm sorry that my father called during breakfast," she apologized and sat down.

"That's perfectly all right." Uncle Gustav examined her. "Is everything all right?"

"I'm not sure. I have to call my father back."

After breakfast, Lieschen and her relatives went to mass at the Hofkirche. Lieschen's soul had been drawn to God ever since her faith had been founded by her mother, and fostered by the teachings of Mother Marisa, Sister Gertrude, Sister Margarita, and other sisters and instructors at St. Germain. Yet, she could not help questioning God why he had put her through the torment of losing her mother so early and under such awful circumstances, and why her parents' relationship had been so ill-fated; why she could not find her grandmother; why Sigi could instill such terrible pain and shame upon her, and her father could not recognize Sigi's wretched side of his character. These were only some of the unanswered questions Lieschen had been grappling with.

During mass, she prayed for a happy relationship with Robert. She prayed intensely because that was now uppermost in her heart and mind. And she prayed that her father would be agreeable.

After church, they drove to the Pilatus Mountain to take the aerial cable to the summit, but found it under repair and closed. They decided to drive back to the Vierwaldstaetter Lake for another boat ride.

While Uncle Gustav hauled the paddles through the cool water, he told Lieschen, "Your grandfather loved fishing here."

She knew her uncle was referring to his, her mother's, and Aunt Klara's father, Lieschen's maternal grandfather. She could hardly remember him, though. He had died when she was three years old. And she never knew her paternal grandparents. They had died before she was born. But where was her beloved grandmother? She looked at her uncle and said, "After Mommy's funeral, I could never see my Grandma. Uncle Gustav, what happened to my grandmother?" She had asked her uncle on previous occasions, but his explanation had always been evasive.

Uncle Gustav shifted his head toward Aunt Sylvia. Neither spoke.

"Please tell me where Grandma is," Lieschen pleaded.

"I really can't tell you because I don't know." Uncle Gustav appeared uneasy and sad.

"As you know, we live a long distance from Graz," Aunt Sylvia said, as though the distance could justify not knowing the whereabouts of one's mother or grandmother. Lieschen wanted so badly to find her grandmother before getting married to Robert, to share her happiness with Grandma. She watched a few bubbly lines next to the boat and visualized herself in a long white bridal gown with a lacy veil and a long satin train, and beautiful flower girls, and Robert standing in the nave, with Grandma looking on. Lieschen knew Robert loved her. She felt it deep in her heart. It could only be a question of time when he would propose.

The following morning, while Lieschen made more sketches of Claude Monet's Sunrise at the Mongrit, Herr Oberbauer stopped by. "If you need additional information about the Monet paintings, let me know while they're still at hand," he offered kindly.

"Danke, I appreciate your help, but I can't think of any questions right now." A moment later, Lieschen retracted her response because she could think of an important question. "Oh yes, I can. I'm sorry," she said. "Will you have exhibits of paintings by Vincent Van Gogh, Albrecht Duerer, or El Greco? Or Michelangelo, Leonardo da Vinci, Delacroix, or Joseph Vermeer? Or Henri Rousseau, or Marc Chagall, or Paul Klee?" She was amazed that all of these masters came to her mind spontaneously.

"An exhibit of Paul Klee's paintings is in the works. I will let you know as things develop. How long will you be staying with Fami.lie Schmidt?"

"At least one year."

"Will you be working here in Lucerne?"

"I want to enroll in classes at the RAIK Art Institute. Uncle Gustav and Aunt Sylvia told me it's one of the best art schools in Europe."

"Any art student can roll the dice in his or her favor with a RAIK training," Herr Oberbauer pointed out. "Subject to personal talent," he added with a knowing smile.

Robert approached. "Guten Morgen," he said. Lieschen wondered what happened. Robert was supposed to be at work.

"Uncle Gustav wants me to take you to the RAIK," he told Lieschen.

"We were just talking about the RAIK," Herr Oberbauer disclosed. "A propos, while you're here, I want to tell you that a new customer is interested in your series of the Amsterdam Lagoon paintings."

"Sounds good."

"Listen, my friend, have a safe ride. Hope the morning traffic won't be too sticky."

"I hope not either," Robert said.

They arrived at the RAIK half an hour later. Traffic was okay. Lieschen completed the requisite paperwork for a one-year program.

On the way back to the Mongrit, Robert stopped in front of a Konditorei called *Wiener Schokoladen Stube*. Hopping out of his Talbot, he said, "Be right back." His heels clicked away so fast, Lieschen had no chance to ask him where he was going or what he was doing. When he returned, he handed her a quaint box of Mozartkugeln.

Ah, that's what he was doing. "Danke," she smiled and opened the box. She offered Robert a Mozartkugel, then put one into her own mouth. "Mmm, they're delicious," she whispered as the chocolate melted on her tongue.

"Sorry, I have to rush back to work." Robert resumed driving.

"I can take the bus or walk to the Mongrit. It's not that far from here."

"That's not necessary. I'll take you there, but then you'll have to excuse me. I have a lot of work to do. That's why I've to be back at the office as quickly as I can."

"I understand. I appreciate what you're doing for me."

"Always my pleasure." Robert cast a tender glance at her, then set out to overtake a tour bus.

Lieschen enjoyed the rest of the day at the Mongrit, studying more details of the Monet paintings - brush strokes, light, composition, shape, color, and other components of good artwork.

At closing time, Robert returned with a camera. He took Lieschen to the Vierwaldstaetter Lake where he snapped pictures of her crouching beside a swan. The swan's whitish feathers fluffed up in the cool breeze.

"Can I give the swan a Mozartkugel?" Lieschen asked after Robert had finished taking pictures.

"1 don't think a swan could digest a Mozartkugel. He might not even eat *it.*" Robert put the lid back on the lens and pulled the cover over the camera.

"I don't have breadcrumbs or anything else."

"I believe the swans are well fed here." Robert suggested a boat ride.

While they ventured off shore in an olive-green paddle boat, Robert whistled the familiar tune of Edehveiss. The song reminded Lieschen of the dainty white velvet bouquet Robert had given her at the Geschaeftsball. She still felt sorry that it had disappeared. She knew that the Edelweiss was Austria's and Switzerland's national flower and could only be found in the ravines of the Alps. She had also heard that the Edelweiss was Russia's national flower, but she could not be sure.

Quite far out in the lake, Robert dropped the oars and lowered his hands into the grayish-green water. He scooped *up a* palmful and splashed droplets at Lieschen. She did the same, wetting his cream-colored linen shirt.

When Robert tilted the boat to one side, Lieschen held on to the flanks, wondering what he was up to. "Just testing," he smiled, "though I wouldn't mind swimming with you through deep waters." He let the boat balance itself.

Was this an indirect proposal? Lieschen wondered. She would not mind swimming through deep waters with Robert either, if he meant living through difficult times together.

A fish leaped out, sailed through the air, and plunged back into its own wet world. "It jumped really high," Lieschen said while watching the ripples in its wake.

"Quite a performance," Robert agreed. "My grandfather told me that fish breed well in this lake."

"Uncle Gustav also told me that my grandfather often came here."

Robert wiped his perspiring forehead. Lieschen wondered why he was perspiring. There was a cool breeze. "Are you okay?" she asked.

He nodded, but he looked as if a wasp had just stung him. Lieschen had seen a few wasps at the shoreline, but not out in the lake where they were.

"Did you ever have to give a promise under oath?" Robert asked. "I mean an oath creating a bond. I mean an oath concerning a code of silence, slicing into your life like a paralyzing dagger?"

What on earth is Robert talking about? "No," she replied, baffled. She did not even understand the question.

"Just wondered." Robert paddled back to shore. They hardly talked anymore. Robert's strange behavior perplexed Lieschen.

He drove her home but did not stay for dinner. He looked sad when he left. She worried that she might have done or said something which might have hurt or insulted him. But what could it be?

That evening Lieschen's father called again. "You have to come home," he demanded. His tone sounded uncompromising.

"Pap, I can't."

"What is holding you back?"

Lieschen wanted to say, "Robert", but she could not say it out loud. Instead she said, "I've enrolled at the RAIK Art Institute." She held the receiver close to her ear, while she waited for her father's response.

There was only silence. Slowly she sat down on her uncle's leather chair at the desk in his office.

"What about your obligation to me and to our business?" Her father's voice sounded deep when he finally spoke again.

"Pap, I'll be back in a year." Lieschen shut her eyes and imagined herself returning with Robert as her husband. That would certainly put Sigi in his place, she thought with a sense of deep satisfaction.

"Do you understand what you're destroying?" Her father's tone contained threat.

Lieschen opened her eyes. She would move to the United States with Robert, or anywhere he would want to move, if her father would not accept him as his son-in-law.

"I urge you to come home. You don't want me to take action, do you?" The phone clicked. Her father had hung up, just as he had done during their previous conversation.

Lieschen could not possibly leave Lucerne. She could not live any longer without seeing Robert, hearing his pleasant voice, experiencing his kind gestures. Her father could not take away her happiness. This was the happiest time since early childhood, before she had lost her mother.

CHAPTER 15

The following day, during breakfast, Uncle Gustav expressed his approval for Lieschen's enrollment at RAIK. "I'm sure your father will understand."

Lieschen inhaled deeply and thought their last telephone conversation sounded more like her father might send soldiers to take her home.

"After all, it's your life," Aunt Sylvia said. "We've talked about this before." She drank a little coffee with Schlag.

"I also believe I should be able to decide for myself," Lieschen said, but her resolute tone was laced with worries.

"Me wantin to be a greatest cookin, and nobody willin disturbin me." Despite her squeaky voice, Isolde's conviction sounded clear.

Lieschen smiled at Isolde and scooped up a forkful of pancake with strawberry marmalade.

"Fraulein Liesichen lettin nobody disturbin you ideas," Isolde emphasized.

"I believe, it's best to follow your own ideas and convictions," Aunt Sylvia concurred.

"Me flowin with convixion." Isolde drank coffee.

Lieschen swallowed the bite of pancake she was chewing and again smiled at Isolde, whose comical mannerism helped stifle Lieschen's worries a little.

After breakfast, she went back to her room and prepared herself for another day at the Mongrit. Uncle Gustav had offered her a ride. She had two more days before the classes at RAIK were scheduled to begin.

She wore an ocher muslin dress with a lively orchid- and leaf pattern, seamless nylons, and flat ocher leather shoes, comfortable for walking and being on her feet all day. With a sketch book under her arm, she joined Uncle Gustav.

Outside, on the cemented landing, she stopped because Heinz, the robust, drunken man with whom Robert had an angry exchange at the Geschaeftsball, came up the stairs with a young lady in a navy-blue linen dress. Heinz appeared fully sober now; and the young woman gave the appearance of a blissful mother with child. She held a small package in her hands. Lieschen also noticed the beautiful reddish-golden braids winding like a crown around her fair face.

"Lieschen, I want you to meet Robert's wife Monika and her brother Heinz." Uncle Gustav motioned with his right hand.

Lieschen's sketchbook slipped out under her arm and dropped on the cemented landing. Her chin jerked. She felt as if someone had just stabbed her with a flaming dagger. She staggered forward to pick up her sketchbook, but stumbled into the iron railing and came close to tumbling down the stairs.

Monika rushed to help her. As soon as Lieschen had regained her balance, Monika asked, "Are you all right?"

Lieschen nodded, although she was afraid she might faint.

Monika extended her right hand and said, "I'm very happy to meet you."

"I'm pleased to meet you too . . ." Lieschen's voice faltered. They shook hands.

"Robert has told me many nice things about you," Monika said. Her expressive brown eyes appeared warm and sincere.

"I see ..."

Heinz also shook hands with Lieschen. "Nice seeing you again." A smirk twisted his face.

"Oh, you've met?" Uncle Gustav looked surprised.

"Jeah, we've met." Heinz's smirk lingered on his healthy, round face. His thick brown locks appeared fuzzy.

Monika turned to Uncle Gustav and handed him the package she was carrying. "These are the granite samples from my father."

"You didn't have to bring them over. I could've picked them up." Uncle Gustav took the package into his hands. "I was going to stop by your father's shop later today. You saved me a trip. I appreciate your efforts."

"I wanted to bring them because I also wanted to meet Lieschen." With a friendly smile, Monika turned to her again.

Lieschen felt as if standing on an icy cliff, about to be cast into the gorge below. She did not know how she could hold up and face this reality.

"How much longer will it be?" Uncle Gustav looked at Monika's blissful body.

"I'm going to see Doctor Ambrosius this morning. Probably one more month. I've been really sick, though-"

"I know. I hope you're feeling better now?"

"Not much."

"Listen, if we can do anything for you, let us know."

"Danke." Monika gave a grateful nod, then turned back to Lieschen and offered, "If you're going to the Mongrit, we'd be happy to take you there."

"I'm not going there now, danke." Lieschen desperately tried to conceal her disillusion.

"I hope you'll soon come to our home for a visit."

Lieschen nodded, tears stinging her eyes.

As soon as Monika and Heinz left, she swayed back to her room and slumped on her bed. She buried her head in her arms, on the pillow, and sobbed. Her shoulders heaved.

"What's bothering you?" Uncle Gustav's voice came through the door.

Lieschen lifted her head and exclaimed, "I didn't know Robert was married." Again she buried her face in her arms, on the pillow, and wept bitterly.

Uncle Gustav sat down at the edge of the bed, gently touched her right shoulder and said, "Listen to me! If you're upset because of Robert, I have to tell you something."

Lieschen's head jerked up. "I don't want to hear anything else about Robert!"

"All right. Perhaps I can tell you later ..."

Lieschen shook her head.

Before Uncle Gustav left for work, he offered again to drive her to the Mongrit, but she declined.

CHAPTER 16

Lieschen packed. Aunt Sylvia had left with Uncle Gustav, after she had also unsuccessfully tried to console Lieschen. Only Isolde stayed home.

Lieschen wrapped the portrait of herself with her parents, her treasured graduation gift, and carefully slipped it between the clothes in her suitcase. That photo seemed to be all she had left to hold on to. She slipped off her ocher muslin dress and put on the same ivory suit with the crepe blouse and rusty beige leather purse and shoes she had worn when she arrived. Then she wrote a note to Uncle Gustav and Aunt Sylvia, thanking them for everything; and she explained that she had to depart. She gave the note to Isolde and said, "Make sure to give this note to Herr and Frau Schmidt?"

"Me makin sure," promised Isolde; then she added, "Fraulein Liesichen, not forgettin flowin with convixion."

How can I flow with conviction now? Lieschen nodded sadly and called a taxi.

Approaching the ticket line at the airport in Zurich, she noticed Frau Fritsch, her plump kindergarten teacher whom she had detested as a child. Frau Fritsch was just paying for her ticket at the counter when Lieschen spotted her. The mere sight of Frau Fritsch intensified Lieschen's despair because it reminded her of a time when she had stolen a daffodil for her mother's grave. She had picked the daffodil in the front garden of the kindergarten and was about to bring it over to her mother's grave when Frau Fritsch caught her at the gate. Lieschen would never forget. "You know you're not allowed to touch flowers in this garden, and you're not allowed to leave the school grounds," Frau Fritsch had warned Lieschen while ripping the daffodil out of her hand

and making her go back into the classroom. Inside she ordered her to go to the catheter and put her hands on the ledge. Then she reached for a heavy stick under the catheter and lashed down on Lieschen's hands. It was the first time Lieschen had been punished like that, and the first time she had wet her panties. Consequently, for two endless months, Frau Fritsch had made her spend the recess behind the catheter in the classroom.

Turning away from the counter now, Frau Fritsch spotted her and walked right up to her. "What a pleasure to see you," she smiled.

Leave me alone! Lieschen wanted to tell her. Instead she swallowed hard without talking.

"Do you have eye catarrh?" Frau Fritsch's harsh staccato voice had mellowed; and her concerned look seemed genuine now.

Lieschen nodded, but she would not mention her heartache, which had caused her to weep and make her eyes sore.

"Are you taking medication?" Frau Fritsch asked.

Lieschen nodded again and hoped that Frau Fritsch would leave her alone.

"You have grown tall and beautiful. Wouldn't you rather be back in kindergarten?"

This question fizzed Lieschen's nerves even more. She wondered whether Frau Fritsch even remembered her punishment over the daffodil.

"I certainly would like having you again. You were a miraculous child. Very gifted," Frau Fritsch said.

It was Lieschen's turn to buy the ticket; and she was glad to terminate the conversation with Frau Fritsch. At the counter, she rummaged through her purse and realized that she was out of money. She had used her cash to pay for the taxi from her relatives' home to the Zurich Airport. She had only a few Schilling left, not even enough to pay for another taxi from the airport Thalerhof to their villa in Mariatrost, let alone for an airplane ticket.

"Why don't you step aside and let other passengers take their turn." The brunette stewardess behind the counter made an impatient gesture.

Lieschen closed her purse and was about to step aside, when it occurred to her that she had a prepaid ticket, round-trip, which Uncle

Gustav and Aunt Sylvia had sent her as graduation present. In that lucid moment, she even remembered where she had put it. She retrieved the ticket from a side pocket in her purse and handed it to the impatient stewardess for validation.

In the airplane, Lieschen could see Frau Fritsch taking a seat farther up front. Lieschen dropped into a window seat at row 24. Her head raged as if a hurricane blew inside. Her heart broken, her soul torn to pieces, she wanted to lay her head on her mother's lap and sleep, just sleep, and forget she had ever been born.

Upon take-off, her eyes became too heavy to keep open. Nonetheless, she was aware climbing through the emergency exit onto the right wing of the airplane. It felt cold and swayed like a loose oak limb in a storm. Lieschen clutched the swaying wing. Her feet dangled in the cold air. When she could no longer hold on, she let go and dove into the abyss with terrifying speed.

Midair, she became suspended. Next to her, a pink coffin appeared. The lid opened, and her mother smiled at her from the coffin. Lieschen smiled back, affectionately. Seeing her mother's sweet smile helped her.

"Fasten your seat belt," came the voice of the stewardess who had been shaking Lieschen's shoulder. "Wake up! We're landing."

Lieschen's eyes finally jerked open. She looked at the stewardess, disoriented and, for a moment, could not differentiate between the natural world and the nightmare she just had.

"Can I help you fasten your seat belt?" the stewardess offered kindly. "Danke, I should be okay." Lieschen closed the belt. She had not closed it on takeoff.

From the Airport Thalerhof, she dragged herself to the Strassenbahnstop, where it occurred to her that she had forgotten to pick up her suitcase with the treasured photograph. She felt so forlorn, she could hardly think. Some people looked at her, but she did not see Frau Fritsch anymore.

She staggered back to the baggage claim department at the airport and waited until her luggage showed up on the quasi empty belt. Then she searched her purse and all of her pockets for money to pay for the streetcar to Mariatrost. She could scrape up that much. She did not want to call her father or Aunt Klara to pick her up, and she did not have enough money for a taxi.

Sitting in the green streetcar, she thought that flying to Lucerne on the thirteenth had been a big mistake because it had resulted in bad luck. On the other hand, she might not have seen her mother's lovely smile from the coffin. Her mother's smile seemed to tell her that life was okay.

When the streetcar halted at St. Germain, Lieschen wondered if she should get off. Perhaps I could become a nun? Before she decided to get off, the doors of the streetcar closed and the tram moved on. Lieschen thought of Mother Marisa, Sister Gertrude, Sister Margarita, and the other sisters and instructors.

St. Germain seemed to be a likely place for her to find peace. She closed her eyes and visualized herself wearing a dark habit like Mother Marisa and the other sisters, and serving God and helping people. She could see herself being a good nun. Since she could not have the man she loved, and since she could not associate with Sigi, she seriously considered becoming a nun.

At the terminal in Mariatrost, she called Ingrid from the nearby phone booth. She did not know why she had not called Ingrid at the airport. With her frayed mind she just could not think right.

The ring of Ingrid's phone reverberated in Lieschen's ears like serenading shouts, but there was no response. She looked across the street and saw people going in and out of the Witt Bakery.

Since the suitcase was too heavy for her to carry from the terminal to their villa on the hilltop, she wondered if she should call Werner, but she answered herself, "I can't. Werner would want to know what happened, and I couldn't tell him that I'd fallen in love with a married man, and that he had shattered my life." Falling in love with another man was one thing, painful enough for Werner, but falling in love with a married man would crush him. Werner was such a dear friend with a strong moral character, and Lieschen could trust him with all of her problems, but he loved her with every fiber. Lieschen's love for Robert made her realize how Werner felt for her. Unfulfilled love could be excruciatingly painful.

Once more, she dialed Ingrid's number.

"Did you call earlier?" Ingrid asked.

"Yes. I'm so glad I could reach you now."

"I was outside. Where are you? You seem out of breath."

Lieschen explained and asked Ingrid to take her home.

"I was just going to leave for a dentist appointment. You caught me on time. I'll see if I can reschedule. Wait by the phone booth. I'll call you right back."

Lieschen stood there like a lost sheep, glancing over at the Witt Bakery, with people still coming and going. Some people gawked over at her.

When the phone rang, she grabbed the receiver.

"I'll be there in a few minutes," Ingrid promised. "Wait by the phone booth, so I'll know where to find you."

"I'd rather walk. People are staring at me. I can't stand it."

"Okay, I'll watch for you on the road."

Lieschen meandered up the ascending sidewalk, her handbag strapped over her left shoulder, her heavy suitcase in her right hand.

One young driver stopped and rolled down his window. "Can I offer you a ride?"

"Danke, help is on the way." Lieschen did not recognize the kind, young driver. When she spotted Ingrid's blue Volkswagen a moment later, she dropped her suitcase and waved.

Ingrid drove by, turned around, and then called through the open window, "Ciao!"

"Ciao," Lieschen called back in their colloquial way of greeting.

"What in the world did you find out about your Mom? You look awfully munched up," Ingrid said, then opened the door and stepped out of her Volkswagen.

"I wasn't able to find out how Mommy died, but something else happened."

"Tell me in the car so we won't block the street." Ingrid helped Lieschen load her suitcase.

Inside the Volkswagen, Ingrid said, "Now tell me." She closed the window and pulled away from the curb.

"I've fallen in love with a married man."

Ingrid jerked her foot off the gas pedal. "You monkey! How did you manage that?"

"I met him the day I arrived in Lucerne. He is my relatives' nephew."

"And you didn't know him?" Ingrid put her foot back on the gas pedal. The Volkswagen puffed on up the small, winding asphalt road among fields and interspersed farms and homes.

"He's probably related to Aunt Sylvia's family. I didn't ask, and I didn't care. I just fell in love."

"Grand. Real masterpiece. You didn't lose your marbles, did you?" Ingrid gazed at her.

"I might've," Lieschen sighed.

"How did you find out that he's married?'

"I met his wife Monika this morning."

"Did Monika tell you that she's the wife of the man you'd fallen in love with?"

"No quirks! Not now!"

"Falling in love with a married man can be serious." Ingrid squinted her eyes. "How did you find out?"

"My uncle introduced us."

"And Monika? What did she say?"

"I can't remember. I only know that she was sweet and pregnant."

"And that sweet man - what's his name?"

"Robert Schweitzer."

"And Robert never told you?"

"I don't know if he didn't want to tell me or what. We never talked about his family. Perhaps he didn't want to tell me because he loved me too. I'm sure he loved me." With her fingers, Lieschen wiped the tears on her cheeks.

"Does Monika know that you've fallen in love with her husband?" Ingrid twisted her lively red lips.

"I hope not. I'd feel very bad. She looked so blissful with her unborn baby. And she was also sick."

"Did you make her sick?"

"Can you stop that? I never intended to make her sick. I didn't know Monika was Robert's wife. I didn't know Robert was married."

Ingrid shifted down the clutch and stepped harder on the gas pedal. The Volkswagen gingerly crunched on. Mediterranean-style homes and villas skirted this part of the Mariatroster Hill, with lots of fruit- and deciduous trees surrounding the fashionable homes.

A short while later, when Ingrid drove around a sharp curve, Lieschen saw Frau Kramer in the front garden of their exclusive villa. She was holding a watering can. They waved **at** each other.

"It'll be quite interesting if your father finds out." Ingrid remarked as soon as they passed the curve and the Kramer villa.

"Finds out what?"

"That you've fallen in love with a married man."

"I'm not worried about that." It wouldn't matter since I want to become a nun, Lieschen thought; but she would tell Ingrid after talking to Mother Marisa to be sure that Mother Marisa would admit her to the convent.

"Ugh! You aren't worried about your father's reaction?"

"I mean-" Lieschen did not want her father to find out about Robert; but if he did, she thought it wouldn't matter that much. She knew that her father won because he wanted her to come home, and she was coming home. Lieschen did not dread facing her father, but she dreaded facing Sigi.

"1 think I know what you mean." Ingrid opened her window to chase out a fly that cruised around as if it owned the whole space inside the Volkswagen. "And how about Werner? What if he finds out?" She closed the window as soon as the fly was out.

"I care a lot about Werner, but I love him like a brother, platonically, as you know."

"He loves you with heart, body, and soul."

"I don't know what to do about that. And I don't know what I'd do if he found out." Lieschen could not worry about all of that now. Her stuffed, miserable head was already clogged to the brim.

"I suggest that you give your love relationship with Werner a serious chance."

"Let's not go into that now."

"I just want you to be happy and not worry about a man you can't have."

To be happy! How foreign that sounded. Lieschen's brief happiness with Robert had collapsed like a shooting star at the end of its journey.

"It's really strange. Here you're, surrounded by money and riches, yet you're terribly unhappy."

"I didn't even have the money for a taxi from the airport home."

"That's because you weren't prepared. The point is that your father is one of the richest men in Austria, and you're so unhappy because of your mother's suspicious death, because you can't find your grandmother, because of a man you can't have, because of another man who tries to rape you - because, because, because . . ." Ingrid cast an incredulous glance at Lieschen, then said, "Hans and I have to scramble to build and furnish a small home, and we're very happy."

"That proves that money and material possessions alone don't make people happy. You have each other. That's more precious than money and riches. It's called love. Simple, precious love. I wish I could exchange my father's riches for love."

"All of your father's riches?"

"Depends. I believe love is the greatest treasure." I'd have given anything for true love with Robert, Lieschen thought while her aching heart throbbed.

"Now you're talking. I'd like to have more money though. I believe eventually Hans will earn more, and then we'll add on more rooms for our children."

Lieschen knew that Ingrid and her fiance' Hans wanted to have a houseful *of* children. "Hans is doing well with his construction company, isn't he?"

"He just obtained a new contract from the Goser Brau."

"Good for him. And for you."

"I've a lot of confidence in Hans. He's just a little hot headed when he squares *off* with someone. Or when he has a couple drinks and loses his temper, his thoughts come out head over heels." Ingrid smiled. "Perhaps it's his Irish blood."

Lieschen knew that Hans's parents were from Ireland. "No one is perfect," she said. Hans's outspoken, principled personality and his sense of humor and quick wit appealed to her.

"What's happening with Sigi?" Ingrid asked.

"Why do you mention him? just thinking *of* him gives me the creeps."

"Outside or inside?" Ingrid giggled.

"Both. And that's not funny."

"I didn't mean to upset you any more." Ingrid stopped giggling. "I'm just in a good mood today."

"I don't want to spoil your mood." Lieschen liked Ingrid the way she was, except right now her goofy sense had an ill effect on her.

Along the rose-bed, Ingrid pulled into the circular driveway in front of the Reinking villa and helped Lieschen carry the suitcase inside. Frau Emma came out *of* the kitchen and greeted them. "The home felt empty and cold without you," she smiled at Lieschen. Then right away she stopped smiling. "You don't look okay." With a concerned expression, she asked, "Would you like hot chocolate or something else?"

"Hot chocolate, please." Lieschen hoped that hot chocolate might help her dull her pain.

Frau Emma also asked Ingrid, "Hot chocolate for you? Or another refreshment?"

"Nothing for me, danke. I've a dentist appointment in half an hour. I've to leave shortly." Ingrid helped Lieschen carry her suitcase upstairs to her apartment. "Vow it's stuffy in here!" Ingrid dabbed her nose as they entered.

"I think nobody has opened the windows while I was gone," Lieschen said while inhaling the stuffy air.

"Special instructions?" Ingrid asked as she put down Lieschen's suitcase in her study.

"Could be." Lieschen opened the floral drapes and the window on the east-side of her study. Outside, red cherries had begun forming on the big old cherry tree. She stepped back to her suitcase and snapped open the ledges. "I want to show you something." She pulled out the framed photo of herself with her parents and showed it to Ingrid.

"Uuugh!" Ingrid took the photo into her hands. "That's what I call a treasure."

"Me too. Graduation present from Uncle Gustav and Aunt Sylvia."

"How precious!" Ingrid looked at the photo for a long moment; then, handing the photo back to Lieschen, she said, "You haven't shown me your own paintings in quite some time."

"Would you like to see them now?"

Ingrid glanced at her watch. "I've got a few more minutes."

"Let me put the picture in place," Lieschen said and placed the framed photo with her parents next to a cluster of purple glass grapes and a Meissen vase on an upper shelf of her Danish bookcase that was filled with books and souvenir items.

"Looks neat," Ingrid approved. Then they went into the adjacent painting studio. Everything seemed untouched and a little untidy, the way Lieschen had left it. She always kept her apartment tidy, but not her studio.

"Some of my paintings you've seen. I keep adding new ones as I finish them," Lieschen said.

Ingrid looked at one specific painting of children playing in the snow. "This will be my wedding present?" She smiled.

"You can have it if you'd like."

"I'd love it."

"It's yours." Lieschen took the painting off the wall and handed it to Ingrid.

"That's very nice of you. Danke."

"I'm glad you like it."

"I like it a lot." Ingrid put the painting under her arm and turned to a half-finished painting on one of the three easels near the south window. "How different from your earlier style," she observed.

"Sometimes I like to paint fantasy or semi-abstract themes from my imagination." This image of a snake climbing a ladder had occurred to Lieschen after Sigi had attempted to rape her. Painting used to have a lyrical quality for Lieschen but, after Sigi's attempted rape, it had changed.

"Why not." Ingrid checked the time on her wrist watch. "I've to get going," she said.

"I understand. Danke, Ingrid, for driving me home." Lieschen accompanied her out. Then she went into the kitchen and drank the hot chocolate Frau Emma had prepared for her.

Frau Emma was cleaning fresh string beans on the marble counter by the sink. "Do your father and Aunt Klara know that you're back?"

"Not yet. I'd like to rest a little before I call."

"Why don't you surprise them at dinner without calling?" Frau Emma let water run over the string beans.

Lieschen thought that was a good idea. "Okay, I'll do that," she said. Reserl peeked in and asked how she could remove a marmalade stain from the dining room table.

"I'll be over in a minute," Frau Emma turned back to Lieschen and asked, "Would you like anything special for dinner?"

"Perhaps Apfelstrudel." Lieschen thought that Frau Emma's delicious Apfelstrudel might stimulate her appetite, and she wouldn't have to sit at the dining table without eating anything.

"All right."

Lieschen put the empty cup in the sink and scrambled upstairs where she forced herself to unpack her suitcase. Then she took a warm shower, and slipped on a peach-colored silk nightgown. What an odd time of day to be wearing a nightgown, she thought. She Iiked to be up early in the morning and stay busy all day, like her father and Aunt Klara. Not even when she was sick did she like to stay in bed.

She went back to the Danish bookshelf in her study and, for a long while, looked at the photograph of herself with her parents. She loved this picture no end. Then she began searching for a book to read. She skimmed over various titles: Sophocles' *Oedipus Rex*, Goethe's *Werther* Schiller's *Don Carlos,* Shakespeare's *Hamlet and King Lear,* Tolstoy's *Anna Karenina, The Tale of Gengi* by Murasaki Shikibu, Margaret Mitchell's *Gone With the Wind,* plays by Franz Grillparzer written in the Shakespearean style, and a few books by Herman Hesse. And she looked at a series of recently released novels.

She could not decide what to read and continued searching. When she spotted her own quaint booklet of handwritten poems, she pulled it off the shelf, sat down on the mustard-colored couch and began turning the pages till she came to one poem she had written the summer before her graduation from St. Germain, on a trip with her father to the coast of <u>Rimini</u> in Italy.

She began reading the poem called *Oceanwaves.*
Brushed by wind
Pushed by storm
Caressed by gentle breezes
Shining, sparkling
Music ringing out to the golden sand

From shore to shore
Waves wander on
Trailing, rising, falling
Pulsing with the daily beat of life
Sailors and ships
People and birds touch its swirling foam
Under sunshine, moon and stars
Under dreamy, gloomy clouds
Waves hum their rhythmic tunes
Embracing, swallowing
Caressing, nurturing
Recreating and killing in their mysterious bosom.
Oceanwaves glide on with the eternal rhythm
Trailing, rising, falling
Pulsing with the daily beat of life.

Lieschen remembered when she had written this poem early one windy morning while her father had been asleep in the adjoining room at the Hotel Lambertini. By herself, she had sauntered to the beach on a cemented sidewalk along a nearly empty asphalt road that was lined with palm trees swaying in the wind. Only a few people had ventured out to the cool, windy beach that early in the morning.

On a hump of sand, close to cresting waves, Lieschen had scooted down and, from her shorts' pocket, she had pulled a crumpled sheet of paper and a short dull pencil. She had a difficult time to hold the crumpled sheet and write on it. At one point the wind nearly blew away the sheet. She managed to hold on and finish the poem while watching crushing waves with large white caps.

Being pushed and pulled by crushing waves in her heart and in her head, that's how she felt right now. God, why? She put the booklet with the crumpled sheet of paper back on the bookshelf, pulled out another book of poetry and carried it to her bedroom. She turned on the radio at the nightstand and switched the dial to station 227 for classical music. Then she crawled under her down comforter and started reading. Classical music at a low volume, and reading, usually helped her fall asleep.

She only read a few poems, the last one called, *The Dying Christian and His Soul* by Alexander Pope.

Vital spark of heavenly flame
Quit, oh quit this mortal frame
Trembling, hoping, lingering, flying,
Oh the pain, the bliss of dying
Cease, fond nature, cease thy strife,
And let me languish into life.

Lieschen perceived that the person's soul in Alexander Pope's poem wanted to escape the chains of suffering on earth, just as she felt right now. She thought of Robert and Monika, and her eyes grew very *heavy*. She put the book of poetry on the nightstand, scrambled deeper under the down comforter, and closed her eyes.

Where was Robert? Their love and happiness had dissipated like stubble in a storm. Her chest seemed to be filling up with lead, and soon everything appeared dark.

When Lieschen awoke, she looked at the alarm clock on her nightstand. Ten minutes to four. Still a couple of hours before dinner. She rose slowly, stepped over to the west-window in her study, and looked out. A few fluffy clouds sailed on the blue sky. She tried to pull herself together and went to slip on a veridian, pleaded linen skirt with a white linen blouse and veridian house slippers. Then she tottered downstairs. The semi-high heels of her slippers made a clickety-click sound along the marble tiles in the hallway.

In front of the kitchen she stopped, then walked in. Through the kitchen window she could see Frau Emma and Reserl collecting red and green bell peppers in their vegetable garden. Lieschen knew Frau Emma enjoyed tending to their garden, and Reserl would often help her. They grew a good variety of lettuce, red beets, cabbage, carrots, spinach, cauliflower, onions, string beans, radishes, tomatoes, bell peppers, gooseberries, strawberries, and a wide array of herbs. She reached into the pantry for an apple and began munching while she continued watching Frau Emma and Reserl.

As soon as she had finished eating the apple, she walked down the hall to their family library and into the adjoining music room. The lid of the black Boesendorfer piano glistened like a black mirror, in stark contrast with the caramel-shaded Persian carpet on the parquet floor. Her eyes fell at Albrecht Duerer's Praying Hands on the wall beside the piano. She remembered when her mother had taught her how to pray. She was two years old, and ever since her soul had been drawn to God.

Turning back to the piano, she wondered whether she should play. She had hardly touched the keys during the past two years, but was tempted to do so now. She opened the shiny wooden lid of the black piano bench, took out a book of Beethoven's and a book of Mozart's lyrics and sonatas and began playing Beethoven's Pastoral, followed by a selection of Mozart's Zauberfloete. Her delicate fingers stumbled a little over the black and white keys, but her sensitivity for music, combined with her current emotions, created an engaging performance; except she thought that nobody was listening. When she heard footsteps, she stopped playing and turned around. With tears shimmering in his eyes, her father, together with Aunt Klara, moved toward her. Lieschen rose from the piano bench. Her father embraced her, and she embraced him. Her inner trauma did not get in the way of their reunion. Aunt Klara also gave her a warm hug. Lieschen felt not much animosity against her aunt now. A good part of the blame against her father and Aunt Klara had dissipated since Uncle Gustav had revealed her parents' tragic relationship.

"I knew you'd come home. You're my child. You belong here. This is your home! Your life! Your future!"

Lieschen could tell her father was very happy over her return. She could not remember ever hearing him express his heartfelt emotions like now. "Go on! Go on playing." A happy smile danced on his lips. "How about Bach, or Brahms, or Mendelssohn for a change."

While Lieschen took out the music from the piano bench, her father and Aunt Klara settled into two of the red-cushioned walnut chairs behind the piano.

Lieschen played part of Brahm's Songs of Destiny, then Mendelssohn's Venetian Gondola Song; however, she could not find the music by Johann Sebastian Bach and, regretfully, could not play anything by her father's favorite composer. Although Lieschen stumbled on some notes, her father was visibly pleased and gave her another warm hug at the end of the performance.

In the formal dining room, while serving the main course of their meal, Frau Emma said to Lieschen, "You played the piano so beautiful, like in the olden days. I heard you way out in the garden."

"I'm content that Lieschen played the piano," her father said with an approving nod.

Lieschen smiled a little while her pain remained well hidden. She ate more than she thought she could eat from the serving of Veal Goulash, potato pancakes, tender string beans, and a salad of red and green bell peppers with chives.

All the while her father kept asking questions about Lieschen's visit to Lucerne, and about the Vierwaldstaetter Lake and the swans, but he avoided talking about Uncle Gustav and Aunt Sylvia.

Frau Emma collected the plates and served Apfelstrudel. Lieschen was amazed how much she enjoyed the Apfelstrudel. Then something awful happened.

"Sigi has been asking about you every day," her father said.

Lieschen covered her mouth with her napkin because instant nausea made her feel like vomiting. While she managed to suppress the urge to vomit, the little energy she had regained dissolved like raindrops on the surface of a sea. She got up and said, "I'm really tired, I'd like to go to bed."

"We'll talk more tomorrow. I also have something ..." her father looked at Aunt Klara, then back at Lieschen. "I have a surprise for you at the Plant," he said with an exulted tone.

"For me?"

"Ja, ja, for you my dear Lieschen." Her father's face beamed.

Lieschen was afraid that the surprise would involve Sigi. Everything would involve Sigi, who seemed to reflect her father's desires, his aristocratic bloodline, his business interests, everything. And her father would not, or could not recognize Sigi's wretched side of his personality. She mumbled, "Gute Nacht," and went to bed.

Chapter 17

Early in the morning, before breakfast, Lieschen called Mother Marisa from her study. "May I talk to you about a difficult development?" she requested.

"Would you like to come to my office?" Mother Marisa offered. Her voice sounded neutral as always.

"Would it be all right?"

"Of course. Let me look at my calendar."

When Mother Marisa resumed, she said, "How about eleven o'clock?"

"Okay."

"I'll see you at eleven."

"Danke, Mother Marisa."

During breakfast, Lieschen's father talked about business matters in connection with Sigi, and about the surprise at the Plant. Lieschen's energy kept draining, not because of the surprise, but because of Sigi.

Right after breakfast, she went into their garden and picked yellow daffodils for her mother's grave; and on the way to St. Germain, she stopped at the cemetery. She had to wait for an elderly lady to fill up a watering can at the cemetery fountain.

"What a gorgeous day! Nice to be alive," the stocky woman said. She did not pay attention to her watering can, though, which began overflowing and splashing water on her long, violet dress. "My dress seems to be thirsty," she joked when she noticed the wetness. She turned off the faucet.

Was this supposed to be funny? Lieschen was not sure.

The lady raised her right hand and indicated the nearby crosses and marble headstones. "All these peaceful souls. My brother's buried over there." She pointed toward the vicary.

Lieschen looked over in that direction.

"The road we all must travel—always living on the edge of death. Just think, tomorrow you could be dead."

So could you, thought Lieschen.

"Or today, or the next moment." The lady picked up her watering can. "Have a pleasant day," she said and trotted away toward her brother's gravesite.

"You too. Have a pleasant day," Lieschen called, but she did not know whether the lady had listened and had heard her. She walked on.

While Lieschen filled her ceramic vase with fresh water, she thought about the edge of death and wished she could better understand God's design for life on earth-for people, animals, and all living things. Sometimes, when she had been filled with deep despair, she had wished to be dead. Now she had no wish to be dead. She did not know why she felt as she did-perhaps because her mother's lovely smile in the pink coffin told her she was watching her, and that life was worth living. She arranged the daffodils in the vase and carried the bouquet along a cemented path, among graves marked with crosses and black and white and gray marble headstones. Many graves were tended with flowers, plants, small trees, and pebbles, while some were neglected and overgrown with weeds and grass.

Lieschen placed the bouquet of daffodils in front of an evergreen tree in the diamond-shaped center, in front of her mother's black marble headstone. Then she bowed her head and meditated. She asked her mother, "Mommy, should I become a nun?"

She heard a little finch twitter ecstatically on a pile of wreaths and fresh flowers at a nearby new grave, but she could not detect her mother's response. From the cemetery, she drove to St. Germain where Mother Marisa offered her a seat at her birch-wood desk. "How is your world?" she asked. Her analytical gray eyes, short nose, and pale expression seemed half-hidden under her white bib.

"Not good. Not good at all."

"One of the richest girls in Austria, and life isn't good to you?"

Lieschen did not understand why everybody thought life had to be good to her because she had a rich father. "I don't know why things have gone wrong, but they have. Badly." She inhaled long and hard, and then said, "Mother Marisa, I would like to become a nun."

Mother Marisa examined her with a rather startled expression and said, "My dear child, when things go wrong, that's no reason to become a nun. Can you tell me specifically what made you come up with this idea?"

"I had ... I had a very, disappointing experience." Lieschen almost choked as she thought of Robert.

"Many people have disappointing experiences."

Mother Marisa propped her arms at the edge of the desk and interlinked her fingers. "I don't want to delve into your private life, but if you wish to tell me about your disappointing experience, it might help both of us understand your situation better and find a solution."

Lieschen could not tell Mother Marisa about Robert. Falling in love with a married man was not something she could justify before her Mother Superior; nor could she disclose Sigi's attempted rape and her devastating entanglement with her father's affection for him, the main reasons why she wanted to become a nun.

Mother Marisa waited a little while, then asked, "Does your father know what you plan to do?"

"Not yet. I mean this is what I want to do. It's my life!" Defiance added to Lieschen's frustration.

"I understand that it's your life. Nonetheless, I would think you should feel an obligation to discuss such a significant plan with your father."

Lieschen said nothing.

"Your father told me that he wants you to continue the family tradition of his pharmaceutical business."

"I don't think I'm made for this kind of business ..." with a detestable character like Sigi presiding as general manager. Lieschen kept the last part of her statement to herself.

Mother Marisa pulled out a big white linen handkerchief from a side-pocket of her habit, dabbed her face, then said, "I've watched you grow. I know you're very gifted, but I don't believe you have the makings of a nun. `Just picture yourself wearing the same dark habit day-in, day-out, year round, for the rest of your life, with your beautiful hair cut off."

Lieschen sucked in her lower lip. "I can do that."

"It's not only that. Occasionally you might have to scrub floors and give yourself up completely to the service of other people. You have been served, and now you want to reverse the course. I don't believe you could live up to such a commitment."

Mother Marisa always preached not to judge, the very thing she'd just done. Lieschen resented it. "I can serve God, and I can serve other people," she asserted.

"You don't have to be a nun to serve God and other people. In every-day life you can and should practice love and follow in Jesus' footsteps. There're many good people on earth who practice love every day. A kind smile at a street sweeper, for instance, would be a thoughtful gesture."

Lieschen wondered what Mother Marisa was trying to tell her with that example.

"There're many ways in which each person can demonstrate love-with family and friends, with children, elderly and disadvantaged people, sick people, in day to day relationships with everyone at home, in school, business, everywhere, the way Jesus Christ always reached out." Mother Marisa asked Lieschen to do more soul searching. "Can I make a suggestion?" she said then.

"Okay," Lieschen nodded.

"Why don't you come in once or twice a week and work with our handicapped children. This would be a nice gesture on your part, and it would be a good experience for you. At the same time, it would be a good opportunity for you to serve God."

Lieschen felt awkward about this proposal, yet she wanted to be available to do good deeds. After all, she had just offered to serve God and other people, and Mother Marisa was giving her a chance. "What would I be doing with handicapped children?" she asked.

"You show them love, draw with them, teach them reading, writing, simple math, solve easy puzzles, play and sing with them. We will give you guidelines as you go along."

Lieschen had frequently seen handicapped children play on the school grounds by the Schiller Fountain, but she never thought she could be involved.

"Most of these children are deeply grateful in their hearts and souls. They are quite unselfish, as if they understood better what life on earth is all about."

"What is that?"

"It means we have to carry the cross of Jesus Christ in our hearts, and God will always be with us, through our struggles and suffering, through good and bad times. I believe handicapped children feel this in their hearts."

Lieschen had never thought about it that way.

"And you might consider working part time at your father's pharmaceutical business," Mother Marisa suggested. "You can best learn hands on. At the same time, you can find out whether you want to work in your father's enterprise and eventually carry on the business, as your father wishes."

These suggestions did not seem unreasonable-if I could only keep Sigi at a distance. "I'll think about it," she promised.

"If you still want to become a nun six months from now, we can talk more about it."

"Danke, Mother Marisa."

Lieschen drove to her father's Plant and ran into Sigi in the hallway of the administration floor. He was coming from the opposite direction, together with his secretary, Fraulein Ludmilla Sphinx, a vivacious, dark-haired Fraulein in her mid twenties, and Frau Erika Stein, her father's secretary.

While they exchanged greetings, Frau Erika's smile showed a few wrinkles around her expressive amber eyes. As usual, she had her bright red hair tied with a large pin in the back of her attractive head. Lieschen's father had sometimes cited Frau Erika as an example of a responsible, loyal employee. Frau Erika had lost her husband in the Second World War and had raised her son on her own while working for Reinking & Company.

Sigi put his hand on his chest and said, "My dear Fraulein Lieschen, a stone has fallen from my heart in seeing you back. I couldn't sleep a single night while you were away. 1 worried day and night."

With one eye, Frau Erika winked at Lieschen, indicating that she was accustomed to Sigi's counterfeit tongue.

The two secretaries marched on. Lieschen followed. Sigi grabbed her hand. "I have something very important to tell you," he sizzled into her ear.

Lieschen ripped away her hand. Wild ants began crawling under her skin. She could stand neither Sigi's touch, nor his sight.

He ignored her resentment. "And you must tell me about your trip."

"I must tell you nothing! And you better leave me alone!" With quick steps Lieschen proceeded toward her father's office. At the door, she glanced over her shoulder and was glad that she could no longer see Sigi. She entered her father's office.

He looked up from some memos on his desk. "Oh hi, Lieschen! Come, sit down." He pointed at a chair at his desk, but the next moment he said, "Or better, let me show you the surprise." He rose from his heavy leather chair and led the way to the office next to his own.

"This is your office now." With a sweeping motion of his hands, he indicated the medium-size oak desk and the oak shelves.

My office! Lieschen had to digest her unexpected promotion. She knew the office belonged to Aunt Klara.

Through the clear glass of the tall window, she could see the River Mur. On the other side of the river loomed the Schlossberg, the landmark of Graz. The round clock on the tall tower showed accurate time with its large fingers and Roman numerals. All administration offices on the second floor had views, but this view was special.

For more than two hundred years, her father's company had been situated in this two-story brick building, with its lab in the basement. The company had been handed down from Lieschen's great-grandfather to her grandfather, and on to her father. Reinking & Company stood for prestige and high reputation and was one of the largest pharmaceutical companies in Austria.

"Where is Aunt Klara's office now?" Lieschen asked.

"Next to yours. Aunt Klara wanted you to enjoy this view. And she needed a larger office," her father explained.

"I see." Lieschen had a feeling she'd be proud to work in her father's company and keep art as a hobby, if only Sigi were not general manager. "What would my responsibilities be?" she asked.

"Aunt Klara will fill you in. And we'll coordinate your work schedule with your classes at AKA. Of course, during the summertime, when you have no classes, I would expect you to work a full schedule, similar to Aunt Klara's and mine."

"Pap, can I think about your proposal?" A bitter taste appeared in her mouth because Sigi was part of all of this. She could never spend eight hours a day, or more, in Sigi's proximity. This would be living hell.

"What is there to think about?" Her father looked disappointed.

"Pap, I appreciate your offer. I just don't want to plunge into something which I might regret later. This is all quite overwhelming. I'd like to have a little time to think it over."

Her father frowned.

"Thank you for this opportunity." Lieschen embraced her father, but his hug was not warm at all.

If only Sigi were out of the picture! If only! If only! kept racing through her head when suddenly something sparked. Perhaps this will be my chance to get rid of Sigi. If I gain enough control, I might be able to oust him. "Yes, Pap, I accept your offer. I appreciate this challenge." Lieschen's voice filled with sudden excitement. She dropped her purse on the desk as a sign of being ready.

Her father's frown deepened as he scrutinized her. "Okay," he said slowly.

She thought her father could not know why her attitude had changed. He could not read her mind. She watched him open the upper right drawer of the desk. "You can start familiarizing yourself with these accounts. Aunt Klara will brief you further. And tomorrow, during the board of directors meeting, I will introduce you to the directors."

Lieschen thought the board of directors meeting should give her insight into the workings of her father's company and into Sigi's authority. Thus she could gain a clearer picture as to how she could battle him. A coup against Sigi appeared to be the most exciting new prospect.

Shortly after her father left the office, Aunt Klara came in. "Uncle Gustav would like to talk to you." She indicated the telephone on the desk.

Lieschen reached for the receiver and pressed the blinking button. "Hello!" She could not hear anyone on the line and looked at her aunt. "Is this a hoax?"

"Why don't you press the blinking button once more," Aunt Klara said.

Lieschen did and could now hear her uncle's voice. "I'm sorry, Uncle Gustav, our connection didn't work well," she apologized.

"Sometimes our connections don't work as well as we'd like, but we keep trying." Uncle Gustav's baritone voice sounded warm as always.

Lieschen understood the double entendre. She could not blame her uncle for having fallen in love with Robert, but she could blame him and Aunt Sylvia for not having told her that Robert was married. Yet, there was no use complaining now. Nothing could be changed.

"Lieschen ..."

"Yes ..."

"I understand that you're going through a crisis because of your experience with Robert, but one day you'll find that this experience has a deep meaning."

Lieschen's hands began to tremble.

"I don't want to preach, but you should be happy that you met Robert and that you had a good time together."

Uncle Gustav can easily talk about my earth-shattering experience since it didn't affect his heart, thought Lieschen.

"Aunt Sylvia also sends you her love," Uncle Gustav said.

"Danke. Would you give her my love too."

"Of course. You have to come again soon for another visit."

Lieschen was not certain if she'd ever find the courage to go back for another visit and face Robert. She also wondered whether Uncle Gustav had told Aunt Klara about Robert.

"Let us know when you decide to come."

"Okay."

"Take care."

"You too, Uncle Gustav."

Lieschen's hands continued to tremble after she replaced the receiver. "Would you like to go over the files and ledgers now?" Aunt Klara indicated the top right-hand drawer.

Lieschen nodded and thanked her aunt for letting her have her office. "I hope one day you will realize that I love you. I always have." Aunt Klara swallowed hard.

Lieschen scratched her throat. Aunt Klara had been good to her while her mother had been alive; but then came the dreadful night when her aunt had treated her so cruelly, and when she had locked her in her bedroom, and her mother had died.

"It might not always have seemed that way because unusual circumstances caused friction between us," Aunt Klara said.

Lieschen did not want to respond or pry. Not now. "You wanted to show me the files and ledgers," she said.

Aunt Klara explained details and pointed out, "Your father wants you to have a good overview of the entire business in order for you to carry on, if it should become necessary."

"I don't understand."

"Your father's health."

"Is it that serious?"

"As you know, your father hardly ever talks about his illness, but his heart condition is worsening."

For several years Lieschen had been aware of her father's afflicted heart, but his energy level remained high with long working hours, private enjoyment on hunting trips, political involvement, concerts, and other stimulating activities; therefore, she assumed her father's heart was okay.

The phone rang. Lieschen answered. Her hands were no longer trembling.

"Herr Sigi Prinz would like to take you down to the lab and show you around." Her father's official tone sounded businesslike. Sometimes her father addressed Sigi as: Herr Sigi Prinz or Herr Prinz, and sometimes by his first name, Sigi.

Blood surged into Lieschen's head. She wanted to be good to her father and avoid strain. But how can I be good if Pap has such unreasonable expectations? To Lieschen Sigi had the lowliest character of any person she ever met, and her father wanted her to work and associate with this awful man. All she wanted was oust him, not work with him. She could never understand her father's affection for Sigi and why he could not recognize his rotten side. Her clever father could be so deceived and manipulated! It seemed incredible to Lieschen, yet this was the reality.

"Lieschen, did you hear me?"

She took a deep breath and said, "I don't want Sigi to show me around in the lab."

"Why not?"

"Because 1 feel uncomfortable with him."

Silence followed. When her father resumed, he asked in a muted tone, "Would you prefer that I or Aunt Klara take you around?"

"Yes." Lieschen's emphatic tone resounded in the receiver.

"Is Aunt Klara in your office?"

My office! Upon hearing it a second time, it occurred to her that she had attained status because she was the daughter of her prominent father. "Yes, she is here," she replied.

"Let me talk to her."

Lieschen handed the receiver to Aunt Klara.

Upon finishing the conversation, her aunt asked, "Would you like to go to the lab now?"

"Okay." Lieschen was glad that her father had accepted her rejection of Sigi. It gave her hope.

They proceeded downstairs to the lab. Employees in white overalls worked with instruments on long, white tables. The monotonous, white laboratory struck Lieschen like a different world. Her father had told her how they had modernized the entire lab; but if that was supposed to be a modernized lab, it did not look attractive to Lieschen. She turned to Aunt Klara and said, "If I had my way, I'd break up this white monotony with color."

"Which color?"

"Any color-green, blue, magenta, orange, yellow . . ." She pointed to one corner of the lab where she saw colorful vials stacked away. "I'd take these and spread them throughout the lab."

"Perhaps one day you can do that."

"If I have a chance, I want to make a difference in this Company." Lieschen thought of her biggest challenge: ousting Sigi. This idea had taken root and kept stirring in her head.

"You wouldn't be a Reinking if you didn't want to make a difference," Aunt Klara said.

A lab employee's hidden veridian eyes gleamed at her through his mask with a distant glow, as if he were a creature from another planet. "He is Ingrid's cousin Jakob," Aunt Klara told her.

Jakob lifted his mask and smiled at Lieschen. She smiled back since she now recognized him. Jakob's wavy brown hair had been squashed by the mask and made his long face appear shorter.

Herr Klug, the lab manager, approached and signaled to Jakob to flip his mask over his face.

"He isn't supposed to take off the mask while working with anaplastic cells," Herr Klug informed Lieschen and explained the function of the various instruments, especially the ones used for the research and experiments of Xiron. Herr Klug did not wear a mask, but he wore a white lab coat.

Having begun his tenure under Lieschen's grandfather, Herr Klug had been with Reinking & Company as scientist and lab manager for thirty-nine years; and he had been her father's loyal friend. Lieschen had always been impressed by Herrn Klug's refined personality whenever he had come to their villa for dinner or when she met him at other occasions. His dark hair had turned white over the years, but his eyebrows had not changed. His white hair and his dark eyebrows gave his oval face an arresting contrast, especially as he faced Lieschen tete-a-tete. Herr Klug was about six centimeters taller than Lieschen. Since she wore high heels, the difference appeared minimal.

Aunt Klara also listened as Herr Klug pointed out the importance of the development of the Xiron formula. He talked in his relaxed manner, defining alkaloids and other terms such as eucapnia, anaplastic cells, carcinogenic chemicals, duodenum, jejunum, sarcomas, etcetera. All these terms sounded foreign to Lieschen, but she listened with interest and showed appreciation for Herrn Klug's efforts. She also knew that it was in her own best interest to learn more about the Xiron formula and about all of the associated terms.

That evening, Lieschen's father came up to her apartment. She had already changed into a white, colorfully embroidered negligee and linen robe. Her father handed her a list of the board members. "Come sit by me, and I will explain." He pointed to the mustard colored couch, where he sat down.

Still standing next to her father by the couch, Lieschen held the list of the board members in her hands and looked at the names.

"It is important for you to get to know all of the directors and ranking officials. So far, you only know a few."

"Okay," Lieschen replied and was about to sit down when she noticed her father's expression changing. He appeared to be in sudden pain. "Are you okay?" she asked.

He rose, walked to the Danish bookshelf and stared at the framed photo of Lieschen with her parents. "Who gave you that?" His tone sounded gruff.

Lieschen joined her father and told him that Uncle Gustav and Aunt Sylvia had given it to her as graduation present. She asked, "Do you like it?" Since she loved both of her parents, she thought her father must see why she loved the photo. Her parents' tragic relationship had not diminished her love for either of them. The only thing that had punctured her love for her father was her mother's suspicious death and her grandmother's dubious disappearance. And to this day she still did not know how her mother had died, and where her grandmother was.

Her father did not respond to her question about the framed photo. He only said with a deep voice, "We'll talk more tomorrow." He turned away and left Lieschen's apartment. She could not stop him.

She continued to look at the beautiful photo, thinking of her parent's futile relationship. She could not help asking whether destiny or people's own actions determined such futility.

CHAPTER 18

Around the oblong conference table at the Reinking Pharmaceutical Plant, fourteen members had assembled. Lieschen joined on her assigned seat next to her father. As usual, he presided the meeting. After addressing the board members, he said, "It is my pleasure to acquaint you with my daughter Lieschen, who will gradually assume my own responsibilities. Some of you already know my daughter." He motioned toward his left where Lieschen was seated.

She was glad that her father was no longer upset with her; however, various members reacted with a cold expression. Lieschen knew the upper management comprised a men's world. Her father made a big exception with her inclusion; and she intended to live up to her father's expectation and trust and stand her ground.

Herr Klug and Frau Drexel, a white-haired lady who served as head of human resources, sent a smile her way, giving her encouragement. Aunt Klara and Frau Drexel were the only female board members.

Her father proceeded talking about phase III of the development of Xiron; and he emphasized the necessity of building new clientele in Austria and in other countries for the distribution of their pharmaceutical products. Then he reverted to his initial announcement. "I know my daughter is quite young, but she is intelligent, and she has proven to be independent and responsible. I fully trust in your support for my decision."

Lieschen wondered if her trip to her relatives in Lucerne and her subsequent return had influenced her father's evaluation of her maturity. If Pap only knew!

"My health is no longer what it used to be. I need to prepare for the future." At this point, her father swallowed hard.

Lieschen now believed in the progression of her father's illness, although he had appeared strong and dynamic and had never complained. He kept his pain bottled up and expected her to do the same. Secrecy seemed to be her father's motto. Why?

In closing, he said, "It is my daughter's turn to speak to you." He motioned toward Lieschen.

She squeezed her fingernails into her palms, but she would not show her tense emotions. She rose, lifted her head, straightened her shoulders, and began to speak. "Thank you, father." She made a formal bow toward him; then she turned to the members of the board.

"Esteemed Board Members! Since it is my father's wish that I follow in his footsteps in the operation of our Pharmaceutical Company, I would appreciate your cooperation and assistance. It is an honor for me to serve in this new capacity. I shall do my utmost to satisfy your expectations, and I will put every effort into earning your confidence and trust."

At this point some members applauded.

Amazed at her own bearing, Lieschen realized that she had been brought up with a business orientation in mind. At the end of her speech, she shook hands with most of the directors and company officers and thanked them personally for their cooperation and assistance in this process. She did not shake hands with Sigi, though. She ignored hitn.

Back in her office, Lieschen called Mother Marisa and informed her of the recent development.

"You have decided to work in your father's company during summer, and you will attend the AKA Business College in fall and work part-time in your father's Company," Mother Marisa clarified her understanding of the status quo.

"Yes," Lieschen confirmed.

"I knew you would make a wise choice. You will carry God's armor and succeed."

"I'll try," Lieschen said, but she did not mention that her goal to oust Sigi had taken center stage. After pausing for a moment, she asked, "When would you like that I work with the handicapped children?"

"I'm delighted that you resolved to volunteer. It will help you grow in love and understanding of life."

Lieschen suggested a tentative schedule which she had to coordinate with her work schedule. "I have to confirm the schedule with my father," she pointed out.

"Of course."

Just as her phone conversation with Mother Marisa ended, Sigi entered her office with a bouquet of long-stemmed red roses in a shiny, black vase. He placed the vase with the bouquet on her desk and congratulated her on her newly attained position. Then he sat down across from her. Lieschen had not invited him to sit down, but he did as he pleased. She wanted to take the roses and throw them in his face so that every thorn would sting him.

"Fraulein Lieschen, you must understand that we have to work together for our Company's continued success. And we must let our mutual love flourish!"

Lieschen gasped. "How can you possibly assume that I love you?"

"I know you love me. And you must know how much I love you!" A seductive smile danced on Sigi's lips.

"I swear before God that I don't love you."

"I beg your pardon?" The seductive smile on Sigi's lips changed into a sardonic twist.

"You don't have to beg my pardon." The next moment Lieschen reminded herself not to jeopardize her relationship with her father and some of the gains she had made so far. She had to pretend to cooperate with Sigi while handling this intricate dilemma in a diplomatic manner. "I'm busy right now," she said.

"We could go to a movie and talk in private," Sigi suggested.

Never again will I go out with you! Lieschen sucked in her lower lip and kept silent.

"I'd like to invite you to see 'The Grasshoppers' at the Annenstein Theater this evening. It's a newly released movie with challenging adventure. I believe you'd enjoy it."

Lieschen felt ants crawling under her skin. She had tried to get rid of this creepy feeling in connection with Sigi, but she had not succeeded. "I have an art meeting this evening. I cannot go to a movie. And right now I'm very busy."

"All right, we can go to see the movie tomorrow."

The phone rang. Lieschen snatched the receiver as though it were a life saver.

Frau Drexel was on the line to discuss payroll matters. Lieschen prolonged the conversation with Frau Drexel by asking unrelated questions until Sigi finally left her office.

After the phone conversation, Lieschen took the roses over to Aunt Klara and put them on her desk.

"They're beautiful." Aunt Klara smelled the roses. "Who gave them to you?"

"Sigi. But I don't want them."

"I see."

"May I leave them on your desk?"

"If you'd like." A faint smile crossed Aunt Klara's lips. "Are you going out with him?"

"Is that what you'd expect me to do?"

"I don't know."

"You should know," Lieschen said and exited Aunt Klara's office.

Later at home, she spotted a letter from the Courthouse among a stack of mail on the small side table in the formal dining room, where Frau Emma usually kept their mail. Could this concern Mommy or Grandma? Although Lieschen knew about her parents' futile relationship, she still had to find out how her mother had died; and she had to find her missing grandmother.

Since she was not allowed to open her father's private mail, she held the letter toward the window to see if she could make out the subject matter. She could not read a single word and put the letter back on the stack of mail. She hoped her father would disclose the content to her.

She went to pick out a red apple from the fruit basket in the pantry and headed upstairs, where she munched the apple while skimming the headlines of the Grazer Zeitung on her balcony.

At dinner, Lieschen asked her father, "Did you see the letter from the Courthouse?"

"Yes, I received it," her father replied without further comment.

Why isn't Pap telling me what it's about? If it concerns Mommy or Grandma, I have to know. I've a right to know!

The following morning, after her father and Aunt Klara left for work, Lieschen dashed into her father's office and searched his desk and his drawers for the letter from the Courthouse. Since she could not find it, she thought her father might have put it into his vault. She would open the vault to find out, but first she had to make sure that nobody was watching her.

Frau Emma tended flowers in their garden. Reserl put away dishes in the kitchen. Joseph, their gardener, and one helper, Christopher, worked in the orchard. No one else was around. It's safe, Lieschen confirmed to herself and immediately searched for the key, which she found in her fathers desk drawer. She opened the vault and lifted out documents, letters, private bills, and whatever other paraphernalia was neatly stacked inside. She put everything on her father's desk and examined each item.

When she heard her father's Mercedes stop in front of their villa, she threw everything back into the vault, locked it, and put the key behind the boxes of staples in the middle desk drawer where she had found it. She was not fast enough, though, to get out in time. She had only reached the door when her father came in.

"What are you doing?"

"I brought you a letter which was in my mail. I put it on your desk." Lieschen pointed at a letter while biting her tense lips.

Her father checked the letter. "Nothing important," he said and put it back.

Lieschen knew it was not important. She had referred to an advertising letter and was glad she could use it as an excuse. She was allowed to enter her father's office, but he expected her to respect his privacy, especially his private mail and his private vault.

"I forgot the Krambinski file," her father explained and pulled out the upper left desk drawer.

"Oh." Lieschen clenched her teeth and hoped her father would not open the vault.

He took the file, closed the drawer, and headed for the door. "See you at the office," he said and rushed out.

Lieschen followed her father into the hallway, then climbed the stairway to her apartment. Through the west-window in her study, she observed her father hauling his Mercedes away from the circular driveway.

As soon as he was out of sight, she dashed back into his office, opened the vault and straightened out the documents and paraphernalia which she had tossed in earlier. She was too nervous, though, to continue with her search.

When she arrived at the plant, her father summoned her to his office. Did Pap find out what I've done? With clenched teeth she entered his office. He motioned for her to sit down and questioned her about a phone call from Mother Marisa. Lieschen told him that she had agreed to work with handicapped children at St. Germain.

"What in the world gave you such a grotesque idea?" Her father's forehead wrinkled.

"Mother Marisa suggested it."

"When did you talk to her?"

Lieschen would not tell her father that *she* had gone to see Mother Marisa because she wanted to become a nun. She simply said, "I went to see Mother Marisa the other day."

"I do not approve of having you work with handicapped children."

"I think it would be a good experience for me."

"Do you want to turn into a social hypocrite?"

Shocked, Lieschen stared at her father.

"It's not fitting for you!"

"I just want to do good deeds and help a little if I can. In fall, I probably couldn't continue."

"You will not even start!"

Lieschen thought of her father's health and modified her approach. "Pap, Mother Marisa said this would be a good learning experience for me. I'd like to do it over the summer. I'm only scheduled to work two afternoons a week. Please, Pap!"

Half-hearted, her father relented.

In her own office, Lieschen worked hard all day, primarily on ledger keeping; and she had one meeting with Frau Drexel concerning employee files.

When she returned home, she found a fine-grained, cerulean-blue envelope in the stack of mail on the small side table in the formal dining room, addressed to her. Did I get a letter from the Courthouse too? she wondered. The letter did not contain a sender's name, and it did not look like a letter from the Courthouse. From whom could it be? She examined the postage stamp. The letter had been mailed in Lucerne. Could Uncle Gustav and Aunt Sylvia have written to me? She recalled no mention of a letter during her recent conversation with her uncle. Or could it be from Robert?

With the letter in hand, she zipped up to her study. Since she could not put her hands on the letter opener right away, she ripped open the flip with her fingers and pulled out a cerulean-blue note with a photo of herself posing beside a whitish swan at the Vierwaldstaetter Lake. She remembered when Robert had taken photos, and she remembered the fluffy feathers of the swan, which clearly showed on this photo. She dropped back on her couch and began reading the note.

Dear Lieschen,

I'm sorry you departed so soon. Forgive me if I offended you, I didn't mean to hurt you.

Tears welled up in Lieschen's *eyes* as she continued reading.

Hidden forces stood between us

Monika and I hung one of your photos with the swan on our living room wall. We enjoy it a lot, and I hope you will also enjoy the enclosed photo.

Thinking of you often, I remain with cordial greetings,

Robert

What hidden forces is Robert talking about? With trembling hands, she held the note and the photo. The next moment, resentment prevailed, and she tossed both the photo and the note on the coffee table and leaned back on the couch. Her heart thumped while tears rolled down her cheeks. She wondered if she should tear up the note and the photo, but something deep inside her heart would not let her. She still wanted to hold on to something very precious which she could not have. She continued thinking, reflecting, and agonizing. Then she picked up the photo again. Her experience with Robert had been the happiest of her life. She could not toss it away. Even if she tore up the note and the photo, she could not tear up her heart. Robert would always be there.

She rose and walked over to the picture window on the east-side of her study. Clasping her hands, she looked beyond the old cherry tree, which was now full of red cherries. She prayed, "Dear God, please help me! My heart feels like bursting." She wanted to shout at the top of her lungs to make sure God would hear, but she did not shout because she remembered when Sister Gertrude had told students in class to petition God quietly. "God will answer all petitions in His own time, in His own way," Sister Gertrude had explained.

In a little while, Lieschen stepped into her bedroom and put on chocolate-colored pants, lavender socks, and a lavender linen shirt. She intended to go into her studio to paint, hoping thus to calm down.

In her studio, she reached from one tube of oil paint to another and squeezed paint onto a large palette-vermilion, sap-green, cobalt-and ultramarine-blue, alizarin crimson, orange, yellow, burnt sienna, and titanium-white. She squeezed out more paint than she needed. Whatever. She could not squeeze it back in. She gazed at the full palette and dipped a number six bristle brush into liquid medium and into alizarin crimson and resumed working on the abstract depiction of apes strolling through Herrengasse in Graz. She had started this painting after she had returned from Lucerne.

Suddenly she dropped the brush because she messed up what she had painted earlier. Her painful sentiments got the better of her. She needed fresh air or something else. She slipped the palette with the fresh paint into a plastic case to preserve the paint and decided to go horseback riding. Once more she changed her clothes to a pair of coffee-brown jodhpurs and boots, but she did not change out of her lavender linen shirt. She tucked it inside the jodhpurs.

Just as she opened the door to leave, the phone rang. She rushed back to answer. "Ciao!" she heard Werner's voice on the line.

She was surprised. "Ciao!" she said and right away continued, "I haven't heard from you in so long."

"I haven't heard from you either. Ingrid told me that you're back from Lucerne." Werner's disappointed tone implied, "Why haven't you called me?"

Lieschen could not call Werner because her life was wrecked, and she could not tell Werner what happened. She hoped that Ingrid had not told him about Robert either. She regretted, however, that she had neither written nor called Werner from Lucerne. "How have you been?" she asked in an apologetic tone.

"I guess okay. Did you enjoy your visit with your relatives?" She took a deep breath and said, "I saw a Monet exhibition."

"I bet that was inspiring."

"Very interesting. And I saw the ancient Chapel Bridge and historic sites of the Swiss Confederation going back to 1291, when Lucerne was a vassal city of the Hapsburg House." With a painful reflection Lieschen visualized her happy stroll with Robert across the Chapel Bridge.

"Your ancestry."

"I believe so," Lieschen nodded into the receiver, then said, "And we went for boat rides. And my aunt took me to see my uncle's Architecture Firm. And she took me shopping, and to lunch. And I saw a little church called Santa Maria degli Angioli, with beautiful frescos, fashioned after a church in Italy, after Saint Francis of Assisi."

"What else did you do?"

Werner sounded as if she had omitted something. But how could he know about Robert unless Ingrid told him? Ingrid had promised not to tell hiin. To Lieschen, their stars seemed crossed. Werner loved her and she loved Robert. "I can't think of anything else," she said. "I spent a lot of time studying the Monet originals. What have you been doing?"

"I worked at my grandparents' farm."

"Did you have a good time?"

"I helped give birth to a calf."

Lieschen tried to picture giving birth to a calf. She did not know anything about farm life. She only had little knowledge of horses because of Grande and because of her father's horses, but she knew Werner loved to be on his grandparents' farm. He used to tell her that staying close to the soil mattered most to him. Lieschen also knew that Werner enjoyed riding a bike, hiking, horseback riding, and skiing. He could do all of that near his grandparents' farm. "Are the calf and the cow healthy?" she asked.

"The little creature tottered around in the hay the moment it saw the light of day. It seemed so happy to be alive. And the mother cow licked the calf for a long time."

"How lovely!"

"Listen, would you like to go to a movie tonight?"

"I was just on my way to go horseback-riding."

"Alone?"

"Yes."

"Is it okay that I join you?"

"Sure."

"I have to take my Mom to the Krenn Butcher Shop. Then I'll meet you by the boathouse. Okay?"

"Okay." Lieschen was glad that Werner called, and that he did not hold her behavior against her. She looked forward to seeing him.

While strolling toward the stables, she saw Ralph riding a stallion in the practice rink. She signaled with her hands, and Ralph rode toward her.

"Do you want to go riding, Fraulein Lissi?"

Lieschen had been accustomed to Ralph addressing her as Fraulein Lissi. Different people called her different versions of her name. Her parents called her Lieschen, or Princess while she was little. Other people called her Princess Lieschen, or plain Lieschen. When she came of age, most people called her Fraulein Lieschen or Fraulein Reinking. Lieschen had derived as a nickname from her mother's name, Elisabeth, which was also Lieschen's official first name. "Yes, I'd like to go riding if Grande is in a good mood," she replied.

"We'll see." Ralph guided his stallion next to Lieschen.

"How's Figaro?" she asked.

"I be racing him soon. Herr Reinking promised that Figaro will always be me racing horse."

"I hope you'll win many races." Lieschen's father had told her that a coach had been working with Ralph and Figaro twice a week now. "I brought sugar cubes for Figaro." She reached into the pocket of her jodhpurs, pulled out three cubes, and showed them to Ralph.

"Figaro will liking it. If he don't, I'll eat the sweetly sugar."

"Okay," Lieschen smiled.

At the stables, while Ralph dismounted his stallion, Lieschen could see a golden cross under Ralph's checkered blue and white shirt. She wondered if Ralph's father, who served as assistant deacon at Maria Strassengel, had given him the cross.

As they approached Figaro's stall, his slender neck and proud head arched from his savagely beautiful, bay body. Lieschen stretched the palm of her right hand with the sweet cubes over the wooden railing.

Figaro pricked his ears, but he did not budge.

"You'll like the sweetly sugar," Ralph said. "You don't have to be a fearing."

Lieschen always considered Ralph's horse-talk humorous, and she was used to his dialect.

Figaro took a step back, as if distrusting the whole proposition.

"Irregardless, let's be patient," Ralph said.

In a little while, Figaro ventured a step forward, then another, then slowly he tasted a cube. After the first taste, he sucked the other cubes out of Lieschen's hand. She could even stroke his bridge and mane.

"Bribed him." Ralph snapped a few fingers.

"Last time I couldn't bribe him with sugar cubes."

"Got to pick the right timing." Ralph ventured away. From a short distance he turned back and said, "I'll get Grande for you."

"Okay." Lieschen stayed a bit longer with Figaro. She enjoyed talking to him and stroking his bridge.

While she galloped with Grande toward the Mariatroster Lake, located near the west flank of the Rinden Creek, the water of the creek murmured and splashed over rocks and twigs, and over a fallen birch tree. The fragrance from the luscious green canopy and from the wildflowers laced the warm air. Soon she spotted Werner and Sprint at the rustic boathouse. They had arrived before she did. Werner looked good in his maroon riding pants with high maroon leather boots, thought Lieschen. And he wore a shirt slightly less intense in the maroon hue. Sprint was tied to a wooden railing at the boathouse. He ogled Lieschen and Grande as if he was glad to see them. Lieschen knew that Sprint belonged to Werner's whole family, but Werner usually rode him.

"Ciao!" Werner smiled his contagious smile.

"Ciao!" Lieschen was happy to see him. He helped her dismount, fastened Grande's reins next to Sprint, then turned and hugged Lieschen. "Good to see you back," he said. She responded with a warm hug, but when Werner wanted to kiss her, she pulled away. He let go. "Would you like to go for a boat ride?" he asked with a disappointed tone.

"I told Frau Emma I'd be back for dinner."

"In that case let's just ride to the crest, so you'll be home in rime." They remounted their stallions and trotted back to the Rinden Creek and along the rugged trail under the leafy canopy toward the crest.

"I started working at my father's plant," Lieschen told Werner. "And my father has enrolled me at the AKA Business College for fall."

"Are you excited?"

"I have mixed feelings."

"Have you been crying, Lieschen?" With his clear blue eyes Werner examined her.

"Why?"

"Because your eyes look sore."

"My eyes are a little sore because I'm worried."

"About what?"

"Different things ..."

"Which things?"

Lieschen shrugged.

"It's a different life now, isn't it? Graduation bygone-"

Lieschen nodded, then asked, "What have you been doing at your grandparents' farm? I know you helped give birth to a calf. But what else have you been doing?"

"I had a good time with my grandparents."

"That's nice."

"Of course, on the farm I helped with forestry work, tending fields, mowing grass, tending horses, cows, calves, pigs, chicken ..."

"That's what you enjoy?"

"As you know, I like working with the soil and with animals better than anything else. I wish you `d like it too." Werner looked longingly into Lieschen's eyes.

"I adore nature and animals. I could sit for hours by a pond under a tree, and sketch or paint, or write a poem. Or just sit still on a quiet, hilly meadow on an Alm and take in the harmony of nature, with cows or sheep or goats grazing, but I don't like farm work."

Werner guided Sprint around a mud puddle. Lieschen led Grande around the other side of the puddle, on a stretch where the trail narrowed.

"Do you ever ride your gold bicycle anymore?" Werner asked then.

"You must be kidding. You know it's too small for me."

"You could still ride it."

"Like a clown? Is that what you'd like to see me do?"

"No, just for fun. I like to remember the fun times we had together when we were little. Watching you ride again would make this happy memory come alive."

Lieschen smiled. As a little girl, she had also enjoyed riding her gold bicycle with Werner, and playing with him in his tree house; but these times were no more. They had grown up. "Perhaps one day I'll ride my gold bicycle again," she said then.

"I wish you would."

The leafy canopy thinned out as they neared the crest. The fragrant air had cooled, and the sun rolled down behind the mountains.

"Would you care to see the premiere of 'The Grasshoppers' at the Annenstein Theater tonight?" Werner slowed Sprint because he trotted faster than Grande.

"That's supposedly a good movie?"

"That's what people say. Adventure and good acting."

"Sigi invited me to that movie."

"Would you prefer going with him?"

"Do I have to answer that question?"

"I think I know. You wouldn't want to go out with that arrogant buff. He's one of the few guys I'd rather do without."

"Makes two of us."

"I think Sigi's father is a good man, but Sigi is another matter. Some people say Sigi has multiple personalities."

"I heard that too. I just wish I wouldn't have to work with him. I try to avoid him as much as 1 can."

"You can tell your father that you don't want to work with him, can't you?"

"Unfortunately it wouldn't help because my father is so biased in favor of Sigi and his family." Lieschen let out a deep sigh.

"That must be hard on you?"

"I want to oust Sigi."

Werner looked stunned. "Serious?"

"I don't want him in my father's Company. Fortunately Aunt Klara doesn't care for Sigi either. She hasn't expressed it in so many words because she has to heed my father, but I can tell."

"If your aunt doesn't care for Sigi, that's part of the battle, isn't it?"

"I hope so."

"Listen, we got sidetracked." Werner checked his wrist-watch. "You didn't tell me if you want to see 'The Grasshoppers' tonight?"

"Yes, I would."

"It starts at eight. And you told Frau Emma to be home for dinner. We better head back." They agreed to meet at the Annenstein Theater at seven-thirty.

When Lieschen descended the stairway to leave for the movie, she heard voices in the game room, next to the family room. She looked in and saw her father, Aunt Klara, and Herr and Frau Kramer playing chess.

"Gruess Gott," she said, looking in at the door.

Everybody turned toward her and returned her greeting.

"Won't you come in?" her father said, and she walked across the rich, sap-green Persian rug toward the game table.

"Would you care for a match?" Herr Kramer offered.

"Not tonight, danke. I have to go to an art meeting."

"How have you been, Lieschen? I should say Fraulein Lieschen," Frau Kramer said. "You have graduated. You're a grown-up lady now."

"Lieschen is fine," Lieschen replied with a smile.

"Do you enjoy working at your father's Plant?" Herr Kramer inquired.

"It's interesting."

A complacent smile appeared on her father's lips as he watched her express interest in his Company. They chatted a bit more, then Lieschen checked the time on her wrist-watch and, with a friendly "Auf Wiedersehen", she took leave.

Werner had been waiting in line at the entrance to the Annenstein Theater, punctual as usual. The moment Lieschen joined him, she spotted Sigi farther up front, near the entrance. A red-haired woman in a tight-fitting purple dress and high-heeled purple shoes stood next to him.

When the red-haired woman turned around, Lieschen recognized her as the young woman who had attached herself to Sigi's Porsche like a lioness the night Lieschen went to the Opera Haus with Sigi. Suddenly Lieschen's cheeks began burning because she saw her gold necklace with the pyramid-shaped emerald pendant around this woman's neck. Right away she realized that she had lost the necklace during the struggle in Sigi's Porsche, and Sigi must've given it to that woman, she was certain. What a shameless act! Lieschen wanted to storm up and reclaim her necklace, but she could not get into a quarrel in front of Werner and everybody else standing in line. She worried that some people would recognize her, and Sigi would tell her father that she had gone to a movie with Werner.

"What's the matter?" Werner blinked.

"Sigi's up front. I don't want him to see us." Lieschen did not mention her necklace because Werner knew nothing about that awful evening with Sigi. She would not even know how to tell Werner about Sigi's attempted rape. Instead of watching the movie, she squirmed and pondered how she could get her necklace back.

From the cinema, they went to the Meridian Cafe and were seated at an ornate white iron table on the terrace. A romantic candle flickered in the middle of the round table. Fragrant pink roses climbed up on the surrounding trellises. Lieschen paid no attention to the lovely surrounding. All she had in mind was to get her necklace back. But how?

A friendly waitress took their order of fruit ice cream with chocolate cream wafers, which she served promptly. Werner and Lieschen had chosen the same kind of fruit ice cream. Lieschen looked at the appetizing dish in front of her but, instead of eating, she continued to fidget and squirm.

People on nearby tables observed her. She could not conceal her irritation over Sigi's shameless action - taking her beautiful necklace, which her father had given her for her eighteenth birthday, and giving it to that woman!

What's bothering you?" Werner ate another spoonful of his fruit ice cream. "I can see that something is wrong. Quite wrong!"

Lieschen could not explain. She simply couldn't.

Werner kept watching her until, abruptly, he pushed his half-full dish of ice cream toward the middle of the table, next to the flickering candle. It was one of the few times Lieschen had seen him lose his temper.

"If you cannot trust me enough to tell me what's bothering you, I want to go home." Werner's lips compressed. "All evening you fidget and fidget, and you cannot tell me why."

"Werner, please, I trust you fully. I . . ." Lieschen did not know what to say or do. She had hardly patched up her friendship with Werner, and now this!

"Let's go home!" Werner rose.

Lieschen knew that his patience went a long way, but at this point it had run out. IIe paid for their ice cream, and they left the Meridian Cafe, their friendship uprooted again.

CHAPTER 19

Driving to work along Mariatroster Kay in her new Porsche, Lieschen's mind continued to reel over Sigi's shameless action. Over and over she kept asking, How can I get my necklace back? It was pitiful that a despicable character like Sigi held such a prestigious position in her father's Company. Lieschen's determination to oust him became more and more crucial. She had already tried different allegations against him, but they had all fallen on deaf ears with her father.

As she crossed Karl Rainer Strasse, she remembered the elderly gentleman who had stumbled into the hood of Sigi's Porsche at that intersection. She hoped that he was okay.

In her office at the Plant, she responded to a phone message from Ingrid's cousin Jakob in their lab. "Brace yourself." Jakob's tone sounded urgent.

"Why?"

"I can't tell you over the phone."

"Can you come to my office?"

"Okay, I'll be there shortly."

When Jakob came in, Lieschen was talking to Frau Drexel on the telephone. She motioned for Jakob to have a seat. "Why am I supposed to brace myself?" she queried as soon as she replaced the receiver.

"You might also want to catch your breath." Jakob stabbed a few fingers into the air.

"Don't keep me in suspense!"

"All right." Jakob pulled back his fingers and placed his hand on the desk. "Sigi wants to replace Herrn Klug with Dietrich," he said with a sharp tone.

"Dietrich Wulst?"

Jakob nodded, screwing up his face in disgust.

"Dietrich doesn't have the necessary qualifications?"

"Does Sigi? If you ask me, Sigi is an arrogant sleazebag just like Dietrich."

Lieschen tapped her pen on the desk, thinking and wondering what to do.

"It would spell disaster."

"I know it would."

"Dietrich would jackknife everyone who doesn't tie in with his and Sigi's crooked ways."

"We have to prevent it," Lieschen agreed. "I'll talk to my father."

"You better!" Jakob removed his hand from the desk.

"He's never undercut old-timers. Not that I know of. And Herr Klug is also my father's good friend."

"Which should help. I would not want to work under Dietrich, I tell you that much." Jakob rose. "Listen, I've a test brewing. I've got to go back to the lab. Just had to tell you."

"I'm glad you told me. I do what I can."

"Holler if you need me."

"Okay. Danke Jakob."

Lieschen was sure that Sigi wanted to get rid of Herrn Klug because he wanted to control the lab. And there was something else: Herr Klug had told Lieschen that Sigi intended to divulge the formula of Xiron to a competitor and pocket a sizable payoff if she didn't marry him. Herr Klug had overheard this conversation between Sigi and Dietrich, but he had advised Lieschen not to tell her father.

She walked over to her father's office and sat down at his desk when he motioned for her to sit down. She asked him straight out about Herrn Klug's transfer.

"Who told you such nonsense?" Her father slipped the pen he was holding into the fancy penholder with the gold imprint *Reinking & Co.*

"I heard it this morning. There's this rumor floating through the grapevine."

"Don't be vague. Who told you?"

Lieschen could not tell her father because she could not get Jakob in trouble. While she searched for an explanation, her father reached for the telephone and summoned Sigi to his office. He promptly came and sat down beside Lieschen. Ants began crawling under her skin. Instantaneously. Her father asked Sigi for the status quo concerning Herrn Klug.

"I find the coincidence quite remarkable." Sigi cast an acid glance at Lieschen. Then, turning back to her father, he said matter-of-factly, "I intended to confer with you about prospective improvements."

Improvements! Lieschen squeezed her fingernails into her palms.

"Let's talk about Herrn Klug," her father demanded.

Sigi thrust his chin up and said, "I believe Herr Klug's expertise would best serve our Company with customer relations, since we need to expand this department. However, I will not finalize the transfer without your approval."

Her father took a deep breath and, with an edge in his voice, he said, "We will not consider such a transfer."

Lieschen was grateful for her father's response.

Herr Klug remained in his position as lab manager, but Lieschen worried that Sigi might find other means to get rid of him.

Later at home, comfortably settled around the coffee table in the living room, Lieschen brought up the controversy concerning Herrn Klug. "Pap, Sigi is not a good manager," she said. "I've expressed my concern to you before. He just isn't fair. He exploits good people. And loyalty and integrity mean nothing to him. Herr Klug is the latest example. I believe Sigi shouldn't be general manager."

Her father's eyebrows furrowed. "Anyone can make a mistake." He spoke snails' pace.

From her father's expression, Lieschen detected regret over the whole controversy with Herrn Klug. "This isn't a question of a mistake. It's Sigi's pattern. He just undercuts good employees and good people." Lieschen took a deep breath and continued, "The other recent examples are Frau Drexel and Herr Schneider. Sigi is coming down on them without justification."

"In the case of Frau Drexel, she shouldn't have released information to Brigitte Sommers. And Herr Schneider admitted his own wrongdoing," her father pointed out.

"Pap, Brigitte told me that Herr Schneider had authorization from Herrn Klug to release the Eucapnia samples, but Sigi had removed the authorization from his desk. Frau Drexel saw it. Then Sigi lied about it and blackmailed both. I believe Herr Schneider doesn't want trouble, that's why he swallowed the falsified accusation and said it was his own fault."

"I've obtained different information." Her father looked uneasy. "We'll investigate further." He crossed his legs and said, "As to Sigi, I believe he's the best qualified manager we can have. I have thoroughly trained him. Nonetheless, who do you think should be general manager?"

"I should, in due time."

Her father seemed to admire her statement. "That's what I had planned for you all along, and I will accept your proposition to carry on the management together with Sigi. I'm sure you realize that a respectable gentleman officer is essential in our business milieu. And you need Sigi's strength and knowledge to carry on the vast responsibilities."

God, why does Pap underestimate me? Lieschen knew she had to learn a lot, and she would learn at AKA and on the job. She felt confident that she could handle all responsibilities in due time. She also counted on the cooperation and assistance of employees and high-ranking officials. She intended to establish good relations with everyone, except with Sigi. As far as Sigi was concerned, she was prepared to go beyond fair play because he was so contemptible.

"You couldn't handle all responsibilities without Sigi," her father stressed once more. "You have to rely on my judgement."

Lieschen could not rely on her father's flawed judgement, and she would never share management responsibilities with Sigi.

CHAPTER 20

Through further inquiries at the Coroner's office, Lieschen could finally obtain Dr. Tschingelbaum's address, but she could not find him despite having driven to his home at 113 Herrgottwiesgasse in Graz several times. This time she would try to locate him early in the morning, on her way to work.

She rang the door bell. As before, the chiming reverberated throughout the one-story Mediterranean-style home, but again there was no response; and all curtains and drapes were drawn. Nothing stirred inside, as if ghosts occupied Dr. Tschingelbaum's home.

Across the street, Lieschen saw a white-haired lady watering flowers on a veranda. She walked over.

"Excuse me," she said and waited till the lady had put down her watering can on the wooden veranda floor and straightened up her short, full figure. Then she asked, "Would you know when Dr. Tschingelbaum will be home? I'd need to talk to him urgently."

"The good Doctor might be home in three, four, five months ..." The lady's coarse voice sounded uncertain but kind.

"Are you serious?"

"Why wouldn't I be?"

"I don't know."

"The Doctor, his wife, and his grandchildren are vacationing in Palermo. It's uncertain when they'll return. Come in," the lady invited Lieschen and waddled in front of her like a penguin. "My foot is killing me. Last week I had surgery on my left knee," she disclosed.

"Oh, I'm sorry." Now, Lieschen understood why the lady walked like that.

In the quaint kitchen of her Tyrolian-style home, Lieschen saw a Persian cat sleeping on a soft blue cushion, on a white chair. "She's cute," she said.

"Her name is Mingi."

"May I pet Mingi?"

"Go ahead."

Mingi responded with a gentle purr.

"Let me give you my card," the lady said then. She pulled a card from a drawer of her white credenza and handed it to Lieschen. "You can call me from time to time to see if the good Doctor has come back."

Lieschen looked at the card. "Danke Frau Dr. Stiglitz," she said.

"Why don't you give me your phone number too."

Lieschen did.

"We'll keep in touch."

"I appreciate your help. And take care of your knee." Lieschen put Frau Dr. Stiglitz's card into her purse and drove to work.

Members of the board of directors had begun assembling as Lieschen arrived. She joined at her assigned seat next to her father. This time, her father had a different agenda. As soon as all members were present, he began talking about an upcoming Heimkehrerfest, a traditional autumn festival for veterans.

Every year, residents of Graz and various provinces of Austria, as well as visitors from other countries, participated at the Heimkehrerfest; and important dignitaries, including Lieschen's father and Sigi's father, held speeches.

After the board meeting, Lieschen's father called her to his office and assigned the speech-writing for this year's Heimkehrerfest to her. It was the first time her father gave her such an important assignment. He also handed her copies of previous speeches as guidelines; and he pointed out that she had to attend the Heimkehrerfest with Sigi. "You have to represent us in the proper light. You understand?"

Sigi representing proper light? Lieschen did not understand, but she did not say anything because Sigi just entered.

"Have a seat." Her father pointed to the chair next to Lieschen. "We're discussing the Heimkehrerfest."

"I brought literature for you, Fraulein Lieschen. Sigi handed her pamphlets with information concerning the Heimkehrerfest. Then he sat down on the chair next to her.

Ants began crawling under her skin. Instantaneously.

"I advise that you consider the interests of your father and our Company as your primary responsibility," Sigi pointed out.

Conspiracy between my father and Sigi! But without me! Lieschen checked her wrist-watch. Turning to her father, she said, "Excuse me, I have to attend to my obligation at St. Germain." She rose and stepped to the door where she glanced back at her father. "Good-bye," she uttered and exited.

At St. Germain she escorted the handicapped children to the playground by the Schiller Fountain. She watched the youngsters swirling watercolor on pink, yellow, *green,* and blue paper. Sister Gertrude had given her the supplies and guidelines for this afternoon's activities, and Lieschen had shown the children how to hold a brush and how to paint, but most of the children preferred painting with their fingers. Painting seemed to be one of their favorite subjects, just like singing.

While painting a tree, Manfred, an eight-year old boy with the mind of a three-year old, announced that he had to go to the bathroom.

"Go ahead, Manfred, I'll follow you," instructed Lieschen. "Put down your brush. Don't take it to the bathroom."

Manfred dropped his brush and ran toward the bathroom. Lieschen made sure that all children were okay before she followed Manfred. As she entered the bathroom, Manfred was squeezing his pants in the sink. She explained that he only needed to wash his hands, not his pants, after going to the bathroom. On second thought, she wondered whether Manfred might have wet his pants because he was in a big hurry. She took a dry pair out of the locker cabinet and helped Manfred put it on. Then she finished washing Manfred's pants in the sink. She felt awkward about doing this, but it was part of her duties.

As they left the bathroom together, Heinz trotted toward them, pointing a ruler at his tongue.

"What do you want me to do?" Lieschen waited patiently for the four-year-old Heinz to explain. He could not talk much, but he kept stretching out his tongue and tapping it with the ruler.

"Don't hurt yourself." Lieschen reached for the ruler, but Heinz would not give it to her.

"He wants you to measure his tongue," called Marianne, who looked up from her artistic composition. Marianne was a year older than Heinz.

How can the children understand each other so well? Lieschen wondered and told Heinz that a tongue could not be measured with a ruler.

Meanwhile Manfred had jumped into the Schiller fountain and was swirling purple paint around, straight out of the tube. Lieschen lifted Manfred out of the fountain and took away his tube of purple paint. She had barely placed him in yet another pair of dry pants when the closing bell rang. The children wanted to continue painting, but the fun time for that afternoon had come to a close; and Lieschen was glad.

At home, during dinner, her father resumed the conversation concerning the Heimkehrerfest. "You have to understand that it is absolutely necessary for you to represent us in our respectable tradition. I will not pass over the impropriety of your public appearance with Werner." With his silver fork, her father picked up a slice of Naturschnitzel.

Ah, my father is aware that I've been seeing Werner! Is he spying on me? Lieschen had an uneasy feeling.

"This would have severe consequences," her father warned.

"I will not go to the Heimkehrerfest with Sigi." Lieschen also picked up a slice of Naturschnitzel from her plate.

"This time you will have to put our Company's interests first. By now, you must've learned to keep your priorities in line. I love you dearly, but you have to follow proper objectives. Our objectives!" Her father dipped a forkful of mashed potatoes into cherry sauce and guided it to his mouth.

Over my dead body will I go to the Heimkehrerfest with Sigi! Lieschen refrained from expressing this thought, but she stopped eating because her stomach churned.

After this unpleasant dinner, she went to bed and read a short story by Friedrich von Schiller, while listening to classical music. When she drifted off to sleep, sinister creatures swarmed across distorted crimson streaks on the horizon. Then loud sirens of a fire truck awoke her, and she could not go back to sleep.

In the morning, at the Plant, Sigi came into her office shortly after she arrived and reminded her of her obligation concerning the Heimkehrerfest.

Lieschen asserted, "I'm the one who will determine the priorities of my obligations." She had arranged to go to the Heimkehrerfest with Werner, and with Ingrid and Hans. She had reconciled with Werner after the incident at the Meridian Cafe'; however, to this day she had not gotten her necklace back.

CHAPTER 21

When Lieschen and her friends arrived at the Hauptplatz, the Town Hall Square in Graz, many people had already gathered. They joined and found a convenient location near Sporgasse.

The atmosphere of the Heimkehrerfest reminded Lieschen of a carnival. People of all ages participated in the merriment and thanksgiving for veterans. Most people wore traditional costumes. Lieschen thought that Werner and Hans's tan-colored Styrian suits and hats, and her and Ingrid's dirndl dresses with fashionable scarves and Edelweiss pendants fit well.

She watched her father and other dignitaries congregate on a temporary pinewood podium in front of the Rathaus, the Gothic City Hall. From her vantage point, Lieschen had a good view. She also glimpsed a Veteran's band marching through Herrengasse, a major business street with variety shops, museums, banks, and galleries. The musicians in brisk Veteran's attire played Johann Strauss' Radetzky March on trumpets, clarinets, horns, trombones, flutes, saxophones, bass drums, bass tubas, and oboes. When they reached the Hauptplatz, they assembled in a semi-circle on the west side of the statue of Archduke Johann.

During weekdays, this whole market square accommodated open-air vendors selling flowers, fruit, vegetables, hot sausages, freshly baked rolls and doughnuts, warm pretzels, hot chocolate, coffee, and other drinks and snacks. From her office at her father's Pharmaceutical Plant across the .River Mur, Lieschen enjoyed strolling here for a snack or a quick lunch. Sometimes Frau Drexel or other colleagues would join her.

As in previous years, the open-air stalls had been dismantled and cleared away, and a temporary pinewood podium had been installed in their place, accommodating the festivities of the Heimkehrerfest. Lieschen also saw cheerful welcome signs on the surrounding four-, five-, and six-story buildings, that huddled together with narrow gable roofs. The quaint facades in rainbow colors, with green shutters on the upper floors, housed legal and commercial offices; and variety shops occupied the ground floors with attractive large display windows.

Herr Welleiter, mayor of Graz, stepped on the platform behind the lectern on the pinewood podium and welcomed all participants. He had hardly begun speaking when airplanes with silver linings appeared and drummed through the air at a low level, in salute of the veterans. As soon as the airplanes sped off, Lieschen could see white streaks•in their wake.

Herr Welleiter resumed his speech. "I can't talk as loud as these dazzling airplanes," he jested, "but I wish to express our appreciation for our heroic Veterans, who always keep us shielded. In this protective spirit, we have to hold on to our main goals of maintaining freedom and peace in order to secure a promising future for our children, and for all of us at home, abroad, everywhere. And we have to ..."

Sigi's friend, Bruno Krenski, distracted Lieschen as he plowed toward them through the packed crowd. He did not say anything. He only stared at Lieschen with a peevish grin, like a perverse clown. Bruno was known as a clever village bozo with the nickname "Crazy Bruno," but Lieschen knew he was not as crazy as he made himself out to be. Hans had told her that Bruno just liked clowning, which he also did professionally at the Mainard Circus.

When Lieschen saw Bruno drudging on, she asked her friends, "Wonder what he was up to?"

"Mischief. What else?" Hans sounded annoyed.

"Perhaps Sigi sent him," Lieschen wondered aloud.

"He'd better stay clear!" Werner grunted.

"He'd better," Hans echoed.

Meanwhile people applauded the speech of Lieschen's father. Lieschen regretted not having heard it, especially since she had written the speech for him. General List, Corporal Weintropf, and two other dignitaries, Herr Schwarz and Herr Braun, delivered more elocutions, closing the formal ceremony.

The play Milch *Geld* followed on the agenda. This colorful play portrayed people's meager but happy alpine life. Boys in Lederhosen and girls in colorful dirndl dresses performed lively folk dances and yodeled and sang during the play. Sigi's girlfriend Petruschka played the guitar and sang the song *Mein Heimatland*.

"I believe Petruschka is wearing one of her modeling dresses," Ingrid remarked.

"Oh-la-la," Hans snickered.

Lieschen noticed the small frills around Petruschka's decollete on her feminine figure, while her straight, coal-black hair cascaded over her round shoulders. "Does Petruschka still model at the Sternsaal?" she asked.

"Yes, twice a week," Ingrid replied.

"That snob couldn't have found a nicer girl," Hans gruffed.

Lieschen knew that Hans liked Petruschka and her family, but he deplored Sigi.

"I've told Petruschka she's stupid to be so nuts about Sigi," Ingrid said.

"I don't think he understands the stuff love is made of." With longing eyes, Werner looked at Lieschen.

Hans grinned. "I wonder how Petruschka models in bed, with all of her Gypsy passion. I should find out."

"I suggest . . ." Ingrid took a long breath, then uttered slowly, "I suggest that you don't find out!"

"Why not? I might not be allergic to her."

After a while of charged silence, Hans added, "I know I have some crazy marbles in my head but they don't distract me from being just and loving you." He looked straight into Ingrid's eyes.

Lieschen knew that Hans enjoyed teasing, just like Ingrid. And she also knew that Hans loved her with all his heart.

When Petruschka finished her performance, she bowed gracefully. A little girl in pink, about five years old, carried a bouquet of red roses to her. Petruschka gave the little girl a tender kiss on the cheek.

Celebrations continued in restaurants and ballrooms. Lieschen and her friends went to the nearby Rasthauskeller, a restaurant with banquet rooms and a large dance hall. Many local residents patronized the Rasthauskeller.

A young waitress with a red ponytail, tied together with a big white bow, welcomed them and asked them for a little patience to be seated. Just then, a waiter whisked by with a full serving tray of sausages, fried potatoes, and Sauerkraut. Lieschen savored the aroma. She was hungry.

In a short while, they were seated and enjoyed a tasty meal of Sauerbraten with red cabbage, pickled mushrooms, potato salad, onion rings, and Wiener Sachertorte for dessert.

Before leaving the Rasthauskeller, they reserved a table for four to return for a festive dance after the boat ride. Lieschen looked forward to the idyllic boat ride, which they had planned in advance.

At the Mariatroster Lake, they left their hats, neckties, and scarves in their cars. While strolling over to the rustic boathouse, Werner and Hans opened the top buttons of their white shirts. At the pier behind the rustic boathouse, Werner scooted down and pulled the chain of his wooden boat from the eyelet, and he and Hans hopped in. They held out their hands for Lieschen and Ingrid to join. All four settled on the wooden benches. Hans reached for the oars and began hauling them away from the shore.

Lieschen could hear birds twitter in the larch-, birch-, and needled evergreen branches that grew in profusion adjacent to the shoreline. The chirping of the birds sounded like an orchestrated serenade and grew faint as they moved farther out in the lake. Only a few wooden boats drifted about in the quiet, shimmering water. Motorboats were not allowed on the Mariatroster Lake.

"What happened there?" Lieschen pointed at a scar on the side of Han's left cheek. She had not noticed the scar before.

"Love scratches." Hans showed his white, slightly crooked teeth that contrasted his tanned face and rich, rusty brown hair.

"Worse than that . . ." Ingrid gently touched Hans' scar and explained, "A board hit Hans at his construction site at Goetzstrasse."

"Caught me by surprise," Hans admitted.

Suddenly Crazy Bruno showed up in a bright-blue boat. His bulky body hunched over his wooden seat likes a stuffed , cowering cabbage.

His cobalt blue shirt hung loosely over his battleship-gray pants. He was barefoot.

'What's he doing here?" Lieschen asked her friends. She felt annoyed over his intrusion.

"Clowning, what else. Look at this goofball with his idiotic grin! In a contest for loonies, he'd win first prize," Hans snubbed.

"Everybody can be great at something." Werner wrinkled his nose.

"Yeah, it's all in your head, crazy or not crazy." Hans's square nod underscored his irritation.

"I guess," Werner chuckled.

"Greetings." Crazy Bruno skirted their boat and dropped the oars. "You don't have to guess any longer. I have a message for you." With his piggy eyes he looked at Lieschen.

"What message?"

"You know, you're not supposed to be here with these folks." He pointed his bulky hands at Lieschen's friends in a derogatory manner, as if they were below humanity.

"Who gave you the right to tell me such a thing?"

"The proper authority." Crazy Bruno's voice sounded as if his heart lodged in his throat.

"Get the hell to the point!" Hans demanded.

Bruno rolled his piggy eyes, lifted his loose shirt, and pulled a gun from the back of his pants. With his bulky fingers, he aimed the gun at Lieschen. "Here's the point." He pulled the trigger.

The shot hit the left flank of their boat. Water gushed through the bullet hole. Bruno fired several more shots. "Need to get unloaded. You asked for it." His mockish grin reached from ear to ear while he watched the water flooding their boat.

Lieschen and her friends leaped into the lake because their boat was sinking.

Bruno hollered, "This is a warning. Take it to heart." He maneuvered his own boat around and paddled away.

"What a slug!" Hans's muffled voice barely rose above the sound of splashing water.

Lieschen and her friends shuffled with their hands and feet, trying to swim to shore.

"I can feel the ground," Lieschen called when they neared the shoreline.

"Be careful that you don't get stuck in that silt," Werner cautioned loudly while Lieschen's head bobbed in and out of the murky water. Hans signaled with his hands and shouted, "Don't stand up!"

Lieschen knew that quite a few people had drowned in that vicinity. She personally knew two young women. She tried to remove her feet, but the more she shoved the more she got pulled under. When she managed to emerge above the surface, she cried, "Help!" The next moment, her feet burrowed deeper into the billowing silt, and she immersed completely.

Werner, Hans, and Ingrid rushed to her rescue and pulled her out, saving her from drowning.

Exhausted, wet, cold, and muddy, they reached the shore. "Girl, you were in trouble." Hans ran his hands across his dripping hair.

"I know, I couldn't remove my feet anymore. I didn't realize until it was too late. Danke for helping me." Lieschen pulled at her wet dirndl that clung to her skin like glue.

"You know your boat's lost," Hans said to Werner.

"Thank Heaven Lieschen didn't drown. I can replace my boat."

"I bet that rat-I mean that Sigi rat-wanted to wreck our day. He could've cared less if you had drowned." Hans looked at Lieschen while shaking his knotted fist in the air.

"Perhaps that's what he wanted." Werner squeezed water from the sleeves of his jacket.

"How diabolical!" Hans's voice pierced the quiet air.

"I feel terrible," Lieschen sighed. "This whole thing happened because of me." She was still trying to catch her breath and get rid of the billowing silt in her mouth. It tasted awful.

"Don't worry about anything now," Hans said. "The main thing is that you're alive. We'll settle the score."

"Danke." Lieschen appreciated her good friends. At the same time, she realized how thin the line between life and death had brushed up against her. Sometimes, when life seemed unbearable, she longed to be dead, but not now. Now she had to <u>fulfill</u> a main goal-ousting Sigi from her father's Company. She realized, however, that she did not have much control over life and death. In an ironic way, she remembered what the lady at the Mariatrost Cemetery had told her about living on the edge of death; and she also realized that life seemed more fragile than soap bubbles in the air.

They agreed to meet at the Rasthauskeller at seven and drove home to take showers and change clothes.

The same lively waitress with the red ponytail and the big white bow, who had waited on them earlier, ushered them to their reserved table near the rostrum in the main dance hall. Everything seemed normal again while in reality it was not. Lieschen felt tense. She anticipated retaliation because she knew that Hans was not ready to accept such an evil deed.

"For starters, do you wish hors-d'oeuvre, pastries, wine, champagne? What would you like?" The waitress pulled a notepad and a short pencil from her lacy white apron.

They reviewed their orders and, on mutual consensus, Hans ordered a bottle of white Riesling wine and an assortment of freshly baked pastries. The waitress scribbled notes on her pad and left.

Hans asked Lieschen, "Where's your father?"

"After the closing of the ceremonies on the Hauptplatz, he went on a hunting trip with his friends. They went to his estate in Stainz."

"Why didn't he take Sigi along?"

"I don't know." Lieschen shrugged, then looked at the rostrum where musicians in marine-blue suits tested their horns, trumpets, and other instruments. Yellow and orange lanterns draped the ceiling above the rostrum.

As soon as the musicians started playing a Rapsurka, people gathered on the dance floor. Lieschen and her friends did not dance. They nibbled on the freshly baked pastries, which the waitress had promptly served. The pastries included Lieschen's favorite Vanillekipferl and almond biscuits. Then they ordered the main serving of crispy golden-baked chicken with minced mushrooms, roasted onion potatoes, mixed salads, and a dessert of a fluffy Black Forest Cake. While eating they talked about a strategy on how to get even with Sigi and Bruno.

As soon as they finished their delectable meal, they followed Hans's suggestion and descended the cobbled stairway to the bar in the basement. Hans said that it was a likely place for Sigi and Bruno to show up. He also mentioned an incident during which Bruno had helped him with a flat tire near his construction site in Goesting a few months ago.

"Paradoxical, isn't it?" Werner remarked.

"It seems Sigi dangles Bruno around his fingers," Hans snubbed.

Down in the basement, people drifted about, drinks in hand. Others sat on barstools, chatting, laughing, smoking . Lieschen could neither see Sigi nor Bruno.

Hans ordered the liqueur they had selected - plum brandy for himself and for Werner, and cherry liqueur for Lieschen and Ingrid. A dark-haired bartender in a crimson suit served the drinks on the shiny mouse-gray marble counter while Lieschen noticed another bartender tapping on the facing of one of the three oversized, brownish beer barrels in the back of the bar.

She and her friends had just reached for their drinks when Werner motioned toward the cobbled stairway and grunted, "You name the devil!"

Hans lifted his brandy as if announcing a celebration. He gulped down the hot drink and slammed the empty glass on the counter. Lieschen watched in trepidation as Sigi and Bruno strutting toward them.

Near the bar, Sigi stayed behind while Bruno swaggered on. He gazed at Lieschen cross-eyed as he paraded by.

"Like a donkey on a joy ride." Werner's angry tone rumbled through Lieschen's ears.

"Like a left-footed ass!" Hans gruffed. "And you dare to show up!"

Cuffing and cussing under his breath, Bruno paraded on. He was no longer barefoot. He wore gray leather shoes and socks with the battleship-gray pants and the cobalt blue shirt he had worn earlier at the lake, except he had his shirt tucked into his pants now; and he wore a necktie. At the far end of the counter, he slouched into a barstool. His bulky bottom drooped over the seat of the stool like a huge, melting doughnut. He coiled up in the shape of a retreating snake.

Now Sigi pranced toward Lieschen and her friends.

"We're flattered to see you!" Hans's voice rasped.

Sigi ordered a plum brandy and challenged Hans for a toast.

"My left foot! What prompted you to send that nut with a gun?" Hans demanded.

"What are you talking about? What insulting nonsense!" Sigi looked indignant.

"Scumbag! Bloodsucking scumbag! That's what you're. Why don't we go outside and settle the score," Hans challenged Sigi.

"You're intoxicated." Sigi turned to Lieschen. "I must take you home, that your father will not hold me accountable for having seen you in the wrong company."

Lieschen shuddered.

"If you refuse to go outside, we can settle the score right here." Hans punched Sigi in his chest. He swayed back and ogled Hans like an angry peacock.

One of two men, standing nearby, said, "Bullfight in the making." The other man replied, "No admission."

Sigi steadied himself and advanced. Hans straightened his arm, bent his elbow, and smashed his hand into Sigi's jaw. Lieschen heard a thud, like splintering wood. Sigi straightened up and doubled his punches until both of them ended up rolling and kicking on the cobblestones in front of the bar.

Everybody had moved away from the fighting zone and watched from a safe distance. Lieschen stood next to Werner and Ingrid, squeezing her fingernails into her sweaty palms. Her cheeks burned. When Hans and Sigi scrambled up, Lieschen saw blood curds dripping from Hans's nose. She was astonished at his courage. She had never seen him fight like that.

Sigi's eyes blazed. People gawked, but did not interfere. With his left palm, Hans touched the wrist of his right hand and advanced toward Sigi. He squared his sturdy shoulders, rolled his palm, and gave Sigi a blow to the side of his neck that made him keel over like a tree under an axe. Sigi sprawled on the cobblestones.

"Finally," Ingrid hissed.

Lieschen's stomach knotted. Her cheeks blazed.

Hans waited a moment, then trudged over to Bruno, who gawked at him like a sick clown. "Idiotic ass! An ox has more brains than you do." Hans seemed out of breath.

"Ju-u-u-st followed orders," Bruno stammered.

"Which orders?"

Lieschen could hear the discourse because everybody was silent, as though waiting for a special announcement. Bruno did not reply, but Lieschen knew that he was referring to Sigi's orders.

"Get lost." Hans gave Bruno a heavy punch on his right shoulder. He toppled off the barstool. From the cobbled floor, he gazed up at Hans like a captured rat.

"I'll torch your ass if you'll ever come near us again!" Hans turned and signaled for Lieschen and her friends to leave.

While they tottered up the cobbled stairs, Werner complimented Hans.

"That scumbag was more difficult to knock out than I'd expected." Hans wiped his bleeding nose with his fingers. His breathing was still rough. Ingrid took out a rose-colored handkerchief from her purse and dabbed Hans's bleeding nose. Lieschen also gave Ingrid her avocado-colored linen handkerchief to absorb all the blood that was coming from Hans's nose.

Outside, sirens blasted.

"Someone must have called the police," Werner said.

A Volkswagen with blue, pulsating roof lights squealed to a stop in front of the Rasthauskeller. When the sirens and the blue lights went dead, three police officers bounced out of the Volkswagen and scurried inside.

Lieschen and her friends marched to their cars and drove off.

CHAPTER 22

The morning after the Heimkehrerfest Lieschen attended the board of directors' meeting at their Pharmaceutical Plant. Sigi elaborated on the Xiron formula. While he talked, Lieschen noticed bruises on his face. She was convinced they resulted from the fight with Hans the previous evening; but Sigi made nothing of it, as if he were above such cinches. And her father said nothing either-no reproach, nothing about the entire day. Lieschen still felt sick over the whole incident, nonetheless she was determined to hold up.

"I've strained over the development of Xiron as if it were my own child and, in a sense, it is." Sigi flashed a savvy grin at Lieschen's father.

Always scoring points and taking credit for other people's achievements! Lieschen could not stomach his presumptuous declaration and said, "Excuse me, it is Herr Klug, Herr Probst, and Herr London who are responsible for the development of Xiron." Herr KIug had kept her informed, and she wanted to bring the facts to the attention of company officers who might not have been aware of individual responsibilities and accomplishments.

"You're distorting facts!" Sigi's savvy grin changed into an acid glare, aimed at Lieschen.

"I can prove that *you're* distorting facts," Lieschen asserted with controlled agitation.

Her father intervened. "It was a combined effort, initiated by Dr. Eugen Prinz, who closely cooperated with his son and with Herrn Klug, Herrn Probst, and Herrn London."

Lieschen knew that Herr Probst had passed on; and Ingrid's cousin, Jakob London, had only been involved in the recent development. Her father's deep tone of voice, and his sharp glance indicated that she had overstepped her authority. She wanted to tell the board members that her father always supported Sigi, whether or not it was justified, but she gritted her teeth and refrained.

Herr Briggart, vice president of research and development, said, "As far as I can remember, Herr Prinz Junior hasn't been with our Company when Herr Klug and Herr Probst began developing the Xiron formula."

Sigi flicked poisonous darts at Herrn Briggart, while Lieschen appreciated these comments.

"Let's not talk about petty matters," countered Dietrich Wulst, Sigi's friend.

"It's not appropriate to take credit for other people's achievements," noted Aunt Klara. "And this is not a petty matter."

Vow! For the first time Lieschen had heard Aunt Klara speak in opposition to Sigi, in front of her father and other board members. Her father adjourned the meeting, called Lieschen to his office, and censured her. She defended her position as well as she could. In the end, Lieschen believed this whole incident helped put Sigi down. And it showed that he was not universally liked by the board members, as her father had led her to believe. She had the impression that her father wanted to impose his affection for Sigi upon company officers, just as he wanted to impose this affection upon her.

Shortly after this confrontational encounter, her father left for a business engagement with Herrn Kramer at his brick factory in Weiz. Lieschen decided to take this opportunity to continue her search for the letter from the Courthouse and for other evidence concerning the cause of her mother's death and her grandmother's disappearance. She had to solve these painful enigmas and told Aunt Klara she would take an early lunch.

At home, Frau Emma was mending a dress in the sewing room and Reserl was cleaning the kitchen. Lieschen could not see anybody else around and entered her father's office. She opened the vault and pulled out document after document-grant deeds which she had seen before, certificates, letters, personal invoices and various licenses. She could not find the letter from the Courthouse. What she just spotted, however, was an invoice for seventeen thousand Schilling paid on behalf of her grandmother to Dr. Ludwig Praust in Stainz. What in the world is this? She inspected the invoice closely. This is something substantial! she concluded and made notes. Then she put the invoice, together with all other documents, papers and paraphernalia, back into the vault.

She rushed to the Plant and questioned Aunt Klara, "Do you know Dr. Praust?"

With a startled look her aunt replied, "Yes. How did you find him?"

"I'll tell you later. I want to know if Dr. Praust has been treating Grandma."

"Yes."

"Where is Grandma?"

"In a hospital."

"Why can't I see her?"

"You can."

"When?"

"In due time."

This was no longer satisfactory for Lieschen. "Please let me see Grandma today," she pleaded.

"Let me make arrangements." Aunt Klara's uneasy tone showed Lieschen that she had rattled her aunt's equilibrium.

"Which arrangements?" she asked.

"I'll explain later." Aunt Klara's firm motion with her hands indicated that she wanted the questioning stopped. Later at home her aunt explained that she could not yet make arrangements.

"How long will it take you to make arrangements?" Lieschen questioned.

"You have to be patient." Lieschen remained at odds with Aunt Klara over this vague explanation.

Two days later, on Friday morning, Lieschen joined Mother Marisa and the handicapped children in the School Chapel at St. Germain for her last meeting before her classes at AKA were scheduled to begin the following Monday.

Gretel handed Lieschen a picture made of sawdust, glue and paint, a lovely melange of shapes and forms and color. "This is from all of us," Gretl announced with great excitement. Lieschen thanked Gretl and all the children. Then they said the Lord 's Prayer inside the Chapel. From there, they wandered over to the Schiller Fountain, where they sang the songs which Lieschen had taught the children: Kuckuck Kuckuck ruft aus dem Wald (Cuckoo is calling from the forest); Kommt ein Vogerl geflogen (A little bird comes flying); Fuchs, Du hast die Gans gestohlen (Fox, you stole the goose); and Eia popeia, was raschelt im Stroh (Eia popeia, what's crackling in the straw).

Lieschen thought these songs were quite an achievement for the handicapped children; yet, while she taught them, it seemed a natural process, like birds learning to sing.

At the end of this inspiring engagement, Hansel, Heinz, Waltraud, Marianne, Manfred, Richard, Rudolf, Gretl, Liesel, Anna, and Erich gathered around Lieschen. Heinz stretched out his tongue.

"It's very big, and *it* will grow bigger," Lieschen assured him. By now she better understood the thought process and communication of handicapped children.

"We must say good-bye," Mother Marisa said to the children and, turning to Lieschen, she emphasized, "And you must come back to visit us, especially at Christmas and Easter. You belong here too."

"I will gladly come back. Thank you for the opportunity to work with these special children."

As Mother Marisa had predicted, the children helped Lieschen grow in understanding of life, love, and compassion.

"You're welcome," Mother Marisa said with a warm smile. "We also appreciate your contribution. May God continue to be with you."

CHAPTER 23

Contrary to her expectations, Lieschen enjoyed her studies at AKA. She put serious effort into building her knowledge and confidence for the business world. Her main goal in her father's Company remained to oust Sigi and replace him as general manager. However, this goal had proven to be much more difficult than she had anticipated. Her father's affection for Sigi, and his quest to bring them together seemed unbreakable.

Lieschen had little private time as the autumn days marched on; and she could not paint much at all. Nonetheless, she took time out to look at flowers and the changing autumn leaves in their garden, in their orchard, and everywhere. Colors of leaves changed from green to red and gold, and many shades in between; and soon they began to drop, molt, and die. Flowers collapsed, and the merry sound of birds hushed. Snow laced the roofs, trees, meadows, and fields. A white sealer crusted the whole countryside. Winter had come too soon for Lieschen.

While she continued her studies at AKA, she worked part-time at her father's Pharmaceutical Plant, always trying to ward off Sigi. And she continued her secret investigation concerning her mother's suspicious death. She kept in touch with Frau Dr. Stiglitz. Herr Dr. Tschingelbaum had not yet returned from Palermo. And, as hard as Lieschen tried, Aunt Klara managed to keep her at bay concerning her grandmother.

One Thursday morning, when her aunt brushed her off anew, Lieschen's cup ran over. She decided to violate their family code and call Dr. Praust directly. Frau Irmgard Klee, secretary of Dr. Praust, told her that Dr. Praust would return her call. Lieschen waited and left more messages, but no return call came.

Two weeks later, early Saturday morning, Lieschen ventured on a snow-crusted asphalt road to Stainz; and, with the help of local residents, she found Dr.Praust's Clinic on Andreas Hill. An unassuming, small man in his sixties, wearing a white coat, came out of the office just as Lieschen approached the door. "Dr. Praust?" she quickly asked.

"Yes. How can I help you?"

Lieschen introduced herself and brought up her grievance.

Dr. Praust would not let her finish. "Special instructions from your aunt and from your father are necessary in order for me to release information concerning your grandmother."

"I am a close relative. I am my grandmother's granddaughter," Lieschen protested.

"Young lady, doctors have to observe a professional code and keep patient information confidential. My hands are tied. I'm sure you will understand. And now you will excuse me." Dr. Praust motioned with his hands and walked away.

Understand? Lieschen looked after Dr. Praust and broke into tears. She had tapped into a substantial source, yet she could neither see her grandmother, nor get information.

In her Porsche, she wept bitterly. Her tears would not stop while she drove to Ingrid's home. The moment she arrived and Ingrid, together with Tasso, welcomed her, the tears stopped.

They settled on the comfortable tan couch in the living room along the oblong coffee table. Tasso snuggled up at Lieschen's feet while she told Ingrid about her dilemma. "Dr. Praust requires a release from my father and from my aunt to give me information and to let me see Grandma. My own grandmother! Can you believe that?"

"I can't, really. But why won't your father and your aunt give you such a release?"

"That's also my question. I don't know why."

"What kind of humanity would prevent you from seeing your own grandmother? I mean, you have a legal and a personal right to see your Grandma."

"Legal right, personal right . . ." Lieschen let out a despondent sigh, then said, "I don't know where to turn anymore."

"I wonder if your grandmother really knows what happened to your Mom and, for that reason, you're prevented from seeing her."

"I suspect that must be it. I couldn't think of another reason either."

Ingrid offered Lieschen gooseberry juice and poured it from a crystal glass pitcher into two tall glasses. Lieschen sipped the tarty juice, then asked, "How is Hans?"

Ingrid put her glass of gooseberry juice back on the coffee table. "You wouldn't believe what happened the other day." She took a deep breath and said, "Hans was nearly killed."

"What on earth are you saying? That's no subject for joking!"

"Joking? I still tremble thinking about it. Just picture this . . ." Ingrid threw her hands into the air. "Two days ago, Hans fell from the fourth floor at his construction site in Goesting and got caught in an iron mesh on some cross boards." She dropped her hands. "A few workers told me that Hans would've plunged to his death if he hadn't been caught in that iron mesh between the boards. Just can you imagine?"

Shocked, Lieschen folded her hands in front of her chest.

"I told Hans if he'd been killed, I wouldn't want to live. That's how I feel. But thank Heaven, Hans is okay." Ingrid drank more gooseberry juice, so did Lieschen.

"When will you go on the ski trip to the Teichalm with Werner?" Ingrid asked then.

"After Christmas, in January. That's when I'll have semester break from AKA. And Werner could arrange the timing."

"Your father will be happy, I'm sure."

"He doesn't know yet." Lieschen had never been anywhere with Werner overnight, but she wanted to give herself and Werner a chance for a close relationship, which Ingrid had suggested earlier.

Ingrid invited Lieschen to stay the rest of the day and to have dinner with her parents. Lieschen enjoyed the meal and the socializing with Ingrid and her parents. Tasso also participated, eagerly chewing chicken bones. Lieschen left a little extra meat on her bones for Tasso.

CHAPTER 24

Lieschen loaded the back seat of her Porsche with teddy bears and various stuffed animals, dolls, building blocks, color crayons and pencils which she had bought for the handicapped children. Dressed in festive attire, the children had already gathered in front of the Tannenbaum in the community hall at St. Germain when Lieschen arrived. They watched with sparkling eyes while she spread the gifts under the glittering fir tree, adorned with colorful candles and ornaments.

Father Cassedi came over to talk to Lieschen. "How kind of you to bring gifts for the children," he said. "And it's good to see you."

"Nice to see you too, Father." Lieschen rose from the floor.

"How have you been?" Father Cassedi asked.

"I've been fine, danke," Lieschen replied. Just then she noticed Sister Gertrude signaling with her right hand from across the hall.

"It's time for the children to sing," Father Cassedi told Lieschen. "You will sing with us, won't you?"

"I'm happy to sing along."

Lieschen hummed along while Father Cassedi directed the children. They sang, "Leise rieselt der Schnee" (Quietly the snow falls); "Oh Tannenbaum" (Oh Christmas Tree); "Stille Nacht, Heilige Nacht" (Silent Night, Holy Night); and "Alle Jahre wieder kommt das Christuskind" (Each year the Christ Child returns).

Following this animated choir, St. Nikolaus with a long white beard and a thick curly mustache, dressed in a coral-red suit, handed out nuts, oranges, candies, chocolates, and the presents under the Tannenbaum. Krampus stood guard at the entrance. He held a bitch rod and a heavy chain. He looked like a humanized animal with horns.

While Lieschen joyfully watched Hansel, Heinz, Waltraud, Gretel, Liesel, Manfred, and all the handicapped children open their presents, Mother Marisa came to talk to her. She inquired about AKA, and about Lieschen's part-time work at her father's Plant. Mother Marisa approved what she was doing.

Leaving St. Germain in her Porsche, Lieschen turned on the windshield wipers because it was snowing. She drove slowly and reminisced about the special Christmas gathering with the handicapped children; but she dreaded Christmas at home because her father had invited Sigi and his parents to celebrate with them.

Uncle Gustav and Aunt Sylvia sent her a surprise Christmas package with a lovely gold brooch in the shape of a dainty twig with rubies. Robert sent her a Christmas card and a picture of their baby girl Monika, who was now six months old. Lieschen thought little Monika looked darling on the photo. She resembled Robert, and she had her mother's expressive brown eyes. In the note, Robert explained that little Monika had been born prematurely and was named after her mother.

Although Lieschen's pain over her crushing experience with Robert had subsided, he remained buried in her heart like the sunken Titanic at the bottom of the ocean. She returned Christmas greetings to Robert and Monika, with special wishes for little Monika, and she sent a Christmas card with a thank-you-note to Uncle Gustav and Aunt Sylvia.

After the disappointing experience with Dr. Praust, Lieschen had been bugging Aunt Klara to let her visit her grandmother before Christmas and, finally two days before Christmas Eve, Aunt Klara relented. Together they set off for Andreas Hill in Stainz. Lieschen knew that Dr. Praust had his clinic there, but she did not know that her grandmother was there too.

"You have to be brave when you see Grandma," Aunt Klara warned Lieschen as they neared Andreas Hill.

"Why?„

"You'll understand when you see Grandma."

Lieschen felt endlessly annoyed and frustrated because she still could not understand her aunt's evasive attitude.

At the parking lot behind Dr. Praust's Clinic, Aunt Kiara parked her green Opel Kadett next to a white BMW. Before opening the car door she cautioned once again, "Remember, you wanted to come here!"

Stop your admonition! Lieschen's heart wailed. "Yes!" she responded with an emphatic tone. She could not wait to see her grandmother.

Stepping out of the Opel Kadett, Aunt Klara reached for a package under a sweater on the back seat. "This is a Christmas present for Grandma." She showed Lieschen the nicely wrapped package with a big Christmas bow.

"I didn't bring anything." In her excitement, Lieschen did not think to bring a present.

"Don't worry, this present is from both of us." Aunt Klara locked the car door with one hand and held the gift package and her purse in the other hand.

"Can I help you?" Lieschen offered.

Aunt Klara handed her the package.

"What did you buy?"

"A blue angora sweater and a warm nightgown."

Inside the building, Lieschen nearly fainted when she realized they had entered an asylum for the mentally ill.

"God, no!" Her breathing stopped when she saw her shriveled grandmother sitting in a rocking chair in a far corner of the community hall. Snow-white hair crowned her Grandma's wilted face.

"What happened?"

"I'll tell you later." Aunt Klara put her index to her lips. She took the package from Lieschen and put it among other colorfully wrapped packages under the tall Christmas tree. Ornaments glinted between the green needles of the fragrant Tannenbaum. When Aunt Klara straightened up, she said, "Let's go and see Grandma."

Lieschen proceeded unsteadily next to her aunt.

Grandma wore a simple gray woolen dress with long sleeves. She held out her bony hands, and Lieschen took them eagerly into hers.

Does Grandma not recognize me? Lieschen had anticipated a big hug. While little, her Grandma would always give her big hugs and many kisses. Grandma pulled back her hands and turned to a companion next to her on another rocking chair. "This is my sister," she introduced Lieschen.

She knew her grandmother did not have a sister. Or is Grandma introducing me as her sister? The elderly woman acknowledged Lieschen with a brief glare. Other patients on nearby rocking chairs paid no attention.

"Grandma, I'm not your sister," Lieschen gasped.

"I know." Grandma pressed her bony fingers toward her chest. There were no diamond rings on her fingers now. "Remember when we were young and went skiing on that high hill where we chased each other. Remember?"

"Grandma, I-I-I'm your grandchild!" Lieschen's blood seemed to curdle in her veins.

"And remember when we couldn't get up on that hill fast enough. Remember?" Grandma's excitement grew.

"Grandma!"

Aunt Klara signaled for Lieschen to be quiet.

Baffled beyond herself, Lieschen listened to her grandmother talking about things that only existed in her own world. Suddenly Grandma bent over and slapped her calves with her bony hands. "These black spiders keep crawling up. Up, up, up . . ." She continued to slap her calves.

Lieschen could not see any black spiders, but she remembered the big black spider with the red cross which had crawled on the wall behind her mother while they had dinner on that fatal evening. Is Grandma gobbling up her memory about that horrible night?

Aunt Klara whispered, "Time to leave. If we stay too long, we might upset Grandma too much."

Hot tears stung Lieschen's eyes as she gently said good-bye to her grandmother, who looked like a confused soul in a shell of worn and withered bones and skin.

Walking toward the exit, Lieschen's feet dug into the wooden tiles. The heaviness of her heart seemed to ooze down through her feet.

On the wall by the exit hung a small, framed landscape, with happy birds floating through the air. A verse in calligraphy adorned the lower part of the small landscape. Lieschen started reading the verse:

There're no crazies in a nuthouse,
Only lost souls.

Therefore think twice,
and look in the mirror.

Chilled and bewildered, she turned to her aunt. "Did you read this?"

"Not yet, but I will." Aunt Klara retrieved her glasses from her purse and also read the verse. Then, looking at Lieschen with an uncertain expression she said, "Perhaps there is no such thing as insanity. Perhaps the people here have a health condition that can be cured. That's what I had hoped for your grandmother."

This only confused Lieschen more. Why is life so unreliable? So sad? She felt like howling, howling like a hungry wolf in a steppe.

"We have to trust in God. God is good, and God is Love. And God knows why things happen. We don't have to know." Aunt Klara took a deep breath.

Lieschen thought she had to know, and back in the Opel Kadett, she asked her aunt for an explanation.

"After your mother's funeral, Grandma lost her capacity to reason. Remember when Grandma fainted at your mother's funeral?" Lieschen remembered very well and nodded sadly.

"That's when it happened."

"But why?"

"I believe Grandma couldn't bear losing your mother, which caused her to have a stroke. And consequently she also lost her capacity to reason." Aunt Klara inserted the key in the ignition. "Now you can understand why I never took you to see Grandma. I hoped that she would regain her mental health. And your father didn't want you to visit Grandma in her dilapidated condition in this asylum."

"How unfair!"

"I'm not certain that it was unfair. It would've been better for you to see Grandma in good health, especially when you were little. But don't worry now."

"Why?"

"Because Grandma's mind has shut out all worries. She lives in her own world. And she is well cared for." Aunt Klara maneuvered her Opel Kadett out of the parking space. The BMW that was parked in the adjacent space had left in the meantime. A silver Audi had taken its place.

"Life has taken a turn. Life takes many turns." Aunt Kl.ara shifted into second gear and drove down Andreas Hill. "It's nonetheless very sad," she said.

"Very, very sad!" Lieschen echoed. Only one odd thing happened. This whole event strengthened her trust in Aunt Klara because she could see that her aunt had told her the truth. She looked through the rear window, back at the asylum, and whispered, "God, why? Why all this?"

Aunt Klara drove slowly on the snow-crusted road. "I would like to tell you something," she said.

Lieschen turned toward her aunt.

"I'm sorry if I hurt your feelings in the past." Aunt Klara swallowed hard. "Sometimes, the load I had to carry seemed too heavy."

"Is that why you were so cruel to me during the night when Mommy died?"

"I never wanted to hurt you, I want you to know that."

Strangely, Lieschen believed Aunt Klara now. "I'm also sorry if I hurt you," she said.

"You don't have to feel sorry. You had every right to be angry and hurt. But I knew God would bring us together. I've been praying for this." Aunt Klara paused. "You see, there is a road you and I must travel together on this earth. And our road turned out to be steep."

"Is this what you meant by destiny?"

Aunt Klara nodded. Warmth seemed shrouded behind her aunt's stern veneer but, in questioning her aunt further, Lieschen had the distinct feeling that she was still hiding something.

In Mariatrost, Lieschen spotted Ingrid sitting on a bench at the Hilmteich entrance, putting on her white ice-boots. Lieschen knew Ingrid enjoyed skating at this community lake. She could also see children and grown-ups in colorful outfits gliding, dancing, and circling about on the glassy ice. "Would you toot the horn?" she asked Aunt Klara. She wanted to catch Ingrid's attention and wave to her.

The moment her aunt tooted the horn, Ingrid looked up. They waved at each other. Lieschen intended to call Ingrid later and tell her the sad news about her poor Grandma.

In a short while, Aunt Klara veered into the circular driveway in front of their villa.

CHAPTER 25

Christmas Day, early in the afternoon, Sigi arrived with his parents, Dr. Eugene and Frau Iris Prinz. They were the only guests invited for Christmas at the Reinking Villa. Lieschen's father assigned Sigi to sit next to her, and his parents on the opposite side of the lusciously decorated dinner table in the formal dining room. The soft gleam of silver cutlery and silver candle holders with burning red candles adorned the red damask table cloth. Auergarten plates and glimmering wine and champagne glasses completed the festive setting. Although Lieschen felt wild ants crawling under her skin, she would cooperate for a little while. She had to cooperate to accomplish her goal.

Frau Emma and Reserl, dressed in lively red and green Christmas attire, served a variety of deviled eggs, garnished Salami and cheeses, small butter balls, tiny herrings, caviar, pate', and other hors d'oevres, followed by two main courses of Veal Cotelettes and Sauerbraten with appetizing vegetables and salads. Lieschen ate very little.

Frau Emma poured Herzog Champagne and served dessert of Sachertorte, Chocolate-Mooncake, and Eggwhite Fluffies. Her father lifted his glass of Herzog Champagne and announced Lieschen's engagement to Sigi. Although Lieschen knew it was coming, she quivered. She looked at her glass of champagne and whispered, "Without me!" She could never understand how her father could make such an outlandish announcement after all of her objections. Pap must know that I could never accept Sigi as my husband. Or could his illness affect his judgement so badly? In any case, she had formulated her own plan.

Her father toasted Sigi's father, then everyone else. Lieschen clinked glasses with her father and with Sigi's parents, who had been talking to her in a kind manner. Lieschen felt sorry for them for having such a detestable son. Sigi smiled enticingly at Lieschen as he held his glass toward her. Instead of clinking glasses with him, she looked inside her own glass and said, "Today, I don't drink champagne." She put down her glass.

Her real response came after Christmas when she spent New Year's Eve with her friends Werner and Hans and Ingrid, and with Ingrid's relatives Berthold and Erika Strom, at their pinewood chalet on the Praeding Alm. They danced, chatted, laughed, and ate delectable food. At midnight, Werner popped a bottle of Moister Champagne. This time Lieschen toasted happily with Werner and with everyone, and she drank a little champagne. Her unwavering New Year's resolution remained to fight Sigi tooth and nail while trying to maintain a good relationship with her ill father. And she finalized the ski trip with Werner to the Teichalm.

During the first week in January, on the evening before the ski trip, Lieschen took her skis over to Werner's home. When she came back, she joined her father and Aunt Klara around the coffee table in the living room. They had a pleasant conversation about the day's events until Lieschen's father piloted their talks toward her engagement to Sigi. "You must see my health is deteriorating. I have to make sure that you and our Company are well taken care of before I die. You have to marry Sigi promptly," he said. His tone emphasized urgency.

Lieschen felt sorry for her father's afflicted heart, but that was no reason for her to marry Sigi. She would never marry Sigi. She could never marry Sigi. She folded her hands on her lap and said, "Pap, no such marriage is ever going to take place."

Her father looked incredulous, without speaking a word now. Lieschen turned and gazed through the window at the intensifying dusk, wondering how to tell her father about her ski trip with Werner. She could not leave on this trip without telling her father.

"What did you say?" he questioned after a prolonged silence, as if he had to digest Lieschen's objection.

She replied, "Pap, I don't want to cause you disappointment and heartache, but I could never marry Sigi." She announced, "Tomorrow, I'm leaving on a ski trip to the Teichalm with Werner."

Her father's hands shot into the air. "This is out of the question! Think of the public image!"

"The fake mirror. How sad!" Lieschen longed for a harmonious relationship with her father, but his attitude undermined her efforts.

Her father lowered his hands. His eyes glowed. He turned to Aunt Klara, who remained silent.

"Pap, I've been trying to curb my emotions about Sigi, but I can no longer handle it. Lieschen paused, then asked, "What would you do if somebody put a cup of poison in front of you? Would you drink it?"

Her father's eyes popped as he uttered, "You make no sense!"

"Sigi is a cup of poison for me," Lieschen clarified.

"Stop this idiocy!"

"Pap, to me Sigi is a treacherous monster. He has no conscience. He must have fallen from God's grace a long time ago. His moral conduct stinks, and I don't want to have anything to do with him, let alone be engaged or married to him." She could not stop her verbal assault. Her emotions got the better of her. In an odd way, her temperament, as well as her secretive disposition, emulated her father's. She could not help herself and continued, "Sigi is a devil in sheep's clothing. He flatters and deceives, and you cannot recognize his fake character. And you want me ..."

Her father rose and stepped behind his chair. He clasped the backrest with both hands. Behind him was a mahogany cabinet, filled with her mother's beautiful collectibles of silver- and gold artifacts, antiques, exclusive porcelain, figurines, and vases. Two mahogany-framed glass doors protected the precious collectibles. The cabinet had been removed from the wall because the back panel needed repair; however, the repairman had called to reschedule. That's why the cabinet was still removed from the wall.

When her father resumed speaking, his voice sounded deep and harsh. "1 will not have you talk in such a derogatory manner about a respectable gentleman like Sigi!"

Lieschen remained seated. "It is such a pity that you cannot recognize Sigi's malignant character. If he has any good sides, I don't know of any. And they could never outweigh his malignant side." A woeful sigh made her pause. Then she continued, "Pap, Sigi has cast a dark spell over you, and he will destroy our relationship. Everything. I love you, and I want to be good to you, but you keep pushing Sigi into my life when you know I can't stand him."

"Sigi cares deeply about you. Can't you see? You need him! And his character is impeccable. Open your eyes!"

"I've opened my eyes. If being ruthless, deceitful, and manipulative are attributes of an impeccable character, then perhaps you can justify ..." Lieschen suddenly panicked because her father's face began twisting. He put his right hand on his heart as if in pain.

"Pap, please, 1 could never love Sigi," she said softly to reduce the agitation.

Aunt Klara coughed. She observed them as though she found the whole situation hopeless.

Her father remained standing behind the chair, his hands on the backrest. "When will you come to your senses?" With his linen handkerchief he dabbed his sweaty forehead. "I have shown patience, but one day my patience will run out. So will my health."

"I'm deeply sorry about your health. As to my senses-I've always been in touch with my senses. I've never liked Sigi, and I never will. And considering **his** evil deeds and the heartache he has caused both of us, and..."

"You're totally mistaken about Sigi's fine character," her father interrupted. "Can't you see the deep meaning? You're destined to marry Sigi."

Lieschen gasped, "Why?"

"Because Sigi is the only qualified man to be my son in law. He comes from our bloodline. You'll have pure children, and Sigi will take great care of you and the children. And he is well positioned to manage the vast responsibilities of our Company. You have no choice but to marry Sigi."

"Pap, why can't you let me make that judgement?"

"Because you're naive. I know what's best for you, and for our business."

Lieschen thought she'd go mad. Her desperation nearly suffocated her breathing.

"You and Sigi are the perfect match," her father emphasized. "Going on a ski trip with Werner defeats this purpose. I will not allow you to go on such a trip."

"Pap, why do you disregard my feelings as if I were made of clay?"

"What you just said has no merit. I know what is best for you and for our business, and you have to accept my judgement. I will not relent."

"I will never marry Sigi. I'd prefer you put me in front of a firing squad." Lieschen felt as though all of her emotions were draining.

"What did you say?" Big pearls of sweat covered her father's forehead.

"I should marry a man who attempted to rape me! And who wanted to see me drowned!"

"What nonsense are you talking about? Sigi told me of some incident in the car, when he wanted to put his arm around you." With his handkerchief her father dabbed the heavy sweat on his forehead. "My dear Lieschen, you're so naive, so inexperienced in manly matters. Sigi would never do anything to hurt you. He swore to me that he loves you. And he will always protect you and take utmost care of you."

Utmost care of raping me! And seeing me drowned! Lieschen's breathing came in spurts. Her stomach shriveled. She felt helpless in light of her father's affection for Sigi. And now she also knew that he had lied to her father about his attempted rape. And he had not even mentioned the incident at the Mariatroster Lake. But what else could I've expected? Since she had no way of proving anything, she only said, "Pap, can you accept that I don't love Sigi, and that I have my own feelings, my own heart, and my own soul. You cannot take that away from me."

"One day you will see that I made the best choice for you. For your happiness."

"Neither my heart nor my feelings can be chiseled like a piece of wood or marble. I could never love Sigi. For me love comes before anything else. If my heart is in the wrong place, all the money and power are meaningless. With Sigi my heart would be poisoned and dead. Then nothing else would matter. Without love, golden horses and golden bicycles are meaningless."

Her father looked deep into Lieschen's eyes and warned, "Do you know what I can do?"

"What?"

"I can disinherit you."

Lieschen never thought her father would say or do such a thing in favor of Sigi. She became very calm. She could always become a nun, she thought and replied, "Go right ahead."

Her father let go of the backrest and stumbled against the cabinet behind him, hitting it so forcefully that it came crashing down. The mahogany-enclosed glass doors and all the beautiful collectibles shattered. Broken glass and shards and splinters scattered on the parquet floor and on part of the Persian carpeting.

Lieschen worried that her father had become faint; but when he stormed out and slammed the door shut, she knew that it had not been faintness which had caused him to stumble into the cabinet. She and Aunt Klara rose and stared at each other and the upside-down cabinet and all the shattered mess.

"I hope this is not symbolic of what's going to follow." Aunt Klara had a peculiar expression on her face.

"I don't know if I care anymore." Lieschen's eyes burned.

Frau Emma came running in. Folding her hands on her chest, she exclaimed, "Dear God, Frau Reinking's collectibles all broken!"

"Destruction can happen fast." Aunt Klara's peculiar expression did not change.

Lieschen felt as if her heart were part of these shattered pieces. She looked at Aunt Klara as if she were supposed to have an explanation, but her aunt had no explanation.

Frau Emma said, "I'll clean up everything."

"Call Reserl to help you," Aunt Klara said.

"Okay." Frau Emma turned and left.

Aunt Klara said to Lieschen, "I was afraid it might come to a confrontation about Sigi."

"Why?"

"Because your father liked him too much. This is why I wanted you to move away from home and build your own life."

"Because of Sigi?"

"Primarily."

"Why didn't you tell me? You never even mentioned Sigi."

"I couldn't because you would've told your father. He warned that I had no right to interfere with his decisions. And you wouldn't have believed me anyway."

Lieschen believed Aunt Klara now and wondered why things had to happen that way.

"As you know, your father promoted Sigi because he's the son of his long-time friend, Dr. Eugen Prinz from our aristocracy. And your father believed that Sigi is the only qualified person to be your husband and carry on the pharmaceutical business together with you." Aunt Klara paused. "Here you have it in a nutshell."

"I don't want it in a nutshell. I don't want Sigi in any way, shape, or form."

"By now I've gathered as much. But your father had already adopted Sigi as his son in law and successor to his business." Aunt Klara paused, then added, "Your father believes that you have to merge our bloodline with business and love."

"What do you think?"

"I think you should've recognized that I wanted to protect you. Sometimes a sacrifice is necessary for one's happiness and welfare. If you had moved away from home, you could've prevented such clashes." With her hands, Aunt Klara indicated the shattered pieces.

"Could I've really prevented this?" Lieschen gazed once more at the shattered mess, then staggered up to her apartment and collapsed on her bed. After a wrenching while, she drifted off to sleep. The sky lined with ominous clouds and streaks. Lieschen lurched into a deep trough of a giant wave, with sharks closing in around her. "Help!" she screamed. A black hole appeared on the streaky sky. A huge black spider with a red cross crawled out of the hole. Blood-covered deer began falling like hail during a tempest. Voluptuous ghosts with fiery eyes flocked toward her. A huge shark was about to drive his sharp teeth into her legs when she leaped out of the treacherous water and found herself on the Mariatroster Hill. On her gold bicycle, she careened down. Her father and Sigi followed, trying to catch her. An image of her mother appeared through the streaky clouds, as if her mother had heard her cries from the far universe. Lieschen clung to her mother's image and awoke from this nightmare, shivering violently.

She switched on the light. The clock on her nightstand showed two minutes past midnight. She took three Aspirin to calm down and go back to sleep.

The timer chimed at four in the morning. Lieschen turned it off. She had calmed down from her nightmare and hoped that it was not a bad omen for her ski trip with Werner. She took a quick shower and slipped on a marine-blue ski jumpsuit with a cuddly mustard-yellow pullover.

Downstairs, she tiptoed into the living room. All the shattered glass, shards, and collectibles had been cleaned up. What a pity to lose all of my mother's beautiful collectibles! Lieschen swallowed hard. Then she wrote a note for her father that she was leaving on the planned ski trip with Werner to the Teichalm. She asked her father again for his understanding to let her have freedom and make her own decisions. She left the note on the table in the breakfast nook, next to her father's Auergarten plate.

When she arrived at Werner's home, he had their skis already fastened on the ski rack of his Jeep. He had insisted on driving to the Teichalm in his old black Jeep. "It's better than your Porsche for driving on icy mountain roads," he had told Lieschen. She had not objected. She also knew that Werner had a special fondness for his Jeep because it was a present from his grandparents. He had always been close to his grandparents. As a child, he had stayed at their farm for almost a year when he had rheumatic fever, when he would have been in fourth grade. Lieschen had missed him during that year.

Gretl, Werner's petite blonde sister of twenty-two, wished them a nice trip and waved as long as she could see them. Lieschen had been good friends with Gretl, although they did not see each other very often. Werner's six brothers were still asleep.

North of Graz, snowy hills, and sleepy houses along the River Mur skirted the icy asphalt road; but soon the world began awakening with cars coming from the opposite direction, carrying people to work to shops, schools, professional offices, hospitals, breweries, factories, and other cultural, commercial, and industrial centers in Graz.

A short distance farther north, they passed the Erzberg, Austria's rich iron-ore mountain. A thousand snowy crystals glistened on the Erzberg, reflecting the rising sun. Pap is probably up by now, Lieschen thought and wondered how he would react to her note and to her trip with Werner.

In Lanegg, a mountainous village, they stopped for an early lunch at a country inn restaurant called Schoener Hirsch. Across from the Schoener Hirsch was a quaint white church with a tall steeple. The rustic restaurant bustled with people. Lieschen and Werner found a table by a window and enjoyed a hearty lunch of Bratwurst, Sauerkraut, and onion potatoes; and both drank hot cider.

Leaving the restaurant, Werner pointed at a nearby hill. "Look!" he said.

"Look where?" Lieschen did not see anything unusual; but she was suddenly afraid that Sigi's friend Bruno, or someone else might have followed them.

"Up there, by the treeline."

Lieschen looked but could not see anything out of the ordinary. "See what?" she asked.

"A deer, near the small Tannenbaum." With his gloved hand, Werner kept pointing at the treeline.

"Oh, how lovely!" Lieschen smiled when she spotted the deer. She told Werner of her concern.

"Let's not test our luck." Werner raised his eyebrows.

"Okay," Lieschen agreed, then said, "I'd like to feed the deer."

"We don't have seeds, or anything ..."

"I'll go and ask the cook in the restaurant for a little food."

Lieschen received a whole cup full of wheat from a young cook. "We feed the deer all the time," the friendly cook told her.

Holding the cup of wheat in her hands, Lieschen waded through the deep snow up the hill. Werner did not go with her. He stayed by the moss-green doors of the Schoener Hirsch and watched her.

The deer ate the wheat right out of Lieschen's hands. Overjoyed, she could even stroke the deer's forehead.

"Satisfied?" Werner smiled when she came back.

"The deer has such cute eyes. I would've liked to take pictures, but I forgot my camera."

"Darn, so did I. We have to keep mental pictures, I guess."

Lieschen agreed regretfully. She went back inside the restaurant and returned the cup to the friendly cook.

After a challenging climb on an icy dirt-road, Lieschen was glad to see curling smoke coming out of the chimney above the pitched, snow-covered roof of the Tyrolian-style Alpenhaus on the Teichalm, for which they had a reservation for two adjoining rooms.

"Look at these icicles! Like sculpted cones." Lieschen indicated the roofline.

"They look cold, don't they," Werner smiled.

"Very cold." Lieschen also saw colorful skiers catapulting across the slope on the east side of the Alpenhaus. A little girl in a red ski jacket just tumbled into the snow, but was back on her skis in no time.

"If you fall, I'll help you up," promised Werner. From his contagious smile, Lieschen could tell he was happy. "Danke," she smiled back. She thought she might need help because Werner was more experienced in skiing.

Inside the Alpenhaus, opposite the pinewood reception counter in the rustic reception room, orange-red flames spewed from the logs of a brick hearth. Two female skiers, seated on one of the two couches in front of the hearth, reached for their drinks on the elongated coffee table between the couches.

A slightly overweight alpine hostess, dressed in a woolen Prussian-blue Tyrolian costume with large gold-leaf buttons, welcomed them. "Schoenen guten Tag. Ich bin Sennerin Mathilde." She blinked cheerfully with her big olive eyes. Thick auburn braids formed a crown above her low forehead.

Sennerin Mathilde requested Werner's driver's license and made entries in a log book at the reception counter. "You will stay with us for one week, right?"

Werner glanced at Lieschen, then confirmed, "Yes."

Handing back the driver's license, Sennerin Mathilde asked, "Do you need help with your luggage?"

"I guess we would," Werner nodded and put his license back into his wallet.

Sennerin Mathilde called Alexander, a young porter and instructed him to bring the luggage to Room 24.

Turning back to Werner and Lieschen, Sennerin Mathilde explained the system of the lockers in the ski rooms; and she explained the layout of the underground parking. Then she reached for a set of keys on the pinewood wall behind the counter and led them upstairs on the small stairway alongside a pinewood railing.

"All rooms are the same size. Only the decorations *vary,*" Sennerin Mathilde explained as she opened the door to Room 24.

Tucked under the roof with a slanted ceiling, the room looked cozy, rustic and simple with one twin bed against a wall, a pine closet along the other wall, and a pine table with two chairs by the window. The pine furniture blended with the friendly pink Almenrausch design of the tablecloth, wallpaper, curtains, drapes, and bedcover. An alizarin rug ran along the pinewood floor. Lieschen could smell the pinewood which seemed to be one of the main features of the entire Alpenhaus.

She looked out through the small window behind the table and remarked, "The sky seems close here."

"We're close to heaven. That's why," Sennerin Mathilde gave a serious nod.

"So you're angels up here?" Werner wrinkled his nose.

"Haven't you heard, there're no sins in the Alps?"

"Would you bet on it?"

"Certainly." Sennerin Mathilde winked at Lieschen with one eye. Then she opened the door to the adjoining room.

Lieschen peeked in. The room looked identical, except the design was deep-blue Enzian instead of pink Almenrausch; and the rug had a Prussian- and Cobalt-blue pattern. Lieschen remembered when she had gathered Enzian and Almenrausch on the nearby Gaberl Mountain. Many cows had grazed on that Alm during the summer when she had visited. She had enjoyed the cows and the clinking of bells. One speckled cow had even licked her hand.

"If you need anything, let me know." Sennerin Mathilde took leave.

"She probably prefers being a hostess to working on a dairy farm," Werner said.

"Probably." Lieschen knew that a Sennerin's primary duty entailed working with dairy products, making cheese and other milk products.

Alexander brought their luggage, and Werner slipped him a tip.

While they unpacked, Werner called from his room. "I've space left in my drawers if you can't fit in all your clothes?"

"I could fit in everything. Danke, Werner," Lieschen called back and put away the last sweater from her suitcase, an ecru Cashmere sweater. Then they scurried to the basement and gathered their skis. They wanted to get a few runs in before the lift closed.

Their boots squeaked through the snow as they plowed to the open air lift, which lugged them to the peak. On the slopes, as they picked up speed, Lieschen's poles began dancing in the air. After a brief struggle, she managed to regain her balance without crashing into the snow. They could get in quite a few runs before the lift closed. Lieschen only crashed once into the white powder. She could not measure up to Werner's expertise, but she enjoyed skiing.

Back in the Alpenhaus, by the hearth, they pulled off their gloves and stretched their cold hands over the spewing, orange-red flames. Lieschen felt a tingling sensation in her fingertips and toes.

"Feels good, doesn't it?" Werner held his hands close to Lieschen's.

"My feet are colder than my hands." Lieschen looked down at her feet.

"Snow probably got into your boots."

"I'm going to take them off as soon as we've eaten." Lieschen wiggled her toes and asked Werner, "You aren't cold?"

"I don't feel snow in my boots," he smiled.

More and more people gathered around the brick hearth. A middle-aged man with a Zither, an antique cithara, began playing traditional folk songs. People, including Werner and Lieschen, joined in the merry choir. The crackling pine added a romantic touch.

In a little while, Werner and Lieschen went to the alpine restaurant on the east wing of the Alpenhaus to have dinner. They settled on a table for four. It was the only table which was not occupied. While waiting for their food, they looked at winterscapes on the pine-wall behind them. Iron chandeliers from the tall ceiling accented the colors of the winterscapes.

"It seems the same artist painted all of them," Werner observed.

"It seems, doesn't it."

"Quite pristine."

Lieschen nodded.

A young, slender Sennerin with short chestnut braids served a hot beef broth with liver dumplings. For their second course they had chosen a spicy Veal Goulasch with home-made Bemberg noodles. And they had Lebkuchen and a glass of wine cider for dessert. When Lieschen tasted the hot cider, she took a deep breath and said, "Quite spicy."

"If you don't like it, we can ask for hot chocolate," Werner suggested.

"The cider is fine." Lieschen drank the whole glassful and no longer noticed the tingling sensation in her cold fingertips and toes.

After their appetizing dinner, they jaunted back to the hearth and rejoined the merry group, which included boys and girls. The man with the Zither had left, but one boy with thick golden locks, about five years old, sang with a clear voice that captured Lieschen's senses. She adored the voice of this little boy. "He should be in the Vienna Boys Choir," she whispered into Werner's ear.

"Perhaps he is," Werner whispered back.

More people joined the gathering, singing and humming. Some voices sounded tipsy and muffled the little boy's voice.

"Too much cider," Werner remarked.

Lieschen eyes also began drooping. "I'm getting tired too," she said.

"Why don't we have a good night's rest, and hit the slopes early in the morning." Werner gently touched Lieschen's hand. She did not pull away.

Back in their rooms, Lieschen closed the drapes in front of the curtains. As she turned away from the window, Werner stepped close to her. Looking longingly into her eyes, he murmured, "May I kiss you?"

Lieschen blushed and felt awfully awkward. She did not know what to say or do.

With one hand, Werner gently tipped up Lieschen's chin. His eyes searched for her response. She did not fight him. She was willing to give him her virginity if he was ready to take it that night.

Werner kissed her passionately. When he lifted his lips, he swallowed hard and said, "You don't love me ..."

"I do love you, Werner, but not this way. You know you are like a brother to me." She wanted to give their relationship a chance for intimacy but, as she just found out, she could not conjure up intimate emotions or feign passion which did not exist. She wished she could love Werner as she loved Robert.

"Sleep well," Werner said with a disheartened tone, turned and went into his room.

"Sleep well, Werner." Lieschen wanted to call him back, but hesitated.

Werner closed the door.

CHAPTER 26

In the morning, Werner did not hold a grudge against Lieschen. He remained the same kind, considerate friend he had always been. He only looked a little sad.

After a savory breakfast of homemade raspberry omelettes, and hot chocolate for Lieschen and coffee for Werner, they headed for the lift. A thirty-meter long line of skiers in bright ski suits had already formed. Werner and Lieschen joined the line.

An elderly man of medium stature in front of them turned back and said hi. He wore a cream-colored ski jacket with a red scarf and a red ski cap. His cracked lips on his weathered face were partly hidden between a white cuddly beard and a full white mustache. To Lieschen, his face almost resembled that of a Santa Klaus. "Where are you from?" he asked Werner in his husky voice.

"Graz, Styria."

"Good to know you neighbor. I'm Dr. Moor. I had my practice in Klagenfurt."

"In Carinthia?"

"Yes."

Lieschen knew that the neighboring provinces of Styria and Carinthia shared a long borderline.

"When my Irma left this earth to live in eternity, I took to the mountains and became a spiritual physician," Dr. Moor disclosed. "Now I'm ninety-two, and I'm still a spiritual physician."

Lieschen wondered what the occupation of a spiritual physician entailed. She had never heard of such a profession. Because of a rumble in the sky, she looked up. Heavy dark clouds swirled about.

"That's where I'll be sailing one day, above thick clouds, joining my Irma." Dr. Moor's smile added wrinkles to his coarse, pleasant face.

"How do you know?" Lieschen asked.

"Right in here you know." Dr. Moor patted his chest. "Our lifeline with the eternal Spirit is in our heart. Our soul lives in our heart, together with the Holy Spirit. That's how God made us with body, mind, and soul. And God loves each and everyone of us."

"Can you tell us more?" Werner inquired.

"Well, what else would you like to know?"

"Everything about God and eternity."

"Everything is asking too much. Only God knows everything, and he ain't telling. At least not while we're earthbound."

"What can you tell us then?" Lieschen asked.

"I can tell you that God is our big Spirit, and we're His branches. We're all citizens of our earth, and of our universe and eternity. And mind you, when you seek and obey God, you will be safe on this side and on the other side of eternity."

"How do we obey God?" Lieschen asked.

"We have to have faith and live upright in God's ways. It means you have to be good and just, and obey God's commandments through Jesus Christ, our Lord."

"I guess, we better watch out," Werner said.

Their conversation ended because it was Dr. Moor's turn to get on the lift. "And always count your blessings," Dr. Moor called back as he boarded a chair next to a young man and ascended the white hill. Werner and Lieschen followed in the next chairs.

They enjoyed skiing until mid-afternoon, when clouds thickened and the wind increased. Large snowflakes began dancing in the air like little puffs of cotton. Werner and Lieschen were about to board chairs for their next run when the lift closed.

"Why couldn't we go back up at least one more time? It would be fun to ski when it's snowing." Disappointed, Lieschen stuck the rear part of her skis into the snow.

"They have to take precaution. They'd be responsible if something went wrong?" Werner swung his skis over his shoulders and waited for Lieschen to do the same.

Reluctantly she hoisted her skis over her shoulders, and they sloshed through the packed white crystals toward the Alpenhaus. When Lieschen heard another heavy rumble in the sky, she said, "In winter, there shouldn't be thunder." She looked at Werner in strange wonderment.

"It's unusual, but it can happen."

Inside the Alpenhaus, by the hearth, Werner slipped off his orange gloves and ski cap and asked Lieschen, "Did snow get into your boots again?"

"Not this time."

"Good." With his fingers, Werner rubbed his gloves over the spewing fire. Icy crystals fizzled in the hot flames. Then he touched his growling stomach. "I don't know about you, but my stomach's telling me something."

"1 wouldn't mind a five-course meal either," Lieschen jested.

"I'll join you for four." Both laughed.

They were still stretching their cold hands over the bright, spewing flames when Sennerin Mathilde waved from the reception counter. She is really friendly, thought Lieschen, and waved back.

Sennerin Mathilde continued to motion with her hands.

"What does she mean?"

Werner shrugged. "Why don't we find out."

Lieschen stepped over.

"There's a message for you." Sennerin Mathilde reached for a notebook and turned back one page. "Your Aunt Klara wants you to call urgently."

"Where can I call?"

"Right here." Sennerin Mathilde shifted the phone toward Lieschen.

"Danke." While she dialed, she worried.

"I've been trying to reach you all afternoon," Aunt Klara said the moment they connected. "You have to come home immediately. Your father had a heart attack."

"Where is Pap?" Guilt assailed Lieschen because she had left on this trip with Werner against her father's will. She was afraid it might have caused his heart attack.

"In the Landeskrankenhaus," Aunt Klara replied.

Lieschen knew the hospital. The Landeskrankenhaus was the largest hospital in Graz. "I'll come as quickly as I can." She dashed over to the hearth and told Werner.

He agreed to leave right away and informed Sennerin Mathilde. Then they scurried to their rooms.

Lieschen gaped through the window. "What about this storm?" she asked Werner.

"Let's hope we can get to the valley before the storm hits hard. We don't have much choice, do we?"

"I don't think so." Lieschen scooped up her clothes and belongings from the closet and drawers and tossed everything into her suitcase, while Werner cleared out his room.

When Lieschen heard another rumble in the sky, she opened the window and looked out. The curtains flew up, and icy-cold air rushed in. A piece of paper blew off the table. She stretched her head through the window and could see thick dark clouds racing like fairy-tale monsters. "Werner, look at this!"

He joined her to look through the window. "There's nothing to be afraid of," he said with a soothing tone.

Somewhere downstairs a door banged, as if a poltergeist had slammed it. Lieschen could hear people's excited voices while they hurried down the narrow stairway. Sennerin Mathilde instructed them to sign a warning not to drive in these dangerous conditions. "It's a legal requirement," she explained.

Werner signed and handed the form and pen to Lieschen.

"Bureaucracy and red tape!" Lieschen signed grudgingly and returned the form and pen to Sennerin Mathilde.

"Legal guidelines aside, I believe you'll put yourselves into serious danger if you drive in this storm." Sennerin Mathilde sounded anxious.

"We have no choice." Lieschen dug her fingernails into her cramped palms.

Dr. Moor was there too. "This storm is a monster. I wouldn't be caught out in the open," he said.

"But my father had a heart attack. We have to leave." Lieschen felt overwhelmed. Her father might die, and she had not even said good-bye to him before going on this trip. "Dear God, please don't let Pap die," she prayed silently.

Dr. Moor's eyes rested upon her. "If you drive in this storm, you might not reach your destination."

"It's not good to be by yourself on such a deserted road in a storm like this. It's too dangerous." Sennerin Mathilde alerted once more.

"It's foolish to leave now," someone else said.

Lieschen did not appreciate these remarks. "This is an emergency." She looked pleadingly at Werner.

"If you want to go, we leave right now. I'm ready," Werner said.

"We have to go." Lieschen's heart thumped.

Alexander fetched Werner's Jeep from the underground garage and helped with their luggage. Then he strapped their skis on the ski rack. While Werner double-checked the straps, Lieschen looked at the swirling dark clouds.

"These clouds can put on a dramatic display, can't they?" Werner said over the rooftop.

"It's like a theatrical play," Alexander smiled.

Lieschen's eyes followed the sinister ripples until a heavy blast gushed into her face.

"Let's go." Werner slipped Alexander a tip, and they bounced into their seats. With her fingers, Lieschen cleared her eyes and saw Alexander waving as they drove off. The wind whistled through the closed windows like hissing waves. Dusk fell swiftly.

A short distance down that icy dirt-road, Lieschen gripped the dashboard because the Jeep slid all the way to the edge of that steep cliff. A gust nearly toppled them over. With a tight grip Werner held the steering wheel, but the Jeep skidded on.

Lieschen gazed at the headlights cutting across the drenched mash of ice and snowflakes. Her vision became more and more obstructed because the windshield wipers could no longer remove all the heavy snowflakes.

In the next turn, the wheels swerved. Werner withdrew his right foot from the gas pedal and barely touched the brakes, but the jeep kept sliding and skidding until the engine stopped. Werner attempted to restart the motor. It sputtered, then went dead again.

Lieschen clenched her fists while Werner tried to restart the motor over and over. It just sputtered and choked and went dead. "I'm afraid the engine's stalled." He looked at Lieschen with remorseful eyes as though it had been his fault that the motor gave up.

"We have to reach the hospital!" Lieschen's fingernails dug into the skin of her palms. She was not wearing gloves.

"I wish we could." Werner cast a helpless glance at her while the wind howled and whined over the rooftop like a forlorn ghost that had lost direction.

"We can't stay here?" Lieschen gasped.

"I'm afraid this time it's beyond our control."

Werner pulled a linen handkerchief from the pocket of his ski pants and wiped his hands.

"Do you mean we have to wait till we're snowed in?"

"I don't see what else we can do if the car won't move."

Lieschen opened the door on her side.

"What on earth are you doing?"

"I want to see if I can push the car."

"Push us where? Down the cliff?"

"Along the road." Lieschen opened the door wider. Icy snowflakes whipped into her face.

Werner grabbed her hand.

"I have to see my father!" She wanted to grow instant wings and fly with the stormclouds to her father in the emergency room. The wind howled on with wild persistence.

"Do you honestly think you could push us out of this?" Werner looked at her incredulously.

"I can at least try."

Werner held her left hand tightly in his right hand. "I won't let you. If you step out, you might slide down that cliff to your death in no time. What good would that do you or your father? Shut the door!" he commanded.

Lieschen obeyed. She was not used to Werner's sharp tone. After a few frantic moments, she asked, "What are we going to do?"

"Good question." Werner let go of her hand. He reached for a thick blanket on the back seat and wrapped it around them. "This storm won't last forever. Right now we can't do anything."

"I don't want to stay here. I'm afraid it might get worse, and I've to see Pap!" Lieschen's impulses jangled her nerves.

"In spite of the emergency, we have to be sensible."

"What if Pap dies?"

"If his time is up, we cannot change that either. I wish I could bring you to the hospital right now, but I can't. I've tried."

Lieschen knew that Werner had tried. Hot tears flooded her cheeks. "There're certain things in life man cannot change." Werner put his arm around Lieschen's shoulder and pulled the blanket up a little higher.

"Your father's, as well as our fate is in God's hands. Only He has the power to see us through."

Lieschen had a feeling that Werner would not mind dying right there, almost as if he welcomed death together with her. She wondered whether Werner's attitude was like that because he had finally realized that she only loved him platonically, like a brother.

Sitting side by side, nearly motionless, they could no longer see through the snow-crusted windows. The only world left to them remained inside the Jeep. Outside, the storm howled on mercilessly.

Cuddled close to Werner under the warm blanket, Lieschen experienced a strange sensation. She became calm in the shelter of Werner's arm, and soon she could no longer feel anything.

CHAPTER 27

A sudden noise jolted Lieschen out of her daze. "What is it?"

"Ssshhh . . . let's listen. I think someone kicked our tires." Werner also sounded half asleep.

The next moment, someone ripped open the door on Werner's side. Dawning light flashed over them. Four men, each holding a shovel, stood knee-deep in the snow next to the jeep. One of the men cleared their windows; and Lieschen saw a big snow plow in front of them. The storm had quieted, and the road had been cleared toward the valley. A few sporadic clouds drifted along the cold morning sky.

One of the four men asked, "Did you plan a north-pole-expedition?" Lieschen resented the question.

"Just got caught in the storm." Werner blinked to adjust to the dawning light.

"Got caught in a fairyland with a fairy-maiden," said the tallest of the rescuers. He was about forty, and appeared to be the spokesman of the group. All four men wore bright-yellow ski jump suits, with caps a little more intense in hue. The spokesman gazed at Lieschen, shaking his head.

She felt awful. Although she had cuddled next to Werner under a thick blanket, her fingers and toes felt numb. She tried to move her fingers, but she felt no tingling sensation, nothing.

"We'd rather be down in the valley where we're supposed to be," Werner said. Cold steam formed in front of his mouth as he talked.

"Let's clear them out." The spokesman gave a signal to the other three men, and they began shoveling snow away from the Jeep.

"You must know it takes brains to leave the Alpenhaus in such a wild storm," the spokesman said to Werner over the roof-top while scraping off snow around their skis. Werner also removed snow on the other side of the rooftop.

"It's dumb? Crazy dumb!" indicated one of the other rescuers who picked up a shovelful of snow by the front tires and tossed it over to the side.

"How did you know we left the Alpenhaus during the storm?" Werner asked.

"Sennerin Mathilde phoned and told us. That's why we're here, trying to get you out of the deep end."

As soon as they had cleared away enough snow, Werner pulled out four hundred Schilling, handed the notes to the spokesman and said, "We appreciate your help."

Shoving the money into his pocket, the spokesman urged, "Just use more brains next time. You must know you could be dead now." He turned to his companions and said, "Let's give them a shot."

They helped Werner jump-start the engine of his jeep and, within ten minutes, they were on their way down to the valley. Lieschen's hands and feet began thawing as the inside of the jeep warmed up. She could move her fingers and wiggle her toes.

One hour later they reached the valley and, close to twelve o'clock, Lieschen charged into the emergency quarters of the Landeskrankenhaus. A sturdy nurse stopped her inside the double doors. "Visitors are not allowed in here," she said.

"I have to see my father!" Lieschen's heart thumped. Finally she had arrived, and this nurse wanted to stop her from seeing her father.

"Who is your father?" the nurse asked.

"Herr Reinking. Herr Walter Reinking. Chief executive Walter Reinking."

"I'm sorry, Herr Reinking is still in critical condition. You cannot see him now." The nurse made a firm motion with her hands.

"Is my father awake or asleep?" Lieschen thought that would make a difference.

"He wakes up sporadically."

Lieschen tried to control her impulses. "When would I be allowed to see my father?" she asked.

"Possibly tomorrow morning, with Dr. Becker's permission." The nurse's tone remained firm.

"Can I talk to Dr. Becker?"

"I've to see if he is available. You have to wait."

"Okay." Lieschen sat down on a chair alongside the wall.

"You have to wait outside in the waiting area down the hall," instructed the nurse.

Just as Lieschen sat down on an empty chair in the waiting area, she heard cries, like the squealing of a sick crow. The next moment she saw two nurses in white overcoats wheeling in an overweight man in a greenish-black uniform and a black cap. Shiny gold-plated buttons trimmed the jacket of the uniform and the cap.

Squealing on, the man yanked his cap from his head and flung it on the floor. One of the two nurses-she had short copper-red curls-picked up the cap. The uniform and the cap must be that of a guard or a train conductor, Lieschen guessed. From the looks, it couldn't be a fireman's, that much was certain.

The stranger tumbled off the cart. The two nurses caught his arms. He swayed next to the cart. Blood dripped from his left arm. "Th-there's an ea-earthquake under m-my ff-feet," he stammered.

"There's an earthquake in your head." The other nurse, who had long brown braids, said as she tried to steady him.

"I-ve t-told you to leave m-me alone!" The stranger yanked away his arm and began singing, "I hob an duli duli je ..."

"Everybody can see that you're drunk. You don't have to advertise it." The nurse's angry tone reverberated in Lieschen's ears. She wondered how she could assist the two nurses and moved toward them, but right away, she retreated because the drunken man staggered toward her. Stretching out his bleeding arm, he muttered, "Y-you ww-want a t--taste?"

"How awful!" The dripping blood churned Lieschen's stomach.

"You're stone-drunk. Get back on that cart," commanded the nurse with the long braids. She attempted to help him, but he pushed her away.

"Hurly burly, a ff-fiddle-stick's end." He lifted his bleeding arm higher and gazed at Lieschen.

"Th-that's th-the wine ff-from my brake-fast."

"If you drank wine for breakfast, no wonder you crashed through the window," the nurse chided.

"H-hell, I d-did noht crrr-ash th-through the win-dow, the w-window crr-ashed through me-e-e."

"Sure, the window came right at you."

The two female nurses turned to a tall male nurse in a white suit, who approached with quick steps. "That's all quite interesting," observed the male nurse.

The drunken man lifted his head for recognition. "Sss-ee, I'mm interrr-essing."

"People are looking at you," the male nurse confirmed.

People in the waiting area gazed at the scene while the stranger's head jerked higher. His legs kept swaying.

Lieschen thought of Shakespeare's line: *All the world's a stage.* She did not know why she thought of Shakespeare right now-probably because this scene looked staged, yet it was so real.

"What's your name?" the male nurse asked the drunken man.

"Hhh-Herr Fii-nnk ..."

"I tell you what, Herr Fink, we better get your bleeding arm taken care of." He reached for his arm, but Herr Fink snatched it away and poked his fingers into the air. "Mm-my o-old b-bitch h-hurt meee."

"How come?"

"Sh-she toook my bb-bottle aaa-way. I w-wanted t-to catch h-her."

"I see."

"Sh-she said I sh-should hh-hang on a c-clothes-line t-to dry u-up."

"That's ff-funny," mimicked the male nurse.

"Th-that's noot ff-funny. Sh-she's a cr-cruel b-bitch. Vv-ery cr-cruel." Herr Fink stared accusingly at the female nurses.

"I can see what you mean." The male nurse winked at Lieschen. Then he said to Herrn Fink, "But we have to go on in this cruel world."

Just then, Lieschen noticed a distraught woman running toward the waiting area, straight toward Herrn Fink.

"My dear, dear husband, I've been looking for you everywhere." She embraced him.

"I've b-been w-waiting f-for you . . ." Herr Fink wrapped his bleeding arms around his wife's shoulders. Together with the nurses, they proceeded down the hall.

Lieschen kept waiting until Dr. Becker admitted her to his office.

"The chances for your father's recovery are fair," Dr. Becker, a white-haired physician, informed her. He explained that a clogged artery had debilitated the dilatation and contraction of her father's heart in three of the four chambers.

That sounded Greek to Lieschen, and very scary; but she was grateful that her father was alive. "When can I see my father?" she asked.

"In the morning, if no unexpected complications develop. The visiting nurse will advise you in the morning."

Lieschen thanked Dr. Becker and left the hospital.

The following morning, Frau Christina Ebner, the visiting nurse on duty, admitted Lieschen to her father's intensive care unit.

In shock, she stared at her father's sunken eyes, his shriveled skin, his blue lips. In his sleep, his grim face seemed bathed in pain. He looked like an old, broken man. Once a pillar of strength and power with a determined regal personality, her father lay now helplessly confined to a hospital bed. Lieschen kissed his forehead and lightly touched his arm. He did not react.

Frau Ebner told her not to disrupt his sleep and to come back the next morning.

From the Landeskrankenhaus, Lieschen drove to Ingrid's home, where Tasso greeted her at the wooden gate, happily wagging his tail. His reddish-brown fur looked fluffy and seemed freshly washed.

Ingrid came to open the gate. "I've got exciting news. Come in." They settled on the tan couch in the living room. Tasso joined, snuggling his furry head on Lieschen's lap.

"He just had a bath," Ingrid told Lieschen.

"He looks happy too."

"He likes getting a bath and playing with water." Ingrid paused, then said, "What I wanted to tell you is that Dr. Klaus, my gynecologist, confirmed that I'm pregnant." An exuberant smile lit up Ingrid's face.

"How exciting!"

"Since we don't want the baby to be born out of wedlock, we'll get married within a few months. We haven't finalized the exact date."

Tasso lifted his head as though he needed to pay close attention.

"I'm very happy for you," Lieschen said.

Ingrid snapped her middle finger on top of her index. "So am I." Her lively face kept glowing. "How was your ski trip?" she asked then. "You came back so soon."

"My father had a heart attack."

"When did that happen?" Ingrid's expression changed.

Lieschen explained. "And I couldn't come back as quickly as I wanted. A snowstorm hit us. I tell you, Ingrid, it was dreadful. I've never seen anything like it. Werner hasn't either. A rescue team came to help us. Thank God, we made it through, and my father is alive."

Ingrid looked shocked. "How is your father now?"

"Recuperating, ever so slowly."

"And how is Werner? Exciting news? Wedding plans?"

"I couldn't. And Werner is a gentleman."

"I've always known that." Ingrid took a deep breath and, with a disappointed tone, she asked, "What are you going to do now?"

"I'll take one day at a time. I'll continue with the business program at AKA, and I hope my father will soon be well again and stop pushing Sigi into my life."

"Good luck." Ingrid squinted her eyes. "How about Werner? Is he crushed?"

"I feel sorry for Werner, but he understands."

"He always understands. He's that kind of person. All I know is that he loves you dearly."

"I know." Lieschen also thought of Robert and wondered why their stars had to be crossed like that.

"Well, it's your life."

Lieschen nodded. Then they talked about her Grandma. Lieschen had told Ingrid the sad story by phone, but now they talked some more. Ingrid had never heard of Dr. Praust's Mental Clinic in Stainz.

When Lieschen returned home, she called Werner. His brother Michael told her that Werner had left to spend a few weeks at his grandparents' farm in St. Joseph. Since his grandparents did not have a telephone, Lieschen could not call him there.

Chapter 28

"Your father is out of intensive care," Fraulein Angelika Grimm, a friendly brunette nurse on duty, told Lieschen and led her to her father's private room.

What a difference a few days had made. Her father touched her arm lovingly, and they communicated with their eyes. His face no longer appeared bathed in pain.

Lieschen reached for a chair in the corner of the room and sat down beside her father's bed. She watched Fraulein Grimm adjust the lines of the I.V. Then she observed her father and the monitor. Fraulein Grimm stayed in the hospital room while Lieschen visited. She was allowed to stay for ten minutes.

"You can come back tomorrow morning," Fraulein Grimm told her when the ten minutes were up.

"Danke." Before Lieschen left, she kissed her father's cheek. Her father responded with his eyes.

From the Landeskrankenhaus, Lieschen drove to Dr. Praust's Clinic in Stainz to see her grandmother, hoping from the bottom of her heart that her grandmother's condition had also improved. Even a little change for the better would make her very happy. When she approached, her grandmother ignored her. "Grandma, please can you talk to me. I'm your grandchild," Lieschen pleaded, to no avail. Her grandmother seemed sleepy; but after a little while, she raised her bony fingers toward the ceiling. "Can you see the fish nest in that apple tree?" she gobbled. "And the crawling spider. Can you see it?"

With a pitiful sigh Lieschen gazed at the bland ceiling, and back at her grandmother's bony fingers.

"That's where the stork breeds children," Grandma explained. She seemed more awake now.

Lieschen felt goose bumps. She listened to her grandmother as she relayed how a stork breeds children in the fish nest on that ceiling. Gradually, when Grandma became more awake, she pushed back her blanket and slapped her calves. "These spiders keep crawling up! Up, up, up ..."

Lieschen realized that her visit and her efforts had gone too far. With a sinking feeling, she said good-bye to her forlorn Grandma. All of her hopes for her grandmother's recovery had been dashed anew.

From the asylum, she drove to her office at the Pharmaceutical Plant and tried to catch up with ledger keeping. She had to return to AKA the following Monday. By then she had to be caught up. Aunt Klara told her that Sigi had left for an appointment with Herrn Grunewald. Lieschen wished that Sigi would never come back. She worked till eight o'clock that evening and could bring her ledgers current.

Day by day her father's health improved, making Lieschen very happy, until ... Oh, until! Her father expected her to come with Sigi to discuss business matters in the hospital.

"I can handle business matters without Sigi," Lieschen contended.

"Sigi's presence is necessary because we have to discuss our next board meeting."

Back to the old grind! Lieschen let out a woeful sigh.

Her father adjusted his mattress to an upright position and said, "When would you like to come with Sigi?"

Why is Pap challenging me like that? I'll go berserk. The thought of having to sit next to Sigi in his Porsche where he had tried to rape her burned like hot sawdust in her head.

"You must see the significance of a close relation and cooperation with Sigi, don't you?"

"I don't." Lieschen did not want to upset her father, especially not now. She wanted to guard his health. But how can I do that if Pap tramples on my feelings?

Sweat broke out on his forehead. He reached for a handkerchief behind his pillow, wiped his face and said, "Sigi will provide leadership and security for you and for the future of our business. With Sigi you'll continue our bloodline, and you'll have pure children. With Sigi you will flourish. Flourish! Flourish!"

Where does love come in? Lieschen wondered. She felt like vomiting.

"You must see the condition *of* my health. I want your future and the future of our business to be secure before I die."

That broken record. Lieschen had heard it so often. She tried to suppress her vomiting. She had been pulling so hard for her father's recovery, but not to have new confrontations because of Sigi. Why can Pap not stop before a disaster happens? Why does he expect me to betray my own heart? She inhaled deeply and said, "Pap, I'm sorry about your health. Very sorry. But I cannot understand why you're so blinded by Sigi's feigned chivalry."

Her father put the handkerchief on his forehead. His lips twitched. His mouth under his shortly clipped mustache opened as if he wanted to say something, but no sound came out.

"Please, Pap, don't be so unfair. I love you, but I could never love Sigi." Lieschen choked back tears.

The blue veins on her father's temples protruded alarmingly. His cheeks turned pale as if blood was draining before her eyes. His breath erupted in heavy spurts. Lieschen panicked. She dashed over to the bathroom sink in the corner of her father's hospital room, grabbed a towel and soaked it in cold water. She squeezed out the surplus water, scrambled back, and put the wet towel on her father's forehead. "I'm sorry! I didn't mean to upset you," she said. "I just hoped that your attitude would change if you saw how unhappy I was over your attempts to bring Sigi and me together." She settled back on the chair. "It is so painful when you ignore my feelings." She could not comprehend why she had to repeat the same thing over and over, and her father still ignored her feelings.

He grabbed the cold towel and hurled it on the iron-gray linoleum floor. "Not even when I'm gravely ill can you fulfill my wishes!" He gasped for air.

Blood surged into Lieschen's head. Pap might die before my eyes, and I'd have caused his death! That would be too much to bear. She pressed her fingernails into her sweaty palms and said, "Pap, what do you want me to do right now?"

"I thought I'd made it clear. I want you to come with Sigi to discuss our next board meeting."

"Okay." Lieschen rose and stepped over to pick up the towel her father had flung on the floor.

"Why don't you call Sigi and arrange a time for tomorrow. Here is the phone." With his left hand her father indicated the telephone on the nightstand beside his bed.

Lieschen's nerves seemed to crack. She turned away from her father and walked into the bathroom where she hung the towel on the towel bar. Her thoughts reeled, I'm very much afraid that a tragedy is about to happen because I cannot endure this pressure. She crossed back to the nightstand and, with trembling hands, picked up the receiver.

"You know the number." Her father sounded impatient.

Lieschen dialed a wrong number. "The line is busy." She hung up.

"Let me try." Her father bent over.

"I'll try again." This time Lieschen dialed Frau Erika's direct number and asked for Sigi. She hoped that Frau Erika would not connect her, or that Sigi would not be in his office and fly a kite somewhere.

She heard some clicks. Her stomach knotted. Her father watched her. "Hello, my dear Fraulein Lieschen," Sigi's voice came in, loud and clear.

Lieschen could not talk to him and hung up. "We were disconnected." She looked at her father.

"Hand me the phone." Her father dialed and talked briefly with Sigi. Then he handed the receiver to Lieschen.

She forced herself to talk. "It is my father's wish that we discuss business matters here at the Landeskrankenhaus." Although she trembled all over, she tried to hold up.

She saw her father's expression changing. "We can meet here at the Landeskrankenhaus after my classes at AKA," she proposed to Sigi.

"We also have to stop by the Internal Revenue Building to sign and submit tax forms," Sigi pointed out. "Remember, the deadline is tomorrow."

"Okay." Lieschen's father had previously informed her of this requirement.

"I'd prefer that we meet at the Plant," Sigi said. "From there we can go together in one car."

"Okay." Lieschen had no intention of complying with Sigi's itinerary and getting in his car ever again. She replaced the receiver and looked at her father. "We'll be here tomorrow afternoon."

"Good." Her father's expression told her that he was satisfied.

As soon as Lieschen left her father's hospital room, she called Ingrid from the wall phone in the corridor and explained her problem. "Sigi is a pest. He sticks to my father like a leech. Like an evil spirit. If I could, I'd shoot him." Her exasperated voice echoed in the receiver.

"Why don't you." Ingrid cackled.

"Why don't I do what?"

"Shoot Sigi."

"I wish I had the nerve." Holding the receiver close to her ear, Lieschen looked down at her ocher leather shoes, which she wore with an ocher flannel suit and a black pullover. "But what do I do for tomorrow?" she asked. "I don't want to go with him to visit my father."

"Shoot him tonight." Ingrid cackled on. "Listen, call me tomorrow," she said then. "I've dill sauce boiling on the stove. I've to go back to stir it. I expect to be home all day tomorrow. Perhaps we can come up with an idea to solve your problem. I'll ask Hans too."

"Danke, Ingrid. Ciao."

Driving away from the hospital, Lieschen turned on the windshield wipers because it was snowing. If I had the nerve to shoot Sigi, I'd do so because he's so evil. He shouldn't be living in this world! Lieschen shuddered at her own thoughts. Nonetheless, she resolved to shoot Sigi if he tried to rape her again. But for that she needed a gun.

CHAPTER 29

Lieschen called Sigi from AKA. "I cannot make it back to the office in time. We could meet in front of the Internal Revenue Building. From there we can go together to see my father." This time Lieschen would turn the tables.

Sigi agreed reluctantly. Lieschen would not give him another choice.

"By the time you arrive at the Internal Revenue Building, I shall have all the tax forms signed and prepared for you to sign. Then it shouldn't take but a few minutes for you to sign them," Sigi said.

"Okay." Lieschen thought her plan should work.

From now on she intended to scheme with Sigi as he had done with her. She always wanted to be good and upright, but with Sigi she did not know how else to handle her dilemma because her father was so prejudiced in favor of Sigi. "Would you call my father and inform him of the status quo," she said.

"I shall."

Lieschen sensed more resentment in Sigi's tone of voice. "And I shall meet you in front of the Internal Revenue Building a quarter to three."

"Okay."

She was punctual and found Sigi pacing in front of the mouse-gray, four-story building of the Internal Revenue offices. With a knotted stomach she strutted toward him in her navy-blue leather boots with semi-high heels which she wore with a navy-blue woolen dress and matching jacket. A cold wind from the north tousled her hair and blew strands into her face. Batches of snow and ice covered the sidewalk and the road.

"The documents are prepared for you to sign. I've already signed them. I shall wait for you right here," Sigi said. He gave her direction to the office on the second floor, Room 201. While he talked, his lips twisted.

Lieschen passed through the entrance and immediately searched for a second exit. She wanted to leave Sigi stranded and use the second door to escape. She would never again get in his Porsche and sit on that treacherous seat where he had attempted to rape her. Since she could not find a second door, she rushed to the public phone in the hallway and called Ingrid, who had been expecting her call.

Ingrid answered on the third ring. Lieschen explained her predicament and asked Ingrid to help her with her plan. "Please disguise yourself as anything you can think of. And would you bring some old clothes from Hans for me to wear, so we can sneak by Sigi without being recognized."

"Sounds like fun."

"Please, Ingrid, hurry. I'll go and sign the tax forms in the meantime. Then I'll wait for you on the second floor, in front of Room 201."

She could not recognize Ingrid when she stalked toward her with a cane, dressed as an old Gemuesefrau (vegetable vendor), wearing a ragged old wig with gray hair above a powder-white face. "Good enough?" Ingrid sneezed.

"Great job. Hans would be proud of you."

"He'd probably send me off to Mars on a broomstick."

"He wouldn't. He'd miss you."

"I guess he would." Ingrid smiled and opened the shopping bag in which she carried Hans' old work clothes-cobalt blue pants, a shirt in a slightly lighter hue, an old hat, and an old pair of dark-blue shoes that proved three sizes too big for Lieschen. Ingrid had brought along crumpled newspaper to fill the extra space.

They rushed into the W.C. where Ingrid helped Lieschen change. Then they looked into the square W.C. mirror to examine their appearance and burst into a hearty laughter because they looked so weird. Ingrid had also brought a false crooked nose and a pair of glasses for Lieschen, which she put on.

When they recovered from their laughter, Lieschen stuffed her own clothes and shoes into the shopping bag in which Ingrid had brought Hans' work clothes. A lady in an orange-red suit came in. Looking at them with a baffled expression, she asked, "What's the occasion?"

"A theatrical play," Ingrid replied.

"In the W.C. of the Internal Revenue Building? Great place!" The lady proceeded into a stall.

"This trick will work. I know it will," Ingrid said as they exited the W.C.

"If Sigi recognizes us, it might blow in my face." Lieschen became nervous.

"He didn't even look at me when I walked in," Ingrid said.

Lieschen stumbled because the shoes were so big and clumsy, and because she became more and more nervous as they neared the exit. Through the open door she could see Sigi pacing back and forth on the sidewalk. She clenched her fists and squeezed her fingernails into the bag she was carrying. The bag ripped and fell to the ground. She picked it up and shoved *it* under her arm. "I'm not sure we should go on ..." She stalled.

"You can't chicken out now." Ingrid walked on.

"I don't want to chicken out ..."

"Come on!" Ingrid stalked ahead and Lieschen behind her in an upright posture. Although she stumbled a few times in Hans' oversized shoes, Sigi paid no attention to them.

About thirty meters away from the building, Lieschen turned back. Again, the strong wind from the north blew into her face. "It worked," she said when she saw Sigi still pacing in front of the Internal Revenue Building.

"Don't look back," Ingrid cautioned. "We might still blow it if we aren't careful."

They hurried to Ingrid's Volkswagen.

While Ingrid drove, Lieschen changed in the back seat. She put on her navy-blue woolen dress, matching jacket, and navy-blue leather boots with semi-high heels; and she stuffed Hans' old clothes and shoes and facial items back into the bag. Then she glanced through the window at the restless gray clouds.

"What are you going to tell your father?" Ingrid slowed at the intersection of Ludwig Strasse.

"I've to make up a story." Lieschen cleaned her face and combed her hair. "I hate lies, but I have no choice."

"Just be glad you tricked Sigi."

"I am. Danke for your help."

"Glad to help." Ingrid drove through the intersection. Then she told Lieschen, "Hans and I went to see Father Cassedi last Sunday."

"About your wedding plans?"

"Yes. We'll get married on the last Saturday in May. And Hans wants to finish building our home before our baby is born."

"How exciting!"

"As you know, he has the cellar completed. Now, he cannot do much work, though."

"Because of the weather?"

"And because it gets dark so early."

"I understand."

"Hans usually works on weekends now when he doesn't have to work on his construction business."

"No matter how long it takes, it'll be your own home, and you won't owe anybody anything."

"That's the good part." With a happy smile, Ingrid glanced at Lieschen and said, "Hans leaves the decorating to me. I've already started to look for wallpaper. My father will help me with the wallpaper. And I've started to look for fabric to make curtains and drapes and valances. My Mom will help me with that. I want to have it all in cream and olive and pink."

"Should look nice."

"I'll sew the drapes and curtains and valances myself, to save money."

Lieschen knew that Ingrid was good at sewing. "That's wonderful," she said. Her own heart, however, was sore and full of pain. *God, what would I give for true love with Robert! And for peace and harmony with my father! Without Sigi!* The next moment she reminded herself that she had no right to think about true love with Robert. She had already come to grips with that reality, but every now and then she could not help longing for Robert.

At the Landeskrankenhaus parking lot, she grabbed her handbag.

"Good luck! I'll wait here." Ingrid turned off the engine.

"Danke, Ingrid." Lieschen hopped out and scurried through the strong wind to the hospital entrance, and to her father's private room where she found him in good spirits. She was amazed how substantially his eyes had revitalized.

"Where is Sigi?" he asked, fueling Lieschen's frustration. Is that really all Pap is concerned about?

Her father's mattress was in a semi-upright position. "I asked you where Sigi is!" He adjusted his mattress to a fully upright position.

"I don't know where he went." Lieschen tried to retain her composure. She pulled a chair from the corner of the room and sat down beside her father's hospital bed. "We were supposed to come and see you together," she said. "That was my understanding. We met in front of the Internal Revenue Building. Sigi said everything was prepared for me to sign upstairs, and he would wait. When I came back, he was gone."

"Perhaps he had another urgent matter to take care of." Her father spoke now in a moderate tone.

"Perhaps."

"You can come back tomorrow."

Lieschen clenched her teeth and nodded in trepidation.

"Or-" Her father briefly paused before he said, "Dr. Becker told me this morning that I should be able to go home within a few days."

"What good news!"

"Then we could meet over dinner at home, before our next board meeting. We have so much to do." Her father looked pensive.

"Oh, yes. Yes!" Lieschen would do anything to postpone a meeting with Sigi and, hopefully, find another way out altogether.

They talked a bit more before she left.

"How did it go?" Ingrid asked when Lieschen scooted into the passenger seat.

"So far, so good."

"Did you tell your father that you'll make sure to come with Sigi next time?"

"Of course."

"In that case, everything's hunky-dory?"

"My father might be released from the hospital within a few days."

"Sounds good."

"For the moment, but my father is still rampant to bring me and Sigi together. So I don't know what will happen."

"You'll find a solution."

"I hope." Lieschen sighed deeply. She felt desolate about her father's fondness of Sigi, and about his intention to bring them together.

"Also remember what my Mom used to say: people's sinful actions will turn back on them. This is how the Universe works."

"I remember when you told me, but this doesn't help me now." Lieschen swallowed hard.

Ingrid drove her back to her Porsche.

"Thanks a lot, Ingrid." Lieschen hopped out.

"Glad to help. And we had fun. Ciao." Ingrid drove off.

Three days later, Lieschen prepared a large bouquet of white and blue lilies for her father's homecoming. She had bought the lilies from Fraulein Roswitta at the Mariatrost Florist; and she had made a personalized card, which she had placed in front of the large crystal vase with the bouquet of lilies on the coffee table in their living room. Aunt Klara had also signed the card.

When Lieschen, together with Aunt Klara, brought her father home from the Landeskrankenhaus, he was visibly pleased with the bouquet of lilies and the personalized card.

CHAPTER 30

Seated around the conference table at the Reinking Pharmaceutical Company, with fifteen members in attendance, Lieschen's father talked about his stay at the Landeskrankenhaus. "They were anxious to get me back to work," he said with a content smile.

"We're glad to have you back," Herr Klug said.

Lieschen was delighted over her father's recovery; and she was surprised and encouraged because neither her father, nor Sigi, had mentioned the incident at the Internal Revenue Building; and they had no private dinner with Sigi.

During the conference, her father elaborated on the last phase of the development of Xiron. He also mentioned the importance of a business trip to Vienna for the purpose of introducing some of their products to Reinhard & Sons and Kreisler G.m.b.H. And he mentioned a trip to Munich and Paris. Lieschen assumed her father's health was up to par again because he made all these traveling plans.

The next moment, she felt a rattlesnake curling around her neck when her father announced that she and Sigi would make the trip to Vienna. Why does Pap make such decisions over my head? Does he assume I'd accept it if he doesn't discuss it with me? Or does his afflicted health really affect him like this that he cannot consider my feelings?

She managed to grasp a hold of her sudden jangle of nerves. She recognized the importance of expanding and nurturing their client base, but she could not understand why she should have to make such a trip with Sigi. She did not voice her objection in front of the board members, however. Quietly she began formulating in her mind how to dissuade her father from this outrageous idea.

In the evening, Lieschen joined her father at the coffee table in the living room at their villa. He folded the magazine he was reading, moved forward on the couch, and promptly veered their discussion to the planned business trip with Sigi.

Lieschen had expected it. "I can make the trip with Frau Drexel or by myself," she responded. She wanted to make a serious effort to avoid another argument in order not to jeopardize her father's health further.

"You must realize that the pharmaceutical industry requires a respectable gentleman-officer for a proper representation."

"Pap, we live in different times now. Women are accepted in the business world."

Her father's lips twitched.

Gone too far! Lieschen warned herself. "Pap can I get you a glass of water?"

"Water won't cure this problem. You follow my instructions and my advice, and everything will be okay."

"Okay." Lieschen listened to her father's unreasonable agenda. Then she walked out into the garden and dropped on the chipped, wooden seat of the swing under the old cherry tree. Looking through the bare tree branches at drifting clouds, she prayed, "Dear God, I cannot go on this trip with Sigi. I cannot! I can't! Dear God, you know that Sigi has tried to rape me, and because of him I nearly drowned." She sighed deeply, then continued, "Dear God, you must listen to me! Otherwise I'll shoot Sigi!"

God had never responded to Lieschen's prayers in a tangible way, but somehow she felt He had been with her. She could not explain why she felt this way, but that was how she felt. "Dear God, how can I get out of this?" she continued to pray. Her chest swelled as if a thousand soldiers mobilized inside her for the war against Sigi.

She heard her father leave. From the sound of the motor she recognized that he was leaving in his Jeep.

A moment later, Frau Emma called her to the telephone. Lieschen bounced off the swing and rushed to answer the call on the wall phone in the hallway.

"Werner, you're back!" She was so glad to hear his voice and sat down on the Baroque chair adjacent to the wall phone. The cord of the receiver was long enough to reach to the adjacent chair.

"Can I talk to you? I mean in person?"

"Of course. When? Where?"

Werner invited Lieschen out for ice-cream at the Meridian Cafe' in Mariatrost for the following day.

Seated inside the cozy cafe'-it was too cool to be outside on the terrace-Lieschen felt happy to be with Werner. A lively young waitress with short wavy blond hair took their order of a double scoop of Spumoni (Italian fruit ice-cream), and a cup of hot chocolate for Lieschen, and Viennese chocolate ice-cream with raspberry and hazelnut topping, and a Cappuccino for Werner.

As soon as the waitress left, Werner told Lieschen about his engagement to a girl named Marianne.

In utter amazement, Lieschen's breathing seemed to suspend.

"It's true." Werner paused. "I guess God knows what's best." He sipped from his Cappuccino.

Lieschen was happy for Werner, but she had to collect herself from this unexpected turn of events. "How long have you known Marianne?" she asked.

"I met her years ago while I stayed at my grandparents' farm, when I had rheumatic fever. Remember?"

"You were in fourth grade."

Werner nodded. "But I never knew Marianne as I know her now."

"What does she do?"

"She works at her parents' farm. She went to the Wells-Landwirtschafts-Schule to learn about agriculture, and about cooking and sewing. She's an only child, and her parents need her at home."

"When will you get married?"

A sheepish twist appeared on Werner's lips. "At the beginning of May." He scratched his forehead. "Hope you'll come to the wedding?"

That's even sooner than Ingrid and Hans' wedding, thought Lieschen. "I'll be very happy to come. I'd like to extend our friendship to Marianne. Do you have a picture of her?"

Werner reached for his wallet and pulled out a 3 x 5 centimeter photo. "I only have this small picture."

"This is fine." Lieschen carefully took the photo into her hands. Bluish-gray eyes, long curly chestnut hair- "She looks pretty," she said.

"She's a nice girl." Werner glanced at the photo, then at Lieschen, as if comparing her with the photo. "I think I can be happy with her."

"Are you going to live together with her parents?"

"Her parents will stay downstairs in the old farmhouse, and we'll be upstairs. It's a two-story house. The rooms upstairs are small, but cozy, like the rooms in the upper story of the Alpenhaus on the Teichalm."

"You always liked farming. Now you'll become a farmer."

"And I'll be close to my grandparents. They need me too."

"That will be good."

"Life takes unexpected turns, doesn't it?" Werner ate another spoonful of his ice cream.

Lieschen nodded and sipped hot chocolate. A special thought crossed her mind. She would give Werner and Marianne her gold bicycle as a wedding gift, so they could enjoy it with their children. She remembered how much Werner had wanted a gold bicycle like hers. She felt *it* would make a nice gift, and she hoped her father would not object.

CHAPTER 31

Lieschen's father had a set-back in his recovery; therefore, he postponed Lieschen's trip with Sigi.

Nonetheless, the time came much too soon when her father summoned her to his private office at their villa on a Saturday morning.

On his desk Lieschen saw a large pad labeled: *Itinerary - Trip Vienna.* Right away she knew what was coming.

"Have a seat." Her father indicated the chair opposite his own at his desk, and she sat down.

What must be, must be! The nagging echo of the treacherous past with Sigi nearly suffocated Lieschen's breathing, but she reminded herself to curtail her emotions and stay calm in order not to upset her father.

"I'm sure you understand the importance of this trip together with Sigi." Her father scrutinized her.

She did not say a word. Her stomach shriveled.

"The representation has to conform with our standards and tradition, which require a respectable gentleman officer, as we discussed."

Lieschen continued to suppress her desolate emotions and mumbled, "Okay."

"I can see you have matured." A complacent smile danced on her father's lips.

Lieschen would no longer argue because she realized she could not change her father's mind; and she did not want to cause further deterioration of his health. In trepidation she listened to the full itinerary, then went up to her bedroom, sank to her knees at her bedside and prayed, "Dear God, I don't know anymore what to do with my father and Sigi." She reminded God again what Sigi had done to her, and she also warned God once more that she would have to take deadly action if Sigi tried to rape her again.

The following day, when she came home from AKA, she went to see Ralph at the stables. He was riding Figaro in the rink. She signaled with her hands, and he rode toward her.

"August 25 will be me magic day," he announced.

Lieschen knew that Ralph was referring to the races because her father had told her. "I'm looking forward to watch you and Figaro win," she said.

Ralph's lips curled with excitement. "You want to go riding, Fraulein Lissi?"

"Not now. I'd like to talk to you."

"I'm here," Ralph said as if it had not been obvious. He did not dismount Figaro, though. He talked down to Lieschen from the saddle.

"Do you still go hunting with your father?" she asked.

"Why, Fraulein Lissi?"

"You see, I would like to learn how to shoot and go hunting with my father."

Ralph cast a skeptical glance at her, almost alarmed, as if he had a hunch that she was after something bad. "Do you have a gun, Fraulein Lissi?"

"Not yet. This is what I'd like you to do. Since you shoot so well, I thought you could tell me what type of gun I should buy, and where I should buy it." She paused. "Or could you buy a gun for me?"

Ralph's skeptical glance intensified. "Herr Reinking!"

"You must not tell my father. It's a surprise. That's why I want you to teach me to shoot as well as you do."

"Irregardless, Fraulein Lissi, Herr Reinking!"

It took Lieschen some convincing to get Ralph to agree.

"Me and me father practice at the Kloister Target Range," he explained.

"I know." Lieschen was aware that police-officers and firemen practiced sharp-shooting there too.

"When do you want to practice, Fraulein Lissi?"

"Can we practice now? Or tomorrow afternoon?"

"Tomorrow is better," Ralph said.

"Could you buy me a gun by tomorrow?" Lieschen pulled out her wallet from the pocket of her butter-cream cotton dress.

Ralph looked pensive. "Irregardless, you can pay me tomorrow," he said.

The next day, Lieschen arrived at the Kloister Target Range ten minutes early. She was dressed for spring in a dove-gray linen dress with an oval cut and a navy-blue trim, and nave-blue sandals. On the target boards, she could see the sun's glimmering reflections. Nobody else practiced right now.

When Ralph arrived, he told her that he had not yet purchased a gun; but he had his own gun with him for her to practice.

Again, Lieschen held the money toward him. "Please buy me a gun by tomorrow."

Ralph agreed and showed her with his own gun how to aim and shoot at a target. Then he handed her the gun. Lieschen hated the feel of the gun, but she was determined to learn handling this deadly monster. She aimed at a target board but missed more shots than she would have liked to miss. When a group of police officers showed up and observed her, she became more and more nervous. It was obvious that some of the police officers had recognized her.

"That's enough for today." She handed the gun back to Ralph. "Danke," she said.

She would have liked to tell the police officers and the whole world that she did not want to harm anybody. It's Sigi. He is evil. He attempted to rape me. And because of him I almost drowned. Yet, my father insists that I go on a business trip with this evil man. My father cannot recognize his evil side. Can you see why I need a gun?

"Whatever, Fraulein Lissi." Ralph secured his gun and finally, two days later, handed her a new gun, black and shiny; and he gave her further instructions. "Fraulein Lissi, I advise that you not practice with the new gun. It's all loaded and ready for shooting." Ralph held the gun in his hands.

"Can you show me?"

Lieschen paid close attention as Ralph opened the drum and showed her the bullets. "It's good for five roundings," he explained.

Lieschen continued to practice with Ralph's gun. There were no police officers or firemen around now, but many of her shots went off yonder because her hands were not steady; and she had an awful feeling in her stomach.

At home, she put the gun into her dresser, under her underwear. She hated the feel of this gun, but she kept telling herself she needed it.

CHAPTER 32

Lieschen trembled from head to toe as she sat down on the passenger seat in Sigi's midnight-blue Porsche in which he had tried to rape her. Her father wished them a successful, joyous trip. Lieschen would never be ready for this trip, but the afflictions with her father and Sigi had escalated to this horrible reality.

Sigi started the engine. While he inched away from the circular driveway, her father waved with a happy smile. Lieschen perceived a deadly current, as though her father commandeered her at knife point while she was standing on a continental divide, facing the biggest battle of her life.

Barely out of her father's sight, venom seemed to ooze through Sigi's breath when he said, "Look at this pleasant day, especially designed for you and me."

Lieschen did not reply. Sigi's buttersweet tone and his exulted voice penetrated her blood and bones, deep into her soul.

"Can't you see the beautiful sky?" Sigi motioned with one hand, while holding the steering wheel with the other hand.

"I don't feel well. I had to take six Aspirin this morning. I shouldn't be talking," she replied. She wanted to scream, Shut up and disappear before I shoot you! Such mannerism disturbed her, but she could not help her desolate emotions.

"In that case we should've postponed this trip." Sigi cast a sideways glance at her.

"I'll be all right. I just need a little quiet." She reminded herself she had a gun for protection; and this horrible matter had to be resolved.

Farther along the wide two-way asphalt road, Sigi suggested, "Why don't we stop for a delectable breakfast at the Semmering Mountain Inn. That should cheer you up."

"I couldn't eat," Lieschen replied.

Sigi frowned and shifted the clutch down because a tractor chugged in front of them. They had reached a steeper stretch of the Semmering Mountain, climbing between dense fir- and deciduous trees on both sides of the road.

Just leave me alone. Go to Jupiter, or to hell! Only get out of my life! Lieschen's painful sigh alerted Sigi. With a strange expression he glared at her. She could not understand why neither her father, nor Sigi, could accept how she felt.

At a quarter to twelve they arrived at the grandiose Baroque hotel, Bassadores, with its majestic facade and pillars. Lieschen's father had told her that the Viennese owner of the hotel had married a sweetheart from Greece and had named the hotel after her.

Sigi's secretary, Fraulein Ludmilla, had made advance reservations for Lieschen and Sigi for three nights at the Bassadores. Her father had selected this hotel because of its central location.

In front of the Bassadores, Sigi stepped out and handed the keys for his Porsche to a young valet. Lieschen pushed open the door before the valet reached her side. She inhaled the cool, fresh air and glanced at the rain clouds in the sky, then at the grandiose entrance. She dreaded to step over to the shiny double glass doors with gilded frames. She felt as if a bunch of tigers waited inside to mull her up.

The young valet held the car-door until she scrambled out. At the hotel entrance, she stopped.

"After you," Sigi made a gallant motion with his hands.

Lieschen swayed through the glass doors. Her feet felt like heavy blocks of wood.

At the reception counter with coral-pink marble facing, a professional clerk in a crimson suit completed their registration and assigned their rooms on the third floor, numbers 304 and 305. He handed the keys to an elderly porter in a black suit.

In the hallway on the third floor, golden light fixtures protruded from the coral-pink wallpaper, and the plush, magenta carpeting felt soft. The porter unlocked the doors to their rooms.

Before Lieschen entered, Sigi invited her to the Prater, Vienna's favorite amusement park with the well-known ferris wheel. "Since we don't have appointments for the afternoon, we could spend a delightful time together." Sigi's lips curled seductively.

Lieschen wanted to spit at his fake smile, but she knew better. "I still don't feel well," she said. "And I have birthday shopping to do for Aunt Klara." She quickly entered her room, elegantly furnished in the Baroque style, and closed the door.

A short while later, she left the Bassadores for a stroll to St. Stephen's Cathedral. Drifting along Kaerntnerstrasse, she glanced into attractive display windows with beautiful dresses and designer suits, hand-knit sweaters, blouses, skirts, scarves, designer shoes, purses, embroidery, jewelry, and an array of card- and souvenir shops with smaller display windows. Nothing stimulated her. She did not do any birthday shopping for Aunt Klara either. Her heart seemed to weigh a thousand tons, as if set adrift in a sea of temptation to commit murder.

Cigarette smoke mingled with the aroma of delectable pastries and Cappuccinos in front of a terrace cafe' which she just passed. Outdoor cafes had been a Viennese tradition for hundreds of years. And Lieschen had learned at St. Germain that Vienna merged tendencies of a village with an international scope. Timeless, yet ever changing like a kaleidoscope, Vienna had evolved into a city of music and culture to which the Danube River added a sentimental touch.

She trudged on among a brisk stream of pedestrians strolling in both directions. When she reached the end of Kaerntnerstrasse, she realized that she had gone in the wrong direction. St. Stephen's Cathedral was at the other end. "All roads of Austria lead to St. Stephen's," Sister Margarita had told the students in class, but going in the wrong direction did not help. She turned around and walked back.

Despite her troubled mind and heart, she remembered when Mother Marisa had mentioned that she should smile at a street sweeper. She did not know why she remembered that now. Perhaps because she just saw a street sweeper at the entrance to St. Stephen's.

She smiled at the middle-aged sweeper, who lifted his broom and drew circles in the air. Lieschen had no idea what that meant. Whatever .. .

She entered St. Stephen's and sank to her knees in the back row near a statuette of the Virgin Mary in a lovely celestial blue cloak. She looked passed the Gothic sandstone pulpit with its spiral stairway up to the high altar, where candles burned on both sides of the holy cross with Jesus Christ. A dark mist vaporized in her head. Cobwebs appeared. Dark ghosts glowed at her with fiery eyes. Her heart screamed, "Dear God, I've asked you for help. If I shoot Sigi, it's your fault!"

A short while later, she prayed, "Dear God, I don't want to commit murder. Please help me do the right thing, and bless Sigi." She was aware of her conflicting prayers, but she thought one way or another God must respond.

That evening she did not see Sigi and, before going to bed, she checked her suitcase. She had not unpacked. The gun was still under her underwear, in the suitcase on a chair next to a small Baroque table near the window. When she touched the gun, she felt like touching a monster with fiery spikes.

During a restless sleep, she waded through muddy waters. Armed alligators crawled around her. Blood-stained deer floated on the surface of the turbulent waters. A black spider with a red cross climbed on one of the dead deer. An ominous tent shielded the night sky. When a glimmer of light appeared on the distant horizon, Lieschen awoke from this nightmare, trembling and bathed in sweat. It was barely one o'clock in the morning, and she tried to go back to sleep.

At seven thirty in the morning, she crawled down the winding marble stairway. She avoided the elevator.

Since she did not see Sigi in the lobby, she looked outside. Rainy clouds lingered in the sky, but it was not raining. She thought her professional cobalt-violet suit, which she wore with a coral blouse, fit well for business meetings in this type of weather; so did her high-heeled black leather shoes and matching purse.

Back in the lobby, she became more and more elated because Sigi did not show up. Along high walls, she looked at original paintings and replicas by Rembrandt, Degas, and Renoir. What a treat! she thought with a sense of gratitude because it was a beautiful deflection from her worries. Presently she also noticed a small painting of an Indian dancer next to a large painting of the Acropolis. Light from the big crystal chandeliers highlighted these two paintings, which juxtaposed in size, mood, and texture; and they contrasted with the ruby-red wallpaper.

Lieschen glanced around some more and could not see Sigi. Hooray! She felt like shouting with joy, hoping that Sigi had plunged into oblivion. She crossed the lobby and dropped into a soft cushion of a ruby-red Baroque couch behind an oval, deep-pink marble table with a big Baroque vase overflowing with white orchids. Her knees lifted abruptly. She had not anticipated the extra softness of the cushion, which had caused her to bounce like that. She was also preoccupied with jubilant thoughts that Sigi might have disappeared.

The next moment she blushed when she noticed a young, dark-haired man in a light-gray gabardine suit, on the opposite side of the marble table. She realized that he had observed her. "Excusez-moi, Mademoiselle, may I ask you a question?" He held a pamphlet in his hands.

Puzzled and embarrassed, Lieschen replied, "Yes." She straightened up on the couch.

"Mein Name ist Albert Balsac. I don't speak German well, I'm French."

"Je parle un peu francais." Lieschen spoke limited French, but she loved languages and appreciated every opportunity to speak in a foreign tongue.

"Tres bien." Albert's invigorating smile gave away a refined mannerism. "I noticed that you like paintings. So do I," he said in French. Then he asked also in French, "Do you know when the next performance of the Vienna Choir Boys will be? I cannot see this information in the pamphlet." He held it toward her.

"I'm sorry, I don't know," Lieschen replied.

"Do you like the Choir Boys?" Albert's inquisitive gray eyes searched hers.

"Yes."

"I would like to invite you to a performance." Albert put the pamphlet on the marble table. 'Would you give me your phone number? Only if you'd like-"

Lieschen thought she could not give her phone number just like that. On the other hand, she felt a peculiar attraction for Albert. Or could Sigi have set Albert up? Suddenly she felt apprehensive. But if Albert were connected with Sigi, he would know where I live, she reasoned, then said, "I live in Graz. It would be too far for you to drive."

"I'd be happy to come to Graz, take you to a performance of the Choir Boys in Vienna, and bring you back home."

Lieschen hesitated a moment longer. Then she told Albert her phone number, which he jotted down on a sheet of paper from a notepad on the marble table. Just as he slipped the sheet into his wallet, Lieschen's spirits collapsed.

"1 do not wish to interrupt such an animated conversation, but necessity compels me to do so." Sigi cast a reproachful glance at Lieschen.

"Votre mari?" Albert asked with a disappointed expression.

"No, I'm not married," Lieschen answered in French. God forbid I should be married to Sigi!

Albert's expression changed as he whispered, "I'm looking fonvard to seeing you soon."

With a fleeting glimpse, Lieschen nodded gracefully and rose. Together with Sigi, she proceeded toward the hotel restaurant. Sigi ordered a full breakfast. Lieschen had only hot chocolate.

"Would you like to know why I was delayed?" Sigi asked while reaching for his cup of coffee, which an elegantly dressed waiter had just served.

Lieschen did not care what he was doing. She did not care for anything except get him out of her life.

"1 was talking to your father on the phone." Sigi drank coffee.

Lieschen's cheeks flushed.

Sigi put down his cup and watched her while he adjusted his speckled bow-tie around the crimson shirt which he wore with a marine-blue business suit. Then he said, "I told your father that you weren't feeling well. Your father instructed me to take good care of you."

I must not lose control! Lieschen reminded herself. She took a deep breath and uttered, "I feel better today." With trembling hands she picked up her cup of hot chocolate and drank a little. Then she reached for the Wiener Presse in the gold-leafed magazine rack on their table and pretended to read. At least it gave her an excuse not to look at Sigi.

At their first meeting with Reinhard & Sons, Lieschen gained confidence because the businessmen accepted her as a businesswoman. The second meeting with Kreisler G.m.b.H. also went well. But then came the dreadful evening when Lieschen went to dinner with Sigi to the Hungarian Grill, located a short walking distance from the Bassadores.

The animated atmosphere with table music reflected the Hungarian spirit, but Lieschen could not enjoy a single second. Her head buzzed as if a cyclone raged inside, tossing her brain in all directions.

They ordered Hungarian Veal Braten prepared with red paprika and served with a variety of spicy vegetables and a bottle of Traminer wine. Lieschen forced down a **small** serving and only sipped briefly from her glass of Traminer. Sigi ate a big serving and drank three glasses of Traminer.

Back at the Bassadores, Sigi escorted Lieschen to her door. "I wish you pleasant dreams," he said with a valiant nod.

Surprised at the easy separation, Lieschen slipped inside, switched on the light, and instantly locked the door. She felt a strange sense of relief and turned to step across the room. Suddenly she screamed at the sight of a stranger with a black hood, who stood beside the round table by the window, next to the chair with her suitcase, containing her gun. The hooded stranger glared at her.

The door knob turned. Sigi stormed in. Lieschen was sure she had locked the door.

"What is it, my dear Fraulein Lieschen? I heard you scream." Sigi's gaze fell on the masked stranger. "Someone must have played a prank on you," he said matter-of-factly.

Lieschen glared at Sigi, then at the masked creature. "Som-e-one m-u-ust have," she stammered as she realized that the stranger with the black hood was not alive. At the same time, it occurred to her that Sigi must have been behind this ghastly prank. "I shall stay with you," he assured her.

"I'm all right. Please leave my room."

"I can't. I have to protect you." Sigi's eyes darted from her face to her feet.

"Now that I know it was a prank, it doesn't bother me anymore," Lieschen said, but she could not conceal her trembling voice. She dropped her purse on the table and asked, "How did you get in? I locked the door."

"Since your father wanted me to take good care of you, I requested an extra key." Sigi's eyes shifted to the bed, then back to Lieschen. "I can't possibly leave you alone."

"I can fend for myself." Her nerves threatened to burst. She stepped close to her suitcase.

"1 must stay." Sigi advanced toward her.

Lieschen opened the lid of her suitcase. "I am asking you to leave my room," she requested once more while slipping her right hand inside the suitcase, groping for the gun.

"What are you doing?" Sigi kept advancing. "I know you wanted to tell me that you love me. We belong together!" With outstretched arms, Sigi closed in.

You're not going to rape me! Lieschen gripped the gun.

"Tonight is our night!"

Lieschen drew the gun, aimed, and fired.

Sigi fell. Lieschen dropped the gun beside him, grabbed her purse, and zoomed out of the room toward the elevator. Downstairs, she torpedoed by the reception desk, and outside through the glass doors to the first available taxi. She scrambled into the back seat of the taxi and requested through quivering lips, "To the airport, please." The elderly taxi driver of robust build veered into the flow of traffic.

Lieschen's face burned as if singed with dynamite. When the taxi driver stopped at an intersection with a red light, Lieschen asked, "Would you please drive as fast as you can."

"Young lady, I'm not gonna crash through an intersection with a red light." The cab driver did not move an iota. He only asked, "When's your plane leaving?"

"I don't know."

"If you don't know when your plane's leaving, what's the rush all about?"

"I forgot to look at the schedule." Lieschen dug her fingernails into her sweaty palms.

"What's your destination?"

"Graz. I mean Thalerhof."

"That plane departed five minutes to ten. It's now ten thirty." The cab driver turned his head and glanced at her with a sidelong glare, as if he found her crazy. When the lights turned green, he rolled through the intersection.

"Would you stop at the next phone booth. I have to make a call," Lieschen requested.

The cab driver complied.

Lieschen fumbled through the pages of a phone book at a small booth in front of a closed grocery store. When she found the number of Austrian Airlines, she dropped the necessary coin in the shiny coin slot and dialed. A recording of a zoo came on.

I didn't dial the number of a zoo! She dropped the receiver, and once more flipped through the pages to find the correct number and redialed. When Austrian Airlines answered, she found out that the cab driver's information was correct. The last plane from Vienna to Graz had punctually departed five minutes to ten. She replaced the receiver, looked up the number for the train station, and called for departure information. Then she zipped back into the taxi and requested, "Please rush me to the train terminal. I'd like to catch the last train to Graz."

The taxi driver whizzed through the streets with dizzying speed and reached the train terminal twelve minutes to eleven. The express train was scheduled to depart at eleven. Lieschen paid the taxi-driver and included a good tip. "Thank you for driving so fast," she said, then rushed inside.

"You better hurry if you want to catch that train," urged the young, male cashier behind the window.

"I'll hurry." Lieschen slipped the money through the pay sliver, received her ticket, and dashed down the wide stairs to a dimly lit underground passage. She bolted over to another stairway, and up a flight of stairs to gate eight, where an overweight conductor blew the whistle just as she staggered toward the last car of the express train.

"Hurry, young lady. Hurry, hurry!" The conductor in a greenish-black uniform made a fast motion with his right hand. His jacket and cap were trimmed with golden buttons. Lieschen recognized the conductor as the drunken Herr Fink, who had made the scene at dae Landeskrankenhaus while she had been waiting for Dr. Becker.

"I'm hurrying," she replied and dragged her legs up the stairs of the last car where she dropped into the first vacant seat she could spot. With her shaking hands she covered her burning eyes and visualized Sigi's dead body lying on the floor back in the hotel room. Her father and Sigi had driven her to something which she had abhorred all her life: *killing.*

CHAPTER 33

An earsplitting thud jolted Lieschen. Loud cracks followed. Through the train window she saw blazing orange-red flames shooting up like lurid spikes amid billowing dark clouds. She was aware that this was not a nightmare. The next moment she heard an announcement over the speaker. "Demolition with dynamite on boulder thalluses in progress. Everybody stay calm."

The male passenger next to Lieschen said to his blonde female companion seated across from him, "We're about half-way between Vienna and Graz."

"Express train takes on a new meaning," his blonde companion sneered.

Lieschen did not care whether the train ever moved on. Her life seemed finished because she had committed murder. *God's wrath will come over me. I'm forsaken. God will loath me and shut me out. I'll never see my mother again.* More popping thuds blasted in front of the window, and more fireclouds spiked between the billowing smoke. The fiery clouds mingled with the clouds in Lieschen's head.

When the train finally rolled into the terminal of Graz in the morning, Lieschen took a taxi home.

Frau Emma held a jar of marmalade in her hands when she walked in. "I thought you'd come back the day after tomorrow." Frau Emma looked surprised.

"I-I-I- came back early." Lieschen could hardly get a sound out of her dry mouth.

"You look sick."

"I feel sick."

"Would you like that I call your father or Aunt Klara at the Plant? Or a doctor, or an ambulance?"

"Nobody! Nobody!"

"Why don't you lie down then and rest," Frau Emma suggested, "and hopefully you'll feel better in a little while."

"Do you have Aspirin?" Lieschen asked.

"I think so. Go on upstairs. I'll bring you what I have."

Lieschen clambered up the stairway.

"Wait a minute," Frau Emma called when Lieschen was already half-way up the stairs. "There's a message for you. A man called. His name is Albert Balsac. He left a phone number for you to call him."

"I'll call him later."

Lieschen was half-undressed when Frau Emma came in with a bottle of Aspirin and a glass of water on a silver plate. Lieschen stared at the bottle of Aspirin and thought she might as well swallow the whole bottle. "Would you put everything on the nightstand," she requested.

Frau Emma put the silver plate with the Aspirin and the glass of water on the nightstand, then asked, "Would you like hot chocolate or something else?"

"Nothing else, danke."

Frau Emma left and Lieschen slipped on a peach-colored silk nightgown. Then she took four Aspirin, drank the glass of water, and crawled under her down comforter. She pulled the comforter over her head. It was warm, but she needed a cover over her tormented head. She could not help thinking that it was wrong for her to shoot Sigi. Since she had committed murder, she belonged to the lowest scum on this earth. I should've defended myself in a different way! I should've! I should've! But how could I've prevented Sigi from raping me? These tormenting thoughts circled in her desolate head. She pushed off the down comforter, took four more Aspirin without water because she did not have any water left; and soon her suffocating thoughts disappeared.

Aunt Klara came to awaken her. "It's time for dinner," she said in a low voice. "We'll wait for you downstairs."

Lieschen crawled out of bed, feeling drowsy and sick. She slipped on a gray linen blouse and a navy-blue linen skirt and limped downstairs.

Her father and Aunt Klara were seated in the dining room, with tenderloin steak and vegetables already on the table. Her father looked at her without speaking. His *eyes* had sunken deep. His face appeared dark and grim. A dreadful sense told Lieschen that her father already knew what she had done. The bitterness in her mouth dried up her saliva. Since she could no longer bear to look at her father, she looked down at her bare feet. She had never gone to dinner barefoot.

When she heard footsteps, she looked at the door. Sigi entered the dining room, holding a black rose in his left hand. Lieschen glared at him, wondering if he had come back from hell.

"You would've shot Sigi!" Her father's accusing tone sounded as if coming from a deep cellar.

When Lieschen had a hunch what happened, she exclaimed, "Ralph betrayed me!"

"You better be grateful, otherwise you'd be a murderess now," Aunt Klara said with a grave expression. "Your father wanted to test you with blanks, and Ralph and Sigi cooperated. Your father couldn't believe that you didn't love Sigi. That's why he tested you."

Lieschen clasped her head with both hands.

Her father rose from his chair, his face wrinkled in anguish. "One of us has failed to understand," he uttered. "We'll talk more tomorrow ..." A deep gasp drowned out his words. His sunken eyes turned away from Lieschen, and he escorted Sigi outside.

Blinded with tears, Lieschen shuffled up to her apartment. Through the window on the east-side of her study she looked beyond the old blossoming cherry tree in their garden, up toward heaven. "Thank you, dear God!" she exclaimed. "I never wanted to kill anybody, not even Sigi." She realized that God's invisible hand had protected her from committing murder. God must have heard my cries, she thought with deep gratitude. Then she remembered the black rose in Sigi's left hand and wondered if Sigi was facing his own demons and was admitting to be a child of darkness? Lieschen did not know if her father had picked up on that symbolism.

The following morning Aunt Klara awakened her and told her, "Your father died of a heart attack during the night. Dr. Weitzinger just left."

Together with Aunt Klara, Lieschen entered her parents' bedroom and scrambled to her father's deathbed. His wrinkled face had turned stone white. Tiny cracks showed on his thin lips under his shortly clipped mustache. His sunken eyelids were closed forever. Lieschen leaned over and touched her father's cold hands. They chilled her. And her father had stopped breathing. He did not appear human anymore.

Lieschen sobbed bitterly. It pained her gravely to see her father crumble like this over the conflict with Sigi. "Pap, I loved you, but I could've never loved Sigi," she murmured. She attempted to hug her father in one last embrace to show him that she loved him, but her father seemed already so far away.

Attendants from the funeral home came for her father's body. Aunt Klara escorted them outside.

Lieschen stayed in her father's, respectively in her parents' bedroom. Dazed with grief, she prayed. She would always pray for her father's soul as she had been praying for her mother's soul.

CHAPTER 34

Uncle Gustav and Aunt Sylvia arrived from Lucerne for the funeral.

After the memorial service, Aunt Kiara had a private talk with Lieschen in the living room at their villa. They were seated next to each other on the soft cushions of the couch. Aunt Klara disclosed, "According to your father's will, you're the only heiress, and I will be your legal advisor until you're twenty-one."

"And Sigi?"

"Together we'll make sure that he won't be a problem any longer."

"God, I hope!" Lieschen told Aunt Klara of her struggle with Sigi when she had lost her gold necklace with the pyramid-shaped emerald pendant, which her father had given her for her eighteenth birthday.

"Remember when I came home from the Opera Haus all messed up?"

"I do remember."

"That's when Sigi attempted to rape me on the way home."

Aunt Klara looked shocked. "I thought something had gone wrong because of the way you looked," she said.

"In the struggle, my necklace must have fallen off in Sigi's Porsche because I saw one of his girlfriends wearing it."

"Petruschka?"

"Not Petruschka. I don't know the girl's name." Lieschen paused, then emphasized, "I do want my necklace back, especially since Pap died. It has a deep meaning for me."

"We'll see that you'll get it back." Aunt Klara shifted on the couch and said, "Uncle Gustav and I must tell you something else, something we couldn't tell you during your parents' lifetime."

"What is that?"

"Let me call Uncle Gustav." Aunt Klara rose and stepped out.

When both came back in, Uncle Gustav settled on one of the cushioned chairs next to the couch. Aunt Klara sat down next to Lieschen again and, looking at Uncle Gustav, she said, "Your turn."

"All right." His head shifted toward Lieschen, and he began to speak. "Your puzzle and our puzzle has been profoundly painful. We had to promise your father to keep the family secret during his lifetime. This code of silence carried a lethal stamp which your father guarded with his and our lives."

What in the world is Uncle Gustav talking about? Lieschen could not follow.

"You do remember Robert Schweitzer?" Uncle Gustav continued.

Robert? Lieschen's heartbeat surged.

"I'm sure you do remember." Her uncle's baritone voice remained even.

What does Robert have to do with my parents? Lieschen curiosity soared.

"Robert is your brother. He is your mother's illegitimate son," Uncle Gustav disclosed, sinking deep into the cushion of his chair.

"He is your half-brother," Aunt Klara clarified.

Lieschen's breathing seemed to stop. "Does Robert know?"

"Robert has known all along. He wasn't allowed to tell you. He was bound by the same code of silence. So was Monika. She also knew," Uncle Gustav said.

Baffled beyond herself, Lieschen remained silent for a long moment. Then suddenly she bounced from her chair, as if someone had slipped a lightening rod under her. "I have a brother! Robert is my brother. Robert and I will continue my father's business. And Monika too," she exclaimed. She sounded as if she wanted to announce it to the whole world.

"You don't know if Robert will want to do that," Aunt Klara said.

"Why not? I'm going to call him right now." She turned to walk toward the door.

'Wait!" Uncle Gustav motioned with both hands. "Sit down. There's something else you must know."

What else could there possibly be? Lieschen stepped back and sat down again on the couch next to Aunt Klara.

"Monika, Robert's wife, passed away on New Year's Eve," Uncle Gustav said.

Lieschen sank far back into the cushion of the couch and covered her cheeks and eyes with both hands. Then, lifting her hands, she uttered, "You didn't tell me!"

"I'm telling you now." Uncle Gustav looked at Lieschen with a sad expression. "Monika had been ill for quite some time."

Lieschen knew that Monika had been ill. She dropped her hands on her lap. Tears blurred her eyes. "I'm deeply sorry!" She remained silent for a long moment, then asked, "How is little Monika?"

"She is fine." Uncle Gustav swallowed hard.

"She will also be my child. I'm her legitimate aunt," Lieschen said with a soft voice. She pictured herself helping her brother take care of little Monika. It was as if she had graduated to a different kind of love, which included a brother and a child. She always wanted a big brother. She raised her eyes. This new reality appeared to be a dream, yet it was very real. Unexpectedly Albert Balsac's image appeared in her mind. She had not called him back yet, but she would soon call him.

Uncle Gustav and Aunt Klara continued to explain the intricate web of circumstances. "While your father loved your mother, your mother loved Robert's non-aristocratic father," Aunt Klara said. "Your grandparents wouldn't accept Robert's father as their son-in-law because he was not an aristocrat."

"That caused the deadly outcome," Uncle Gustav added.

Aunt Klara continued to explain, "When your mother wanted a divorce, your father would only have granted the divorce if your mother had been willing to give you up. Your mother refused. Then, one day, your mother threatened to shoot your father. That was the night when you heard shots, and when you saw the bloodstains." Aunt Klara inhaled deeply.

Lieschen's vision blurred when she remembered the deadly night to which she had unknowingly contributed; so did Robert and Robert's father, and her grandparents. What a sad entanglement!

Aunt Klara continued, "Your mother had pointed a gun at your father. He managed to capture the gun and, in the struggle, he accidentally killed your mother."

"So the death certificate was falsified?" Lieschen uttered.

Aunt Klara nodded. "It was the most difficult night of my life. I was petrified and deeply sorry that I had to treat you so badly. Yet, to this day, I don't know what else I could've done under the awful circumstances. I couldn't call the police. Orders of your father. He couldn't risk such a scandal, which I could understand. And you must know that your mother had provoked the confrontation."

After another long agonizing silence, Lieschen asked, "Can I call Robert now?"

"If you'd like," Uncle Gustav said.

Aunt Klara nodded, tears glistening in her eyes.

"You're my brother!" Lieschen said when she heard Robert's pleasant voice on the line. She felt a strange sense of connection and revival.

"I wish I could've told you during your visit last year. Or sooner."

"I understand that you couldn't. Would you come and visit while Uncle Gustav and Aunt Sylvia are staying with us?" Lieschen requested. She wanted to discuss their future and everything in person.

"I'll be happy to come." Robert promised to call and tell Lieschen his flight schedule.

"I'm very *sorry* for the passing of Monica," Lieschen said then.

"So am I." Lieschen could hear Robert's profound sigh. Then he said, "I'll see you soon," and the phone clicked.

Lieschen detected Robert's pain. She thought that's why he had hung up so quickly. Slowly she put back the receiver. Robert's pain also lodged in her heart while one question arose in her mind: why did God allow Monica to die so young and leave Robert and little Monica? Was this destiny, or was it something else? God must have allowed it to happen, just as God must have allowed my parents' ill-fated entanglement to happen. And God must have known. And He must have a reason. But what reason? Lieschen only remembered when Aunt Klara had told her that God knows the reason for everything, we don't have to know; but Lieschen wanted to know so badly.

Three days later Lieschen watched the airplane with Robert and little Monika on board descend in a steep curve to the airport

Thalerhof. Together with Uncle Gustav and Aunt Sylvia, she waited by the runway.

When Robert came through the exit of the airplane, he held little Monika in his arms. At the bottom of the metal stairway, he set Monika on the ground and led her by the hand. They walked slowly. Monika looked adorable in her pink dress and matching hat with tiny pink carnations that covered part of her golden curls. Lieschen also noticed a small bouquet of Edelweiss in Robert's left hand.

He smiled as they came through Customs. Lieschen remembered his tender smile, but the chemistry between them had changed because now she knew that Robert was her brother. "Hello," he said and handed Lieschen the small bouquet of Edelweiss. The dainty velvet stars resembled the bouquet he had given her at the Geschaeftsball in Lucerne, which had disappeared.

"Danke." Lieschen looked at the delicate bouquet.

Little Monika watched with her big, trusting brown eyes, capturing Lieschen's heart. Carefully holding the Edelweiss in her left hand, Lieschen lifted Monika into her arms and kissed her lovingly. "You're my child too," she said tenderly, feeling radiant warmth in her heart.

Uncle Gustav and Aunt Sylvia also gave Monika a bunch of kisses.

Some passengers looked at them. Others scurried by without paying attention.

When Lieschen set Monika down, she and Robert led her between them. Together with Uncle Gustav and Aunt Sylvia, they walked through the exit, on to a new life.

Helga Schweininger was born and grew up in the countryside of Graz in Austria. She graduated from the Handelsakademie, a four-year business college in Graz. Marriage to her husband Ferdinand brought her to Southern California, where she has been living with her family since 1962.